# THE LAST CHAMPION OF EARTH

To Roxane

Best Wishes

&

God Bless!

Matthew 5-7

# The Last Champion of Earth

▼

*Donald I. Templeman*

**Writers Club Press**
San Jose New York Lincoln Shanghai

## The Last Champion of Earth

Writers Club Press
an imprint of iUniverse.com, Inc.

For information address:
iUniverse.com, Inc.
5220 S 16th, Ste. 200
Lincoln, NE 68512
www.iuniverse.com

ISBN: 0-595-16944-9

Printed in the United States of America

To Christen & Tracy for Illumination & Fellowship

# CONTENTS

# SAND

2174 A.D.

Albuquerque Earth Science Station:

"Don't you think that somewhere in this universe, there's a power that expects more from us than this?" an exasperated monitoring technician pleaded into his receiver.

"Yo', Albey station!" a loud voice interrupted from an audible speaker. "This is Mare Crisium! I got a hot flash for you guys! Anybody home?"

The technician frowned at the interruption.

"Hold that thought, honey! One second, there's another call! Don't leave! Yeah, Moonbase 3, this is Albuquerque! What's new?"

"I got a big hunk 'a rock on my grid that's headed your way and it looks like it means business, partner!"

"Old news, moonbase! We've been tracking that thing for months! Once it hits the asteroid belt, it's history!"

"Newsflash, Albey! The belt just got called out on strikes! That sonovabitch blew by like an old Ryan heater! Not a scratch! What's worse, it took a couple of turns around Mars, picked up momentum and is headed our way!"

"Um…what was that last part, moonbase?"

"Something wrong with your audio, Albey?"

"Uh, no moonbase. I got my girl on the other channel. Say again?"

"Since when did Albey station allow personal calls during 'business hours'?"

"Since Vogue Day weekend started without me! And my girl's threatened to go back to her nasty girlfriend 'cause I gotta' work! That's when!"

"Sounds like my Vogue Day on Earth last year. My boyfriend blew me off for a floating orgy on the Seine."

"Yeah? That's how I met my girlfriend last year."

"Really? And you've been seeing her this long? Man, sounds almost cultish."

"Actually, I was kind of hoping it was. We had some really special times."

"Man, you're an old fashioned boy aren't ya'?"

"I never thought so, but the last few months were really good…besides sex, y'know. We were gonna' stay together this holiday. Maybe do some traveling. Now she's talking about a quad with some broads her old girlfriend met. Just 'cause I have to work!"

"Spirit of the holiday, Albey: 'Try something new, no matter what or who you do!'"

"I hate that commercial."

"But that's the way of the world! Guess that's why I chose Mare assignment for awhile."

"Well listen bud, I'd love to chat, but my girl's about to hop back into the blender!"

"You listen, cult boy: When you're done, relay my message! Some people on Earth may not want to die just yet!"

"Gotcha' Mare!"

"Mare Crisium, out."

# II.

Peking, China:

"I am so sorry, Mr. and Mrs. Tse-Lun," pronounced the doctor, "but as best we can determine, your child has been born sightless."

The mother covered her eyes and began to sob on the father's shoulder.

"What can we do?" the father asked.

"Well, you can raise the child in a world of blackness," the doctor answered grimly. "There are ways for a blind person to function, with much assistance, in a sighted society. Of course, the cost of raising such a child would be significant...hardships on it and you would be great."

"Or..." the father led, hopefully.

"Or you can opt for...termination."

The mother raised her head to read the father's reaction.

"Termination," the father muttered.

"Yes." answered the doctor.

"But I thought that was only an option when the child is deformed." interjected the mother. "He's a beautiful child."

"Beautiful now, perhaps," said the doctor. "But when he's crashing and falling about the house everyday, doing expensive damage to your home and your lives, will he still be so beautiful?"

"And think of the pain our child's pain will cause us," added the father.

"But he looks so...healthy," the mother lovingly returned. "How could it be legal to...terminate..."

"World Cartel law provides that the parents are free to choose Child Termination anytime during the first six years of a child's life provided there is documented proof of disablement or disfigurement at the time of birth," quoted the doctor. "Clearly that is the case here. Of course, if you choose to wait, your growing fondness for the child might make termination more unpleasant later. I had a couple in here just last week, whose child was born deaf, but they wanted to try. For four years, they tried to reach a youngster who simply could not understand them. They finally opted for termination—but only after so much frustration. It was very difficult for them."

The father looked into the mother's eyes. Their yearned desperation begged for impassioned mercy. He sharply looked away and rendered his decision.

"We opt for the termination," he said evenly.

The mother began to sob.

"It takes great strength to make this decision, Mr. Tse-Lun," the doctor affirmed with a comforting smile. "Mode?"

"What do you mean 'mode'?" responded the father, still wrestling with his choice.

"The parents must choose: gas, radiation, or cranial laser incision. Each mode is equally painless, particularly at this age. However, some parents are more or less comfortable with certain…remedies."

The father looked at the mother indecisively. Her hands covered both her face and her ears.

"Cranial incision…I guess," he decided.

"Thank you. I'll need your signatures," the doctor concluded, sliding a completed form across his desk.

The father froze for a moment, staring blankly, searching through the whispers of his feint reservations. Then, refusing to display uncertainty, he leaned forward and signed his wavering consent.

The mother abruptly stood up and ran out.

"I'll give you some time, Mr. Tse-Lun," smiled the doctor. "She realizes she can still have others, doesn't she?"

# III.

St. Petersburg, Russia:

Alexander Lvov had grown tired of the cycle of poverty that enslaved his people. As a newspaper columnist, he wrote daily commentary on the depravity which manacled the masses to remain as commoner "Weeds" to the bourgeois "Blossoms". Encouraged by his constituents to assume a role of leadership, he decided to run for political office, hoping to imbue his countrymen with a renewed hunger for equality. So one afternoon, he put down his pen, and opened his heart to a large gathering waiting outside a food dispensary.

"We have all the wine and vodka…heroin and blusilver we will ever need!" he bellowed.

There was a smattering of applause from the rear of the audience followed by low laughter among most of the onlookers.

"…And so do our children!" he added.

An unsettled rustle of bundled bodies quickly displaced much of the slothful joviality.

"When the world united and we were promised more freedom by the Blossom politicians than we would know what to do with, we had no idea how right they'd be! While the quality of our meat and vegetables remains in question, we can now buy a fifth of any poison we choose for less than a gallon of milk…and we do! In the twentieth century, when our great grandfathers were dying well before their time, it was called alcoholism. Thanks to their grandsons, however, we've been told to put down the persecution of our 'culture' and accept it as a way of life. As it was so eloquently put by the first global Beneficent: 'It would be at the very base of criminality to encourage any group of people on this Earth to progress against their natures. To force a Weed to believe it should somehow become a Blossom is cruel and unfair! Likewise, a Blossom born to flourish and capture the imagination should never be trod upon as a Weed.'"

"And so we are free to live off of our menial wages, or the tax dollars of our Beneficent government...and screw each other 'til our private flesh stings raw...and drink and smoke ourselves into a blind fog...until the next film or ballgame comes on satellite. Meanwhile, our children run the streets like twenty-second century Cossacks, murdering and killing each other over hover-quads or burrow boundaries...or a night with one of your daughters who'll pander herself for a fake gold chain or an ounce of imported blusilver."

The faces in the crowd grew blank, guilty with reflection.

"I attended the funeral of a friend's son two months ago," Alexander continued. "His boy, who was fifteen, got into an argument with another boy over change at a sandwich stand. The manager of the stand said my friend's boy was right. But when my friend's boy left the stand, the other boy and his friends tied him up and smashed his skull three...four times with a cornerstone. And as my friend walked away from his boy's gravesite, drunk and distraught, I asked him how we can allow this type of thing to continue! And he looked at me, and said: 'Alex, this is the way we are. Better he should die like a man than trying to live like some Blossom fop!'"

"Yeah!" yelled a single voice in agreement with the imbalanced ideal. The rest of the crowd murmured uneasily.

"'This is the way we are'." Alexander repeated. "Murderers, addicts, whores...Weeds. Second class citizens by our own accord. Second to the Blossoms who truss up their depravity with wealth and prestige."

"We are free!" Yelled an angry, thin, young woman with dark shaved hair, who burst through to the front of the crowd. "We can do whatever we want! Who the hell are you to tell us that we should be like the Blossoms! I'd take the stench of an oily, sweaty miner with vodka on his breath over the perfumed effemination of a Blossom man any night of the week! And I'd much rather do it on a wood planked floor in front of a warm fireplace, than on a cold marble patio with some queer Blossom gender bender!"

Half the crowd gave a cheer. The young woman then pulled a bottle from her coat pocket and took an overlong swig while disdainfully staring at Alexander. She then wiped her coat sleeve across her angry lips and spat a cloud of mist toward the platform where he stood.

Alexander returned to her, a look of pity, then raised his gaze to the rest of the crowd. "At you and I, they laugh. At our children, who scarcely attend the warehouse schools from which we have divested, they scoff. 'Innately ignorant', they say. 'Genetically deficient', they say. 'Only a Weed can leave the world with less sense than he had at birth', they say.

"Are all of you happy living amidst crime and filth? Are all of you content to remain as you are? Are none of you prepared to reach for a better life...not as Weeds...not as Blossoms...but as human beings?"

Again, the crowd weighed his words. It would be easy to remain as they were. Tearing away the age old manacles of tradition would be akin to shunning their beloved ancestry. But what had ancestry's embrace gotten them?

"Mr. Lvov!" called the thin young woman in front. She rocked nervously from her front foot to her back, then looked mournfully over her shoulder at the gathering behind her. "When I first began reading your columns...your ideals...they made me sick! I asked myself how this arrogant sonovabitch, no better than me, could tell me that my ancestors and my children aren't as good as anyone else on this planet. But then I saw the Beneficent on satellite vacationing with his family. No food lines for them! No wondering whether someone they love would be murdered on the way home from work...or in school. Fresh air and fertile land for them to play upon, let 'lone plant upon. I looked long and hard at them...and their smirks and then at myself. And Mr. Lvov, it came to me that...you actually could have a point."

Part of the crowd cheered their support of her testimony. The rest remained unsure of her sudden "enlightenment". With this, she smiled warmly and spread her arms apart as if to offer embrace to Alexander. He trustfully knelt down and firmly wrapped his arms around her, embracing his new role as the herald of a new consciousness for the underclass.

Then as his arms crossed around her bony back, she reached into her oversized coat, pulled out a double barreled hand weapon, and blew a ragged hole straight through him.

"Then again, you may not," she sneered as his bloodied carcass fell away.

His mortally wounded, convulsing body toppled to the ground as the crowd shrieked in terror at the all too familiar scene of violent death. The woman hastily shifted her weapon to automatic and fired low over everyone's head. She then turned and fled hurriedly out of sight. No one found the desire to give chase.

She sprinted, with the gun reconcealed under her coat, through the crowded streets. Then ducked into a narrow, recessive alley where a dark hovering vehicle surreptitiously awaited.

She looked behind her one last time, then slid the car door quietly open. Before her second leg was all the way in, the vehicle shifted, tilting skyward and stealthily sped off.

"Done, Catherine?" asked a cracking tenor voice.

"Yes, Nikolai. All too easy," she responded as she nervously lit an herbal cigarette.

"That is why the Controller's office uses people like yourself," he commented, looking down his long, thin nose at her. "How could any of us hope to duplicate such ergonomic efficiency."

"Now why don't we conclude our business," she glared impatiently.

"Ah yes," answered Nikolai. "Private school for your two babies."

"That's right!" she said impatiently, through a thickly smoked exhale.

"They're already on their way," he said reassuringly.

"What? But I didn't get a chance to explain to them…"

"Don't worry, we did that for you. They understood," he assured with a small grin.

"You fuckers! You know what I meant!"

"The school term starts in two days," he said coolly. "We needed to place them clandestinely, otherwise they would draw suspicion."

Catherine stared out of the side window mournfully suppressing sorrow. Her mind sought to recollect what she'd said the last time she would probably ever see four-year-old Marta and six-year-old Charles. She closed her eyes remorsefully as she remembered only the beating she'd given them when they had walked in on her and Nikolai consummating their deal on her tattered sofa.

"They forgive you," answered Nikolai sensing her regret.

"So what about me!" she snapped coldly.

"Oh yes, a month's supply of blusilver," he smiled. "I guess if I had to have a habit, this would be the one to have."

She scowled ruefully at him. Nikolai only smiled again and signaled to the rear of the vehicle. A large man leaned forward and suddenly snatched Catherine into a full nelson.

"A month's supply, my dear," said Nikolai evenly. "Quite a dosage for one so…petite. But I imagine you've built up quite a tolerance over the years."

Catherine cursed out loud and struggled against the large man's iron lock. Nikolai pulled out a large twin cylindered inoculator whose metallic-blue contents glistened perniciously within its housing.

"Why?!!" she screamed, kicking fruitlessly at the front seat, then Nikolai.

Nikolai did not answer as he skillfully bound her struggling ankles. He efficiently unhooked her pants and then pulled them down exposing her pale buttocks. He then "ergonomically" jabbed the inoculator into her left hind cheek. After another moment, both men released her.

She slumped forward as blue veins began to rise in her forehead and crawl down her cheeks to her neck. Her phlegm spattered lips turned dark purple. Her skin, dead white. The henchmen fitted a rubber sack over her face as she violently spasmed and vomited her last breaths.

The vehicle drew near a remote farm yard and hovered for several moments. After a minute, the bodies of a thin young woman and two children were dumped into a filthy hog sty. Then the deadly black vehicle silently darted away.

# IV.

Liberace Gardens, California:

"Evacuate? Look, kiss my ass! Do you know what holiday it is? That's right! Vogue Day weekend! The biggest money grossing fucking holiday in the goddamn world! I got a resort crammed fulla' horny fucking people who wanna get laid, wanna get high, and wanna get their goddamn money's worth! Look chicken little, you wanna talk to me about meteors? Get me a fucking Lunar mining contract and we'll talk, awright?"

Morri Gruberstein, owner of the Liberace Gardens Resort, slammed down the phone.

"Who was that, Morri?" asked Shari, his vice president of operations.

"Don't worry about it," dismissed Morri.

"What do you mean 'don't worry about it'? she persisted. "Somebody was asking you to evacuate the club!"

"Hey, nobody said anything about any evacuation, all right!"

"But I just heard you say…"

"Fuck what I said!" he exploded. "And since when do you start snoopin' in on my phone calls?"

"Since I started sleeping here in your bed…sir!"

"Yeah, well maybe I shouldn't be fuckin' a broad with ears bigger than her tits, huh?"

"Morri, I thought there just might be something going on I should know about," she reasoned. "After all, I am VP of ops you know!"

"Hey bitch, you're VP of my bedposts, all right? You need to know somethin' when I tell you 'you need to know somethin', got it?"

Stunned, Shari jumped out of bed and looked for her clothes.

"Now what? You're mad?" Morri asked with annoyance.

"I…" Shari fought back tears. "I graduated Yale business school last spring which is more than you can say! I know how to run a business! You hired me because you needed me to…"

"…take the place of my blow-up doll," finished Morri with a disdainful grin. "Only you talk too much!"

Shari gasped in shock.

"Look, you came sauntering in here for a job interview with your bouncy breasts tossin' those sorority letters all over your sweater," Morri spewed viciously. "You didn't even wear underwear 'til after you moved in with me! Now all of a sudden you want to talk to me about your business savvy? Hell, aside from the bathhouse, the main swimming pool and my condo, you don't even know what's in half the buildings here!"

"That's not true! I…"

Morri reached behind his dresser and pulled out a map of the resort grounds.

"Okay 'miss vice president' show me where the riding stables are!" Morri yelled.

Shari blankly stared at the map scanning hopelessly for riding stables.

"Okay, that's easy to miss! We're only talking about a few acres," he badgered. "Why don't you show me the air surf course!"

Again, Shari stared blankly at the map as her vision blurred with tears.

"Yeah, that's what I thought!" yelled Morri pointing his finger at her pinkened nose. "For five months you've been so busy drinkin' and tannin' and fuckin' and suckin, you don't have a clue off your knees or your back! You know what I think? I think maybe I need a new VP!"

"Oh no, Morri please…"

"Yeah. Someone who's office isn't my bedroom! Someone who's old man didn't blow his brains out because he went broke and was about to get evicted into the Weeds. And someone who isn't twenty-one but look's like she's forty from flat-backin' her way through the 'in crowd'."

"Morri…I'm sorry."

"Yeah, you sure are! You're fired! Now get the fuck out of here!"

Shari immediately began to cry uncontrollably. Morri grabbed up her clothes and pushed them and her naked body out of the door and onto his front lawn.

She collapsed on the grass and began pathetically shouting: "but I love you!"

Inside: "Security, this is Gruberstein. Could you come remove Miss Oberberg from the premises. Yeah, out the gate. She's fired."

Morri punched off the communicator. Then he began to laugh as he folded up the resort map, which contained neither a riding stable nor an air surf course.

Elsewhere on the premises, Vogue Day festivities jettisoned into full thrust at North America's most prestigious resort village. Yesterday's arrivals for the pre-holiday celebration were already week-worn from fervid activity. Arrivals such as Liam and Miles, who made their way to the resort's Meet and Greet Nightclub.

"Geez, Miles! I feel like I'm going to die!"

"Li, you can't die from sex," chuckled Miles. "If you could, you'd be dead already!"

"Yeah, but did you see the sores on that last hostess?" smiled Liam wearily.

"Sure, but we both had our cures before we got here, so who cares?" answered Miles casually.

"I know. But still, she was a monster!"

"Maybe that's because she was a he."

"No way!"

"Yeah way!"

"Why didn't you say something?"

"Because you'd spent the last three hours trying to get your name on that stupid board," laughed Miles.

"Well, it was worth it!" boasted Liam. "Forty-seven hostesses or hosts or whatever in three hours got me number four on the record board. I won't have to ask for another date the rest of the weekend. The women will be pounding down my door!"

"So will some men," warned Miles.

"Yeah, well…so what," shrugged Liam enthusiastically. "A married guy's gotta' cut loose sometime."

"So what's the wife doing this weekend?" asked Miles.

"Amazon Dyke cruise," Liam said feigning a mysterious South American accent.

"You guys never spend Vogue Day together, do you?"

"Nope. We know some couples who try to, but it's kind of anti-Vogue if you ask me," Liam answered proudly. "Besides our relationship is so enriched by what we learn from other people! When we get back together, we're refreshed! It's almost like discovering each other all over again. It's wonderful!"

The pounding thump of dance rhythms became audible as they turned the next corner. Both men were drowned by the glowing laser light that illuminated the enormous sign above the Meet and Greet entrance.

As they got closer, the detail of the sign grew perceptible. The sign was a computer generated, 30 second loop depicting a bright red male approaching a light green female at a bar. After brief dialogue, the scenery converts to a boudoir in which the nude male pumps the nude female into a shocking pink glow. The scene then reverts to the bar again, only the shocking pink female approaches a light green male, takes him to the boudoir and pumps him into a bright red. And so on…

"Heaven on Earth," laughed Liam, taking in the sign for the third time. "It doesn't get any better than this!"

Miles smiled, marveling at the severe shallowness of the sign's depravity. When he looked down again, he caught only a glimpse of Liam's shirt tail as he bolted hurriedly into the club.

As Miles entered, he found Liam already glowing green from a laser emanating from the ceiling. In another moment, Miles was glowing bright green as well.

The giant ballroom was flooded with people (in varied degrees of disrobement) aglow in greens, reds and pinks. The bar areas were occupied primarily with greens. The large dance floor was predominantly covered with reds and pinks. Occasionally a green body would flash red or pink right in the middle of the dance floor. An event which ceremoniously drew applause and yells from the other laser-lit patrons.

Beyond the dance floor was a spectacular two-story holographic image of the Madonna performing the Vogue theme, accompanied by two unspecifiably gendered dancers mirroring her every movement. Her hair was short shining platinum. Her eyes were piercing reptilian diamonds garnished by thin black brows. Her red lips hung seductively receptive, occasionally hosting the deliberate snaking movements of her surgically forked tongue. She was clad in studded black leather lingerie that left her glowing white limbs, her buttocks and her bosom, openly displayed.

"She really was a goddess!" gasped Liam as he plucked a drink from a passing barmaid's tray. "I can't believe she was sixty-two when she videoed this! Remind me to do her in the Virtual Reality room tomorrow, will you?"

"Sure Li," answered Miles.

Liam gulped his glass and began his prospecting.

"I can't believe they started you out with a green." teased Miles. "If they only knew…"

"Yeah, well everyone starts out green here," interrupted Liam, "but I won't be that way for long!"

Liam homed in on a woman sitting at the bar. He smirked at Miles, then began his descent upon his unwitting prey. It was difficult to tell whether she was alone or with friends, but it didn't seem to matter. Liam swung his arms underneath hers and began drunkenly massaging her ample chest.

Shocked, the woman turned angrily, but Liam's grip was decidedly firm.

"Hey, I'm a doctor! I know what I'm doing!" slurred Liam.

She grabbed her glass, smashed it against Liam's face and broke his fingery hold. Apparently upset, she then stalked toward the exit. Miles followed her.

Before Liam could react at all, two bottomless pink women picked him up and dragged him to the dance floor. He still managed to smile through bloodied, swelling lips.

Just outside the door, the assaulted woman cursed angrily into the night, visibly shaken.

"I hate this place!" she shouted to no one in particular.

"You too?" came a voice from behind.

It was Miles.

"I apologize for my friend," Miles continued. "He gets a little…rambunctious."

"Yeah?" she responded, still flustered. "Well, before the Bar Laws were passed, I could have had him thrown in jail for that!"

"That's true." Miles answered. "But then again, that's why we have Bar Laws. I mean, I don't agree with what my buddy did, but if you didn't want to get grabbed, maybe you shouldn't have gone in."

"I just wanted a drink, okay?" she shot back. "Can't a person get a drink without getting pawed?"

"Only in the privacy of their own home," answered Miles.

"Yeah, great."

"So if you hate it here, why did you come?" Miles finally asked.

"Because my fiancé is having his bachelor party on some Caribbean fuck-barge this weekend. So I figured I'd pay him back by coming here. Great idea, huh?"

"You tell me."

"Well, it's not."

Miles grinned at her, then smiled as he turned his gaze skyward. He noted a flashing red star that appeared larger than any other he'd ever seen.

"So what are you doing here?" she interrupted. "I mean, you sound like you hate it too."

Miles paused a moment, noting that the star appeared to be expanding with each flicker. Then he looked back to the woman.

"I do…hate it," he answered with divided attention. "I mean it's Vogue Day, right? Has anyone really thought about what kind of holiday we're talking about? I mean the whole idea seems to be to have sex with as many strangers as possible. Has anyone asked why?"

"It's more than that," she clarified. "It's like the old Independence Day, only to the tenth power! It's a celebration of our basic human freedoms to do exactly as we choose; to reach out to others all over the world and celebrate ultimate diversity by touching the lives of as many new people as possible. It's showing your love for them as fellow human beings."

"Just so long as they belong to the same social strata," added Miles.

"That's not necessarily true. My sorority used to spend Vogue Day in an aborigine village—myself excluded, of course. I know lots of people who find the Weeds to be a real turn on."

"Okay, so you have some slummers. The fact remains that Weeds 'diversify' with Weeds and Blossoms 'diversify' with Blossoms. I mean, what Weed could afford Liberace Gardens?"

"I d'know," she replied carelessly, shaking her hair as if growing annoyed with the conversation. "From what I understand, those people prefer their own crude way of having fun. And no one tells them they can't! That's the beauty of freedom, I guess."

Miles again gazed skyward noting that the star was now the size of the moon.

"So what are you doing here?" she asked again.

"Oh…" Miles looked down. "I'm looking after my buddy. This is his favorite holiday. His wife makes me promise not to let him have too much fun. When they get back together though, they just try to one-up each other's achievements since she's pretty much doing the same thing."

"Wow, that's great!" she smiled. "I hope I have that kind of marriage."

"What kind of marriage?"

"The kind where you can be together without…being stuck, y'know?"

The sky began to rumble as the red star had grown to twice the size of the moon. A scarlet incandescent glow began to tint the grounds below.

"What the hell is that?" Miles pondered aloud.

"Probably a Martian shuttle," she threw in. "My best friend's dad uses them on business. I heard their huge...and noisy!"

"Hmmm..." Miles pondered as the rumble grew louder.

"Hey," she started again, rubbing Miles's shoulder. "I really appreciate your coming out here and apologizing, but I think I'm gonna' go back to my...cabin. Um...I don't want you to think I do this all the time, but uh...you are kinda' nice and um...well do you want to come...with me?"

"Huh?" responded Miles immersed in the sight and sound of the thundering red meteor.

The ground began to shake violently as the clatter of the Garden buildings became ominously audible. There were screams from inside the Meet and Greet, but it was difficult to ascertain if it was in response to anything unfestive as the music continued to pulse relentlessly.

From a distance someone could be heard asking: "What's going on?"

The blackness of the evening was now entirely immersed by the fiery reddish-orange glow of the meteoroid.

"I think I'm going back inside after all!" the woman shouted over the mounting rumble.

Miles did not hear her.

She ran back inside almost being hit by a piece of the Meet and Greet sign which had shaken loose.

Miles felt the flesh on his forehead grow hot as if someone had stuck his head into an oven. He opened his mouth to try and clear his ears of the meteor's roaring approach. A trickle of perspiration ran down his back as he knew, full well, it was far too late to run anywhere. The massive iron sphere now appeared to be kilometers in diameter.

Then suddenly, before he could unleash a death scream, he felt his skin split and burn away.

In another instant, there was a resounding explosion that staggered the witless planet Earth. And with immaculate, hellish finality...Liberace Gardens became a spewing infernal maw of molten rock!

# V.

Cannes, France-Inside the Beneficent Palace:

"My lord, I do not think you grasp the depth of our despair…"

"Of course I do!" the Beneficent answered impatiently. "I'm sending food! I'm sending medics! I'm sending agricultural engineers to train your people in the most modern irrigation meth—…"

"My lord!" the African governor interrupted.

The Beneficent scowled at the display of disrespect. The collapse of protocol took precedence over his reception to reason. He set down his jeweled wine chalice and slowly walked toward the open windows overlooking the blissful sandy shores of the Mediterranean.

"My lord," the governor repeated, softening his tone. "My people…our people there…need…relocation."

"What?!" bellowed the Beneficent as if a harmonious dream had been capsized by alien interlopers.

"Relocation, sir."

"Relocation?! Relocation to where? Arabia? It's full of starving people already. North America, perhaps? It's diminished resources can barely support the population there now."

"That's not entirely true, sir. They live quite well…"

"They're teetering on the brink of total collapse there! They just don't know it yet!"

"And so it has been said for over a hundred years, sir. Yet still, their markets are bountiful; their women and children are fat. The people of Africa are beyond collapse. Cannibalism is rampant! Starvation is the number one cause of death there! Two-thirds of our land mass is now desert and it continues to spread. With all due respect sir, a plan of relocation to the Americas and Western Europe is the only solution that will relieve the remaining population. Otherwise…"

"Is this a rejection of the World Cartel's offer of assistance…governor?" The words hung malevolently on the Beneficent's lips as he poured himself another full chalice of Languedoc.

"No sir, but…"

"But you propose that your people, Weeds for the most part, be relocated; flooding struggling, predominantly Blossom regions that bear life-threatening burdens of their own."

"As in the price of satellite entertainment, my lord?"

"Hold that glib tongue of yours, governor, lest I have your ungracious throat elinguated!" the Beneficent yelled wagging a forefinger and sloshing red wine onto his bare feet. "You know damn certain that the aspirations of the Blossom people far exceed that of any Weed. To needlessly disrupt the lives of millions of blossoming families is unconscionable, unlawful and unconstitutional!"

The governor bore the Beneficent's absent humanity with concealed disgust.

"If some unforeseen disaster befell Europe tomorrow," the World's leader continued, "and Blossoms needed to move into the south of Africa where your people now thrive, what would be your response?"

"I would tell them to pack a very large dinner," the governor shot back through tight lips.

The Beneficent hid his frown behind the chalice as he held it to his mouth and drank. When he finished, a smile appeared from behind the jeweled cup.

"Ha!" laughed the Beneficent. "I knew there was a reason behind my appointing you as governor of that surly continent!"

"Sir?"

"That biting uncensored sense of humor! That tenacious unyielding leadership! That powerful…intelligence."

He reached down, filled another chalice, and handed it to the governor. Then he put his arm around the governor's shoulder and spoke into his ear:

"I will offer you food, medics and agricultural engineers. If you refuse it, then I will ensure that your hungry, starving, disease-infected people will know that they remain that way because you said 'No' to me. And I'm willing to wager that soon thereafter you'll be calling me to send the Champion to rescue you from the swell-bellied hordes who'll be demanding your head, for a starter, and your loins as a main course. Besides, as long as the birthrate there continues to exceed the mortality rate, aren't your peoples' futures assured for generations to come?"

The governor felt the Beneficent's fingers dig into his shoulders like the talons of a demonic griffin. He drained his cup, but tasted nothing.

"Thank you, sir," the governor spoke blankly. "The reputation of your generosity…remains intact."

The two men exchanged rehearsed smiles, and the governor then departed hoping to be outlived by the continent under his charge.

The Beneficent smiled and slowly walked back to his coveted view of the hazy blue sea.

He stroked his black and white Vandyke beard and admired the gray hair which decorated his still firm chest and stomach.

"History will mark my greatness," he muttered to himself.

Then an adolescent boy's voice spoke from behind.

The Beneficent turned and saw Val standing in the doorway wearing only a satin cloth about his waist.

The older man smiled, but there was worry in the boy's face.

"What is it?" the Beneficent asked.

"California," the boy's voice shook. "There's been a disaster."

Two floors below, kilometers from worldly concerns:

"Is he gentle?" queried young Anna Maria as she sat still for her auburn mane to be brushed full.

Louisette, nine years her senior, paused for a moment to weigh the question…or perhaps to weigh an answer which her virginal cousin could comfortably digest. Louisette had been with him so many times, so many places, so many different ways. The basic simplicity of the term "gentle" had no context when his stoic face, his powerful body panned across her flesh's memories.

"No?" Anna Maria filled her cousin's hesitation.

Louisette could feel the tender muscles in Anna Maria's delicate bare shoulders tense with the thought that this coming of age could be marred by some unforeseen unpleasantness.

"Yes!" blurted Louisette nervously, as she resumed her broken brush strokes!

"Yes, what?" asked Anna Maria growing apprehensive.

"Yes…" Louisette said carefully. "…he can be very gentle. Very sweet."

Louisette felt her cousin's shoulders grow soft again. Anna Maria's resurgent calm served to dull Louisette's own myriad of concerns.

"Anything could go wrong." Louisette silently fretted to herself. "He could be depressed, angered, drunk or any combination of the above. Certainly, the last thing we need is for her to go in there any more frightened than she has to be. But then, he did promise to be nice…for what his promises are worth. But why does she have to want this so badly? And why does she have to want him?"

"I saw him kill once!" Anna Maria spoke, meeting her own bright gaze in the dresser mirror.

"You did?" answered Louisette feigning less surprise than she felt.

"Yes, on satellite." the girl answered with childlike mischief in her voice. "I'm sure uncle Georges didn't mean for me to see, but he fell asleep in front of the monitor so I snuck into the room and watched the whole thing!"

"How clever." Louisette filled, setting down the brush and inspecting her handiwork.

"It was shocking! And barbaric!" Anna Maria fawned breathlessly. "Yet so astonishingly magnificent!"

"Where was he?"

"Persia!"

"Ah! The Eastern Arbitration of…2171, I think," Louisette reflected fondly. "I'd known him a year already!"

"2172," Anna Maria corrected.

"Oh."

"The announcer said that the Persian Regional had never been beaten," Anna Maria revered. "But neither had he! The Persian pinned him down with gunfire for over an hour in that tiny hole. But he didn't realize that uncle's man had circled behind him! He must have leaped twenty feet from his perch, onto the Persian's back. They repeated it in slow motion so many times! I remember his hair flowing behind him like a golden cape. It was the most beautiful thing I had ever seen. Then he pulled out his knife, stabbed the Persian in the chest, and before he let him fall, shot him through the back of his head with his hand weapon!"

"And father's territorial judgment was upheld," Louisette concluded with little enthusiasm.

"And my life was changed forever!" sighed Anna Maria.

"That's why father didn't want an eleven-year-old girl watching that rubbish! You were too young…too impressionable," Louisette scolded mildly. "Now stand up!"

"Perhaps," defended Anna Maria. "But it's been over two years. I'm a completely different person now. I've become a woman! And the fires ignited that fateful eve burn brighter with love's passion today, than the child I was could ever have conceived!"

"Love!?" Louisette frowned. "What do you think you know about such a thing!"

"Enough to know that it's what's missing from our world today," Anna Maria smiled. "All I see is a preoccupation with sex and money and prestige and position and none of the things that have anything to do with the one element which sustains the human heart: Love!"

"Well," Louisette exhaled as she pulled straight, the silk lace panties covering little of her cousin's bottom. "If it weren't for money and prestige and position, you wouldn't be here now talking about a man other women, on and off of this planet, only dream of. And believe me, if it weren't for sex, you probably wouldn't be standing here in scant lingerie babbling about 'love' at all!"

"But that's just my point. Don't you see?" Anna Maria asserted with untried conviction. "Love and sex…are not the same thing. I mean, people would lead you to believe that they are, but they can't be."

"Is that so?" Louisette filled, as she tied the large bow binding her cousin's thickly curled hair.

"Yes, I'm positive," Anna Maria pouted at Louisette's implied skepticism. "Look at this weekend—a holiday where people all over the world are having it off with one another. Most with people they don't even know! People they probably will never see again! You can't tell me they're all 'making love'."

"Then what are they doing?" teased Louisette.

"Why…they're having sex!" exclaimed Anna Maria.

"Ohhh." Louisette accepted with a smile.

"Lou! You can't be missing the point, can you?"

"Which is?"

"Which is…" Anna Maria clasped her hands together, hastily scrambling to construct her philosophy into words, "…that there are only two ways for a woman to be with a man. She can be with him for herself, which is sex. Or she can be with him for him, which is love!"

"And it's that simple?" contested Louisette with growing annoyance.

"Remarkably so," Anna Maria proclaimed.

"Anna…"

"Listen to me, Lou. This didn't just dawn on me today. I've been weighing this for years!"

"Years? You haven't got many—and more than half of those playing with dolls."

"Lou, do you know what the number one cause of death for people between the ages of thirteen and thirty-five is?"

"Drug overdose."

"Excluding Weed class, Lou."

"Ummm, overdose still, I thought."

"No. It's suicide. And do you know what the number one reason is?"

"Bad looks?"

"No, silly. Bad relationships."

"Oh, come Anna! Who could tally such a number?"

"Uncle Georges commissioned a study of Psychiatry Ports, which accounts for ninety-four percent of the Blossom population. In fifty-eight percent of the suicides, people were observed by their counselors as being significantly despondent over their sexual relationships. And that doesn't even include deaths tied to drug use brought about by other bad relationships."

"It's just numbers, Anna!"

"How can you say that when your best friend, Elizabeth, killed herself last year?"

"She didn't kill herself."

"Oh, that's right. Her father had her swallowing those thirty pills ruled an accident and the note she left a hoax. Still, when Jonah told her he was tired of her, she got really depressed, disappeared into some Vietnamese Weed slum and turned up dead 'by accident' a few months later!"

"I hate to tell you this, dear cousin, but you don't have any idea what you're talking about."

"I hate to tell you, cousin, but though you may have me in years, I've read a great deal more in my thirteen and a half years than you'll read in your next twenty. Love is Heathcliff and Cathy in the Wuthering Heights. It's Romeo and Juliet in the fields of Verona. Pauolo and Francesca defying Satan. Joseph and Mary…"

"Oh, Anna! Storybooks…!"

"Edward VIII and Wallis Simpson in Hyde Park. John and Jacqueline framed by a New England sunrise. Napoleon and Josephine on these very shores."

"Anna," Louisette took her cousin's hands and held them tightly, "Maybe that's the way it should be. But that's not the way it is. Trust me, please."

"For you, perhaps." Anna Maria spoke with sudden impetuous disdain. "You know I'm going to take him from you today, don't you?"

"What?!" Louisette responded with a surprised smile.

"You heard me," the young girl addressed with a coolness unsuited to her years. "How long have you and he been together now? Two…maybe three years? And in all that time you took everything from him you could—but you never gave him anything."

"Anna, that's enough!"

"I've overheard the two of you argue. I've heard the anguish in his voice."

"You've heard what you've wanted to hear," answered Louisette, still stunned by the turn of the conversation.

"I've heard him call you selfish!"

The word rang in Louisette's head as she eased back into a chair and stared into nothing. His favorite weapon, she reflected.

"And I hear how, no matter how scornfully he repels your possessiveness, you brag to anyone who'll listen about how strong he is. How huge he is. How he'll one day succeed your father as Beneficent of the world…and how you'll be his wife! No wonder he detests you! No wonder he now looks to me."

"Anna, don't be ridiculous! I arranged this for you…"

"Did you have a choice? You've seen how he looks at me now. I remember how jealous you were the night he read my poetry aloud."

"I wasn't jealous, Anna. I was embarrassed. He was perverting it."

"In your eyes, maybe. I think, for the first time in his life, he saw a woman that understood the meaning of commitment and understanding and true love—something you cannot grasp."

"Anna, he likes you. He likes you a lot. But he's doing this because I asked him to…so that the first time would be…special for you."

Anna Maria stared at her lean burgeoning figure in the mirror with stern resolve. "Not for me, Lou. For him. I love him. And in a few hours he will be certain that he loves me. For I will take nothing! And I will give him all that I have to give. In the end, he will come to see things as I do. And the world will then become much the better for our joining."

Louisette began to massage her temples with her fingertips. Everything was suddenly all wrong. If she could have put a stop to her cousin's imminent meeting, she would have. But it was the eleventh hour and Anna Maria would only have interpreted any intervention at this late juncture as an extension of Louisette's "jealousy". Of course, she could head Him off, but she knew how he so detested final minute detours…especially in such matters as this.

"She'll have to see for herself how things are." Louisette silently concluded. "It'll be a letdown for her, but she's smart. She'll have to deal with it."

"Well," Louisette spoke aloud in a condescending tone, "I hope you're right."

"Don't patronize…"

"I'm not, I'm not. I know better. It's just that I can remember the first day I held you in my arms. It's hard to believe you're…a young woman now."

"Buttering up the 'new competition', Lou?"

"No, Anna. For no man, would I ever compete with my flesh and blood."

The young girl's brows suddenly softened. She looked away, swallowed hard and exhaled deeply. Just as quickly as Anna's coolness had blown in, it seemed to dissipate upon those words.

"Oh Lou, I'm sorry. I'm just…"

"I know." Louisette comforted. "Nerves. It's only natural. There's no harm done. I just hope you reviewed the videos I gave you."

"No."

"Anna!"

"No, Lou." she said softly. "This can't be done your way. Trust me."

Growing fear reclaimed Louisette, but she refused to let it show. She embraced Anna Maria and handed her a pink and violet Iris bouquet. She then pulled the lace shawl closed across her cousin's bare bosom and kissed her for good luck.

Louisette watched as Anna Maria then embarked upon the long march down the palace corridor toward his room. With each clattered shuffle of her cousin's steps along the black marbled floor, she could see terror and apprehension unsteady Anna Maria's strides. For a single moment, Louisette thought or hoped that the girl would turn around, run back and become simply her brainy little cousin a while longer.

"It'll be fine," she muttered doubtfully. "It'll be fine...and I could really use a dose of silver now."

In another moment, Anna Maria's frail figure disappeared behind the mammoth oak doors leading into his living quarters. Louisette felt a shiver as they loudly echoed shut.

The vestibule of his quarters was like a great shrine paying tribute to his many accomplishments. Gold and silver plaques dating back to his boyhood covered the dark wooden walls. Each inscription detailed some immaculate physical feat on some seemingly infamous date in history.

Anna Maria ran her delicate fingertips along the sharp edges of several awards, and sighed deeply—scarcely noting that she'd been holding her breath for several seconds.

She slowly passed along the walls wishing there were time to take in each and every tribute. She had studied him through media periodicals for years, yet all she had learned seemed insignificant in comparison to being here. Weight lifting awards, track and field awards, survival camp titles, weaponry certifications and...

"My God," she whispered.

A swirling white and green marble bust of him sat upon a pedestal wherein were carved the words: "With undying gratitude from the Greek-Italian Region for settlement of the Adriatic Dispute-2167.

"The first one," she recalled from her reading.

There were many other ornate monuments and trophies similarly inscribed with the offerings of thanks for his resolution of worldly conflicts.

"The North American Initiative-2169," she read on. "The Blossom-Weed Reapportionment of Russia-2170. The East Indian Combination-2173. The Israeli Dissolution-2171. The Colombian Coca Export Ruling-2173. The Martian-Lunar Mining Agreement-2174. And...the Eastern Arbitration-2172."

Anna Maria's heart pounded fiercely as she found herself short of breath. The date of the Eastern Arbitration was, to her, the date she had been born into womanhood. She collapsed at the base of the golden jeweled obelisk he had brought home for his service to mankind. She unconsciously laid down the bouquet, then pressed her body against the carving of his name.

"The mountains doth tremble at his gaze, the very skies darken upon that which he frowns! '*That I might gain he that is without law,*'" she whispered with her eyes closed. "'*I am sick when I look not on you.*'"

"Anna Maria," called a heavy voice from behind.

She squeaked involuntary at the shock of another presence. She snapped up the bouquet and whirled to her feet.

He was a giant in every aspect. Six feet, eight inches tall and heavily muscled in a way that no sculptor's chisel could aptly depict. Veins rained down his neck into tributaries that filled is massive arms. His azure eyes were bright like a noon sky, only with pupils that appeared illuminated by lightning. And the long golden hair that spewed from his scalp, fell regally upon his barreled bare chest and his broadened square shoulders.

"Victor," she mouthed silently.

"Anna Maria?" he repeated not reading her frozen lips.

"VICTOR," she managed audibly the second time.

"Yes," he said with a perplexed smile.

"Our...appointment," she said, surprised by her own nervousness.

"Appointment?" he said with a still perplexed look.

"Yes. Lou, um, Louisette said…"

"Ohhhhh," he seemed to recall with a grin. "Yes, I remember."

He placed his heavy hand gently on her back, which frightened her at first, but then felt comforting. It was the first time she had ever been alone with him—or any man not old enough to be her father.

He guided her into his bedroom where she saw portraits of him at various stages of life with Uncle Georges and other important Earth, Lunar and Martian dignitaries. There was even a picture of him and Louisette near a closet, though it was partially obscured by several plants.

The entire room was done in burgundy velvet and cream satin. There were large shoes, underwear, and tunics strewn about. Papers and books lay everywhere. It was strangely and decidedly masculine to her, but not entirely unsettling. After all, Louisette had mentioned that men were this way.

He lumbered toward the king-sized bed unlike the great idol she had come to admire from afar. He rolled onto his back, reached for a long curved bottle, and took a prolonged drink.

She stood in front of him, rigidly clutching the bouquet. It was almost as if he had already forgotten she was there.

"Drink?" he then offered playfully with arched eyebrows.

"Um no. I don't." Anna Maria answered, concealing her single encounter with the vine.

"Oh, come now," he engaged, "that's not like Louise's sister."

"Cousin," she corrected.

"Cousin, yes," he repeated. "Well, your 'cousin' drinks like a pelican."

"I don't," Anna Maria smiled, cheerfully ignoring the insult.

"Well, maybe you should consider it," he said not smiling.

"Maybe later," she agreed apprehensively.

He rolled his eyes back and drank again, spilling wine down the center of his tanned pectorals and into his dark navel.

She panicked that she might already be losing him. "I can't fail this soon," she thought.

"I brought these for you!" she spoke hastily, offering the bouquet with another cheerful smile.

"Oh," he said poorly masking his indifference. He clutched the bouquet with his large hand and reached under the bed pulling out a silver vase. He clumsily stuffed the bouquet into the vase and carelessly sat it by his feet at the end of the bed.

Anna Maria's heart began to pound again, only this time out of shear terror that the biggest moment of her life would pass as a yawning afterthought.

"So how old are you, now?" he asked with a limp smile.

"Um, fourteen," she exaggerated.

"Wow," he said inspecting her for the first time. "You've grown up nicely."

"I'm taller than Louisette by two inches," she blurted.

"And wait 'til you really fill out," he said matter of factly.

Anna Maria looked down and away self-consciously. She had considered her maturation to have been substantial over the past year. Now he had made her unsure.

"Hey, you look great," he feebly tried to make up. "Really fresh and…quite attractive."

"I'm failing," she thought to herself. "Louisette will laugh and he'll never think of me again. Joan. I've got to be Joan."

Tears began to form in her eyes as she began to rub her arm with her hand and shift her weight to one leg.

"Anna Maria," he said, sitting up, "maybe this isn't the right time for you. I mean…"

"No!" she yelled wiping her eyes. "You have to know…I…I love you!"

"What?" he said with a chuckle.

"I love you," she said, relieved to have relinquished the words.

"Anna Maria, do you have any idea what…"

"Don't ask me that!" she said desperately. "I know how empty you really feel! I know what's been missing for you!"

"Oh, really?" he said, tilting his head with mocked interest.

"Yes!" she said as her voice wavered. "Truth. Love. And…something else…larger and more wondrous than all the universe."

He inspected her scarcely nubile form again as he sipped from the stem of his bottle. Her firm young derriere sat perkily beneath her shear lace panties. Her thin slender limbs were youthful but actually exquisitely feminine. Her breasts were tiny, compared to Louisette's implanted bosom, but alluring in their modesty. Her long unblemished neck beckoned for the clench of his teeth. And of course, he considered other uncharted territory that playfully tickled his libido.

And there's that child's face, he thought, that the make-up can't conceal. Those big, empty, innocent eyes. That coyish girl's smile.

"All right," he said with a wolf-like smirk. "Show me."

"What?" she asked nervously.

"Show me…how much you love me," he cajoled with sarcasm that sailed well beyond her.

She walked purposefully toward him and alighted on his lap, for a moment appearing to know exactly what she wanted to do. She placed her hand on his chin and kissed him on the mouth. He waited for her next move, but she only met his eyes and smiled again.

"And?" he said impatiently.

Anna Maria's heart pounded so hard, now, that she felt the blood surging into her skull. Totally unsure of herself, she wrapped her arms around his huge neck and kissed his ear. She pulled back again and looked into his perturbed face.

"I honestly thought Louise would've prepared you better," he said leaning his mass aggressively forward.

She tried to hurriedly launch into the statement she'd prepared for him weeks ago, but violently, he snatched her wrist and twisted her arm behind her back. With the other hand, he reached behind her head and yanked apart the bow that bound her hair. He then clutched a fist of curls, wrenched her head backward and began gnawing savagely on her throat and shoulders.

Anna Maria became too confused to scream. Overcome by the physical deluge, she fitfully tried to make some sense of what was happening. But Shakespeare, Emily Bronte, and her recent studies provided her no viable points of reference. She wanted to pass out, or disappear, or something until it was over—but she could not.

In seconds, her carefully tailored undergarments were torn away by huge, violating paws that seemed to be everywhere. He rolled her over like an infant and pinned her under his hulking frame. Gradually, she began to feel much like the dead and conquered Persian: helpless, worthless, lifeless.

Victor, meanwhile, was absolutely certain that awestruck little Anna Maria, if any measure of her shallow cousin, would someday recall having the time of her empty little life, losing her virtue and virginity to the Champion of Earth!

# VI.

The Palace Operations Center, three floors above:

The Operations' central staff was stunned by the Beneficent's mere presence here. It had long been established as a matter of course, that this leader cared nothing for the mundane details of any event, crisis, or catastrophe. All of the particulars of any such occurrence were, by decree, succinctly crammed into a one-page memo by the staff and forwarded through Val, the Beneficent's young page. Once the memo was digested, the Beneficent would quickly decide what Operations branch would be best suited to defuse the matter quickly and dispatch a recorded message, (three-quarters of which usually consisted of a reading of the aforementioned memo) to the assignees who would be given direct orders to "fix it", "handle it", or "kill it".

Only the Champion would ever be given a personal briefing regarding actions of necessity. Some said it was due to the critical importance of staging World Cartel settlements so as not to raise the ire of the losing contingent. A swift victory at the hands of the Champion was considered to be an insult. A prolonged struggle, however, albeit resulting in defeat, left the ill-favored region or faction with its pride intact and made settlements generally more palatable. Of course there were others who rumored that the Beneficent enjoyed meeting the Champion in private simply to contrast his time spent with Val.

"So what does this all mean?" blustered the Beneficent to the sprawling room of computer terminals, video monitors, and central staff members.

Manda Martine, Cartel Operations Coordinator, toyed with the idea that the Beneficent might, after eighteen years, finally be asking what it is her people do in this World Cartel nerve center. But she was certain his query was probably directed at the memo he'd received an hour ago (which shockingly spilled over into a page and half), detailing the obliteration of Liberace Gardens.

"It means, sir, that 47,000 Vogue Day vacationers were incinerated by what appeared to be a meteoroid of unspecific composition," Manda capsulized.

"Unspecific?" filled the Beneficent, feigning a grasp of the disaster's magnitude. "Why 'unspecific'?"

"Because at this point, our science personnel are just now setting up along the perimeters of the scene. Mare Crisium station was only able to report frozen methane, iron fragments and huge amounts of hydrogen and helium as it tanned past the moon. Albuquerque was able to confirm, but this thing emitted such a wide spectrum of light and radiation, that getting any reliable type of spectro analysis was close to impossible!"

"So we have no idea at this point what it is!" the Beneficent exclaimed.

"You're essentially correct, sir." Manda conceded.

"Well that won't suffice Ms…"

"…Martine."

"Yes. I want answers!" he finished.

Manda seized the opportunity to involve her top aide who sat nearby, unable to work because of the projection of the Beneficent's voice.

"Sir, I'd like you meet Jean-Paul Vendemiaire," Manda introduced. "He's the one who picked up the meteoroid's initial trajectory and was able to determine its approximate point of impact."

"You mean we knew exactly where this thing was going to land?" the Beneficent addressed Jean-Paul. "Couldn't we have warned those people?"

"We tried to, sir," answered Jean-Paul as Manda reached behind him and tore down a satirical drawing he'd made of Val and the Beneficent in an unflattering position. "Unfortunately, a Mr. Gruberstein saw fit to rebuff our urgent plea for evacuation of his resort. Between obscenities, he groused something about 'profits' and 'a busy time of a year'. Perhaps he figured his insurance would cover the twenty square kilometers of inhabited terrain that were converted into a molten crater."

"Twenty square kilometers!" the Beneficent repeated, stroking his beard. "How big was the damn thing?"

"Well, as Manda said, spectro readings were pretty unreliable," said Jean-Paul. "But we estimate it was somewhere between .25 and .65 K's in diameter. Quite a monster. They felt it from Hawaii to parts of Manitoba. Fortunately, the hydraulic tectonic plates reacted well. There's been quake activity all over the northern half of the western hemisphere, but minimal tidal activity. Still, the death toll is still going to be pretty high before its all over—especially in the Weed regions where the slightest disruption of routine leads to violence and rioting."

"Manda, have the magnetic containment lockes been activated around the Blossom regions?" the Beneficent prioritized.

"Yes sir." Manda answered dryly.

"Good. We don't need any Weed barbarism bleeding over onto good people," the Beneficent said with conviction. "Let those cretins kill each other. They'll grow tired eventually."

The Operations room fell silent except for audio-visual transmissions and humming computers. Everyone froze on the hate-filled words of the Beneficent. They were all Blossom class now, but no one considered it culturally acceptable to publicly castigate the Weeds for their "chosen" lifestyle. Part of the original Blossom-Weed Edict of Separation sixty years ago called for "outward tolerance and acceptance for the sake of harmony". This, and the fact that many Operations people had distant family on the other side of those magnetic lockes, made the Beneficent's bigoted aloofness taste all the more sour.

"You people are all doing an excellent job." The Beneficent spoke to break the silence. "And I realize this is going to be difficult on all of us."

The Beneficent then lowered his voice to Manda and Jean-Paul: "Keep me apprised of everything that goes on with that meteoroid. Two-page memos if you have to. I don't know if any of us are ready to deal with a goddamn invasion. Let's hope we won't have to."

The leader of the entire planet smiled and waved to the people in the Operations room, then pivoted, and strode out of the sliding exit.

"Invasion?" Jean-Paul asked, as he replaced his drawing. "Who said anything about a bloody invasion?"

"He just did." Manda answered flatly. "I guess if you're the undisputed ruler of the known, docile universe, that would be the one thing you'd fear the most. Something out of your control. Something UNknown."

# VII.

Tegucigalpa, Honduras:

"Apocalypse!!!" yelled Manuel above the gunfire, looting, and cries of chaos that rambled ruthlessly through the streets of Tegucigalpa. "Repent! Make your peace with God!!!"

The words of the minister, who had closeted his spartan parish in the basement of his grocery store, fell completely unheeded.

From the moment the quake had hit and the power lines failed, this city roiled into a murky cauldron of savage anger. Festering debts were being settled with irrevocable finality as factions systematically sought to vanquish their hated rivals. Schools became besieged fortresses. Storefronts became battered bunkers. And the humans became less so, stealing and killing until they, themselves, became victims of the blood bath. Libertad Avenue was literally ankle deep in shell casings, empty weapons, and putrefying, exsanguinated corpses.

Hours ago, Manuel had been leading prayer beneath his store. The few who were still beholden to the words of Christ had become his pillar, since murder and addiction had stolen away his wife and children. When the lights went dark after the quake, everyone knew what would follow: pillaging, violence and death. So he warned everyone to stay below, hidden away from the horrors above. They quietly listened to the herd of plundering looters as Manuel's livelihood was ransacked and gutted.

"They can steal away all we have, but they cannot take our souls," he comforted the frightened men, women and children huddled on the basement floor.

Then, the hidden trap door was yanked violently open over their heads.

"Who's down there?" called a young man's voice from above.

"No one to concern yourself with," answered Manuel.

The young man poked his gun followed by his head into the opening and observed the candles and crucifixes surrounding the huddled gathering.

"It's a fucking cult!" he called to someone behind him.

Manuel no longer bristled at the insults to his faith. He pitied the unenlightened.

"You!" the young man called to him. "Get up here, witch-doctor!"

Manuel complied, hoping to divert attention from his followers. He climbed the wooden ladder through the trap door opening. As he rose to the ground level he was not surprised by the sordid sight of his ravaged place of business. He was, however, taken aback by the gun-butt a second young man used to split open his face.

Dazed and bleeding, Manuel staggered helplessly into a shattered display case. He tried to speak through broken teeth, but could only think what he wanted to say.

"Cults almost fucked up this whole planet!" the first man spoke. "Got everybody fighting everybody else! And over what? Some words written by some drunk shepherds thousands of years ago? Some 'holy land' so dead you couldn't grow marijuana in it? Some god you can't see? Some…shit nobody's dumb enough to believe anymore?"

As if on cue, a third man kicked Manuel in the rib cage. Then the three armed men began to laugh.

"I always wondered why I got sick every time I ate from this place," the first man continued. "I used to think that maybe you stink so bad you make the food rot. But now I know you weren't giving a shit about me or the people who waste their hard earned money in this place. You were worried about poisoning our people with your fucking cult shit! Well, let me tell you something: The days of the brainwashing cults is over! Today, we do a little cleansing of our own."

The second man appeared with a large, nozzled container and began pouring the contents through the trap door opening. The sharp odor of the flammable liquid was unmistakable. Manuel tried to jump to his feet, but was shoved back onto the broken glass that littered the floor. In another instant, the first man fired a shot into the basement, and a fire ignited.

Deafening screams of anguish shrieked from the trap door opening. A man on fire crawled up through the door and was immediately shot through the temple, spraying blood, hair and brains against a near wall. A boy followed and was likewise, shot and kicked back down into the flames. The first assailant then, stomped the trap door shut, and locked it tightly with a bar of wood, like the lid to a medieval incinerator.

"Mi amigo, I guess it's time to pray, eh?" the first man said with a chuckle, as his two friends dragged Manuel's limp body into the street.

Manuel awoke hours later only to view his smoking storefront collapsing within itself.

"*...for they know not what they do,*'" he muttered, staggering to his feet. "*O faithless and perverse generation...*'".

From that point onward, he walked amidst the gunfire, shouting scripture and warnings as he had once feared to do. Bereft of everything he had cherished on this Earth, the spirit of his convictions held him up as never before. He could not weep for the familiar faces on the dead bodies that lay all about him, for their time had already passed. But for the living...the wretched murderous unrepentant souls, yet unsaved, his work could still be done.

Manuel shouted above the gunfire and the chaos, determined to use his final breaths preaching God's will. And he secretly prayed that an end would soon come to everything this unholy Earth had become.

# VIII.

Cannes, France-The Beneficent Palace:

Louisette was flush with invigoration after her warm floral bath and her late afternoon dosage of blusilver. Previous concerns over Anna Maria's sexual inauguration now seemed absurdly belabored. Even the panic which now embraced the Palace staff, due to some large rock from outer space that had killed some handful of people in…"California?" she tried to recall. No, Florida, I think," seemed distant and unimportant.

She laughed giddily at her own lack of concern and the absence of the need to be.

"Well, wherever!" she chuckled to herself in the mirror. "Only, why do the places with the prettiest beaches have to be prone to so many natural disasters? I guess it's like being a beautiful woman. Every day you're the envy of everyone around you. Then one day…hmmm. Well, I guess that's not a good analogy. Anna Maria is so damn good at those kinds of things. In fact, I'm sure she's dazzling Victor with her adolescent wit and her educated notions on world affairs at this very moment. But I fear that school girl charm won't be enough to turn him from me when the sweat starts to fly!"

She started to laugh again, but then faded to seriousness as she scrutinized her buxom nude form.

"Polymer-cellulose injections again?" she asked herself as she held her oversized breasts in her hands. "He always said, 'too much today is too little tomorrow.' And I could swear he gets enlargements himself, though he swears not. But these things are uncomfortable enough!"

She turned and regarded her rear and thighs. "Damn, I remember when I was thin like Anna." she said, disdaining her own perfect legs. "Computer! Set the microbe lounge to reduce my size nine ass to a seven!"

The microbe reduction lounge eased out from under her bed. (The device injects fatty tissue-consuming hybrid microscopic Martian parasites under the skin to reduce weight and bulk.) But when it came to a halt, a warning signal sounded.

"Based upon your reduction sixteen days ago from size ten to size eight, this action could result in serious nerve and cell damage!" advised the computer.

"Override!" she yelled angrily.

"By order of Dr. Canard, 'Override' command has been disabled!" the computer replied flatly.

"Damn you then!" she screamed kicking the lounge violently until it receded under the bed again. "Where the hell is my goddamn bulimia when I need it, anyway! This machine has been a curse from day one!"

She rubbed her temples and recalled the incident last year when Victor had unlovingly referred to her as being 'porcine' on her twenty-first birthday. As a result, she locked herself away that day and overrode the computer to eat her down from an eleven to a five.

"God, I almost killed myself!" she reflected. "Now I've got a stupid lounge without a stupid override. Men just don't understand!"

She leaned forward into the mirror and examined her face.

"Computer," she called, "What about cheekbone injections?"

"Last, injection was four days ago. No alterations advised for another seven days." replied the computer.

Louisette tensed up in anger again but consciously calmed herself.

"What about a nose reduction?" she asked impatiently.

"This will exhaust your nose alteration limit for this twelve month term." the computer stated.

"Who asked that? Just accept the coordinance!"

"Affirmative."

Louisette spoke the coordinances for the alteration as a helmet sized dome lowered over her head. Laser light flashed across her face causing her nose to sting slightly. Then a cooling salve tickled the edge of her newly formed feature, and the dome lifted.

"Excellent," she smiled.

Louisette then, barefooted over to the closets, yanked out something red and short, and tied it around her body. She returned to the mirror and brushed her black, shiny, curled hair madly until it sat twice the height of her head. She tucked her inoculator into her cleavage, hastily crammed her feet into her tight spiked heels and pranced out the door.

Sauntering through the corridors as the Beneficent's beautiful, beloved daughter and the Champion's coveted consort had become her favorite means of reaffirming her sense of importance. The dislike of the female staff members was a proud medal of accomplishment by her reckoning. For surely, even beyond her ever-changing bounds of beauty, Louisette's life of privilege and irresponsibility was reason enough to be the envy of any woman alive. Their placative smiles and scornful whispers behind her back only heightened the deluded pleasure of simply being Louisette. Though in rare sober interludes she often wondered how, though almost her equal in status, dear, sweet, cousin Anna Maria had failed to earn her fair portion of popular resentment.

The men were, to her, as caged animals restrained by their fear of violating her station and/or incurring the wrath of the great Champion himself. Though, from time to time, like a naughty toddler, she would wander into one of the cages for an illicit evening, so that the teasing of the other "animals" would carry realistic possibilities.

She swayed past a group of maids, standing idle during one of their cleaning breaks. Predictably, one maid managed a forced smile while the others passively beckoned her passing with stiff jaws.

Louisette giggled to herself as she strutted onward with added emphasis on the loudness of her heels.

She turned a corner wondering where next to make an appearance when she saw Jean-Paul, the Operations staff assistant walking hurriedly in her direction.

"How the devil do I cram a bloody catastrophe into a two-page memo!" he exclaimed to himself reading over a scroll of data trailing behind him.

He was about to walk by without paying Louisette any notice at all. Being hated, she didn't mind. But being ignored was intolerable.

"Jean-Paul!" she called, clumsily accosting him by the waist and shoulders. "Uh…so tell me what's going on in Florida."

"Beach volleyball, I guess." he replied impatiently as her finger massage made his skin crawl.

"Isn't something important going on?" Louisette asked ignoring his desire to move on.

"Yes," he said, blinking against the heavy perfume that stung his eyes. "But I think you're talking about California, not Florida."

"Same difference, right?" she smiled.

"Sure, Louise." Jean-Paul answered noting the light blue haze in the whites of her eyes.

"So what's going on?" she purred, trying to pull him closer.

Jean-Paul could not suppress a heavy sigh which capped his total contempt for her. He was knee deep in preliminary analytical data that needed to be condensed into something Manda could somehow pass on to the Beneficent in two pages. The meteoroid disaster was now half a day old, and the last thing he desired was to regurgitate facts to a blusilver-inebriated "princess" who would carelessly expunge the bewildering information back into a warm palatial bubble bath. Nonetheless, he respectfully tried to cliff-note succinctly.

"A large meteoroid hit Liberace Gardens last night and killed a lot of people," he said slowly.

"My god," she said attempting to muster concern. "Are they closed now?"

"I'd say so, Louise," Jean-Paul said as he began dismantling her hold. "There was nothing left!"

"Wow," gasped Louisette fighting to understand through her blusilver rush. "Does…does my father know about this?"

"Yes. He's meeting with the Champion now as a matter of fact. And he's waiting for a memo from Manda. Look, Louisette, I have to go." Jean-Paul turned and regained his quick strides.

"Well, when you're done," she called to his back, "do you want to come up to my room and do some…stuff?"

Jean-Paul disappeared down the hall bearing the burden of the universe on his neck.

Louisette pouted at another missed attempt to seduce the "handsome intellectual" from Ops.

Then she wondered: If Victor was meeting with her father, what had happened to Anna Maria?

# IX.

Beaufort, South Carolina:

Anthony Denison was immersed in the midst of an unusually enjoyable evening. His son, Lang, had been possessed by one of those incredible eight-year-old zones of boundless energy, prepared to wrestle his father dauntlessly, for the "Title" of the living room. His wife, Mikki, had served an unrivaled supper, highlighted by a juicy Duck a la range, a sweet, rich raspberry torte, and a bottle of Pinotage saved from their honeymoon ten years ago today.

Youth and stamina triumphed as Lang inadvertently headbutted his father in a vulnerable place collapsing him into immediate submission. Having asserted his preeminence over aged adulthood, the boy proudly marched off to bed with little resistance, brashly refuting the adage: "…uneasy lies the head that wears the crown."

The "vanquished" Anthony rolled up onto the couch and clicked on the satellite monitor. He programmed the channel to jazz and closed his eyes to revel in the rare comfort of his own home. Then he felt Mikki's hands run up his back and over his shoulders and didn't attempt to suppress a thankful smile. He opened his eyes and saw his wife appearing more beautiful to him than the day they had married. He silently thanked his fortune for Lang and Mikki, both.

"Lights," he called as the room dimmed to black save the red and blue stage light emanating from the monitor.

Anthony reached up and gently pulled Mikki over the back of the couch. It was only at that moment that he realized she wasn't wearing a shred of clothing.

"Whoa!" he laughed just above a saxophone's amorous coo. "What's the deal?"

"You're the deal, sweetheart," she smiled. "You're home. Happy anniversary."

Their smiles melted away with the acknowledgment of how important this evening really was. Anthony was the head of Operations-Space

Anomalies Division stationed on Mars. His job required him to be away for three quarters of the year during which he could only watch his son grow up through weekly sub-space communiqués. Mars was settled, "but no place for my family," he had explained to his wife. And besides the fact that he relished the division between work and family, he needed them on Earth, so as to always ensure that he would return home to his coveted Carolina roots.

Mikki was a good wife, but had been no saint during the early stages of her husband's imposed sabbaticals to the "Red Rock". Early on, a series of affairs almost destroyed their union. But when one particular indiscretion saw a near stranger physically threaten her and her son, she came to realize that the choice between her husband and infidelity had to be certain and unwavering.

Anthony, in the meantime, had no problems remaining faithful. His addiction to pills, however, had become another matter. An incurable workaholic by all accounts, Anthony loathed fatigue when he was on about something. As a consequence, to maintain his optimum alertness, he had developed a cycle of medicinal usage that virtually arrested his patience for the shortcomings of others. At work, this made him brilliant, but difficult. But on the visits home, it made him an insufferable domestic boor. Two years ago, at Mikki's insistence, instead of returning to his family, Anthony spent the Winter Holiday under the care of a dependence counselor.

The following year's three-month reunion had been a great improvement, although aggravatingly tense as they struggled to rediscover one another. But the correspondence over the past several months had been much more comforting for them both. Finally, the fatty burden their relationship had once lapsed into began firming into a powerful, lean muscle both had chosen to work at and rely upon. Anthony and Mikki, soon realized that though the universe was vast and endless, in all of it, they had only each other…and their son.

"So how does it feel to be home?" Mikki nibbled on his ear.

"Better than I could've hoped," Anthony smiled. "If I'd known it was going to feel this good, I'd have flown home without a shuttle; just flapped my arms in space until I hit Earth's atmosphere."

"And then you'd have burned up."

"Oh no," Anthony caressed her thigh. "I'd have smoked a man-sized hole right through the ionosphere, I'd have been so hot to get home again."

"Just for me," Mikki massaged his chest.

"No," Anthony grinned. "Actually, for that raspberry torte you finally mastered. Is there anymore of that left?"

Mikki hissed playfully, and punched her husband in the chest, momentarily abandoning her delicate ministrations.

"Hey…ow!" Anthony grabbed her fist. "That's it! My son disembowels me and now you want to finish me off. I'm outta' here!"

"Well if you're disemboweled, what good are you anyway?" Mikki poked his pelvis.

"So that's all I'm good for?" he grabbed her other hand.

"So you say," she stuck out her tongue.

Anthony grabbed a pillow and smacked her across the head.

Mikki then, dove at him with her free hands and began tickling his rib cage. Anthony started to laugh uncontrollably until he was able to seize her wrists. Then they smiled at each other and kissed.

"So how does it feel to be home?" Mikki asked, holding his eyes with her own.

"Like three months leave may be too short this time," he spoke in earnest. "Like…maybe I'll figure out a way to stay away from the Red Rock for good."

"Don't say that unless you mean it, hon." Mikki grew serious.

"I do." Anthony pushed back her hair. "I just don't know if I can make it happen."

"Then let's not talk about it," she frowned.

"I just thought you should know, I'm thinking about it." Anthony rubbed her shoulders.

"I don't want to know what you're thinking," Mikki shook her head. "I want to know what you're going to do."

Anthony sighed deeply. He had badly wanted to share his thoughts with her, but somehow the mood began to veer toward something less pleasant. He mindfully shifted subjects before the air began to chill.

"Remember Donald Farhi?" Anthony asked lazily.

Mikki broke out into uproarious hysterics.

"Bad complexion, talked to himself a lot, afraid of his own shadow..." she said laughing.

"...and wouldn't leave you alone." Anthony finished.

"Until you came along and started bullying him. You were so mean!" Mikki teased.

"I wasn't mean," he lightly defended. "I just knew, even in high school that you and I..."

The satellite monitor suddenly flashed bright, then went dark. Mikki froze, waiting to see what would happen next. Anthony sat up, already anticipating the familiar pattern of this forthcoming interruption.

In another instant, the pudgy round face of Manda appeared on the screen.

"Good evening, Anthony, Mrs. Denison." Manda said dryly. "Happy anniversary."

"Thank you," answered a stunned Mikki, who quickly sat up and scooted behind Anthony to eclipse her sudden embarrassment from the satellite camera.

"Manda, you've got to be joking!" Anthony said with plain annoyance.

"No joke," said Manda with mild regret. "I know you just got home yesterday, but we need you in California."

"California?" Anthony replied "Isn't that a little out of my jurisdiction?"

"Yes, it would be." Manda continued. "Except that that meteoroid you and your people had been tracking hit us last night."

"Impossible!" Anthony insisted.

"Possible," responded Manda. "Haven't you been watching the media? We have a twenty K crater and a lot of dead and unaccounted for."

"But we had that thing set to miss us by half a million miles!" said Anthony, who had put his home on media black-out for the week. "It should be on its way to Sol by now!"

"We know. But it seems to have picked Earth for a layover."

"Damn." he cursed, knowing what she would ask next.

"It's here, Anthony. And Beneficent Georges is crawling up my crack."

"I thought he used Val for that."

"Not when it shakes up a quarter of the planet, bud."

Anthony rubbed his hand over the stubble he had planned to grow into a beard and resisted looking back at the predictably unhappy face Mikki would not be able to contain.

"Well," he said with resignation. "Give me an hour to say good-bye to these strangers I call my family…and I'll meet my team in…"

"…Santa Cruz," Manda filled in.

"Yeah. Santa Cruz."

"Anthony, you know we…I wouldn't have called if this wasn't real bad," Manda said apologetically.

"I know, Manda," he responded. "I guess it comes with the fat wages."

The screen went dark. Anthony let loose a deep sigh.

Mikki rubbed his back with consolation.

"Don't worry about us," she said. "This isn't a few years ago. I know you have to go…and I know you want to go. Just hurry back."

Anthony stood up and took his wife by the hand. He kissed her lovingly on the cheek, then decided to take an extra hour to say good-bye.

# X.

The Beneficent Palace:

"'*For the great day of his wrath is come*'," quoth the Beneficent in a deep foreboding tone, "'*and who shall be able to stand?*'"

The Beneficent sat the open book in front of Victor and took up his bejeweled wine chalice again. In passive defiance, Victor continued to inhale from the tip of his thick herbal cigar, ignoring the offer to share in the enlightenment.

The Beneficent scowled at Victor's arrogant, entrenched skepticism.

"What would you have me say, Georges?" Victor addressed him informally. "That some two millennia aged demon, in the form of this meteoroid, has returned to Earth to avenge itself on humanity?"

"I never said such a thing," the Beneficent defended.

"Then why in the hell have you been bombarding me for the last hour and half with quotations from that goddamned moth-chewed relic of yours?" asked Victor from behind a cloud of white smoke. "Why don't you just pack it back to the Louvre archives where it belongs?"

"Because…" the Beneficent said with rare uncertainty, "if there be even a shred of truth in the text of this 'relic' (as you say), then this Earth, this paradise which we've built from the ashes of oppression, repression, bigotry, violence, and all of those ills which once inhibited the celebration of life; the splendor of the human spirit, will be obliterated!

"Look here: '*And in those days shall men seek death*'," read the Beneficent, "'*and shall not find it; and shall desire to die, and death shall flee from them.*'! Monstrous!"

"Georges…"

"And look here: Alleged edicts from some 'higher force' that curves its gnarled roots about the very essence of human nature. '*Thou shalt not kill*', when we know that there are a myriad of circumstances under which a person may be forced to undertake such an action for the sake of self preservation. '*Thou shalt not commit adultery.*' I ask you, what is adultery in a world where consenting adults are free to choose whomever they desire to lay with so long as it is mutually agreed upon? '*Thou shalt not covet thy neighbour's wife,*' with no regard for the women's right to choose if she desires to be coveted! '*Nor his manservant, nor his maidservant*', even if he be willing to offer a better wage! '*Nor his ox*' whether or not thy neighbor sees fit to make good use of it! '*Nor his ass*', obviously in opposition to one's freedom of sexual preference! And '*Thou shalt not steal.*' Bah! Woe unto those who protect not themselves from people's inclination to steal, I say! "

"Georges…"

"'*Broad is the way, that leadeth to destruction…narrow is the way which leadeth unto life*'! Yet we know that it is the acceptance of any and all philosophies of life that make us rich in diversity and wisdom. For who is one man to tell another how he is to weigh his fortunes. Granted, the existentialist may have more solidity in his favor than say…the astrologist. And certainly, the scientist will scratch closer to the surface of facts than any of us. But to proclaim a way that is narrow…the very sound of it smacks of, nothing short of, binding limitations on the freedom of the living, thinking person."

"Georges…"

Unhearing, the Beneficent riffled through the pages of the tattered book to another marked passage: "'*Lay not up for yourselves treasures upon earth, where moth and rust doth corrupt, and where thieves break through and steal:*'. These fiendish words speak of a man's earnings as if they were a canker on the face of his life, rather than a homage to his worldly accomplishments. '*But lay up for yourselves treasures in heaven, where neither moth nor rust doth corrupt, and where thieves do not break through nor steal:*'! Well, we know that this 'heaven' or haven as it were is supposed to be somewhere in space! And we know that the creation of rust is impossible in the airless void! And certainly no moth could possibly live there! But what charlatan could conceive of a plan whereby human beings of that time would dispense their wealth toward some non-existent plain! Ohhh

Victor, this is the ilk of specious chicanery that brought those wretched Cult institutions crashing down for good in the mid-21st century. Impoverished, hopeless, deluded followers begging for a miracle that would never come. And in the end, only their fellow man was there to rescue them from the despair in which their so-called morality had tried to drown them. Only their fellow man brought an end to the starvation and disease. Only their fellow man brought an end to the violence, suppression and guilt. Only their fellow man was able to say live and let live. Blossom be free to flourish! Weed be free to be as thou wilt. And cherished freedom for all doth reign supreme. But now this."

The Beneficent punched on a wall-wide monitor displaying the molten whirlpool left in the meteoroid's wake. The darting lights of science aircraft were visible only as specs above the fiery maw.

"And now this!" the Beneficent yelled angrily as he slammed the book onto the glass table in front of Victor.

"Georges," Victor began calmly, for the fourth time, "I think you need a sedative."

"A sedative!?" the Beneficent shouted. "A sedative!? Yes. Let me rest! Or should I fiddle while 'Rome' burns? Victor, that damn thing is here to destroy us, I know it!"

"Georges, it's a fucking rock for god's sake."

"'*and, lo, there was a great earthquake;*'" the Beneficent recited. "'*And the stars of heaven fell unto the earth…*'"

"Enough." Victor demanded with annoyance. "You're talking about old Christian Mythology that holds about as much matter as the old 'Big Bang' theory did."

"Yes," the Beneficent answered, breathing heavily after a deep gulp of wine. "But historically, every myth, has had its basis in fact. Have you ever wondered: what if advanced alien creatures visited our planet millennia ago and planted the seeds of this…'religion' as a means of arresting our advancement as a species…for the purpose of preventing us from rivaling them sometime in the future? And what if they found, centuries later, that we had broken away from their control and were now incapable of being fooled again? What recourse would be left to them but to destroy us?"

"Georges, I always wondered why Louise was such a little flake," Victor said disparagingly. "Now I know where she gets it from."

"Don't mock me, Victor!" Georges warned. "You may be the Champion of Earth, but the people of this world won't bite the hand that feeds it!"

"Even if that hand has the shakes from too much Languedoc?" Victor challenged.

The Beneficent reached into his robe, whipped out a single barreled hand weapon and fired it at Victor.

Before the laser light could singe his flesh, Victor skillfully leaped from the couch dodging the beam with margin to spare, and slid across the glistening marble floor.

"Come, Victor," the Beneficent offered. "Come kill me now, that you may rule this world that much sooner."

"You shot at me!" Victor exclaimed in disbelief.

"Yes," the Beneficent spoke evenly. "There's your provocation!"

"You were my father's best friend." Victor said with sincerity. "And you've been my mentor from the day he died. Why would I kill you?"

"Why, indeed," said the Beneficent. "Why, when you know full well it means one thing to be Champion—but it's another matter entirely to be king of the universe. It means wielding both power and knowledge as an artisan wields a brush to canvas. It means being precisely all things to all human beings so that they may never question your station. It means walking a tightrope over a Martian canyon, with no ship waiting to catch you if you slip. It means a special kind of responsibility that frankly, scares you to death, doesn't it...Victor?"

There was a silence which cast its shadow of truth betwixt them.

In another moment, the door chime sounded and Val's thickly perfumed aroma preceded him into the room. He wore a pink silk cloth flowered loosely about his narrow pelvis. The click of his high heels pittered rhythmically across the room. The boy wore no top. He rarely did. Only a selection of rings, necklaces, bracelets and dangling earrings gifted to him by his liege adorned his soft creamy flesh.

The effeminate male nymph took his position under the Beneficent's arm and handed over a three-page memo. Then as he massaged the Beneficent's hairy chest, he turned his elegantly painted gaze at Victor who remained on the floor, unsettled by the familiarity of their affectionate pose. Val coquettishly winked at Victor, then seductively ran his tongue across his bright pearlish teeth.

Victor, disgustedly, looked away.

The Beneficent frowned at the length of the memo and began to skim read aloud: "Spectography…Metallurgical …Denison on his way…death toll…diameter…2000 Kelvin …no life signs!"

The Beneficent crunched the memo in his hand as an aura of confidence returned to his face.

"No life signs!" the Beneficent exhaled excitedly. "Do you know what that means, Victor?"

"It means it's just a rock." Victor said evenly.

"That's right!" confirmed the Beneficent triumphantly.

The older man swept his young nance off his feet as the boy clung around his neck. Val began laughing giddily in the voice of a young adolescent female.

"What about a swim?" the Beneficent asked the boy.

"But I just got made up!" Val playfully pouted.

"Then I'll just unmake you!" the Beneficent laughed loudly.

Val began kicking his legs excitedly as he let out squeals of pleasure. Cackling loudly, the Beneficent, carried the boy up two stairs and disappeared into the private pool area.

Val protested mildly between his own screams and the Beneficent's howling laughter. Then there was a loud splash, and soon thereafter, the festive noises became quietly intimate.

Victor hoisted his giant frame from the floor, while trying to block out the echoing voices from the pool area. As he strode out of the Beneficent's room, he took up the frayed relic that sat on the table. He decided it would be a good day to forego his scheduled workout, visit the palace library, and bone up on his mythology...and his history.

# XI.

Santa Cruz, California:

"So when does Denison get here? When dis crater dries up and begins sprouting plant life?" asked Amritraj from aboard the hovering lab vessel.

"He's on his way." Manda confirmed. "We had to dig him out of vacation, you know."

"Yes, well we are trying to configure a sonar matrix dat will allow us to probe de inside of de crater and figure out what's inside." Amritraj updated. "Unfortunately, de intense decametric radiation emanating from de meteoroid's core is distorting all of our readings. One scan makes it look like dere might be a ship in dere of some kind. But den de next scan looks like molten egg yolk. We take a dird, and we get turbulence, a fission reaction and doubled radiation levels. Wid de fourd scan we get what Mitchell called 'mineral whales', appearing fifty meters long and swimming in a giant circle. But den dat disappeared too! Widout Andony, we might as well be charting a kaleidoscope!"

"Agreed, A." said Manda. "Denison developed the sonar matrices that allowed us to map the core surfaces of Jupiter and Saturn while he was still an undergrad. This should be a penny puzzle for him."

"If he ever gets here."

"A, he'll be there."

"Den I'll just sit tight!" resigned Amritraj as he cut off his computer console. "So what is de Palace saying about all of dis?"

"Well," Manda answered carefully. "We just sent Beneficent Georges a three-page memo we knew he wouldn't have the patience to read, saying very technically that no one has a clue. For now, he seems content to let the media peddle it at face value. With the holiday this weekend, he figures no one will give two shakes."

"Ah, yes. Vogue Day in Madras." Amritraj said fondly. "Lots of tourists! Lots of curry! Lots of steak! Lots of horizontal hayrides! What would my ancestors say?"

"'Where's the poverty?' probably," answered Manda.

"And I'd tell dem 'about 400 kilometers to de nord…on de oder side of de…line." said Amritraj without fondness. "'Two dousand people to de square mile. You can't miss dem! And don't worry, de Beneficent says dey're all happy!'"

"Careful, A. This is a monitored frequency."

"Dat's true. I wouldn't want anyone in de Controller's office to get de idea dat I am against de rights of starving anarchists to butcher each oder and deir families!"

"A! It's not that bad. It can't be," said Manda trying to curb the tone of the conversation.

"No?" charged Amritraj. "Manda, in dese madders I'm afraid dat you are still a naive, Ohio farm girl."

"A…"

"A cute one, mind you," he lightened momentarily. "But naive, nonedeless."

"Thanks…I guess."

"Manda, I told you how my family made it to soudern India, didn't I?

"Yeah. Your father dealt bootleg opium and saved enough money to buy your family out of the Weeds."

"Dat's essentially correct. But dat wasn't until I was ten years old. Before dat time, twelve of us lived in a two-room, government-subsidized, straw shack. I grew up believing dat fresh air was supposed to smell like baby's urine and animal excrement. I walked home from school every day expecting to have to defend my life from roving gangs who killed people out of sheer boredom. And many times I did have to fight! Of course I lost a sibling or two when dere were too many gang members to stave off, and I had to turn and run to save myself. But…according to everyone from Cannes to Bombay, we were 'happy'! We could go where we wanted, so long as it wasn't too far soud, and we could do exactly as we pleased. And while dere wasn't always enough food or medicine, dere was certainly a bountiful supply of alcohol and recreation drugs."

"Well, there was lots of drug addiction where I grew up." Manda put in. "But I guess I always had this identity problem as a kid. I felt like highs would only take me further away from who I really was."

"But Manda, in Nord America you have Voluntary Rehabilitation Hospitals. You have Psychiatry Ports. You have strict laws against any form of violence. You have educational requirements. And certainly, de people dere are not packed togeder like canned rabbit's feet!"

Amritraj reflectively rubbed his forehead as if trying to knead the unpleasant thoughts from his conscience. "But in de Weeds, law is anoder word for oppression. Hard work is considered slavery. Help is undue interference."

"It's their choice, A." Manda attempted to console.

"So says de Beneficent." Amritraj concluded. "So says de World Cartel. And I ask myself why I even care. I have a nice home, a great job, and a preddy girlfriend I don't see enough of..."

Manda smiled and momentarily lowered her eyes from the screen.

"...but de doughts continue to hound me," he finished.

"Well," Manda said thoughtfully, "I guess that's what it is about you that I..."

A beeping signal on Amritraj's console cut in. He immediately clicked his computer back on. As the glowing orange and yellow crater reappeared on his monitor, he intercommed downstairs.

"Gary, what's de problem?" Amritraj asked noting no change in the crater's condition.

"No problem, sir," returned the voice from below. "I just thought you'd want to know that 'the expert' just came on board."

"Denison?"

"Aye, sir."

"Send him up!" ordered Amritraj. "Manda,—"

"I heard. Call me when you come up with something I can run through the strainer for Beneficent Georges."

"I will."

"And be careful."

Amritraj frowned as Manda's concerned face faded from the viewscreen. He then ordered his computer terminal to pull up all the information available for Anthony Denison's briefing.

## XII.

The Beneficent Palace:

Louisette's head ached from the inside as if her brain had sprung a slivered leak. Her skin had turned cold and clammy as even the sunlight from the corridor windows touched her flesh like a cool draft. She always loathed coming down from a blusilver excursion. Today she hated it more because cousin Anna Maria had seemingly vanished.

She had hurried to Anna Maria's room the moment Jean-Paul had informed her of her father's meeting with Victor. But the room appeared undisturbed since the late morning: bed made; books stored; stuffed dolls meticulously positioned at their stations.

From there, Louisette had gone to Victor's room. But amidst the disarray of clothing and magazines and trophies, her young cousin was no where to be found. Indeed, the only evidence of Anna Maria having been there at all, was the silk ribbon she had used to bind the girl's hair, now discarded over a tilted lampshade.

Louisette had searched the Palace library, although for her, locating the library had been a chore in and of itself. But no one there had seen Anna Maria all day.

She checked the palace gym, a place where Anna Maria had been known to work out difficult questions on the parallel bars, and where Louisette often enjoyed free-lance man-hunting, but her cousin's name did not appear on the registry there.

So Louisette, then scoured the beach for hours hoping to catch some glimpse of Anna Maria, perhaps gazing out over the sea, attempting to intellectualize her 'fascinating' new experience with Victor—but the girl apparently had not been so inclined.

She communiquéd to a number of Anna Maria's closest friends thinking that she may have felt some strange need to share her encounter with someone other than family. But none of them had heard from her for days.

In the end the search left Louisette exhausted and frustrated. Being a woman who loathed physical exertion outside the boundaries of sexual activities, she determined that she had exercised more in the past few hours, than she had since…she had discovered sex.

Louisette flopped onto a velvet bench in the palace corridor to rest before she returned to her own room. With some effort, she pried off her high-heeled shoes, then poured sand onto the thick oriental carpeting.

"I should've taken them off," she realized, belatedly. "I killed my ankles!"

Louisette asked one of the maids for an herbal cigarette to settle her down. She then laid over on her back, propped her feet up, and stared at the ceiling paintings of historical and mythological figures flowing in and out of colorful, imaginary settings.

"How can that girl be so selfish?" she mumbled to herself in a cloud of smoke. "If it weren't for me, she'd have never had her precious Victor. Maybe she's just embarrassed that he didn't accept her the way she expected. 'Poor' girl. He probably didn't even spend more than a few minutes with her. He's not very damned patient. In fact, he's not very damned anything…except the most egotistical man I've ever met! Of all the pictures and portraits in this entire palace, I'm certain his favorite is the ceiling mirror in his bedroom!"

As Louisette sighed deeply and closed her eyes, a disturbingly dark thought crept into her sobering conscience. But before it could take shape, she hastily forced a long drag from her cigarette, hoping to burn the shadowy notion from consideration.

"Louisette!" called an urgent young man's voice.

She opened her eyes and saw Wesley, a thin, bookish boy, hopelessly smitten by the mere mention of Anna Maria's name. Though bright and energetic, Anna Maria had walled away his persistence in a prison of friendship, charitably refusing to allow it to become anything more than platonic. Wesley, dauntless to the brink of tragedy, had unproudly accepted the role of her neutered male associate for the past three years.

"Yes, Wesley?" Louisette perked up, certain that he, of all people, would know of her cousin's whereabouts.

"I'm looking for Anna Maria!" Wesley spoke with a breathless pant.

"I haven't seen her." Louisette slumped, instantly annoyed by his sudden uselessness.

"Oh, gee. She's late!"

"Late for what?"

"Um, she and I and some other students were supposed to make a presentation to the Cartel Committee twenty minutes ago!"

"What for?" Louisette asked, surprised that students had gained an audience with the Committee during a holiday when governors could barely do so in states of emergency.

"Well, you know she's been working on this project for Weed Literacy for months now. She got us together so that we could propose a system for providing Weed kids with a broadened literary exposure."

"Oh." Louisette commented with disinterest.

"It was all her idea—she had it all planned out—and now she's missing! I can't believe she'd do this! All she talked about was how important this is. Now the other kids and I are about to get bounced on our collective rears by the Committee because we don't know what we're talking about without her."

"Well, can't you just wing it?" Louisette offered.

"In front of the Committee?" Wesley gulped. "My dad's out there! He'd kill me!"

"Well, I'm sorry, Wesley. I can't help you," Louisette sat up rubbing her arches. "I've been looking for her too."

"Well…" Wesley hesitated with the request of a favor dangling from his lips.

"Well, what?" Louisette jammed her feet back into her shoes.

"Well, Anna Maria had most of the proposal on a cartridge. If you could get it for me, we might be able to…'wing it'."

Louisette huffed to her feet and arched her back until it cracked. She signaled for the boy to follow her and tottering much like a skinny duck on over-large feet, he did.

As they walked toward Anna Maria's room they were observed by many passersby who seized the opportunity to accost the pair with whistles, catcalls and grunts.

"You should be ashamed, Louise!" called one maid from a doorway.

"Ashamed of what?" Wesley asked Louisette.

Louisette answered only by hastening her strides. "What do they take me for?" she thought as she pulled up the sagging top of her red wrap.

"I hope you know where this cartridge is," Louisette said as they approached Anna Maria's door.

"Oh yeah." said Wesley confidently. "She has a cartridge file she keeps in her cedar chest. It's better organized than the library's."

Louisette voice coded into the room. Wesley popped in closely behind and darted toward the chest. Across the room, Louisette noticed the satellite monitor playing quietly next to the bed.

"Got it!" called Wesley.

Louisette did not hear him.

Wesley frowned for a moment then bolted back out the door, running to salvage the meeting.

Louisette walked slowly toward the bed that was now disheveled. On the monitor were two women performing limber acts of coitus with an oiled male torso that almost rivaled Victor's in musculature. She stopped for a moment and noted dark smears tracked into the white shag carpeting. With her eyes she followed the smears to the bed where the edge of the white quilted comforter was unmistakably stained with two or three large dark red blotches that ran off to one side. Behind the side of the bed, Louisette saw two thin legs laying across each other still wearing the white bowed slippers she had picked out for Anna Maria earlier that day.

"Shit!" Louisette said breathlessly. "Anna Maria?"

Louisette quickly ran to the side of the bed and saw her cousin laying discarded in the tall white carpeting like a shattered, despondent Lladro figurine. Her dim, glazed eyes were open but stared no where in particular. Her hair was frayed on one side of her head but smashed on the other. Her right arm clutched the shredded lace shawl to her bosom. Her torn, blood-soaked panties were tied around her hip.

"Anna Maria." Louisette said softly again, hoping the girl would at least blink to indicate that she was alive. But there was no movement.

Fearfully, Louisette knelt down to touch the girl's face. It was only then that she saw the purple and blue teeth prints swollen about Anna Maria's slender neck and shoulders, and the scarlet raw abrasions on the insides of the girl's lean thighs.

"Anna Maria." Louisette repeated again as she touched her cousin's pallid complexion.

"Lou!" Anna Maria shouted as she sat up seemingly shocked from a deeply entranced fugue.

"Oh, sweetheart," Louisette spoke as tears crept down her cheeks. "What..?"

"He's not much for flowers." Anna Maria interrupted in a shaken voice that struggled to recover itself. "That was a serious miscalculation on both of our parts. And he's not much for ribbon either. But he likes hair, though."

Louisette took Anna Maria into her arms as her cousin's broken voice cut through her heart.

"And I definitely should have reviewed these," Anna Maria said, turning her head to the moaning, gyrating trio on the satellite monitor. "I had no idea that this is the way it was supposed to be."

"Well, maybe next time…" Louisette tried to comfort.

"Oh no." Anna Maria broke in. "No next time for Victor and I."

"Why not?" Louisette followed. "You don't love him anymore?"

"Oh...yes." Anna Maria continued, bowing her chin to her bruised chest. "I still love him very much. But it was obvious to me...today...that he hates me."

"Oh, Anna..."

"No, Lou. You weren't there. From the moment he laid eyes on me I could see that he thought I was the most ridiculous little thing. He never heard anything I said, and it was an effort for him to even pretend to care how I felt. When I confessed my love for him, it was as if I had soiled his dignity. When I kissed him, he became angry...attacked me...and I was sure he was going to kill me! I couldn't think...I couldn't even breathe!"

"He couldn't have been angry," Louisette spoke as Anna Maria began to hyperventilate. "Not at you."

"Oh yes...he was," Anna Maria said with sorrowed certainty. "He was very angry at me. He began growling obscenities... calling me names...biting with his teeth, hitting me with his knee. He pushed his fingers, his ...everything...everywhere."

Louisette shuddered.

"It was hatred, Lou!" the girl remorsefully concluded. "Only fierce, untempered, hatred could bring so great a man to act on my guileless advances as he did. Hatred for my being arrogant enough to think I could offer him love. And hatred for being such a horrible lover. I thought he was going to kill me...and I wish he had. It would have been so easy for him...like a rodent or an insect. But I wasn't even worthy of dying by his hands. Uncle Georges called him on the com, and he just pushed me onto the floor, got dressed and left. And now I have to live as the... repugnant object of his undying disdain!"

"Anna..." Louisette fumbled, "...he's a very large man, very strong. Almost three times your weight. It's possible you misinterpreted what he..."

"Dammit, Lou!" Anna Maria strained. "I know you think I'm hopelessly naive, but he wasn't careless! And he wasn't at all gentle as you said he could be! He wanted to hurt me. He wanted to hurt me so badly that I'd never have the audacity to look on him again! And he succeeded."

Louisette found her vision blurred with tears. Yet she noted that Anna Maria's own anguished shock prevented the young girl from crying herself.

"I've read about love…as God would have it." Anna Maria continued, taking her cousin's hand. "And romance. And it's a very real thing…two people caring and giving to each other for the rest of their lives. Sometimes I think I even wanted it more for Victor than for myself. But there was no chance. None at all. I failed him so miserably…and in doing so, failed the world! I was so foolish! I refused to prepare as you asked me to! I was so pathetically sure of myself! Now I know better, but it's too late.

"Look at me, Lou," asked Anna Maria, shamefully looking away. "Another opportunistic succubi cast down for not even the sake of pity. I tried to…tell him how I felt…tell him…what I meant, but…

"How could God have erred so greatly in my misbegotten creation?"

"God?" Louisette said with dismissal. "Now you're talking nonsense. No wonder you've taken this so hard."

Anna Maria's brow furled, then melted to resignation. She dropped her head to Louisette's shoulder and tried with futility to purge the stinging nightmare.

"Anna, darling," Louisette said softly. "What you need…what we need…is to get out of this place for awhile. Now, I was planning to go to Monte Carlo with some new friends for the holiday. And…I think maybe you should come along."

"Lou…"

"Don't argue. A little sun, a lot of men!" Louisette said before she could catch herself. "And…we can talk some more."

Anna Maria's expression did not change. Louisette had never wanted so badly to make things right for her; to restore the girl's signature glow. She reached into her top and pulled out her inoculator and three vials of blusilver.

"Welcome to the adult world, sweetheart," Louisette spoke tenderly. "You've never been down before, but it happens to everyone. This is how you get back up. A half vial for now, half for when we get to Monte Carlo and two for whenever else you think you might need them. By the time we get there, you'll be so high, you won't even remember…what's his name. Trust me."

"'…*there's rue for you; and here's some for me…*'" Anna Maria recited taking the inoculator and vials into her palms.

Louisette made no sense of the remark, but hoped that the drug would whitewash the damage.

"Do you want Dr. Canard?" Louisette asked. "I think you've got a bit of a tear."

"I'm okay." Anna Maria answered, blankly somber.

"Do you want me to call someone to help you wash up?"

"No. I'll manage," the girl answered stiffly.

Louisette rose to her feet and almost fell again noting that her headache had increased significantly. Resigned that she had done all she could, she unsteadily wobbled toward the door.

"Call me if you need anything, Anna."

Anna Maria crawled up onto the bed and sat still.

As Louisette stepped forward, the room doors opened.

"Lou," Anna Maria, called.

Louisette halted in the doorway.

"Did he ever treat you this way?" Anna Maria begged an answer. "Ever?"

Louisette swallowed hard and reflected over her tumultuous relationship with Victor. A hundred painfully violent images of doing anything and everything imaginable to remain the Champion's woman hacked through her memories. All for fleeting status. All for elusive pride.

"No," Louisette lied. And she stepped through the doors which closed quickly behind her.

# XIII.

Santa Cruz:

"Sonic particle conduit?" quizzed Amritraj. "Look, I understand acoustic inertance, but what in de world is a Sonic particle conduit?"

"Think about it a moment," Denison said as his eyes danced around the pulsing spectrographic image of the large molten crater. "Our readings have been shredded by all that radiation billowing out of the center of that crater, right?"

"Correct." Amritraj responded like a lab student.

"And here we are, hovering right above that crater soaking up all those lethal, gene altering rays, right?"

"Well, not exactly. Dis vessel's dermonuclear engine generates a field around us dat protects us from harmful radiation. We've been using de same technology in space for half a century now."

"True." Denison observed wagging his forefinger as a pointer. "So why can't we simply extend the field into the crater, which pushes the acoustic inertance aside and allows us to take our sonar readings a section at a time?"

"Well, for one ding," Amritraj contested, "it would take an inordinate amount of power to extend de field more dan a few K's. Dis vessel was built for Eard after all. And even if we could extend de field farder dan a few K's…say ten or fifteen maximum, we'd have to get so close to dat ding dat we would be endangering every life aboard!"

"How close, is 'so close'?" Denison asked, still fixated on the monitor image.

"Now wait just a damn minute 'Mr. Mars'!" Amritraj said rising to his feet with perturbation. "Dis is not de Big Red Rock! Dis is Eard! All of de well-to-do equipment for dis kind of work is out dere wid you and your frontier fraternity bredren! Dis lab vessel is nearly 'dirty years old and it functions well enough, but it is not suited for your kind of flying trapeze maneuvers!"

"Hypothetically…how close?" Denison asked, calmly deflecting Amritraj's protestations.

Amritraj's eyes narrowed at Denison's insistence on formulating a high risk plan for a seemingly low priority phenomenon. "Hypodetically…Mr. Denison, we would need to double our engine output which might (and I emphasize 'might') quadruple our shielding which in turn 'might' allow us to addain a maximum perigee of say…half a K from de surface."

"Sounds like you'd already given the matter some thought, Mr. Amritraj." Denison lightly teased.

"I have also recently given dought to cliff jumping onto jagged rocks, but I have no immediate plans to partake, Mr. Denison." Amritraj responded coolly.

"Well that's good, Mr. Amritraj," Denison said with only a hint of sarcasm. "I'd hate to lose you before we make a run at scanning the inside of that crater."

Amritraj folded his arms as his countenance darkened into a surly storm cloud.

"Computer," Denison addressed. "I'd like the specs on modular requirements to upgrade this vessel for the following parameters."

Denison ran through a more detailed outline of what it would take to modulate the lab vessel for their experiment. Outranked, Amritraj, took a smoldering stroll toward the back of the room and returned with his ire peaked.

"Mr. Denison." Amritraj addressed tightly, "I request dat you do not jeopardize dis Lab vessel purely for de sake of capricious scientific curiosity."

The specifications for the upgrade of the Lab vessel appeared on screen in response to Denison's requests.

"How soon can Albuquerque transport and refit the needed upgrades?" Denison asked the computer.

"On a 1A priority basis, transport and modulation can be completed in one hour, fifty-two minutes." responded the computer.

"Good. Initiate transport on a 1A priority basis. Command authorization ANDE50733."

"Transport Initiated."

Denison swung around in his chair and met Amritraj's angry glare. Without broaching the sensitive subject, Denison had effectively seized command of the Lab vessel with little observance for protocol.

He did not relish the assumption of this duty and relished the role of Cartel-appointed interloper even less. But there was a job that required him to be here. A job so important, that the palace saw fit to amputate him from his family. If called upon to perform a task, Denison was not inclined to exert himself half-heartedly. He at least owed that to Mikki and Lang, if not to the rest of the world. He concluded that should someone be made unhappy by this sequence of souring events, his own misery would embrace the company.

"Mr. Amritraj," Denison began, "you and your crew were called upon to lead a fleet of science teams to determine what kind of celestial object slammed into the Earth and took the lives of some 47,000 people. You were contracted because, by reputation, there is no Corporation on Earth more qualified to perform that task. Unfortunately, all you and your people have been able to come up with are some very colorful opticals for the evening media and a body count. Because this situation grew a little more complex than anticipated, the Palace called me. Me, who just got the red dust rinsed from under my cuticles last night, and hasn't seen his family in over nine months. Obviously, the palace thinks there is more to this than meets the eye, and frankly, the more information I tally, the more I'm inclined to agree.

"Four months ago, I was on Mars when we first tracked this meteoroid. Initially, we thought it was going to be trapped in Saturn's ring, but it wasn't. Then we thought it was going to smash into Titan, but it veered around it. Then we figured it would get sucked into Jupiter's gravitational field, but it managed the fool us again and use the inertia of several orbits to propel itself toward the asteroid belt. We recharted and recharted its trajectory until we concluded that a month from now, it would burn up on the outer surface of the sun. In fact, we concluded that if it survived the asteroid belt at all, its aversion for colliding into other celestial bodies made it virtually no threat to the Earth whatsoever. But now, here, months later, in spite of the most sophisticated, scientific projections we could muster, that thing landed right on top of a crowded resort village like..."

"Like a missile." Amritraj finished.

"Yeah." Denison concurred. "Like an angry, vindictive invader from god knows where! Maybe it's just coincidence that it smashed into a populated area. Maybe it's because it hit on the most important holiday of the year, at the most celebrated vacation resort in the world, that it's got us all paranoid. Maybe the fact that it simply defied our finite abilities to predict it, has caused us to fear something we couldn't explain with technology. I mean, how dare this...'thing' defy the laws of physics as we've defined them...and allegedly mastered them. The timing. The location. The scope of this disaster. And the fact that we had to sit by and watch it happen. We have to know why this thing is here, Mr. Amritraj. We have to know why and we have to know now. It's our job. Perhaps so that the rest of the world may bask in its coveted ignorance of such things, reveling in their fragile, conceited peace of mind, but it's our job to know why. We didn't understand it when it was millions of miles away. But, for my wager, we'd damn well better understand it now."

Amritraj weighed Denison's words as the man's voice sounded at harmony with the whirring equipment which surrounded them. He felt guilt for any professional jealousy that may have defamed his perceptions of Denison, having never met the man before today. Moreover, he recalled why he had taken to science some thirty years ago, himself. And why promotions never seemed to matter as much as the discoveries that prompted them. And why this man, who sat in front of him with his face awash with the anticipation of discovery, was the Chief Coordinator of the Operations-Space Anomalies Division on Mars.

"All right, Mr. Denison." Amritraj conceded, masking total acquiescence. "I guess...maybe dis is a more urgent madder dan I was willing to...accept. Whatever you require of dis fleet will be offered to you."

"Thank you, Mr. Amritraj. Based upon everything I've heard and read about you, I'm actually honored to have the chance to work with you."

"You can't believe everyding you read, Mr. Denison. And even less of what you hear."

"That's true. But I do believe Manda."

Amritraj swallowed a smile which threatened to break his stoic countenance and turned to prepare his people for the work that lay ahead.

# XIV.

The Beneficent Palace Library:

"Animal!" Louisette screamed at the top of her lungs.

Victor, peered boyishly from behind his library monitor, earnestly shaken by the high-pitched shriek.

The other patrons of the Palace library quietly shifted in their seats as they passively prepared to ingest yet another unseemly confrontation between the purportedly affianced couple of Louisette and Victor.

"Unprincipled, unfeeling, callous, mindless brute of a savage…mandrake!" Louisette yelled as her voice echoed loudly throughout.

"Mandrill," Victor said softly.

"What!?" yelled Louisette indignantly.

"Mandrill," he repeated wearing a brash smirk. "I think you meant to call me a mandrill. ManDRAKE is a plant."

"Well, that's what you are!" Louisette attempted to qualify in her rage. "A spineless, limp, pathetic little plant of a man, who should be trampled by a herd of…cantaloupe!"

A single laugh spilled out from behind one of the library terminals but quickly squelched itself as Victor turned to eye who would dare mock them.

Louisette seized the distraction and pounded an overhand punch into Victor's protruding pectorals. He turned slowly back toward her, his eyes tightly narrowed with abrupt perturbation.

"Okay, I'm sorry." Louisette reversed, suddenly aware that she had encroached upon an established boundary of their relationship.

"Sorry?" Victor responded with ebbing restraint. "You walk in here, interrupt my research, insult me in front of our peers…"

Another snicker from behind a terminal (at the use of the term 'peers' by the renownedly egotistical Champion) went unaddressed.

"…and now you're sorry? Well, my most 'beloved', let's see how sorry you can really be!"

Victor stood up from behind his terminal and reached over it snaring Louisette by her hair. Holding her like a pup by the scruff the neck, he pulled her toward him, then pushed her forward, walking her on her toes to the restroom.

Before the automatic doors could open completely, he smashed them wide with a sweep of his giant elbow. Victor and Louisette then disappeared from view. In another moment three women and two thin men came stumbling out into the reading room as the damaged doors shut, unevenly, behind them.

"Now before I send you bobbing for bowel movement in one of these stalls," Victor said through his teeth, "suppose you tell me what this latest neurological spasm of yours is all about!"

"Anna Maria!" she answered, struggling fruitlessly to untangle his grip on her hair.

"What?" he responded innocently.

"Anna Maria, damn you!" she shouted, finally spinning away from his loosened hold.

"Yes, what about her?" he gestured guiltlessly.

"What about her?!" Louisette responded, astonished by his apparent denial of any wrongdoing. "I just saw her! She's bleeding! She's bruised! And she's completely shattered by what you did to her!"

"Oh? Well, she was somewhat fragile, I'll admit." Victor said evenly. "But, I did nothing you didn't ask of me."

"Uh!" Louisette exclaimed with disgust. "I asked you to give her something special; something she'd cherish for the rest of her days! I did not ask you to…brutalize her like some…slaughterhouse calf!"

"Is that what you are, Louise?" he said, calmly leaning against the wall. "A barnyard animal who relishes being sodomized? I figured you'd think more highly of yourself. After all, I didn't do anything to your dear, sweet cousin that you haven't enjoyed more than a half dozen times, yourself!"

Louisette was inwardly wounded by the scathing truth, but still managed to defiantly collect her oft-soiled dignity. For though she could never effectively defend herself to Victor, defending Anna Maria was another matter entirely.

"Anna Maria is not me," she spoke with her chin uplifted and her eyes ablaze. "She lives in a reality neither you nor I may ever understand. She's warm, intelligent and selfless. She surrounds herself with books and feelings and a special love for all people in spite of themselves. She even said she loves you!"

"I know. She told me." Victor smirked.

"Even afterward!" Louisette confirmed.

Victor's face went blank for a moment, uncertain of what that meant.

"Her only fault was being a girl with a woman's feelings growing inside of her." Louisette acknowledged sadly. "My fault was encouraging those feelings instead of telling her to go back to her room and stay a child a little longer. But you! You couldn't be a decent human being, could you? Not even for an hour! You had to leave your mark…rape her like some sadistic butcher!"

"Rape?" rejected Victor. "I did no such thing! I treated her like a woman!"

"She's only a girl!"

"She's perfectly legal!" defended Victor. "Has been, for months from what you've told me. And I didn't ambush her on some street corner. She came to me willingly."

"But you promised…"

"I did what I promised!" Victor proclaimed. "Which is more than I can say for you."

"What are you talking about?" Louisette asked, as her resolve began to rattle loose.

Victor measured her as a predator measures its cornered quarry. Any assertiveness he had lost in this exchange returned to him, full bore.

"You're pregnant again…aren't you?" Victor asked with certainty.

Louisette folded her lips, trying feebly to contrive a response that might sufficiently deflect the accusation.

"Aren't you?" he pressed.

She looked away, painfully wishing now that she had never confronted him…even for her cousin's sake. This topic was one she was totally ill-prepared to discuss.

"Yes." she answered resignedly.

"I don't hear that shrill, shouting harangue any longer! What's wrong?" Victor poked.

Louisette fell back against the wall and stared at the floor. Dr. Canard, sworn to secrecy, had obviously reneged on his vow.

"We had an agreement, didn't we, Louise?" Victor asked deliberately.

"Yes," she responded, fighting tears.

"And that was what?" he pursued.

"No babies." she whispered.

"That's right," he said with a sneer. "This morning, I overhear two nurses talking about 'our' baby! I was sick to my stomach at the very thought. Then, an hour later your…cousin comes toddling into my room like some trussed-up flower girl looking for a birthday clown. You're lucky it was her and not you. I swear I'd have killed you."

The violent words jolted her as she shook involuntarily against the tile.

"So what do we do?" Louisette asked, trying to block out the thought of Anna Maria having paid for her selfish concealment.

"Get rid of it," he said coldly. "Take another pill."

"Victor, No…" Louisette began to plead.

"How many times have we been through this?" he interrupted. "Six, seven times? And each time what have I told you?"

"'Get rid of it'," she recited sadly.

"That's right!"

"But when…"

"I don't know when, Louise!" he said derisively. "Pull this again, and it'll be never!"

Tears began to roll down Louisette's face. Victor turned away from the scene and checked himself in the mirror.

"Take another pill, Louise. Otherwise, I'll take the damn thing out myself."

Victor strode out of the lavatory repelling onlookers with arrogant, threatening, disdain.

Louisette looked in the mirror. Her eyes had reddened. Her face had drawn colorless. She called the bathroom computer: "Face. Personal code PJT051957."

A plastic circuitized mask lowered from above the mirror. She hastily pressed the mask against her cheeks and ordered it to begin. There was no noise save a high beep that indicated that her facial was complete.

Louisette inspected the makeup, then tossed her hands through her hair. She locked with her unhappy gaze and attempted to mold a more cheerful facade. Then she quickly turned and exited the lavatory.

She could feel the eyes of the people in the library inspecting her for some sign of discontent. She smiled "happily" looking at none of them, and briskly exited into the corridor.

# XV.

And now the news:

Yesterday evening, the Beneficent was in Versailles to kick off the annual Vogue Day festivities that will be taking place this weekend all around the world. He spoke to a large throng of celebrants gathered outside the old Palace gates.

Cut to video:

"My friends, these are wonderful times we live in. For the first time in history, the world has been totally at peace for seventy-five years!"

The crowd cheers and applauds enthusiastically.

"For the first time in history, we know of no disease that is incurable. We know of no treasure that is unattainable. The very universe itself sits before us—a new and boundless frontier awaiting the illumination of mankind's unrivaled glory! But most importantly is the indisputable fact that all people everywhere are absolutely free! Free to do as they want! Free to go where they want! And free to have as they want! Of course, on this great planet of ours, it was not always so. There was a time when we were encumbered by race, religion and guilt. But mankind's destiny for greatness has been irresistible and undeniable. And on this wonderful holiday, we celebrate 'the combination of our diversities, the pursuit of endless possibilities, and the omnipotence of glorious humanity!'"

The crowd again follows with hearty cheers of the Constitutional quotation.

"And I'd like to close with the words of our first Beneficent, the esteemed Snake Clinden as he spoke from this very perch seventy-five years ago today: "'Tradition is the manacle of the human spirit. Ritual is the invitation to mundane self-imprisonment. Associations few, are affiliations poor. History is for those with their heads affixed to the rears. Only that which is new and different marks well the passage of our lives. To live in vogue, is to live in full. So whatever you do, do something that is new!'"

The crowd roars with approval.

"Peace, love and joy to you all! Enjoy the holiday! Enjoy your holiday!"
Cut away from video.

Despite the urging for all people to get out and diversify during the
holiday, the Beneficent, himself, said he would be spending this year's
Vogue Day weekend in Cannes with friends and family. This would be
after a short stopover in Hollywood to promote the satellite release of One
hundred-eighty episodes of "Lunar Command", the action-adventure
series in which Beneficent starred, almost twenty-five years ago.

The World Market, closed for the weekend, saw Alcohol and Cocaine
stock prices rise dramatically in anticipation of sharply increased consumption for the holiday. Good news for consumers, however, is that
while Blusilver stock fell, this was attributed to the current price war being
waged by manufacturers. It appears as though Blusilver will be the drug of
choice this Vogue Day.

If you're planning to spend the holiday abroad this year, you may want
to steer clear of South Vietnam. Weed Saigon physicians say they may
have uncovered a new strain of immune deficiency virus that does not
respond to inoculation. Reportedly, eight people there have died from the
said disease, which is alleged to be spread through oral-genital contact.
While a cure has not been isolated as of yet, the Palace reports that your
biennial vaccinations should prevent you from contracting the disease. If
you're uncertain about your vaccination status, local Vietnamese bath
houses will be offering vaccinations free of charge through Monday.

For those few of you who are looking to diversify fully clothed this weekend, Anthony Warwalls much talked about film, "Mare Cult" opens in
satellite theaters today. The controversial fantasy film documents the revitalization of religion by lunar scientists and the threat such a revitalization
poses to freedom on Earth. The use of ancient religious symbolism and quotations as well as scenes of sermons to mass congregations have caused an
uproar among civic leaders on Earth and the Moon. Parent groups are particularly upset by one scene wherein children are depicted petitioning an
unseen deity. "Tangible, human icons are healthy," one woman said. "But

the portrayal of people, particularly children, worshipping an invisible force is disturbing. I don't know why anyone would want to drudge up such nonsense as the Cults, when they almost destroyed humanity! Films about sex and death at least carry an element of truth in them. The Cults subverted the thought processes of mankind for centuries!"

And speaking of controversy, the Beneficent's niece, Anna Maria Diderot is meeting with the World Cartel Committee at this hour, to propose legislation allowing a literary merger between Blossom and Weed school systems. The measure calls for a worldwide link of library computer systems without regional class restrictions. The popular young teen has been a proponent of this plan ever since her first tour of Southern Africa three years ago. "None of the adults had ever even heard of Dickens or Dostoevsky." she said a month ago. "And the children there, had never even been exposed to common nursery rhymes or fables. It made me quite sad".

While Blossom response has been generally favorable, especially among the young, Weed rights activist Sharpton King had this to say during a protest rally yesterday in New York:

Cut to video:

"If 'dat lil' upty plinthess 'dink she goan poyzon de' mans o' our cheedren she is thadly mithaken! Weed peeples suffa' enuff propergander frun' de' upty blozzoms. We is tellin' our keeds ta' 'tay way frun' dat' nun-sents an' lessen to 'day own peeples. Franklay', I like ta' poo ma' foo' up dat gull's butt!"

Cut away from video:

This rebuttal came as no surprise since the Weeds have held steadfast to the Edict of Separation. The rally itself was dispersed when an illegal nuclear device was detonated nearby killing thousands within a ten-block radius. Details regarding the blast are unavailable at this time.

The chances of Mademoiselle Diderot's proposal being passed by the committee are reportedly good, but the Weeds must also accept the proposal or the issue will be rendered moot.

Parts of North America were rocked by earthquakes last night causing severe damage in many areas. A giant meteor is said to have been responsible for the quakes. The Palace isn't saying much, but has confirmed that the Liberace Gardens resort village was destroyed by the meteor's impact. This has caused the Champion to cancel his Caribbean vacation plans. "I care too much about people to be able to enjoy myself during this time of tragedy." the Champion was quoted as saying. As we speak, corporate science teams are gathering at the crater site and relief efforts in Blossom regions have begun so as not to put a damper on the holiday spirit.

And speaking of the holiday spirit, what will the Beneficent's daughter, Louisette, be wearing when she co-hosts the Monte Carlo celebration on satellite this weekend? She hasn't said, but we'll have some conjecture from our fashion analyst when we return!

Fade into commercial:

(Music)

Man: "My kids quit school and ran off into the Weeds! Should I go after them or wait for them to come home on their own?"

Girl: "I'm going out on my first date with a boy I really like! Should I drop acid, speedball, or dose blusilver before I pick him up? And if he offers me homemade, should I accept?"

Man 2: "My wife just dumped me for my sister. Should I kill myself?"

Woman: "I know it's not wrong to have sex with multiple strangers when I'm partying. It's even fun! But why do I feel so guilty the next morning?"

Voiceover: "Life may be simpler than it used to be, but life's questions can still be perplexing sometimes. At the Crankin' Couch we listen and understand your problems. Our half-hour sessions run twenty-four hours seven, days a week. And unlike other Psychiatry Ports, we offer up to five-minute sessions without an appointment to help you unravel the tangle your life can often become! Subscribe for a full year, and we'll give you a whole week free! And in case of emergencies when it's impossible to visit us, call our Crankin' Couch Hotline (be sure to have your credit I.D. handy)."

Woman 2: "My live-in lover just won custody of my children in court. Should I counter-sue her or just start another family?"

Voiceover: "Remember, before you jump off that ledge, try hopping onto our couch! Crankin' Couch, a member of the World Council on Mental Fitness since 2082."

# XVI.

The Beneficent Palace:

"Manda, we've got problems!" Jean-Paul called, hustling into the Operations center.

"Yeah, I know." Manda said sarcastically. "Forty-seven thousand dead people, a crater the size of a small city, Amritraj and Anthony at each other's throats and the Beneficent demanding that I make it all disappear!"

"Well, that's not all." Jean-Paul added with regret.

"Now what?"

"We're getting calls from all over the world…"

"…from people who's relatives were at Liberace Gardens." Manda finished. "I know that. Public Service has been on it since last night."

"Yes, Manda. But PS is being flooded with calls from people wanting to know about the meteoroid. They're asking things like whether it was launched from outside the solar system."

"Launched?"

"They're asking how many aliens have been captured."

"Aliens?!"

"They want to know how many more of these meteors are on their way that the Palace hasn't warned them about!"

"Good grief."

"And the media's starting to run with it, Manda. This thing is a mess! We're on the verge of a world wide panic if something isn't done soon.

Manda dropped down into her chair and began rubbing her sinuses.

"I tried to tell him that going silent on this thing wouldn't work," she said tersely. "He said the holiday would allow us to gloss over it. 'People won't even be watching the media', he said. Well, he was wrong."

"It's not the first time you've had to clean up behind him." Jean-Paul reminded. "And it probably won't be the last."

"What's that supposed to mean?" chimed a young feminine voice from behind.

Manda and Jean-Paul both spun toward the doorway where Val leaned playing with his feathered bangs in a compact mirror.

"I mean, you wouldn't be implying that our lord had erred in his decision to try to keep things peaceful, would you...Jean-Paul?" The boy accented his question with a wink and pursed lips aimed toward the second in command.

Jean-Paul's jaw set as the scantily-clad youth brashly taunted him with thin arched eyebrows that then, drooped into a mocking pout. When Jean-Paul clenched his fists and started toward the boy, Manda hastily intervened, collaring Jean-Paul by the shoulders.

"Oh, come on, big man." Val teased, rubbing his bare chest with one hand, while running the other down the inside of his loose, turquoise cloth. "You know you want it."

"That's enough, Val!" Manda commanded

"Sorry, Manda." Val said innocently. "But he's the one coming after me!"

"That cloth holding your hemorrhoids okay, Val?" Jean-Paul snarled.

"Only one way to find out, Pauley." Val smirked.

"I said enough, both of you!" Manda demanded.

Jean-Paul turned away and stared out over the Operations hall trying to collect himself. Val, with a careless sigh, returned to primping himself in his miniature mirror.

"Now Val," Manda continued. "It was not our...intent to criticize the Beneficent. But the fact remains that there is obviously some concern out there about what's going on in California, holiday or no holiday. Now based on what Jean-Paul's telling me, I think we need to send out a direct broadcast from the Beneficent himself. It's the only thing that's going to settle people down."

"Well, why don't you just tell them what you told us?" Val asked, hopping up on Jean-Paul's computer desk. "Tell them that there's no sign of life and that there's nothing to worry about."

"That's not what we told you," Manda said with irritation.

"But the memo said, and I quote: 'no life signs'." Val replied, defensively crossing his arms and legs.

"That's right, Val," Jean-Paul said tightly. "No life signs as in: No survivors of Liberace Gardens! We don't know whether that meteoroid brought living cosmic anomalies with it or not! The area's too hot right now!"

"Well, why didn't your stupid memo say so?" Val smugged.

"It did." Jean-Paul said with restraint. "Maybe, the Beneficent skimmed over that part."

"No, he didn't!" insisted Val. "I was right there when he read it!"

"Well, that's not the issue right now." Manda intervened. "The issue is that people are worried and need reassurance—and the only person who can give it to them is the Beneficent."

Val popped off the desk and began pacing.

"Val," Manda asked, "can you tell him we need a direct broadcast?"

"Um," Val paused, nervously rocking on the heels of his heavily embroidered pumps. "He's asleep, right now."

"What do you mean, asleep!" Manda persisted. "This is an emergency! Wake him!"

"I'm only a page, dammit!" Val whined. "If he's asleep, he's asleep! I can't do anything about that!"

"Maybe he's dead, Manda." Jean-Paul put in.

"Dead?"

"Yeah. As in: dead drunk."

Val shot them both a guilty glance he quickly tried to subdue. But Manda and Jean-Paul captured the unguarded confession before he could successfully hide it away.

"Well, I don't give a damn!" Manda concluded. "Go get him, Val. If I know him, he'll blame me. Not you."

With a loud huff, Val pirouetted and clattered out the door, dreading the task of rousing the leader of the world from his inebriated "slumber".

Jean-Paul observed his departure with smoldering disgust.

"Why do you hate him so much?" Manda asked softly. "It's not his fault he's that way."

"It's not like you think, Manda," Jean-Paul said with sadness. "I don't hate him. It's just that, he wasn't always like that. A few years ago he and my little brother were best friends. He was a normal kid, as far as I could tell. Unfortunately, they were in a grammar school play with the Beneficent's niece, Anna Maria. The Beneficent visited the cast backstage after the performance one evening and invited my brother and Val up to his quarters that night for a 'tour'."

Jean-Paul shook his head upon the reflection. "Shit, Manda they were just kids, you know."

"They went?"

"No," Jean-Paul continued. "I wasn't sure what was going on, but old Georges' reputation preceded him. I told my brother he couldn't go. So Val went alone. A week later, my brother came home one day and told me that Val had quit school to become a page at the Palace. And that…was that."

"What about Val's parents?" Manda asked "Didn't they do anything?"

"Like what?" Jean-Paul replied. "I'm sure the Controller's office 'advised' them against making a public issue of it. And besides, legally, it was Val's right to choose."

Jean-Paul sat down to his computer console and began composing the Beneficent's statement regarding the Liberace Gardens disaster.

Manda stared at the open doorway as Val's slender frame faded down the corridor.

# XVII.

Santa Cruz:

"What de devil have you done to my lab?" Amritraj marveled as he observed the robotic maintenance ships finish securing the engine modulation upgrade to his lab vessel. The blinking lights of the pre-programmed drones skirting about the vessel's frame appeared as a squadron of bees working about a fresh bloom, as they darted against the late dusk backdrop, systematically concluding their specified tasks.

"Like the upgrades, Mr. Amritraj?" said Denison as he joined him in admiring the external view of the lab vessel on the giant monitor.

"Dree years ago, I put in a requisition for engine upgrades dat would have finally brought us up to de mid-22nd century." Amritraj said with wonder. "Dey told me to get in line! Ninety minutes ago, you make one call to Albuquerque, and now we're ready for de year 2200. I guess it pays to be connected."

"Not really," Denison answered. "You just never had the benefit of a catastrophe before. Thank the meteoroid, not me."

"I am not prepared to dank anyone just yet," said Amritraj with reservations. "Dese modulations would have been nice under normal circumstances. Unfortunately, it appears as dough we are going to have to take dem out on de 'high wire' wid us before we can peel all de labels off."

"That's life on the cutting edge of discovery, Mr. Amritraj."

"Let us hope dat life continues." Amritraj added cryptically.

"If you like, I can arrange to have you returned home." Denison dug.

"Mr. Denison, dis lab vessel has been my home for de last dirteen years." Amritraj snorted proudly. "Dis fleet of science scouts has been under my direct command for six. In spite of dis less dan desirable situation, I will not abdicate my responsibilities to my profession or my people."

"Good." Denison responded confidently.

"Now Mr. Mitchell and I have been re-tabulating figures for our descent as de modulations have come on-line," Amritraj continued. "It appears as dough when we double our engine output, we will realize a 427 percent gain in our shielding. Dis will allow us to come widin .658 K's of de crater's moud widout risk to life aboard dis laboratory. In addition, we should be able to extend our shields into de crater, creating a particle conduit roughly one hundred meters in diameter dat will dampen de acoustic inertence and allow us to take our readings using sonar. De six science scout ships will prep various sites over de crater before our arrival so dat people here can concentrate on piecing togeder information as it becomes available. In addition, we are also on-line wid Palace Ops so dat everyding we record here will be simul-loaded to Cannes and Albuquerque for immediate concurrent analysis."

"That's excellent." Denison complimented. "This should all go very smoothly."

"So you say, Mr. Denison." Amritraj responded. "Only...I can't help wondering if dere is someding I haven't been told about dis assignment."

"You know what I know," Denison said matter-of-factly, reaching for his cup of coffee.

"Do I?" Amritraj questioned.

"What are you implying?" Denison asked, slightly annoyed.

"I am not implying anyding, Mr. Denison." Amritraj answered flatly. "It's just dat, in all my years on dis vessel, de Palace always trusted my company to do its job. But in de span of a few hours, I get an expert from Mars overseeing my every move and state-of-de-art hardware from New Mexico I've been told I would never need. You seem very sure of where you are going wid dis 'mystery' of ours. Yet everyone else pretends dat dey are in de dark."

"Look, we've been through this," Denison said with a sigh. "Yesterday, I was relaxing on my couch savoring the first home-cooked meal I'd had in almost a year. Suddenly I get a call from the Palace, probably much like the one you got, telling me I was needed here. The only information I received is the information that was downloaded to my shuttle from the

Palace while I was enroute to you! And the only information the Palace has, is what they've gotten from you!"

"What about before yesterday, Mr. Denison?" Amritraj asked with suspicion. "I agree dat I have been on point since de disaster. But what about de monds of tracking you did from Mars before anybody on Eard had a reason to give a damn? What did you know den? What did you dink or hope was going to burn up in de sun?"

Anthony sipped his coffee and silently cursed his own empathetic nature. He wanted to be angry at Amritraj for even suggesting that he might be withholding some dark hidden secret about the meteoroid. But when he placed himself in Amritraj's uncertain position, he fully understood the man's doubtful posture.

"You trust Manda." Denison said. "What did she tell you?"

"I trust Manda more dan you can imagine." Amritraj volleyed. "But she is a very dedicated woman in a very responsible position. I assume dat she has told me all dat she is permitted to tell me, regardless of what she may know. I would not presume to expect less of her."

"Nor I." Denison bridged. "I swear to you, you know as much as I do at this point. You've seen the trajectory data we collected on Mars. We knew its point of origin was clearly outside of our galaxy, but we didn't tag it as anything unusual until it got closer and started dodging projected targets. We couldn't scan it then, for the same reason Mare Crisium and your crew can't scan it now: too broad a light spectrum and too much radiation! I swear to you on the lives of my family that that's all I know."

Amritraj tightened his lips weighing Anthony's insistence. Part of him was besieged with distrust, while the rest of him felt guilty for distrusting. An apology sat on his tongue, but died unspoken.

A beeping signal came over the intercom.

"What is it, Gary?" Amritraj acknowledged.

"All the grunt work's done, sir." said Mitchell's lazy, sarcastic voice. "We're waiting for you brass techs to give the word!"

"'Brass Techs'?!" Denison repeated under his breath with a smile.

Amritraj suppressed a grin. "If everyding is ready, I do not dink de 'brass techs' would have any problem if you began our descent, Mr. Mitchell."

Denison nodded his silent accordance.

"Okay, chief!" answered Mitchell. "The kids are ready to play! Strap in!"

Amritraj and Denison took their places at their respective consoles and began relaying data to one another as the lab vessel began its descent toward the swirling molten face of the gaping crater beneath them.

# XVIII.

The News:

The Palace has promised that Louisette, the Beneficent's daughter, will unveil her new outfit during the direct broadcast of Vogue Day festivities from Monte Carlo. As a bonus, rumor also has it that Anna Maria Diderot, the Beneficent's niece, may accompany her cousin and perhaps be adorned in something equally stunning. Whether the Champion himself will change his plans and join the celebrated femme fatales of France is unknown.

Next Tuesday is the day the world votes to legalize homemade drugs. Don't forget to phone in your vote! Drug companies continue to lobby against the measure with heavy advertising. They contend that "homemade" will only cause greater harm to the public health, since it is obviously impossible for the FDA to regulate its production. Homemade advocates, however, contend that it's their bodies and their right to ingest anything they choose without government intervention. They also contend that the drug companies are simply afraid that the competition from homemade drugs will force lower prices, cutting directly into corporate profits.

In other news, Vogue Day celebrations in the Weeds have been hampered this afternoon by outbreaks of what is believed to be cult-induced protests. News agencies and the Palace have also been flooded with calls regarding the giant meteoroid that destroyed Liberace Gardens, California yesterday evening. Infectious panic has led many to believe that the catastrophe at the celebrated resort was only the harbinger of impending doom on a world-wide scale. Failure by the Palace to relay detailed information has only heightened suspicions that something disastrous may be on the horizon for the entire planet Earth! While we do not necessarily concur with this reasoning, we urge viewers to stay tuned so that we may keep you updated as soon as we learn something new.

# XIX.

Beaufort, South Carolina:

Mikki found maintaining her composure a maddening and arduous mental torture. The distraction of the California disaster had, in the last forty-five minutes alone, caused her to sprain her ankle stumbling over Lang's disassembled Mars Shuttle model, incinerate their lunch because she voice coded "well-done sirloin" into the oven for the cheese and tuna sandwiches she only needed to warm, and cursed out her mother-in-law whose eighth call in the past two hours to check on Anthony had rubbed acid onto her last nerve.

"'Deary, you seem unglued. You're not drinking in front of my grandson, are you?'" Mikki mimicked her mother-in-law's nasally voice to herself. "Senile old shrew! Just because she was a shriveled-up alcoholic mother doesn't mean her son had to marry one!"

Mikki ran her hand through her rumpled hair and limped to the breakfast nook collapsing into a chair. She shook her head with a sigh as she held up her slightly swollen ankle.

"Duh," she frowned.

She closed her eyes for a second, trying to organize her thoughts and collect her emotions. The momentary darkness, however, only served as a blackened landscape for her worst fears. She envisioned Anthony in mortal combat against some insurmountable force. Then she saw meteors raining down on her and Lang with no one there to help them. Finally she could hear Anthony's mother castigating her for being unable to protect her husband and son.

With that, she popped her eyes open again preferring the reality of the smoldering tuna sandwiches still crackling on the kitchen counter across the way.

"I never drink alone. But a cigarette sure would be nice." she muttered to herself. "Mars duty, I can handle. But emergencies…"

She stared blankly for a moment, and the visions crept upon her again. Before they became vivid, she smacked her palm on the table and rose to her feet to busy herself with what could be salvaged for an edible lunch.

As Mikki made her way to the pantry, Lang came marching into the kitchen with his hands clasped behind him. He stopped next to her and looked up with his mouth and brows convergent on the extremities of his nose. It was an odd sort of frown that indicated he was growing weary of being tough.

"Me, too," she thought.

"Mom," Lang began soberly, "is dad going to die in California?"

"What?" Mikki answered, stunned by the boy's frankness.

"I need to know." Lang continued. "The news keeps talking about dead people in California. And that's where dad went. They say that the Palace is hiding something and that something worse is going to happen soon. Does that mean dad's going to die? I'm not going to cry or anything like that. But I just need to know."

Mikki knelt down and looked into her son's eyes. In so many ways he was already incredibly like his father. So bright and so businesslike. The emulations were quite remarkable, considering the fact that Lang and Anthony spent so little time together.

"Lang," Mikki began softly, "the news is just guessing. They don't know what dad's doing. They just want everybody to be scared so that people will keep watching. When they called your dad…they weren't upset. They just wanted him to go out to California and look around because…well…you know…a lot of people died and…he's the best!"

"But he was on vacation." Lang pouted.

"I know." Mikki said with a hug. "But people like the Beneficent and the Champion and your dad don't always get vacation like they want because people need them."

"Because they're the best?" Lang questioned.

Mikki weighed the rumors she had often heard about the Beneficent's private affairs, but waved them off for the sake of this exchange.

"Yeah," she said. "Because they're the best."

Lang smiled. "I hope I'm not the best. I like vacation."

"Yeah?"

"Yeah!" Lang confirmed.

"Well, I bet I know what else you like." Mikki offered.

"What?"

"Pizza!" Mikki said with a big smile.

"Yeah!"

"Why don't you go in my room and look in my top drawer." Mikki prodded. "I got one signaler for the pizza man to come. Bring him up on the monitor and tell him what you want."

"Anchovies?" the boy grinned.

"Half." she compromised.

Lang bolted out of the kitchen. Mikki could hear his footfalls recede into her room, then track back into the living room by the satellite monitor.

With her son preoccupied with ordering lunch, she plucked a pencil from a jar on the kitchen and punched up a Palace security code on her bracelet. A computer generated voice requested that she state her emergency and that someone would get back to her.

"This is Mikki Denison," she spoke quietly. "I'd like Manda Martine to return my call as soon as possible. I'd really appreciate it if she'd let me know exactly what the fuck is happening with my husband!"

Mikki severed the communication, sat back into the chair and closed her eyes again…only for a moment.

# XX.

The Beneficent Palace:

Louisette swung around full circle in front of the mirror to admire the floor-length ocelot coat draped over her body.

"I am toooo much!" she shouted at her reflection as she broke into loud laughter. "Stick by the monitor, Victor! Tonight, Louise is going to smoke your pheasant in front of the whole wide world! Le avenue de Princess Grace will have a new name by the end of this weekend: 'Le Avenue de Louisette!' I'll be turning so many heads tonight that the chiropractors in Monte Carlo will be millionaires by the end of the month!

"'Oh monsieur!' they'll say. 'How did you damage your neck in such a way?'" Louisette played to herself. "'Well doctor, I was bored to death with the Vogue Day celebration when all of a sudden, Louisette walked by! Involuntarily, I whipped my head about to catch a glimpse of her before she disappeared into a lasertheque with a herd of men behind her! My injury was well worth it!' Hah!"

Louisette fell back onto her lounge and laughed with carefree indulgence. Any disconcerting memory of her afternoon conversation with Anna Maria or her confrontation with Victor, had been selectively discarded. Presently, she was feeling quite wonderful—and that was all she would allow to matter.

"Mademoiselle Richelieu," spoke a disciplined voice from the doorway.

Louisette did not hear the voice above her own.

"Mademoiselle Richelieu," he repeated with a mild increase in volume.

Louisette hushed abruptly, aware that suddenly she was not alone. She lifted up her head and met the impassive countenance of Embardee, her personal chauffeur, with her glazed blue eyes.

"Oh!" she giggled with surprise. "How long have you been there?"

"Just now, mademoiselle," he responded respectfully.

"Well, where the hell is everyone else?" she asked as she rolled onto her feet and checked herself in the mirror again.

"In the limousine, mademoiselle. They are waiting for you."

"Waiting?" she smiled. "They should be partying! I still have to go get Anna Maria off her ass! Tell them to pop open another liter of Dom and I'll get there when I can!"

"And the broadcast?"

"Yes?"

"I don't suppose you would want to miss the opening of the broadcast."

"Don't worry about it, Em. The party doesn't start till we get there. Let them play with themselves!"

"As you wish, mademoiselle."

Embardee tipped his cap and rigidly marched out of her room.

Louisette reached into her dresser drawer and scooped up a handful of blusilver vials. She hastily shoved them into her coat pockets, snatched her ocelot bag, and gaily sashayed out of her room.

She smiled as she heard the jingle of the tiny bells strung along the ankles of her suede moccasins for the first time. It contrasted smartly (so she thought) with the high-heeled clicking she had made into her trademark and made her feel ingeniously reinvented.

The Palace corridors were relatively vacant of personnel, except for the occasional Control officer or the Operations people who never seemed to stop working. She instinctively sauntered past everyone teasing them with her "don't you wish you were going where I'm going" look that she always wore before departing for some whimsical engagement. More often than not, the men discreetly implied their approval. As always, the women wore smiles of masked contempt. To Louisette, all was as it should be before the Beneficent's daughter took her glamorous leave.

But the mood of frivolity deserted her as she turned the next corner.

Down the hallway leading to Anna Maria's room, she heard tense commotion. She saw unusually bright lights emanating from Anna Maria's doorway and saw Victor's giant forearm hugging the door frame.

"Get him the hell out of here!" she heard someone yell angrily.

In another instant Louisette saw a member of the medical staff pushing Wesley out of her cousin's room and against the wall. The tall boy was crying wildly and shaking his head in disbelief.

Without noticing, Louisette found herself trotting the rest of the distance until she reached Victor, whose hulking body obscured the doorway.

"What is this?" Louisette asked as she reached up and touched Victor on the shoulder.

Victor turned his blonde tasseled head toward her and met her eyes with a saddened, powerless expression that rendered the Champion's face barely recognizable. The lightening crisp certainty he had always carried in his eyes was completely imperceptible.

Stricken by mounting panic Louisette pushed under Victor's heavy elbow and into the room. To her right she could see Drs. Canard and Anitra along with two medical assistants standing over Anna Maria's bed.

"Stay here," advised Victor in an uncharacteristically tender voice.

But Louisette moved anxiously toward the bed and shoved a working medical assistant to the side so she could see.

The sight levied an agonizing shock through her body that prevented her from making a sound.

Anna Maria lay flat on her back completely inanimate. Her head rested on a pillow soaked with powder blue regurgitation and dark blood. Her bare chest and stomach were also stained thusly, with the exception of a hand smear between her breasts where the doctors had taken readings. Her lips were dried and black. Her eyelids were swollen bulbous. And her face and neck were marked with purple blotches where veins had either burst beneath the skin or capillaries had ruptured.

The only items which appeared to remain vaguely undefiled about the young girl were her curled auburn hair which sat remarkably neat about her discolored face, the torn and stained panties still tied at her hip, and the now vomit spattered white slippers with the oversized bows.

"A straight blusilver overdose." Dr. Canard said with a tinge of remorse. He held up three completely drained blusilver vials. "Clearly, she meant to take her own life."

"She's gone," Dr. Anitra confirmed with decided finality.

Louisette gagged on her tongue. Then her eyes rolled back into their sockets as she fell back into Victor's chest. Victor clutched her gently and walked her semi-conscious body back to the doorway.

"How, Victor?" asked a teary eyed Wesley standing in the hallway. "She never touched any of that stuff before!"

"Get the fuck away from me," responded Victor, never looking in Wesley's direction.

The boy stepped back against the far wall. Louisette held her eyes tightly closed. She bobbed and shook her head frantically as if engaged in a silent quarrel with herself.

"Louise?" called Victor, holding her up by her fur lapels.

"Huh?" she responded listlessly.

"Louise!" Victor called again.

Louisette's eyes began to open slowly, the light blue haze still in evidence. With a limp smile she reached her arms around Victor's waist.

"Oh, sweetheart." Louisette spoke with a chuckle. "I just had the weirdest dream. Anna Maria was dead and I.."

"Louise." Victor spoke directly, trying to clear her eyes with a stern tug. "Anna Maria…IS dead!"

"Uh uh. No." Louisette smiled. "She's waiting for me to pick her up. We're going to Monte Carlo…"

"Louise!" Victor called with another tug. "You just saw her! She's dead!"

Louisette took a deep breath and looked out into the hallway where Wesley leaned dejectedly against the wall with his head bowed. She then turned her head toward the lamp lit bed where the doctors conferred over Anna Maria's motionless body.

Without warning, she began flailing wildly at Victor, inadvertently scratching him under the chin.

"You did this to her!" she screamed. "You animal! You liar! She loved you! How could you!"

Victor, with relative restraint, pushed her to the floor, then checked himself for bleeding.

When Louisette saw him detect blood, she suddenly feared for herself. Victor, however, did not move toward her.

"How did Anna Maria get your inoculator, Louise?" the Champion asked, holding the object up to her. "Did she borrow it? Did she suddenly decide to convert from being a fitness fanatic to a blusilver addict...so she could be like her screwed-up cousin? Or did you seduce her with it, you sick cunt!"

Louisette ran her shaking hand through her hair, then took the inoculator from Victor and clinked it against the vials in her coat pocket.

"If Anna Maria was too...frail to be with me, you should never have suggested that she come to my room." Victor continued. "And if you wanted me in the right frame of mind to...nursemaid her, you shouldn't have pulled another pregnancy stunt! And if you thought that consoling a weak little girl with blusilver would make her silly little problems go away, well...the proof that you were wrong is laying over there...very stiff and very dead!"

Louisette looked painfully down the corridor.

"And I guess since you're off to Monte Carlo, it'll be up to me to break the news to your father." Victor finished scornfully. "Well, do the world a favor when you're there, Louise. Fuck anyone you want, but don't try to help anybody else. At least that way they'll live!"

Victor finished her off with a convicting glare Louisette could meet only out of the corner of her eye. Then he turned and angrily stalked down the hallway.

Louisette tried to recess her mind back into the comfort of her blusilver fugue, but failed.

Wesley knelt down, and helped her to her feet.

"She was wearing this," he said with a whisper, as he handed Louisette a gold chain bearing a diamond studded Latin cross. "And she wrote this."

Louisette took a crumpled note in her hand and recognized Anna Maria's meticulous calligraphy:

> *I realize that by this unconscionable act of selfishness I abdicate my soul's union with Heaven. But I could no longer endure myself as a loathed participant in a society which cares nothing of itself let alone God Almighty. A society that exchanges love for pain, kindness for cruelty, and holds caprice as its greatest virtue. All told, when I consider it, the conclusion of my life on this Earth we've made would have been wrought even had I chosen to continue. Though unworthy of his grace, I pray the Lord's forgiveness.*
>
> *Anna Maria Diderot*

"She was so logical about everything," said Wesley, distraught. "She must've written this after she took all that stuff. I mean, 'God.'? 'Heaven'? Cult stuff! It doesn't even sound like her."

Louisette folded the paper and stuffed it and the necklace into her purse.

"Yeah," Louisette said in a choked rasp. "Not like anyone we should know."

She looked at Wesley as if she wanted to offer some profound eulogy of the young girl whom they had both loved so deeply, but found that her thoroughly impaired senses were tragically incapable of constructing another sentence. So instead, she hurried to catch her limousine, willing only that sorrow should stay well behind.

# XXI.

The Beneficent Palace, Satellite Broadcast Studio:

"I know you guys are busy, but will you work with me on this?" Manda pleaded.

"Why can't the Beneficent just tell the people what we're doing?" Denison asked from the communiqué monitor.

"He said it would be more credible if you guys gave your assessment directly from the crater site," answered Manda.

"Good old Georges," Amritraj said, sticking his face into view. "Why do yourself, what you can delegate to flunkies."

"Shhhh!" Manda warned. "He's right here with me. Now listen, you two. I don't have a choice in this and neither do you. When we go on the air, you're both going to be on standby. You can turn things over to Mitchell for the time being."

"Manda…" Denison began to protest.

"That's it, Anthony," Manda interrupted. "That crater's not going to leap up and bite you while your backs are turned! Now do as I ask!"

"Aye, aye, captain," relented Amritraj.

Manda playfully sneered at the two disgruntled faces on her monitor.

"Oh. And Anthony," Manda added, "your wife left me a message."

"Is something wrong?" Denison asked.

"Nerves." Manda smiled.

"Yeah," said Denison with a sigh. "I can imagine. But I just haven't had time to patch through."

"No problem," said Manda. "In a few minutes, you'll be world wide. She'll know you're okay then."

"Yeah, but do me a favor anyway. Call her back after the broadcast. Tell her I'm thinking about her…and Lang."

"No problem, Denison. Now stand by. We'll be back to you in a little while."

Denison smiled and Amritraj's waving hand then covered his face as Manda clicked off her monitor.

"Help me, damnit! He's going down again!"

Manda spun from her console just in time to witness Val weakly straining to keep the Beneficent from falling face down into the carpeted floor. She was about to run over and assist when Jean-Paul reappeared, grabbing the Beneficent by the collar and belt as Val fell away onto his backside.

The Beneficent's eyes burst open and his head bobbed forward then snapped back as Jean-Paul guided him into a crushed velvet armchair.

"What happened to him?" Manda exclaimed, checking the wall chronometer. "He was fine a moment ago!"

"No. He was not fine." Jean-Paul corrected. "He was simply conscious. Now he's not. To borrow a Weed colloquialism, we need to face the fact that our beloved Beneficent is completely 'sewered'!"

"He is not!" defended Val, jumping to his feet. "He's just…very tired. What with the African governor yesterday and the meteoroid catastrophe and…"

"You can't be serious!" Jean-Paul said with amazement. "You've swallowed so much of his sweat, I think the salt's crystallized your little brain!"

"How dare you!" Val shouted, appalled.

"Care to make an issue of it, 'page'?" Jean-Paul challenged.

"Jean-Paul, that's enough!" Manda said authoritatively. "Him, I can understand. But you know better! Now we have work!"

"Yes ma'am," Jean-Paul said, collecting his professionalism.

Val gave Manda an injured glance she didn't notice, then took an unassuming position behind the Beneficent's chair.

Manda and Jean-Paul focused their attentions on the Beneficent, who sat slumped in regal garb, his jaw hanging from his face like a winter coat slung carelessly onto a rack. His pointed beard and grayed hair had been combed and re-combed numerous times in the past hour. His camera make-up had been touched and retouched. But each time he sunk into inebriated oblivion, his groomings muddied into disarray like a mound of melting frozen desert.

"Val," Manda started, "Is the Beneficent on any drugs besides the wine?"

"You know his prescriptions better than I." Val snapped haughtily. "It's your job."

"I'm not talking about prescriptions." Manda clarified. "I mean recreational."

"He doesn't 'do' recreational." Val proclaimed folding his arms.

"I mean for real!" Manda insisted.

"How dare you!" Val countered aghast. "He's the Beneficent! He would never indulge that way!"

Manda and Jean-Paul simultaneously berated the boy with disapproving scowls. Unspoken, the deafening word "liar" rang through Val's eardrums.

"I mean it!" Val pleaded genuinely. "I know he…likes to drink from time to time. But otherwise, he never trips. Honest!"

Jean-Paul frowned at Val's understatement of the Beneficent's drinking. It was well known that Georges could more often be found without shoes, than without the bejeweled chalice of Languedoc he always carried with him.

"I swear it!" Val implored. "The only time he ever…hit me, was one night when I offered him a dose of blusilver. He got very, very angry and threatened to turn me out of the Palace if he ever saw that blue haze in my eyes again. I think it has something to do with his wife and sister. They were heavy users and they both wound up dead. That, and the fact that he's lost control of Louise. I think he'd ban all rec drugs if he didn't think it would hurt his popularity."

Manda's skepticism began to subside. Jean-Paul, however, seemed unmoved by the boy's convincing plea.

"All right." Manda said. "But if you're wrong, what I'm about to try, may kill him."

"What's that?" Jean-Paul questioned.

"I ordered a blood alcohol suppressant hoping we wouldn't have to use it." Manda answered firmly. "It's a common drug among musicians and school teachers in North America. Kind of a 'gets you through the moment' anti-tox."

"Don't you think you should call Dr. Canard?" Jean-Paul asked apprehensively.

"He's out on an emergency call," Manda said matter-of-factly.

"Hmm. Maybe Louise finally finished herself off." Jean-Paul offered with a tinge of sarcasm.

"Try an overdose of milk and cookies." Manda said as she fumbled with an inoculator. "He's with Anna Maria."

"Oh my," said Jean-Paul with feigned concern. "Another sprained toe dismounting from the parallel bars? Will she still make her dance recital tomorrow night? Oh, I hope so!"

"You hate her, too?" Val accused.

"No, Val," Jean-Paul responded. "Just you."

"No one hates anyone." Manda interceded. "Call it unprofessional jealousy under duress."

Jean-Paul received Manda's diplomatic salvo as a cue for him to discontinue the verbal jousts. He knew that she was aware that part of him was an intellectual Weed at heart—but this was not the time for him to vent his harbored ideological frustrations.

Manda finally clicked the vile into the inoculator.

"Don't worry, folks. It's just like taking a headache tablet," she said reassuringly.

But just as she prepared to inject the Beneficent, he began to stir.

"My people," he slurred under his breath.

"See!" blurted Val, "he's fine!"

"We've seen this before," warned Jean-Paul.

With a heavy gargled clearing of his throat, the Beneficent lurched to his feet, swaying unsteadily. Manda braced herself to recapture her collapsing liege at any moment. With increasing awareness, however, the Beneficent straightened his bowed knees and arched his slouched posture erect. He blinked his eyes thrice and tilted his chin upward. A sudden, stately awareness seized control of his sagging features. With remarkable metamorphosis, a staggering, scarcely conscious drunkard made the immaculate transformation into the leader of the entire planet Earth.

"What goes on here?" he bellowed in a rasped bass.

"The crater, sir! Your script!" briefed Val, popping from behind the chair and offering the Beneficent the printed statement he was to read.

"Ah!" the Beneficent responded with astutely manufactured recognition. "Yes! Yes! Well done, boy."

Manda and Jean-Paul watched impatiently as the Beneficent quickly scanned the prepared statement murmuring every eighth word aloud as was his custom. He then, folded the paper and tucked it into his velvet vest pocket.

"How soon do I go on?" asked the Beneficent with arched eyebrows and an anticipatory smile.

"Um, right away sir," answered Manda who was now forced to lead the Beneficent by following the Beneficent's lead.

The Beneficent strode into his studio-staged office with Manda trailing dutifully behind. He confidently halted before the cameras and checked his appearance before a monitor mounted above the set.

"I believe our makeup people are slacking, Ms. Martine," the Beneficent spoke touching up his cheeks with his fingers. "And can no one but me wield a comb properly?"

"I'll see to it, sir," Manda answered apologetically.

"Never mind," he responded. "The mussed coif makes me look worked. It'll do for the occasion."

"Yes sir. Will you be seated now?" Manda asked hopefully. The thought of the Beneficent passing out on Network satellite made her extremely apprehensive.

"Not in a time of perceived crisis, my dear," he straightened his collar. "I don't wish to appear lax at the very outset. I'll greet the audience's tension first, then I'll slowly salve their worry back into the Holiday festivities. That shouldn't be very difficult—it's what they want. Remember

Manda, people don't really care about anyone but themselves. They have a showman's proclivity to impress upon others that such is not the case, but in the end, if you can assure them of their own well being, it's usually more than sufficient to quell their alleged concerns."

"He's wonderful, isn't he!" said Val, pressed against the outside of the studio window.

Jean-Paul remained constrainedly silent. Seeing Manda and the Beneficent together fiercely baited his kindling ire. She was the most intelligent, competent person he'd ever met in his years of service in Cartel Operations. For all intents and purposes, she coordinated the entire planet as well as the stations on the Moon and Mars. Yet, in the presence of the pompous, arrogant, detached, aloof, yet widely regarded Beneficent, she seemed to unquestioningly accept the role of a sub-essential bureaucratic menial. It appeared to him an inequity that by all laws of decency should someday right itself. Yet, as history had often illustrated, he knew the likelihood of any correction was less than improbable. Val's immature and excessive reverence for the man only heightened his seething revulsion.

Behind him, Jean-Paul heard the outer studio doors swish open and closed. He paid no mind until the giant figure of Victor stopped beside him.

"In there?" the Champion asked presumptuously, glaring at Val who still devoutly clung to the studio window.

Jean-Paul looked up into Victor's face and thought he read a glimmer of dread. But refusing to be read by anyone, the Champion stepped forward concealing his mien from scrutiny.

"Yes," answered Jean-Paul belatedly. "Is something wrong?"

Victor ignored the question and moved slowly toward the window where he parked himself directly behind Val. Then he reached up with his thumb and index finger extended and vice-gripped the boy by the back of the neck.

"Bonsoir, mon jeune fille," the Champion whispered in Val's ear.

Val's body tensed up in numbing shock as Victor lifted him from the window, and unceremoniously plunked him onto the floor. Val scrambled backwards clutching his throat as if he had nearly been strangled. Given the reputed strength of the Champion, he very well might have been.

"Don't touch me!" Val shouted breathlessly.

"But just yesterday, you were so full of mischief, 'nymphe'," the Champion leered.

Genuinely frightened, Val slid down behind the large chair and never looked up.

"Just…don't ever touch me!" the boy stated somewhere betwixt a threat and a plea.

Jean-Paul wanted to laugh at seeing the Beneficent's brat concubine thusly humiliated. But somehow, the mood of the bullying confrontation was devoid of any humor for him.

Just then, Manda exited the studio stage and entered the room.

"I have to see him," Victor stated flatly.

"You can't," said Manda, returning to her familiar, authoritative mode. "Unless you know something about the meteoroid that we don't know, he has a broadcast to do. You'll have to wait."

Victor's face softened for a moment, but quickly recaptured its impassive rigidity.

"Well," the Champion began. "When he's free, you may want to let him know that his niece has died."

There fell an instant of quiet and stillness.

Then they all heard a sobbed "how?" whisper from behind the chair as Val began to cry.

Manda looked up into the Champion's face not knowing exactly what to say or ask. He stared down at her. Any remorse he may have felt was submerged beneath his iron countenance.

When she looked toward the window again, the Beneficent had begun his address.

Manda signaled Jean-Paul to join her in the control room to monitor the broadcast.

"How?" whispered Val again between sobs.

Victor stepped to the window and watched the Beneficent embark upon another performance. He listened intently blocking out all other noise.

"My friends." The Beneficent began with his chest expanded, his stomach inhaled and his shoulders tilted toward the camera. "A great tragedy befell this world of ours yesterday. A giant meteor pierced our planet's atmosphere and crashed into a crowded resort area in Liberace Gardens, California. According to our Operations staff, which has been monitoring this horrible event from its onset, all 47,000 occupants of the resort area lost their lives in the resulting devastation. As has been reported by the media, significant seismic activity has also been a consequence of this disaster, causing structural damage and power outages across much of the northwest quadrosphere. However, relief efforts in all regions have been under way for the past twenty-four hours and purported widespread destruction has been at worst, superficial."

The Beneficent paused for a moment stroking the tip of his beard as if deeply pondering an excruciatingly delicate matter. He slowly, deliberately, and almost gracefully stepped around the stage-propped desk and nestled with feigned discomfort into the high-backed leather chair. With his brow furrowed and an utter look of perplexity carved into his face, he lifted his eyes to meet the uncertainties of everyone on the entire planet.

"This is unbelievable!" Jean-Paul whispered to Manda. "He's not even using the script I gave him. How does he do this?"

Manda responded with a wry smile, knowing that Jean-Paul did not really require an answer. They had seen the Beneficent "perform" often, under an array of difficult circumstances (self-inflicted or otherwise). Presently, the Beneficent's jury-rigged monologue summoned no revelations other than an affirmation of his well-documented affinity for the stage.

"While the area of destruction has been contained," the Beneficent resumed, "and science teams have gathered in Santa Cruz to begin unraveling the mystery of how this meteor could have caught so many unfortunates unaware…there have been other concerns raised that have left me and my colleagues in the Palace…quite astonished."

The Beneficent gestured with open palms, lifted his eyebrows and chuckled only a smidgen.

"Many of you have inquired as to the nature of this celestial sphere we now find in our midst. Some of you have even surmised that this meteoroid might be some sort of...spacecraft bearing pernicious aliens bent on sealing our doom." The Beneficent leaned back in his chair wearing a smile of fond reflection upon the mere thought. "Perhaps, it is our nature to always fear the worst of times when the best of times are at hand. It often seems as though the very pinnacle of ecstasy, which rests serenely in our palms, also lays vulnerable to fate's often cruel chicanery. I mean, here we are in the midst of our most celebrated holiday: the holiday of discovery, diversity and love. Vogue Day. Yet to our nagged discontent, this...thing from our galaxy's outer reaches comes crashing in on our party like an unwelcomed animal from the wild, does injury to some of our friends, and we immediately fall into an infectious malaise which saps the cheer from our spirits...the warmth in our hearts. And on the matter of what? An alien spacecraft? An invasion force? Based upon what I've heard of the latest theatrical releases we should sooner fear the subversive imaginings of our filmmakers rather than any so-called "real" threat posed by nonexistent extraterrestrial life! When my chief of Operations roused me from my slumber to inform me that half the world had gone mad with the notion that the safety of this sphere was in jeopardy, I thought she'd gone and lost her mind. Then she played back some of the calls we'd received and some of the irresponsible media reports. And I realized that we, here at the Palace had not done our duty in keeping you people informed of the facts."

"That means us." Manda winked at Jean-Paul.

"That means: not him." Jean-Paul added.

"I'm cueing up Amritraj and Denison," said Manda. "Whenever he decides it's time, they'd better be ready."

"Now I could read to you, a memo I received just minutes before this broadcast, assessing the current situation in Santa Cruz," continued the

Beneficent with his fingers confidently clasped together. "However, I've determined that it would be much more effective, if I allowed the scientists themselves to convey their findings and stow away your concerns so that we may all get on with the rich enjoyment of Vogue Day weekend."

"That's it!" Manda noted.

Jean-Paul punched up the split screen with the Beneficent on the upper half and where the team in Santa Cruz was supposed to be on the bottom half.

Manda frowned at the delayed feed from Santa Cruz. She reached around Jean-Paul to see if some switch had malfunctioned on the satellite control grid, but before she could touch anything, the bottom half flickered on.

The image was hazed with a snowy transmission that glitched intermittently. What could be seen was neither Denison nor Amritraj cued up as they had been by Manda only minutes earlier. Instead there appeared to be a commotion as several figures rushed in and out of camera view yelling commands and information back and forth. The scene was conclusively distressing as the scientists plainly scurried about, grappling with an emergency, that clearly took precedence over any direct broadcast.

"As you can see," the Beneficent began improvising, "our people are very hard at work assembling the pieces of this mysterious puzzle so that all of us may rest assured…"

The bottom half of the screen abruptly flashed white with the sound of a condensed explosion and an anguished scream that was audibly chilling. That half of the screen, then returned to darkness.

"Oh damn." Jean-Paul gasped gravely.

Manda ignored him, seizing the control grid and a wireless headset. She frantically began searching for a transmission signal from the Santa Cruz crater site that could tell her (and the rest of the world) what was happening.

"Obviously there is a technical problem," the Beneficent reassured the audience jokingly. "But as I've often said: 'where would man be today if he had no problems to try his mettle; no challenges to spur him to greatness'."

Victor remained outside the studio window, watching while a sixth sense of alarm unsettled his churning innards.

Val joined him, peering nervously at the Beneficent as he spoke. The boy prayed silently that his beloved liege could swiftly set everything right again.

"Anything, Jean-Paul?" Manda commanded desperately.

"Nothing yet," he answered as he and two technicians inspected and groped inside the satellite transmission mainframe.

"There's got to be something!" Manda responded, wrestling to submerge her emotions. "There's a giant lab out there with six science scout ships! They should all be transmitting! Any chance we're getting that radiation interference?"

"Not likely. Even that, would show up as interference. We're getting nothing!"

Manda glared helplessly at the grid. Thoughts of Amritraj began to overtake her mind's momentary repose. She snapped to her feet and walked over to Jean-Paul and the technicians who were already ordering a fifth self-diagnostic on the mainframe.

Jean-Paul looked up and met Manda's countenance, which already seemed to be coming to grips with the fact that her fiancé was probably dead.

"Got something!" one of the technicians called with his head still buried inside the mainframe.

"What?" Manda requested.

"Not sure," he answered with mild exertion. "A transmission…from the crater site."

Manda weighed the uncertainty of not knowing what type of transmission had been picked up. It could be Amritraj and Denison trying to let everyone know that everything was all right. Or it could be some sort of desperate distress call heralding the world's most unsettling fears.

She looked up into the studio, and saw the Beneficent continuing to address the camera looking calm, but wearing thin on substantive banter. With a mental coin flip, she quickly rendered her decision.

"Bring it up…on screen," she ordered.

The transmission came up on the screen, remarkably clearer than the previous one from the Lab vessel. Appearing in dim light was a tall haggard blonde man in his mid-thirties wearing a tattered and smudged gold Cartel Science jacket. His long nose was split at the bridge as blood trickled down into his mouth. His face shined with dirty sweat and several abrasions appeared on his forehead and cheekbones.

"This is Suhne, scout vessel 519 class E." The man spoke with a slight German accent. "Albuquerque, Cannes, whoever is receiving...we need immediate assistance here!"

A loud explosion in the background flashed bright red across the man's face and revealed that he was no longer on any vessel, but standing next to a small rocky hill on the ground.

"Mr. Suhne," the Beneficent engaged. "Can you tell us exactly what is going on at this moment?"

It was difficult for anyone to ascertain whether the man actually heard the Beneficent's request, but he walked briskly toward the camera and disappeared behind it.

"I am the only one who survived," he said between labored breaths. "You have to see what has happened."

The view on the bottom screen, slowly panned across the hill. From the left of the image came a luminescent reddish glow that began to yellow and brighten with each passing moment. Immediately recognizable was the edge of the crater itself, whose ominous image the media had beamed around the world for the past twenty-four hours. The undisturbed trees and brush and landscape lining the outer edges of the Liberace Gardens property stood in remarkable contrast to the vast pulverization the meteoroid had left in its wake only meters to the west. In many ways, the image of towering redwoods over the enormous crater appeared as pious parishioners holding vigil over a mass grave of deceased family and friends—a striking vision which seemed more poignant than secular man's capacity to grieve for his own.

In another moment the recognizable bow of the hovering lab vessel appeared very low above the crater; lower than Denison had reported they could go and remain within safety parameters. From the stem, the vessel appeared to be bobbing unnaturally in a manner inconsistent with its design. Knowing the details of the lab's locomotive specifications, this sight alone filled Manda and Jean-Paul with nagging dread.

The crater itself was violently spewing molten rock and matter from its mouth as though an active core was actually generating energy rather than cooling itself into the earth.

More of the lab vessel became visible now and significant damage was in evidence. The alloy outer-hull away from the stem appeared to be fractured. Newly installed rocket nacelles dangled from the body, dark and inoperative.

Then the final horror was revealed.

A giant molten wave, or perhaps more of a tentacle, had wrapped itself around the entire lab and was dragging it down into the crater. Small explosions from inside the vessel could still be seen through the empty windows and giant cracks in the hull.

The Beneficent, a model of professional composure, let his jaw slip before the camera. Though, with so enthralling an image pictured beneath him, it is improbable that anyone among the hundreds of millions of viewers took notice.

Manda, shaken to the well of her soul, grew momentarily faint, and fell back against Jean-Paul, who felt his own heart pounding dangerously close to cardiac arrest.

"My God. What is this?" Val asked the air.

The Champion stood stone still, his muscles tensed, his hands clenched at his sides. He gazed pensively as a warrior, trying hurriedly to assess what perceived opposition could bring about this frightful calamity.

Manda exhaled deeply and quickly her faculties returned to her. She felt Jean-Paul holding her up and subconsciously pushed his hands away as she leaned forward. She signaled the Beneficent through the studio glass asking with her gestures whether he wanted the signal from Santa Cruz to continue.

With a grave look of resignation, the Beneficent discreetly shook his head indicating that cessation of the transmission would do more harm than good worldwide…so he believed.

"Can you see it?" came Suhne's voice over the picture. "The lab! The scout ships! Everything is gone! We need assistance here!"

A mammoth explosion ensued, upon the lab's contact with the crater's liquid surface. As the tentacle melted back into the crater's mouth, only fragments of the vessel remained, sinking slowly into the hellish roiling maw.

"A." Manda whispered under her breath as she successfully held back tears.

Jean-Paul placed a consoling hand on her shoulder, but she could not react.

"I…" The Beneficent began, hastily pasting together another script in his head. "I cannot tell all of you how this affects me. I…"

The crater let loose with another raging burst as fragments of molten matter twisted skyward in a whirlwind of greenish-blue incandescence emitted from its twenty kilometer face.

Then what followed, astounded.

An expansive, flat shape began to emerge from the crater's mouth. At first, it resembled a giant twenty-first century aircraft with a wing span five kilometers wide. It ascended skyward with red bolts of energy pulsing through its enormous hull like a bright network of glowing veins. It stopped in mid-air, folded its wings, and lifted a bulbed head, flat on the top, out from under its breast.

"Oh dear…" gasped the Beneficent. "The damned thing is alive."

Becoming self-aware, the winged creature silently craned its head skyward and purposefully darted upward into the black evening sky, its red pulsation marking its disappearance over the horizon.

No sooner had the first creature disappeared then did a second arise from the molten nest. After a moment, it too, took flight—disappearing in another direction, in much the self-same manner.

The process repeated itself five more times before the giant crater sat still, the swirl of light still winding upward.

"Jean-Paul, get down to strategic defense!" Manda yelled. "Tell Mars and the Mare stations to power up the satellite defense networks right now! And make sure we don't lose track of those damned…ships or whatever!"

Jean-Paul bolted out of the studio control room and through the doors leading into the corridor. He was certain her commands were already being implemented even before their issuance, but he was glad to get away from the ghastly, unsettling pictures from Santa Cruz. He needed anything else to do. He simply could not bear being overwhelmed by any more.

"What is all of this?" Val asked, appearing at Manda's shoulder.

Her only response was to shake her head with total astonishment, never looking away from the studio monitor.

The Champion remained impassive and unmoved, observing these mind-shattering events with dauntless external calm. Only he could feel the dampness in his palms and the narrow stream of perspiration trickle along his spine.

Two minutes had now passed since the last creature appeared. The view of the crater, even after the shock of preceding events, began to take on the look of little more than a geological anomaly entertaining its audience with a light show—molten matter dancing randomly in the beauteous incandescence.

The Beneficent sat before the camera mentally patching together yet another draft of words that might forestall the masses from falling into utter chaos. But before he could begin again, a heavy rumbling began in the satellite image beneath him; the earth around the crater began to crack and shift. In the distance, another row of redwood "parishioners" began to sink away. Moments later, a giant craggy spire slowly emerged from the molten whirlpool. It jutted skyward nearly half a mile, then came to an abrupt halt, fragments of falling rock crumbling away from its formation.

"Now what?" asked Val.

Manda examined the stalagmite structure, then noting an odd movement at its peak.

"The peak," she spoke to one of the technicians. "Magnify, augment and focus."

The figure at the peak slowly drew nearer and became sickeningly vivid in detail.

Its black bipedal form was a fusion of gnarled and roasted bodies from either the Liberace Gardens or the lab vessel. Its arms, its legs, its torso and its head were covered with charred matted protrusions of dead faces and severed limbs. It's own face wore the flesh mask of a broiled, anguished corpse. It turned eerily toward the ground camera as if aware of its Terran audience.

"The Cartel media is next." The Beneficent cut in. "We assure you that details will be passed along as we receive them."

He nodded to Manda to cut the transmission. Taken by surprise, she followed his command and cued up the Media introduction.

The Beneficent stood up with a drained look of imminent defeat on his face. He slowly shuffled out of the studio office as if he were about to pass out from sensory overload.

Val quickly greeted him with his wine chalice. The Beneficent drank deeply, which seemed to restore a glimmer of his diminished aura.

"What now?" Victor spoke evenly, approaching the Beneficent.

"'What now?'" The Beneficent mocked with a cocked eyebrow. "I tried to tell you. That damned relic of mine, remember? You can take up arms my friend. You can challenge this with all your skills and might. But just keep this in mind: we're all going to die very soon. All of us."

The Beneficent exited the satellite broadcast room. Val hastened closely behind.

The Champion swallowed hard and took another long stare at the blank studio monitor where he still could see the alien's horrid face.

That he had neglected to inform the Beneficent of Anna Maria's passing never entered his mind.

# XXII.

Monte Carlo, France:

The limousine door slid open and Louisette ungracefully toppled head over heels onto the curb. She lay there, semi-conscious for several moments, sensing laughter from all directions. Then quickly, Biff, Pogo and Almah were tugging at her arms, lifting her to her feet. Almah replaced two blusilver vials that had rolled into the street, back into Louisette's fur-lined pocket as the crowd outside the Fonda T. Hotel & Casino began to applaud.

The journey above the A8 from Cannes to Monte Carlo had been a torridly licentious testimony to all that the Vogue Day holiday had become. One need only have inspected the squalid remnants of the limousine's rear cabin to register the measure of depravity which had prevailed during the two-hour excursion.

Emptied bottles of champagne were glued to the velour carpeting. Spent vials of blusilver were also scattered about the floor and seats. There was a burned platinum tray where Pogo had synthesized d-lysergic acid-1000 into an experimental compound for his game of O.D. roulette. Tiny packets of cocaine used to season the half-eaten roasted pheasant were discarded on a black ceramic platter. The windows were smeared with greasy hand prints, sticky beverage, and bare buttock and breast impressions. Soiled undergarments were draped over the door handles and music controls. And the velour seats, were tacked and hardened with a mixture of spilled drink, lascivious aphrodisiacs, and sexually-induced secretions.

The foursome staggered along the carpeted and barricaded pathway lined with spectators, toward the entrance to the casino. Louisette was being carried and or dragged most of the way, taking every third step as she dizzily climbed toward consciousness, her moccasin bells jingling all the way.

Waiting at the entrance under floodlights and video cameras was game show host Lars Larynx, with whom Louisette was to co-host the Vogue

Day Party broadcast. Upon the sight of her, his renowned toothy grin sank to perturbation.

"What is this?" he asked her accompanying trio. "We go on in two minutes! If it hadn't been for the extended media flash from California, she'd be an hour and a half late!"

"What's happening with that Florida thing, anyway?" Almah asked in her squeaky high-pitched voice.

Lars stared at the skinny girl in the transparent silk jumpsuit with her hair waxed into a giant question mark. Then he noted Biff who could have passed for Victor's shorter brother and Pogo, a stringy-haired young man with a pot belly hanging out of his black leather vest and pants, greenish tattoos covering his arms.

And of course there was "princess" Louisette, wrapped in her ocelot coat, despite the unseasonably humid air, her dark sweat-soaked bangs shading her dim, blue-hazed eyes.

"You people haven't heard?" Lars quizzed, pushing Louisette's playful hand away from his blonde pompadour.

"'Booouuut what?" Biff belched.

"California, he said," answered Pogo.

"California?" asked Almah.

"No, Florida," slurred Louisette. "I was talking to somebody at the Palace today who said there's a meeeorr in Florida."

"One minute!" called a voice from behind the lights.

"Forget it. Louise, can you go on?" Lars asked holding her face in his hands.

"I can go on an' on an' on…" Louisette smiled, running her hands up and down Lars's rib cage.

The crowd roared its approval.

"I mean on satellite, Louise," Lars clarified.

"Me? On satellite?" Louise acted surprised.

"Oh god," exclaimed Lars.

"No. Jus' kidding," laughed Louisette. "Apothecary!"

Pogo stepped forward and offered a handful of pills of different colors and shapes.

"Hmmm." Louisette paused for a moment. "Better take the pink ones. I hear they keep you horny."

The production crew broke out into laughter.

"All ready!" Louisette smiled at Lars as she continued to rock back and forth.

"Intro is rolling," called a voice from behind the lights. "Ten seconds to air!"

Lars gave Louisette a last look of concern and then began to prep his signature smile.

The crowd cheered on cue. The "On Air" prompt flashed and the script rolled in front of Lars, Louisette and the others, who were still propping her up.

"Good morning, afternoon, or evening wherever you are! And welcome to the 128th annual Vogue Day celebration! I'm Lars Larynx, and I'm sure you recognize my co-host Mademoiselle Louisette Richelieu! We're coming to you live from the T. Fonda Hotel & Casino in beautiful Monte Carlo! We're gonna be rocking and rolling you for the next thirty-six hours so stay with us and enjoy the holiday! We'll also be bringing you up-to-the-moment media coverage of events around the world as we get them in, but in the meantime, 'Try something new, no matter what or who you do!'"

"Hey, I'd like to say couple things." Louisette interjected, ignoring the prompt. "Firs' of all, all you people in Florida who are dead right now, don't worry! My dad will take care of everything!"

There was a murmur in the crowd that carried into tacit applause.

"I'd like to also introduce you to my best friends in the whole wide world. They won the Music Satellite Channel contest to party with me today. I only met them a few hours ago but I love them! What are your names again?"

"I'm Almah Abak from Cairo."

The crowd cheered loudly with a smattering of disparaging remarks regarding her outfit and hair.

"I'm Biff Jones from Melbourne."

The women screamed enthusiastically as he tossed his golden hair over his shoulder.

"And I'm Pogo Jizm from Cleveland. I also have a band…"

The crowd roared drowning out the remainder of his impromptu promotional effort.

"Okay," interceded Lars, trying to regain control of the broadcast. "So what happened to Anna Maria tonight?"

"What?" responded Louisette excitedly upset. The sight of distraught Anna Maria prone on the floor earlier in the day shot through her memory. Then a clouded image of the dead girl lying on her bed tried to follow.

"She was supposed to come with you, wasn't she?" Lars asked.

"Oh." Louisette answered, trying to piece together the gaps of time she'd lost. Suddenly, she realized that no one here had yet heard that Anna Maria had died. She fumbled poorly for an excuse. "Um, she pooped out on us. Books or something."

The crowd began hooting disapproval that Anna Maria had apparently snubbed the holiday in favor solitudinous pursuits.

Louisette was appalled by the crowd's derisive, insensitive outcries. But again, they were only responding in accordance to what they had been told.

"So," she shifted unnaturally into seductive projection. "Would you like to see what I wore tonight?"

The crowd howled and whistled as she slowly unhooked her ocelot fur coat.

"Are we sure a world-wide audience can…handle it?" Lars asked with a warning in his voice, not sure at this point what, if anything, she would be wearing underneath the coat.

"They're big girls and boys!" Louisette winked into the camera.

With that, she whipped her coat open and let it drop to the floor. Her skin glistened with the perspiration which had mounted due to either the drugs, the heat, the coat, or any possible combination of the three.

To Lars's surprise, she was not nude…for the most part. She wore two thickly crusted diamond bracelets on both wrists. And around her neck was the gold chain with the Latin cross which had belonged to Anna Maria. Her top was a sheer lace bustier with a black, cursive "L" which looped and swooshed over the tips of her protruding breasts. And her skirt was a tight, sheer, black laced, diamond studded mini, flapped open down the front revealing a stylishly-coifed tuft of private hair.

The crowd exploded into cheers and whistles of approval.

Louisette staggered backward for a moment as Pogo and Biff held her again. Then she smiled at the crowd and blew them a kiss.

When the noise died down, Lars tried again to regain control.

"Very nice!" he said with a frozen grin. "Only…what is that around your neck?"

"Probably a sucker bite," she grinned.

The crowd laughed, gladly embracing Louisette's tabloid reputation for indiscriminate behavior.

"No," filled Lars. "I'm talking about that symbol on your necklace. Looks like an old Cult symbol to me."

The meaning of the symbol had never dawned on her; that it had belonged to Anna Maria was all that had been important. But while Cult affiliation was looked upon with extreme disfavor all over the globe, her cousin's accepted beliefs, whatever they were, were not to be ridiculed. She found herself bristling at the inquiry.

"Yes, so?" Louisette responded coolly.

"So, what does it mean?" asked Lars, checking the chronometer for countdown into a commercial.

She paused for a moment, wishing she could conjure some profound statement that would honor its previous owner. But her badly impaired senses could barely keep her conscious, let alone thoughtful.

"Well actually, it's a very old Cult symbol," she fabricated. "And I think it means something like: FUCK YOU, MANKIND! FUCK EACH AND EVERY ONE OF YOU!"

Lars's smile was jolted from his face. The production crew began to scramble. The crowd paused unsure of itself, but then blindly cheered her mindless act of characteristic irresponsibility.

To the continuing adulation of the crowd, Louisette turned, wobbled and unsteadily led her entourage into the Hotel-Casino ballroom.

Lars's styrofoam grin collapsed as the network cut to a commercial.

# XXIII.

Beaufort, South Carolina:

Mikki sat on the living room floor with the lights out, trying to savor an herbal cigarette hanging loosely between two fingers. Though the effort was futile in that images of the burning lab vessel, the resultant screams of her horrified son, and the alien's hideous face on the spire made any respite impossible to relish. In fact, the notion of simply being alive had suddenly taken on stark new relevance during the past couple of hours.

Lang now lay in his room, sedated by capsules she'd given him to rescue his young mind from the tortured reality of his father's death.

"He really tried to be strong," she reflected on watching her son view the destroyed lab vessel sinking into the fiery crater. "But no boy should have to watch his father die like that…with a broadcasted blow-by-blow for the whole goddamn world to see."

Lang was not so young that he could not conceive of death's finality. But coming to terms with the passing of one so close to him was a different matter all together…as it would be, in fact, for any adult.

He had bombarded Mikki with so many tearful questions about their future, that her own grief was submerged by the maternal need to assure him.

Only now, alone in the dark, listening to the milling of neighbors in the distance, did she find herself fully assessing the irrevocable wreckage done to her own life.

"I still have the boy," she repeatedly whispered to herself. "And he'll need me as much as I'll need him."

It was like bandaging a severed limb without having ever considered how one might go about it. And the absurd notion that Anthony "might" have survived lingered like the phantom pain of a lost leg.

"And what about the rest of the world?" she considered. "What designs do the creatures who rose out of the crater's mouth and soared over the horizons have for the planet Earth? And if malevolent, what could the Palace do to stop them? Did the Beneficent have a plan? Would the

Champion be dispatched to arbitrate with the being on the stone spire? Could he actually win…and save us all?"

She exhaled a cloud of smoke and shook her head.

"Who cares," she thought. "They've taken my husband, but they'll never take my son. He's all that matters now. Everything else can burn, so long I have him. My life is his life."

The satellite monitor beeped for the third time in the past hour. Someone was trying to reach them, but she refused to answer because it was probably only her mother-in-law searching for somewhere to defecate her own selfish grief. The grating harangue of that woman's voice left little wonder how Mikki's father-in-law had found an early grave.

Still it was possible that someone from the Palace (Manda perhaps) was calling with more specific information regarding what had been broadcast from Santa Cruz.

As the automatic answerer clicked on, Mikki picked up the remote control and pressed "listen". As she suspected, Anthony's mother was warbling away her discontent and cursing her daughter-in-law for not answering to provide an audience.

After hearing five syllables, Mikki pressed "mute" and tossed the remote onto the couch.

Then she stared at the shadows on the wall and recounted making love to Anthony just before he'd left. And she wondered why, somehow, it had not been a sufficient enough farewell.

# XXIV.

Monte Carlo, France-The T. Fonda Hotel & Casino:

Pogo and Biff observed the giant casino ballroom from the lift as they ascended to the Anti-Grav Plunge platform seven hundred fifty meters above the ground floor. The pounding dance music from below pulsed inside their heads as the integrity of omni-digital music remained undiminished throughout the vast hall. Louisette, meanwhile, clung limply to their shoulders, remaining scarcely coherent.

For her, the evening had pretty much evolved into a total out-of-body experience. The preponderance of blusilver, cocaine, champagne, lysergic acid, and synaptic boosters had taken their malevolent toll on the vitiated interior of her perfectly preserved exterior. Her smoothed face was numbed into a placid smile she had learned to don when confronted with situations uncertain or unfamiliar. She could hear her moccasin bells jingle, but could no longer feel her feet. Her delicate, manicured fingers were frozen cold from badly impeded circulation. Her long-lashed eyes, persistent in their closing, focused upon the oscillating colors which danced along the walls. Her thickly-haired scalp now felt tight and balded. And the weight of her head had become cumbersome to the deserted muscle control in her neck.

Louisette could no longer be certain whether she was in Rio De Janeiro, Bangkok, New Orleans, Istanbul, or some other exotic venue to which her whimsical caprice had often carried her. But while her perceptions of reality faded into vague indistinctness, the garish image of dead Anna Maria still hounded the recesses of her core with hauntingly vivid clarity. To her tortured anguish, no manner of self-inflicted impairment proved sufficient to dissuade the persistence of this soul-rendering visage.

"Are you with us?" Pogo asked her.

Louisette paused for a moment, as if hearing the question echoed through an interpreter. Her pupils momentarily rolled back, then returned with glazed comprehension.

"I'm with everybody," she purred, pressing her ample chest against his bare stomach.

Pogo smirked and winked at Biff who had seemingly grown weary of Louisette's "poor rich girl" vacillations betwixt no pride and lofty conceit.

Sensing his growing distance, she grabbed him by the front of the pants, pulled him close and ran her icy fingers along the thick tendons in his neck. All he could do, was smile and shake his head in disbelief.

As the threesome arrived at the top of the platform, a young man dove off the edge. Pogo and Biff intently watched the man's descent as he swiftly shrank from view. Louisette, meanwhile, continued only to revel in the disjointed color patterns that swirled along the walls.

Amid the screams and yells of his friends, the young man ungracefully executed several flips and twirls in mid-air as he plunged downward. The free-fall appeared recklessly fatal. But suddenly, as if rescued by the unseen hand of God, the man came to a halt in mid-air and slowly glided the remaining distance into a giant inflatable cushion.

His friends above, cheered loudly as he rolled off the mat and onto his feet. From below, he enthusiastically beckoned them to follow.

"You're not really going to try this, are you?" Biff asked Pogo.

"Nope," said Pogo calmly.

"Then what the hell are we doing up here?" Biff grew irritated.

"She's going to do it!" answered Pogo, massaging Louisette's cold damp shoulders.

"What?" exclaimed Biff

"You don't think I can?" Louisette challenged as she fought her fluttering eyelids.

"It's not…that." Biff offered, searching the long queue of people for an excuse to deter her. "It's just…well look how long that line is. You don't want to be just standing around all this time, do you?"

"Not a problem," interjected Pogo.

Pogo whirled Louisette around and marched her, jingling, past the long line of party goers awaiting to take the Anti-Grav Plunge. Biff stood alone, wondering what he should do to stop them. With nothing in mind, he followed.

When Pogo and Louisette arrived at the front of the queue, there was an instructor trying to fit an obese middle-aged woman in a fur jacket and gown with a control belt.

"Excuse me." Pogo called to the instructor, as he held Louisette up with two fingers in the small of her back. "This girl is next!"

"I don't think so," said the instructor, not giving either of them a glance.

"You mean, you don't know who this is?" Pogo added confidently.

The instructor looked up, first noting the unkempt young man in the ill-fitting black leather pants and vest. Next to him he saw a short, beautiful, scantily, but luxuriously attired young woman.

"Bonsoir, Mademoiselle Richelieu," acknowledged the instructor coming to attention.

"Hi!" greeted Louisette who smiled and then broke into laughter for no apparent reason.

She then, began to sway unsteadily as Pogo held her up by her arm.

"I assume, monsieur, that you will be accompanying Mademoiselle Richelieu on her Plunge," the instructor spoke evenly to Pogo.

"No, I won't," answered Pogo smugly. "I'm just here to look after her."

"So I see," said the instructor observing Louisette, staring cross-eyed at a strand of hair she had pulled across her face.

"Of course you do realize," continued the instructor, "that we cannot allow anyone to jump if they…are impaired."

"What are you saying about the Beneficent's daughter, 'instructor'?" Pogo charged.

"I'm not saying anything about Mademoiselle Richelieu," the instructor said with restraint. "I simply wish to ensure that she understands the guidelines governing her safety."

"Okay, fine," answered Pogo, putting his arm around her waist. "Baby doll, the man wants to know if you're impaired."

Louisette was again far away, immersed in the colors running along the patterns of the walls.

"Anna, you don't belong here," she mumbled with a frown.

"Louise." Pogo called, shaking her into a momentary lapse of coherence. "This guy wants to know if you're impaired."

Louisette's eyes fluttered to light blue slits. She looked the instructor up and down, then lewdly licked her front teeth.

"Not right this moment," she spoke with a sassily brash grin. "Unless he wants to get paired."

The instructor looked away from the two with regretful resignation.

"See," added Pogo. "She's all right. So quit wasting her time."

The instructor took a deep breath and signaled to one of his assistants that the middle-aged woman in the fur was having trouble with her fitting. The assistant took the woman aside while the instructor reached behind the counter and pulled out a new control belt for Louisette.

Biff now stood behind Pogo and watched as the instructor began to fit her.

"You can't be serious!" Biff protested aside. "She's completely out of it! What if she dies?"

"At the rate she's going, she'll probably die tonight anyway." Pogo whispered with a smirk. "If she does, we'll be able to say we saw it. Maybe even get a book deal."

Louisette wiggled and shifted like an impatient child as the instructor knelt before her, trying to properly fit the belt around her bare waist. Then she began running her numbed fingers along his shoulders, neck, and through his crew cut hair, while groaning erotic noises.

Some of the patrons in the long queue hooted and whistled their approval—but others looked on with growing impatience.

The instructor stood and began offering instruction on how to jump, where to jump, when to listen for the control belt signal and when to press the button to activate anti-gravitational field. He tried to convey the simplistic, but critical information, but Louisette made it impossible. She began mouthing to herself, the familiar words of the song that was being played below and dancing clumsily in place. He repeated the instructions again, but she only smiled and played with his collar, bent on totally ignoring anything he might have said.

The instructor glared at Pogo and Biff. Pogo simply shrugged his shoulders and looked away.

Biff stepped forward to grab Louisette and prevent certain disaster.

"And when she has you arrested for interfering, who's gonna' help you?" called Pogo.

Biff hesitated.

Louisette then staggered off the platform, several meters wide of the inflated cushion seven hundred fifty meters below.

"No!" the instructor yelled.

Many patrons in the queue screamed, while others commented that she had blacked out completely.

As her listless body hurtled toward the solid marble floor, the partygoers below scattered out of the way.

With all the commotion, the band music died down.

"Isn't that Louise?" noted Almah, who was nestled on Lars's lap at the bar.

Lars followed the pointing fingers of the crowd up to the plummeting figure that clearly belonged to Louisette. He quickly swung his head away, so as not to witness the splattering impact of flesh and bone, crushed against the ground.

Then there was a loud groan as the crowd reacted.

"Oh my..." squealed Almah.

Lars, peeking between his fingers, turned slowly, to view Louisette's shattered body horridly embedded in the cracked marble floor. Instead, however, he saw her limp body hovering in space, not more than a meter above the ground. In another instant, her body bobbed and fell the remaining distance, bouncing gently on her backside where she lay motionless.

Lars, Almah, a small crowd, and several cameramen quickly sur-rounded her. Her hair covered her face. She did not move.

Lars knelt down and slowly brushed away her hair. At that moment they could all see that she was laughing as tears ran back to her ears.

"No ploblem." Louisette slurred looking up at them with a lazy smile.

Lars took her by the hand and assisted her unsteadily to her feet. She then posed and smiled for the cameras, waving energetically at the crowd like a circus acrobat, having just completed a difficult routine.

The nervousness in the crowd melted away into loud applause.

"Merci!" she said with feigned graciousness as she disdainfully tore away the control belt. "Don't mind me, I was just getting a little bored."

The crowd laughed jovially.

"I think I know how to keep things livened up now!" she smiled at Lars. Then she winked and nodded toward the camera offering Lars a cue.

"Uh…how's that?" Lars put in with uncertainty.

"Well, since I'm hosting this party…" Louisette started, mischievously, "…and I'm a little girl…why don't we move this dull bash into the little girl's n' boy's room?"

Both men and women hooted their approval at the "imaginative" and "daring" notion.

The crowd and cameramen pushed and carried her toward the lavatory laughing and cheering on their way.

At no point did anyone notice that Louisette was clutching her neck-lace, blood trickling out of her palm.

# XXV.

Portpatrick, Scotland-Walton's Tavern:

"End o' the world, it is!" shouted fat John as he poured down another stein of brown beer.

"Not 'til ya' stop drinkin', Johnny boy!" Case rasped back at his partner.

"That might be sooner than he thinks!" winked Siobhan delivering another full pitcher. "Ya' seen 'is bill this week?"

"Aye," answered Case.

"But have ya' seen the bank balance on 'is card?" Siobhan asked.

"Now just a minute, there…" John intervened.

"No," answered Case with a grin.

"Neither have we." Siobhan continued. "Not for nearly a month!"

"Now what? Ya' gonna go an' ruin me Vogue Day, Siobhan?" John asked with feigned sorrow in his eye.

"What, and save my business by makin' ya' pay yer tab?" Siobhan smiled. "What with the end o' the world nigh I'd rather take the chance on seein' you drink yerself to yer grave tonight, than save a business that'll be gone with the rest o' the world come mornin'.

"What end o' the world?" Case disdainfully hoarsed.

"Did ya' not see the monitor, man?" John leaned forward, red faced. "Ya' couldn't a been drainin' yer vein the whole time!"

"Ya' think?" Siobhan added sarcastically as she paced back to the bar. "If he took the funnies with 'im, I wager he spent twice the time o' Georges' broadcast gettin' done wi' 'Fannie Annie' alone."

John and fellow imbibers seated at neighboring tables laughed uproariously. Case tried to smile at the mockery made of himself but found the images from Santa Cruz too disturbingly vivid to be doused even by several shots of Irish whiskey. Instead, he scrunched his unshaven face into a frown like a child about to cry.

"Aww, come now, Casey boy." John leaned over, patting him on the back. "What're ya' upset 'cause ya' can't be in Monte Carlo grabbin'

Louise's big tits like everyone else? Hell, ya' got Siobhan here, fallin' outta' her blouse right in front o' ya'! Hey Siobhan! Get yer ass over here an' let me put ya' on me tab ta' perk up ol' Casey here!"

The pub broke into hysterics as Siobhan blushed bright pink and tugged the loose sleeves of her blouse up over her shoulders. She then walked back over to John, gave him a scolding scowl, and finished by popping the cap off of his thinning grayed scalp with a snap of her bar rag.

"Hah! Sado-dominatrix that she is!" John laughed, covering his head with his arms. "Better stick to the four-legged woolly ones, Casey boy! This one likes ta' hurt too much!"

"It can't be the end o' everythin'," Case spoke with his lip quivering and his eyes fixed on the frothy carbonation in his glass. "Not everythin'."

"Well, what do ya' think Casey, man." John leaned forward with a smile. "Old Georges gets on the monitor and acts like everythin's under control. Says we got nothin' ta' worry about. Then, tells us that some o' his magicians in Santa Cruz got all the answers waitin' for us. Only when they cut ta' Santa Cruz there ain't nothin' there but one man and a cracked ship bein' drug down inta' the middle o' that 'nothin' ta' worry about' crater. Then we sees seven flyin' monsters like nothin' no man has ever seen, birthed right outta' that burnin' mess, take off for parts unknown, with no good purpose in mind for Earth, t'be sure. And last, we get a crop in o' that dead-faced wretch atop that mountain, surveyin' the land like he just bought hisself a hunk o' prime real estate. Meanwhile, the whole time ol' blustery Georges himself just sits there with a wine bottle up his ass, too stunned for even him ta' drum up his usual crock o' malarkey. Reason enough for most of us ta' realize we're all down the poop shoot when Georges can't sling buckets o' flamingo dung in our eyes with that lyin' tongue o' his!"

"If what happened ta' Liberace Gardens is any indication o' what that alien means ta' do with HIS property," Siobhan put in, "I'll wager he'll not be rentin' nary a closet ta' the likes o' me an' you! Rather we'll be lucky enough if he and his flyin' monsters give us a two foot grave ta' lie in!"

"But…there's got to be some kinda'…hope or somethin'." Casey mouthed with a blank look on his face.

"Well," John began as he refilled his stein and let loose a loud belch, "There was a time before our grandfathers when great numbers o' people were partial ta' the cults. The cult's promised ya' that even when ya' died ya' stayed alive some kinda' way. An' if ya'd been a good cult member, ya'd go to a good place in the afterlife. An' if ya'd been a bad cult member, ya'd go ta' somewhere nasty an' have ta' spend all eternity watchin' old family slides o' yer in-laws or somethin'.

"Well, maybe the cults had somethin'," Case offered hopefully.

"Don't be vulgar in my place, Casey boy." Siobhan sneered playfully. "Never forget that the cults tried ta' take away every livin' bein's right ta' be free. They tried ta' tell ya' what an' when ya' could or couldna' eat or drink. How an' who ta' love. When an' when not ta' sleep with the person ya' choose. When ta' suffer an' try ta' like it! Ta' drop ta' yer knees an' pray ta' someone who ain't even there! An' worst of all, ta' give away almost every-thin' ya' own ta' their…churches they called 'em…so that those shyster cult leaders could ride around in fancy clothes spreadin' the 'word' ta' new members who'd be just as foolish as you. They had no purpose other than ta' make ya' miserable all yer life and die in a state o' delusion. If ya' ask me, it was that kind o' peace-o-mind scam what finally sired the life insur-ance business."

"Aye, lass," John smiled, "an' I'd o' probably been born o' rich man if me ancestors hadn't been guilt-ridden cultists. Now look at me! I'm a fifth generation longshoreman still payin' for the poverty me ancestors embraced over a hundred years ago because some cult told them that dyin' with somethin' means nothin'. What kind o' fool math is that?"

"Likely, the same kind ya' use ta' pay yer tab, John boy." Siobhan winked.

"It just can't be." Case mumbled dejectedly.

"Face it, Case lad." John spoke with a nod of acceptance. "Since the beginnin' o' time, man's been unable to accept dyin' 'til he himself lies dead in the ground. 'An contrary ta' what the cults woulda' had us believe, not one o' the trillions o' people who've walked the earth have ever bothered ta' come back from the dead ta' tell us what a good time he's havin'. When a man squashes a bug under his foot, he doesn't stop ta' think whether it's livin' in some afterworld o' bug folk. It's dead as the smear on the bottom o' yer boot an' that's the end of it! So why should a man…or lassie…fathom him or herself any more complex than that? When it all comes down, we're just flesh and bone with a little finer tastes than the monkeys in the trees. Nothin' more, Casey boy."

"So we just become nothin'?" fretted Case. "Nothin' at all? The whole damn world? Just like that?"

"Well, who knows, Casey," John answered lighting a cigarette. "Maybe ol' Georges'll trade the alien that little concubine nance o' his for all our lives…assumin' the alien is o' that kind. Or maybe he'll trade 'is daughter for that matter. I bet she'd show 'im a trick or two with those big tits o' hers."

"Now there's a girl who might live forever." Siobhan said sarcastically. "She's more polymer and silicon than flesh and bone, I hear!"

"Aye, the best parts o' her got a long shelf life!" John laughed. "Not like you, Siobhan: All sass, ass and a natural bosom big enough ta' nurse half the world's newborns ta' manhood. That's why I like my women poor. Those Blossom women spend a fortune sculptin' themselves inta' mannequins. Why only in the Blossoms can a skinny, blonde straight haired couple have fat, dark curly haired children. But with a Weed girl, ya' always know yer gettin' exactly what sprung from the seed."

When John cupped his hands lecherously toward Siobhan's sagging chest, she pushed him back in his seat. And as the forelegs of his chair lifted off of the ground, she rudely kicked the back legs out from under his copious girth. With a loud crash, John lay back on the floor with his boots dangling up in the air. The pub, again, exploded into loud laughter as Siobhan draped her bar rag over his face as if to triumphantly declare him deceased.

"Can't I wait and die with the rest o' ye?" John spoke from under the rag.

The loud laughter continued as Siobhan swaggered back to the bar.

Case, meanwhile, continued to stare blankly into his glass, pondering the finite terms of his mortal existence.

# XXVI.

Mare Crisium, The Moon:

"Satellite defenses tracking, Manda." Will monitored from his observatory console. "We've got six of those seven birds located. We have one over Ellesmere Island, one over the Laptev Sea, one off the Chilean coastline, one nearing South Mandela, one parked over the Indian Ocean, and one just south of the Hawaiian Islands."

"Good job, Will." Manda spoke from the monitor above him. "Any indication of aggression?"

"None so far." Will answered.

"Shit!"

"Isn't that good, Manda?"

"Not really. If they were attacking, I'd know what to do. With them just sitting there…well, I'd hate to have my unprovoked order to attack them spell the doom of the entire planet."

"It wouldn't really be unprovoked, Manda. Remember the forty-seven thousand dead at Liberace Gardens?"

"All too well. But that tragedy doesn't necessarily constitute an attack. I hate to sound flippant, but that could have simply been a 'bad' landing by beings who have no idea what the value of human life is. I mean, when we first landed on Mars, we trampled our equipment all through gorges of microbiological life forms unaware of the damage we were doing. It wasn't until later that we realized we'd rendered thousands of species of pristine life instantly extinct by our mere presence. Who's to say that these beings couldn't make the same mistake?"

"That's a very cautious and passionate position I'm afraid I don't share, Manda. Destroying Liberace Gardens on the eve of Vogue Day is just a little too symbolic and demoralizing for me to believe it was just coincidence."

"So what would you have me do, Will? Launch an attack against the first extraterrestrial life to make contact on our planet? At best, we may destroy our first contact with new intelligent life needlessly. At worst, we might incite the instrument of our own destruction."

"So what does the Beneficent say?"

"What does he ever say? 'I trust your judgment. Apprise my page of any changes'," she answered with a lazy smile.

"Manda, do you know YOU'RE the Beneficent?"

"No comment, Will. I just do my job."

"I mean, really, between you and the Champion he doesn't have to do anything but give short speeches and take long saunas!"

"No comment. He's the people's choice, and I just do as I'm told. And unless you want the Controller's office on your butt, you'd do well to do the same."

Will sighed and drummed his fingers beneath the buttons along his console. Manda had an annoying proclivity for rationally balancing unalterable circumstances and forging ahead. It was an enviable characteristic he'd found particularly unique among females, which led him to tread lightly upon another question which had been orbiting his conscience during the past few hours.

"Manda…" he began, softening his usually aggressive tone. "How are you doing…about A…about Amritraj."

Manda's face became taxed momentarily, then looked off-screen for a few seconds. Will immediately regretted imposing on her private mourning. He had frequently worked with her and Amritraj over the years, although his relationship with the couple rarely poked beyond that of a professional acquaintance. Still, he knew that they had grown very close. And the Cartel rumor mill had married them off several times, whenever Amritraj occasioned to visit her in Cannes. They seemed uniquely suited for each other: Amritraj, the passionate, outspoken scientist and Manda, the unflappable, seemingly inaccessible Head of Operations, who hid emotion and compassion from all save the few who knew her well.

"Forget it, Manda. That was dumb," Will tried to retract.

Manda collected herself and with a sliver of pain looked back at the screen.

"Fortunately," she began in a voice that wavered only slightly, "I've been too busy to think about myself. After it happened, I had to call Mikki Denison…and her son. Had to try and say something really consoling and trite-sounding like what a great man her husband was and how sorry we all were. That was so damned hard. How could I begin to think of myself when that little boy had to watch his father die? A and I? I don't know. It's just the way things are, I guess. There's so much to do right now, I hope I just live long enough to figure out what I'm feeling."

"I won't insult you by saying I understand." Will wrestled for a response. "But you really do have my sympathy."

"Thanks, Will." Manda nodded. "Now why don't you locate that seventh bird. Not knowing where it is makes me more nervous than staring at our macabre friend on the mountain."

"You worry too much."

"Someone's got to," she said resignedly

"Well, I'll call you when I have something."

"Good night, Will."

"Good morning, Manda."

Will saw Manda check her chronometer and note that sunrise in France was fast approaching. She smiled in acknowledgment then faded from his view screen.

Then he called downstairs for more data on the flying creatures' departure paths from the crater site.

"Nothing yet, sir." came a voice over the intercom. "Increased solar flare activity is topping off our readings at X200. It may show up on its own, but we can't increase sensor specificity for another couple of hours."

"Fine. Let me know when…"

There was a loud crash from outside Mare Crisium Station that sounded like a heavy, dense mass applying pressure to the metallic exterior. Alarms blared, indicating that cessation of the artificial atmosphere was imminent due to structural failure.

Before Will could issue his commands over the intercom, all of the power around him went completely dead. This was followed by an unnerving inertia of calm as the very air fell quiet. He heard the emergency power momentarily struggle to kick in as the lights flickered in and out. Then everything went black for good.

He could hear men and women calling to each other from the adjoining rooms all around him. Then the voices gradually died away as an eerie, alien hum increased in volume.

He knew something was coming, but couldn't surmise what it might be. Suddenly, a pulsing incandescent blue light appeared on the far wall. It began to expand as streams of energy emanating from it spread throughout the room, wrapping itself around furniture, equipment, clothing and even morsels of food.

Will could feel the artificial atmosphere being sucked through the hole created by the spot of light. He felt the very air evacuating his lungs and his decompressing skull about to explode. Finally, the energy immersed his body and before he could feel himself die, he saw the red eye of the seventh giant ship/creature peering at him where the roof had once been. With that, he and everything around him disappeared.

Mare Crisium Station, on the Northeast quadrant of the illuminated lunar face vanished, leaving only stirred metallic sand as evidence of it ever having existed.

## XXVII.

Monte Carlo, France-The T. Fonda Hotel & Casino:

Morning.

"Mademoiselle Richelieu? Mademoiselle Richelieu?"

A cool shiver ran through Louisette's body as she achingly emerged from a near-catatonic unconsciousness. Her first thought was that she'd been sleeping on the hardest pillow she could ever have imagined. But as she opened her eyes, her blurred vision made out an azure sea of creamy liquid swirling centimeters from her face with dark locks of her own hair wafting like flotsam amidst the speckled regurgitation. The putrid odor caused her to recoil suddenly, peeling her glued cheek from the lip of the cold marble toilet.

The jabbing pain piercing her temples left her equilibrium mangled by residual vertigo. And the effort to rise to her feet resulted only in her toppling into a large filthy puddle on the flooded bathroom floor. The jingling bells on her soaked suede moccasins caused several other sleeping leftovers to stir from their respective corners and stalls.

Embardee, Louisette's personal chauffeur, waded toward her and lifted her up into his arms, cradling her like a young toddler. The tall, gaunt servant carried the limp woman out into the dark, vacant ballroom and sat her on a bench near a wall for her to lean against. He took one of her ocelot coats he had brought along and draped it over her nude bottom half.

"Embardee?" she spoke with her eyes tightly closed.

"Oui, Mademoiselle?"

"Where are my bracelets?" she asked of the diamond crusted jewelry that was now missing from her scarred wrists.

"I did not see them Mademoiselle," he said dryly.

"What about my skirt?" she asked.

"I did not see it Mademoiselle."

"Did you look for it?" she became agitated.

"Oui, Mademoiselle."

Louisette snorted in frustration. Then with much effort, she wiggled her toes to see if she could still feel her moccasins.

"I have my shoes?"

"Oui, Mademoiselle."

She tried to think of what she might have forgotten, but the pain in her head made her not want to think at all. Then she flashed a remembrance of the Anti-Grav Plunge which nearly took her life. Instinctively, she reached up to touch Anna Maria's Latin cross necklace which Wesley had given to her the evening before. It was gone.

"Where's my necklace?" she asked forcing her eyes open.

"I did not see a necklace, Mademoiselle."

"Did you look?" she asked with pained desperation.

"No, Mademoiselle. I did not know you had…"

"Well, get in there and find it!" her voiced echoed, stirring awake other leftovers near the bar area.

Embardee dutifully stepped over an unconscious body in the bathroom vestibule and returned to the squalid lavatory area to search for a necklace he had never seen.

Meanwhile, Louisette sat painfully on the bench as her celebratory injuries grew apparent. Her shoulders felt sore and tired as did her back and thighs which blusilver, among other things, had rendered more pliable during the evening. Her knees stung badly as if split at the caps. She rolled back the fur and saw them bruised and scraped. Her private area throbbed, swollen from an apparent thrashing she could not even remember.

"The price we pay!" piped a disturbingly chipper and energetic voice.

Louisette looked up and saw Lars smiling brightly with Almah attached to his shoulder holding a drink.

"You were great, last night Louise!" Lars beamed. "Ratings were fantastic! You even beat the news stations that were covering updates on the crater in Santa Cruz! In fact, our station suspended coverage of the disaster all together because of you! I hope you plan to stick around! We can work you onto satellite again today!

"No…" Louisette groaned, massaging her head. "Gotta' go."

Lars and Almah looked at last evening's mistress of ceremony as if she were a war hero preparing to ship for home. They earnestly admired that there was something "daring" in Louisette that always made her exceed people's expectations.

"Well, happy Vogue Day!" Almah chimed, as the couple tottered toward the elevators leading up to the hotel.

The bathroom door swung open and Embardee emerged holding up something swinging from a plastic stick.

"Mademoiselle?"

Louisette cracked her eyes open slightly, and quickly recognized the gold-chained Latin cross swinging before her eyes.

"Where?" she asked, snatching it from the plastic stick and jamming it into her coat pocket.

"Le toilette, Mademoiselle."

Louisette tried to smile at the pathetic irony. But instead, increasingly clear visions of Anna Maria sprawled across the stained bed accosted her thoughts. Suddenly, she very badly wanted to be high again.

When Embardee helped her to her feet, her knees immediately buckled. So again he swung her up in his arms and carried her out of the Hotel and Casino to the limousine hovering by the outer gate. The chauffeur poured her onto the floor of the rear cabin which had already been cleaned and re-upholstered since its last ill-fated journey only twelve hours ago.

The limousine sped away while Louisette lay trying to induce laughter from the "joy" of her critically acclaimed performance in Monte Carlo, as she also tightly clutched Anna Maria's necklace in her pocket.

# XXVIII.

Cannes, France-The Beneficent Palace:

Victor rolled to his feet and opened fire!

A deafening staccato burst of gunfire riddled his targets with tiny shells that electronically released hydrochloric acid into the bodies of his victims. They shrieked and mechanically collapsed to the ground.

There was no time to admire his handiwork, however. The hum of seven or eight soaring sharp-edged discs caught his ear. He fell backward as one of the metal alloy discs sliced through the barrel of his weapon while another clipped a tassel of his golden hair.

Reaching into his boot, he pulled out a pronged lance. Aiming it at the disc's point of origin, he pressed a release button on the handle and two miniature shells jettisoned outward. In another second there was a fiery explosion—there would be no more discs this morning.

Still no time to relax. Steel cables coiled down from above and strapped about his limbs with the crushing instincts of giant predatory eels. Slowly the cables constricted tightly, nearly cutting into his tanned sinewy flesh. Pressing his fingers into the heels of his palms, he activated the lasers in his wrist bands and quickly burned himself free.

He gasped for a moment, stealing a chance to catch his breath. But suddenly, the scaly gargoyles were upon him, scratching with their talons, biting with their jagged teeth. With a sharp elbow, he split open one's face. With a powerful kick, he crushed another against a wall. The third, he reached behind and savagely wrenched the wings from its back. And before it could fall, he grabbed it by the throat and jabbed out its eyes with two fingers.

Just then a stream of heat singed away the tabard covering his back. Suppressing any urge to yell, he cybernetically activated the nano-carbon filters in his artificial eye lenses. Looking over his shoulder, he saw through the intense glare emitting from the burning wall of gaseous heat, pulled a tool the size of a penlight from his belt and focused a stream of laser light at the heart of the miniature conflagration. There was a loud cracking noise and with the cessation of heat came an enormous crash.

"Is this over?" he wondered.

Not just yet.

From out of the floor a giant hand rose up and grabbed him by the thigh. With his wrist bands he tried, but failed to cut away its metallic fingers. Slowly, a head appeared from the floor beneath him, then a torso followed by thick steel-banded legs. Soon he found himself dangling upside down staring into the face of a smooth featureless android giant.

He pulled out a club from his holster, pressed a button on its handle and a spiked mace formed at one end. With a powerful thrust, he hurled the mace at the android's head and watched it wedge behind its ear (or where an ear should have been). But the only result was a loud distorted noise that simulated laughter from the nine-foot metal giant.

Victor hurriedly pulled out a keypad from his belt. The giant clutched his arm in its other hand and pulled with incredible hydraulic force. He could not tell whether his arm or leg would separate from his body first, if he didn't act quickly. With only one arm left free, Victor punched up a code on the keypad with his thumb. The mace protruding from the side of the android's neck started to hum and glow. Suddenly, a bolt of electricity shot out of the mechanoid, through the mace handle and blasted a hole in the far wall. The android's limbs went limp and Victor freed himself, executing a flip and a two-point landing onto the floor below.

"Over now?" he asked taking a deep breath.

"Training sequence complete," echoed a simulated voice. "Maintenance reset to be initiated in two minutes."

Victor smirked to himself and strode out of the training room.

"You weren't ready for the droid, were you?" Kima asked, greeting Victor as the doors closed behind him.

"What was that all about?" Victor shrugged checking the uneven length of hair sheered by the discs.

"That's not an answer. You weren't expecting it were you?" persisted the thin, modestly built older woman.

"No," he confessed. "Of course you wouldn't expect me to cut your throat with this knife, would you?"

Victor seized her by the collar, lifted her off of her feet, and poised the edge of a sharp hunter's knife at the woman's jugular.

"You never know," she stared coolly into his eyes. "I might like it."

"Don't fuck with me, old bitch!" Victor threatened, lifting her chin with the tip of its glistening point.

"I wouldn't bother, Champ." Kima smiled. "It'd just go over your head."

Victor poked the edge of the blade under the inside of her jawbone and with clenched teeth and a wild gaze, attempted to instill fear in his personal trainer.

"Is this when I'm supposed to cry and shudder and beg, like Louise?" Kima asked evenly.

"You do that," he sneered, "and I'd really kill you!"

Kima started to laugh, but Victor surprised her by pushing her toward the panel where she abruptly rolled into the Training room control grid and fell hard into her chair.

She looked up at him, regarding his "petty" display of assertion as so much silliness. Then began calling up the analysis of his session on her computer.

Victor looked away, momentarily frustrated with her unyielding proclivity for summing him up with such effortless, aloof, conciseness.

"All things considered," Kima scanned her monitor, "you performed quite well. It wasn't your best outing, but with fatigue factored in, your performance was still quite...incredible. I think if we raise your anabolic intake by ten to fifteen..."

"What do you mean 'all things considered'?" Victor interrupted.

Kima shook her head at his immediate assumption of a defensive posture. So proud to be the best, she thought. So scared not to be.

She stood up and slowly walked toward him, then pushed the sweat soaked hair from his angry eyes and spoke softly.

"All I meant was that you haven't gotten much rest in the last twenty-four hours. So much on your mind."

"I was in bed by midnight." he smiled as the tension began to melt away.

"I know," she said running her fingers lightly along his bottom lip. "But you didn't get to sleep until...four or five."

"Who's fault was that...trainer?" Victor rubbed the back of her bare neck and tickled the short hair up the back of her head.

"Could we blame it on Dom?" she purred stenciling her fingernail along the cleft separating his massive pectorals.

"Dom?" he questioned.

"Yeah. That monk, Monsieur Perignon?"

"Ohhhh. Dom." Victor smiled. "I thought there were only two of us."

"Don't worry," she chuckled. "He's blind. He didn't see a thing."

"Good," he sighed heavily. "I like my privacy."

"So do I."

Victor lifted Kima up to him by her waist and held her there as their lips touched and their tongues jousted passionately.

# XXIX.

Harlem, New York-Priest MacDaddy's Lounge:
3 a.m. EST.

Priest MacDaddy's Lounge usually locked its rusted iron gates soon after midnight. Better that, than spinning Russian roulette with the vicious urban Weed streets whose violent nocturnal denizens pillaged the already pulverized concrete landscape as a fervid ritual. But this evening, Priest grudgingly handed the keys over to his frightful teen nephew, B.K. Rebbok. In the spirit of Vogue Day, B.K. and his partner L.A. Neik were entertaining well-to-do guests from the other side of civilization. Babbie and Brittany Hassani: Blossom girls on holiday in the most squalid, depraved Weed slum they could find.

An electric twelve-string sitar blared its solo lazily over the impressive sound system, intermittently drowning out the noises of shattering glass, loud voices and gunfire outside.

B.K. leered perniciously through his lifeless, red-rimmed eyes at the debutante twins who watched him slowly inhale the arsenic gas from the aluminum canister clutched in his làrge filthy paw. Sweat made his muscular, pock-marked flesh shimmer in the dim lamp light. The scraggly, unkempt mustache above his dry, chapped lips twitched ever so slightly as he fought down the burning assault on his nervous system. His heart fluttered a moment but he suppressed any concern. Then he smiled a white and gold capped grin and pushed the canister across the scarred wooden table to Babbie.

Babbie glanced at Brittany who was nervously chewing the pearls of her necklace and fumbling with her gold anklet. She then smiled confidently at B.K. and L.A., and shook her straight dark hair, which she had not washed in a week, off of her shoulders. She lifted the canister with her long, delicate fingers and placed the nozzle into her soft lips, without wiping it off.

B.K. nodded his approval.

Babbie inhaled deeply. Her lungs and her brain felt as if they were set afire. Her skin went cold, then broke into a sweat. She swallowed hard once, to keep herself from vomiting. Then, while her eyes grew pink and lazy, she fashioned a perky grin as if to say: "Is that all?"

B.K. laughed out loud, pounding his fist on the table.

L.A. laughed nervously, wiping his sweaty palms across his smudged and torn "Legalize Homemade" T-shirt.

Brittany tried, unsuccessfully, to smile away her fear.

"Snikkin' L.A.?" B.K. asked sliding the canister in his best friend's direction.

"Nah, mah," L.A. smiled. "Bin sivverin' aw day."

"Wuh? You goan let deese Bossom hoes make you loog lyga' bitch, muhh fukka?" B.K. chided.

"Nah, mah," L.A. looked away. "Bin sivverin', das aw. I ain goan keo mahseff, muhh fukka! Shih!"

"Nah wah ah got ta' be aw dat?" B.K. frowned.

"Aw wah?" L.A. smiled.

"A muh fukka!" B.K. raised his voice.

"You caw me a muh fukka, firs!" L.A. defended.

"Ah ain ax you dat!" B.K. yelled. "Ah ax you wah ah got ta' be a muh fukka?"

"An ah seya ah bin sivverin'!" L.A. nervously asserted. "Ah ain mixin' d'shih!"

"Wah nah?" B.K. demanded.

"Caw d'shih'll keo me dat wah!" L.A. responded.

"Ohh. Ah git it," B.K. relaxed. "So causa' dat, ah got ta' be a muh fukka, huh?"

"Nah, mah," L.A. retrenched.

"Buh dats wuh you sed, doh!" B.K. charged.

"Fuggit it, mah," L.A. asked.

"Wuh? You caw me a muh fukka 'frunna dese laydees an ahm spose ta' jus' fuggit it?"

Brittany tensely scratched the bottoms of her bare feet, tucked under her, as the exchange became heated.

Babbie rattled her slinging bracelets as she twirled a broken strand from her cut-off cashmere skirt.

"Ay, mah," L.A. spoke with irritation. "Ah say'd fuggit it! Stop akkin crazy!"

"Crazy?!" B.K. shouted. "Ah sho yo' azz crazy!"

B.K., all of a sudden, whipped a large-barrelled hand weapon from the back of his pants, jumped to his feet, and pressed it against L.A.'s head.

Brittany let out a loud scream.

Babbie stood up and backed away grabbing her sister by the hand.

"Nah, muh fukka!" B.K. yelled. "Who da' muh fukka nah?"

"Ah am." L.A. answered resignedly.

"Huh?" B.K. savagely clenched his teeth. "Ah cain hee ya'.'"

"Ah am!" L.A. spoke louder.

"An' who da' bitch?" B.K. nudged L.A.'s head with the barrel.

"Ah am!" L.A. said audibly.

"An' who goan do da' snik, bitch-muh fukka?"

"Ah am!" answered L.A..

B.K. pulled the gun away from L.A.'s head and started laughing. With his free hand, he then followed with a loud slap across L.A.'s forehead.

L.A. cringed and tried to smile away his embarrassment.

"Look," Babbie spoke up, "um, if he's been doing blusilver all day, maybe it's not such a good idea for him to do the arsenic cloud."

B.K. snapped a wild rueful stare toward the two girls as they stood away from the table. His nostrils flared with hostility at the thought that a Blossom "princess" was trying to assert some vestige of dominance on his home turf. A maddened, twisted rage built up inside of him as his finger tightened on the trigger.

But then he looked up and down at their firm, smooth legs and their clean bare feet. He looked at their bright, unblemished faces. He looked at their long satin hair which was mussed but still neater…nicer on them, than anything which he had not had to rob or rape…and kill.

"Hah! Hah! Hah! Hahhhh!" B.K. suddenly burst into laughter. "Y'all scayed ain ch'all!"

"Yes," sniffed Brittany on her sister's shoulder.

"Awww c'moan." B.K. grinned broadly. "Me an' L.A. is jus' fukkin roun' wi' ch'all! L.A. mah boy! I ain goan keo dis' muh fukka!"

L.A. lifted his eyes and tried to smile reassuringly at his partner's frightened quarry. Though in truth, he still appeared very frightened himself.

"Oh!" Babbie responded, returning his grin with a bright, convincing smile of her own.

Brittany, however, remained apprehensive.

"Um," Babbie continued. "I think this kind of shook my sister up a little bit, though. This is her first time in the Weeds. Could we be excused to the bathroom?"

B.K. let drool slip from his lips down to the front of his oversized, leather sport shoes as he stared blankly at their tender, lithe figures.

"Yeah," he finally grunted.

Babbie turned Brittany around and the two girls quickly barefooted toward the lavatory.

"Unnnhhh!" B.K. groaned as the girls disappeared behind the crooked, splintered door. "We goan buss sum lil' bossom butt t'nie!"

Behind him L.A. wiped the beads of sweat from his forehead with a napkin.

Inside the bathroom:

"What's wrong with you?" Babbie scolded.

"What's wrong with me!?" Brittany exclaimed with shock. "That B.K. is fucking out of his mind! That's what's wrong with me!"

"What are you talking about?" Babbie frowned. "I mean, he's different. But he's kind of cool!"

"Cool?!" Brittany's eyes bulged. "Their both dirty, filthy, disgusting creatures!"

"So what?"

"So would you date them?"

"No. But I'd fuck them."

Brittany turned away and stamped her foot in disgust. "I can't even understand what they're saying," she admitted with distress.

"Well, what did you expect?" Babbie defended. "You agreed to come with me. I told you what kind of partying we were going to do. This is a great time!"

"Great time?!" Brittany raised her voice. "The guy almost blows his friend's head off!"

"He was only joking!" Babbie affirmed. "They're friends. That's how you joke in the Weeds."

"Ha, ha," Brittany said blankly. "We should have stayed in Havana."

"Havana was boring!" Babbie stated flatly. "Too many pretty little people from school. Pina Coladas and lines of cocaine all weekend. BORING. This is where its happening! This is where you get Vogue! You dress dirty and you hit the Weeds as hard you can. Something different! Something new! It's a rush! Isn't that what life is all about?"

"And what if something goes wrong?" Brittany said, staring at the floor.

"Then I call our transport." Babbie sighed, holding up a tiny flashing transmitter. "The chauffeur comes in and lifts us right out!"

"I want to leave." Brittany said just above a whisper.

"What?!" Babbie exclaimed.

"I want to leave now." Brittany resolutely pouted.

"We can't just walk out on these guys!" Babbie warned. "We said we were staying over!"

"So?"

"So, I don't want to piss them off!"

"You said they weren't dangerous."

"Well…they're not! But it would be awful damn rude to just pick up and leave, wouldn't it?"

"I don't care."

"Brit, we're not leaving."

"If you don't call our transport right now, I'm telling daddy where we've been."

"He'll put both of us in rehab!"

"I don't care!"

Babbie turned away in disgust and pounded her hand against the wall.

Brittany opened a stall door to go to the bathroom. A brood of tiny roaches scattered under the baseboards. She lifted the toilet cover with the tip of her finger nail and lurched backward at the sight of a large rat swimming along side a giant log of bowel movement.

In the lounge:

"You scay'd dem guls, mah." L.A. spoke up after a prolonged silence. "Day goan lee."

"Mah, qui' bein' a bitch!" B.K. snapped as he loaded a full cartridge into his weapon. "I ain scay nobolly! Dat Babbie gul wettn' huh draws awreddy. Om'll buss dat hoe, you wosh!"

"Yeah, bu' dat udda' gul look scay, mah!" L.A. observed.

"Dats caw she dink she stuk wit' yo faggit azz, muh fukka!" B.K. groused. "If you wuz a' mans, she be too bizzy suggin' yo' dig t'be scay'd o' nobolly!"

"Mah, dats da' ploblem." L.A. became irritated. "We gah dese nize azz hoes, bu' aw we goan do is treat'm lak aw d'udda hoes we dun bussed. Mah, dey dink we animos an' shih! Caw we ak lak animos! You…me, we jus' az good az dem bossom bitches. Buh if we goan ak lak animos, how we goan git anybolly's r'spek?"

B.K. paused for a moment, wondering when his "meal" would emerge from the lavatory. Then he turned and looked up and down at L.A..

"Mah," B.K. sneered, "Shud d'fug up!"

The bathroom door creaked open. Babbie and Brittany stepped out, looking flustered. They walked sheepishly back toward the table.

B.K. bared a large toothy grin as he stuck out his tightly muscled chest and clasped his hands behind him.

L.A. read the girls' faces with dread. He already knew what was coming next.

"We have to go." Babbie announced with a heavy sigh.

B.K.'s neck and jaw muscles began to work tensely, suppressing a wild, instantaneous rage.

"Wuh, y'all scay'd?" B.K. asked sweetly.

"Um, no." Babbie tried to fabricate. "It's just that we've been partying all day and my sister feel's…sick."

"Aw, das aw?" B.K. smiled at Brittany. "You wan' sum'm ta' dring?"

"Uh, no." Babbie interceded. "She just needs to go home."

An insane fury rippled across B.K.'s face as he tried to force a smile through his mounting anger.

"Ya'll say ya'll wuz stayin'." B.K. reminded.

"Look guys, I'm really sorry…" Babbie pleaded with her eyes.

"Wayo, dat's dat." L.A. resigned, throwing up his hands.

"'Dat's dat', mah azz!" B.K. growled.

B.K. snatched Babbie by the arm, and pushed the barrel of his weapon under her chin.

"Nah, bitch! Way d'fuk you ding you goan?" B.K. snarled.

"Waya' min mah!" L.A. tried to defuse.

Brittany grabbed B.K., and digging her nails into his arm, tried to break his hold on her sister. B.K. pulled back and pointed his weapon at Brittany's stomach, and the barrel exploded, splattering open the girl's abdomen as she flopped back against the bar.

At the shocking sight, Babbie screamed and kicked madly, unable to break B.K.'s iron hold.

L.A. charged B.K. to try to wrestle the weapon from his hand. But B.K. kicked him hard, and L.A. fell to the floor.

L.A. rolled up onto his feet and found the gun barrel pointed right at his face.

"Dis' ain righ, mah!" L.A. shouted.

"Wus' righ, muh fukka?" B.K. sneered.

The question hung heavily in L.A.'s mind. The answer, however, remained tragically sequestered behind some private window through which he'd always refused to look..

B.K.'s weapon exploded in L.A.'s face, ripping away his jawbone as he staggered, convulsed and fell to the floor in a bloody heap.

Babbie continued to scream and claw and struggle. When the noise and commotion became more than B.K. wanted to deal with, he pressed the barrel behind her ear and pulled the trigger. One side of Babbie's head disintegrated into a spray of blood. He dropped the dead body to the ground and sighed.

"WHY?" B.K. shrieked madly as tears rolled down his face. "Why ya'll hav ta' fuggup lak dis'?"

He walked over to L.A.'s body and vindictively emptied six more rounds into his corpse. Then he did likewise to Babbie and Brittany, screaming obscenities at their lifeless carrions. He set the gun down on the table and took up the arsenic gas cannister once more, inhaling from it deeply. The burning sensation of "the cloud" settled his nerves.

Outside, a bright flood light illuminated the street. An amplified voice called from above: "This is transport HH112645. Please step into the light and display I.D. This is transport HH112645. Please step into the light."

B.K. began laughing hysterically to himself. Then, almost giddily, he shuffled behind the bar and searched for the mop.

# XXX.

Cannes, France-The Beneficent Palace:

Louisette painfully limped down the tall daylighted corridor uncertain whether she'd pass out in her room or pass out face down in the lush hallway carpeting. For all of her twenty-two years, she felt uncommonly fatigued and unnervingly decrepit. And in spite of the bulky, floor-length ocelot fur huddled tightly around her body, she was still absolutely freezing. A scalding bubble bath would have to take precedence, with the first maid who could be found to draw one, she thought.

"Louise!" called a high-pitched voice from some distance behind her.

Bound to answer to no one but her father, she continued on her way with the gait of an aged plow horse hobbling on its last legs. She did not care to hear from anyone who wanted to offer adulation for last night's world satellite display of her ambivalent brinkmanship in playing the game known as her life. Hollow compliments and transient praise were nearly as common to her as "good friends" who faded with the soonest light of dawn.

She heard the voice call again and responsively ignored it again. When she heard someone running after her, she would have run away from it if she could have. A familiar sweet scent pierced Louisette's clogged nostrils before she managed to turn around.

It was Val, her father's perky young plaything, powdered and primped in a flowered wreath and a green and pink, heavily embroidered chlamys, loosely draped about his narrow shoulders, displaying the nude curvature of his frail body from the open sides.

"Didn't you hear me?" Val asked breathing heavily through his mouth.

"No." Louisette lied, trudging drearily onward.

"Are you…all right?" the boy asked, noting her disheveled, haggard disposition.

"It's just morning, that's all," she responded laconically.

"Well, I saw you do the Anti-Grav before I...went to bed," Val said cheerfully. "You were great! Where did you lear..."

Louisette froze for an instant. Her survival of the seven hundred fifty meter drop had been truly miraculous. But the particulars, as she recounted them, had been too mightily disorienting for her to dwell upon at this moment.

"Val, did you track me down just to tell me how great I was?" She cut him short.

"Well..."

"Half the world's told me already!" She snipped. "Merci, but spare me!"

"Well, actually," Val started carefully, "I'm supposed to tell you that your father wants to see you."

"Tell him..." she winced, massaging her sinuses. "I'll see him in a few hours."

"Um..." Val began, drawing a breath, "He said 'Now'. He said: 'Right now!'"

Louisette scrutinized Val's painted eyes and saw the serious worry on his powdered face—an expression suited more to the professional page than her father's frivolous boy lover.

"What is it?" she asked, attempting to mask concern.

Val sheepishly shook his head and looked down as if to convey that he either did not know or could not say.

"All right," she sighed.

Louisette turned slowly, as if the alteration of her path, alone, required considerably arduous exertion. Then she resumed her labored limp toward the Beneficent's quarters.

"Happy Vogue." Val called with sincerity.

"'Try something new'," she responded in a strained voice.

Val watched her hunched, fur-bearing figure slowly plod its path toward the Beneficent's room. Then he drew himself up as he tried not to think about how terribly Anna Maria had died the day before.

Her father's summons unearthed a foreboding alertness in Louisette which she had not felt in days. Even the sharp, pulsing pain in her head seemed to subside in favor of a preoccupation over what would make her father 'demand' to see her.

Had he suddenly taken ill, she wondered. Or had the tragedy in Florida touched down in a more personal way?

Neither of these hypotheses carried much weight, even in her own mind. If her father were ill, Val would have been…more emotional, more upset. And she knew of no one who could have been at the resort, whose lost life would warrant immediate conference between the two of them. In fact, no matter of import, save her "impending" marriage to Victor, ever seemed to intersect her path with her father's.

Then it dawned on her—Victor. For the Beneficent to call her with such urgency, for Val to so officially, so dutifully act on her father's behalf without so much as a glimmer of his renowned effeminate sarcasm—something critical must have happened. And it certainly must concern the man she was destined wed, who in turn was destined to inherit the Earth.

Surprising herself, she managed to hasten her steps to the Beneficent's quarters as the jingling of her moccasins became audible again.

"I can't possibly lose my cousin and my man in so short a time!" she fretted.

Upon reaching her father's giant oak door, it slowly dragged open before she could herald her arrival through the intercom.

The room was dark and still. Usually, the tall balcony curtains were undrawn and light chamber music quietly filled the background. But this morning her father shrouded himself with the trappings of mournful reflection and abject distress. Louisette had not seen him quite this way since her aunt Josephine had passed away some nine years ago. The deja vu of that saddest occasion pimpled her flesh with the recollection of how dark a day it had been. She had never seen so many adults crying in one setting at one time.

"Sit," came a heavy voice from out of the darkness.

He was at his desk.

Strange, she thought. He had never addressed her from there; it was solely a place from which he conducted business—and business was something of which Louisette had never been a part.

She tried to move quietly to the couch facing the large wooden desk and high-backed leather chair where she made out her father's silhouette. Her ankle bells jingled just loudly enough to rob her of any dignity the solemnity of the moment required. Louisette tried to bend her aching knees gradually to be seated. She managed only a quarter of the motion before the pain forced her to ungracefully plop down on the water-cushioned sofa.

There, she waited for him to stand or gesture or yell or launch into some other demonstrative act commensurate with his affinity for high drama. But he only sat. And amidst the thick black shadows which surrounded him, she could not even tell if he was looking at her. She nervously fidgeted with a chipped fingernail as her stomach began to tighten.

What have I done, she thought—as a swell of impending persecution began to unveil itself—to father? to Victor?

She raced through conversations she'd had with both men over the past few days, but nothing extraordinary came to the fore. She had behaved, by her own account, as she always had, with no harm done to anyone save herself. Yet her father's vindictive silence beset her with fear and guilt over something clearly overlooked.

"She..." Georges began, clearing his throat. "She was everything in my life that I had hoped you would be. She was bright and radiant and cheerful and unencumbered by the conformist fears that most people allow to rule their lives. It didn't matter to her what popular views were. She always asserted a need to know the right and the wrong of it. She'd have made a horrible Beneficent, but certainly that's a resounding endorsement for the grain of her character. She was insistent that her life never center about herself. Even at her own birthday parties she would be overly concerned with whether her guests were having as good a time as she. And I remember the one Father's Day I had to attend to labor disputes on Mars. She had a cake made for me and sent to my suite, along with a holographic message of herself reciting a poem wishing that she could be there. She was my niece...professing a daughter's love. I was so moved I kept playing the damn thing over and over again till I almost broke to tears.

"And she carried so much compassion for the damned Weeds. The Controller's office was always complaining to me about how difficult it was to maintain security during her forays into the Weed regions to meet with groups of children where the adults would have sooner cut out her heart simply for being my niece. 'Why do they live that way?' she'd ask. 'What do they read? Don't they need more help?' And I knew the answers I'd always given to diplomats and the media and even the Weeds themselves. But to her, I couldn't give those answers. I couldn't look in those loving, trusting eyes and tell her what my predecessors and I had been telling the entire world for decades—not that I don't believe in the Cartel charter and its doctrines and addendums. But somehow, insisting upon them to her always felt like...a lie. A falsehood behind which we had contrived justification for our comfort.

"I'd often ask myself how this dear girl of my own flesh and blood could so easily render my certainty tainted, when learned scholars and fervid zealots could not. And I concluded that the science of selective breeding remains one, totally inexact. For certainly the rampant nobility that imbued my niece's spirit was foreign to both my late sister and her institutionalized husband— and clearly no such vestiges of decency came through my mendacious lineage. How could they, when all the dross I have to show for my years of siring is her antithesis...you."

"Father, clearly you're upset about Anna Maria." Louisette's voice fluttered condescendingly. "I loved her, too. The whole time I was in Monte Carlo I..."

"QUIET!" The Beneficent's voice thundered, sounding to nearly quake the giant Le Bruns from their wall moorings.

Louisette felt she had jumped a kilometer out of her seat as her pulse hammered violently throughout her body. She had often heard him raise such a tone with grovelling operatives and faceless menials, but never in her life had he ever bothered to channel such naked ire toward her.

"I witnessed your 'remorse' in Monte Carlo as did the rest of humankind!" He growled between clenched teeth. "I watched you tumble out of the limousine with those detestable peasants you referred to as 'friends'. I listened, painfully, as you told the whole world that you didn't even know the difference between Florida and California when our very existence may be hanging by a thread! I watched you flaunt that banned cult symbol and in the same breath curse humanity like some brazen cultist harpy. I saw you, 'grief-stricken' and semi-conscious from drugs, on the dance floor swinging shamelessly from man to woman to man like some under-compensated escort girl living on spartan gratuities. I saw the clumsy fall from the platform during which I must admit I vacillated betwixt whether I even wanted to see you live. And I endured your display of 'anguish' as you led almost a hundred people into the lavatory where you delivered obscenity and indecency to a grand new height!"

"I did nothing illegal, father." Louisette muttered, tucked behind her fur lapels.

"I'm not talking about legality!!" He pounded his fist on the desk, causing her to jump again. "I'm talking about you, my daughter, being a canker on the face of this office! I'm talking about trying to maintain control and credibility while you work double time trying to exhibit what a misbegotten, empty-headed whore you are! And I'm talking about your poisoning and destroying the one flicker of beauty in this wretched Palace who everyone could look to with adoration."

"Father, poisoning…?"

"Three vials of blusilver, Louisette?" the Beneficent's voice cracked. "Anna Maria shot three vials? You could have killed that Arabian Horse of yours with three vials! Not nearly that much killed your mother and your aunt and they were addicts like you!"

The word "addict" hung in Louisette's mind. She knew what an addict was. And she knew that she used several drugs with regularity. But she never once correlated the term with her own usage.

"Anna Maria wouldn't have used blusilver unless she was coerced by you!" he continued. "She always criticized the use of recreational chemicals...even alcohol. Then she up and kills herself with an ass full of the world's number one shoot! What would you have me think, Louisette? That she changed all by herself?"

"No." Louisette whispered, wiping away a tear.

"What then? Were you just plain jealous of her outshining your dimness at every turn? Did you figure to use her naive, unfounded admiration of you to destroy her?"

"No."

"Then what the hell happened?" he yelled. "Why is my sister's child lying on a meat slab in the infirmary, when it should be you?"

There was a short silence as both father and daughter weighed the loveless accusation. Up until now, Louisette had always comforted herself with the notion that her father truly loved her in spite of herself. This morning, however, the illusion evaporated on his every word.

"Um..." she began as her voice rattled. "Um...I gave her the vials because...she was upset."

"Upset? Over what?"

Louisette bowed her head. She did not know where to begin telling her father about the arrangement she'd made for Anna Maria to be with Victor—and how everything had gone horribly awry.

"Over what?" his voice thundered again.

"Um, well..." she stammered, "she liked Victor. She...uh...liked him a lot. And...um...he hurt her."

"Hurt her? Hurt her how?" the Beneficent asked, perplexed.

"Well...she was going to be fourteen soon. And...um...her...body was...changing. And...um...she had begun asking me...about men. So I told her some...things about...love...and about Victor and me."

"So?"

"Well, it turned out that she'd been having feelings...for Victor. Strong feelings. So I told Victor and asked him if he would...show her...or be her first..."

"My god, Louise!"

"Well, she's roughly the same age I was when I...well. She and I both agreed it was time. But somehow, things went...wrong with Victor. I mean...it wasn't what she expected. I mean I tried to tell her beforehand, but she had all these storybooks in her head..."

The Beneficent loudly slammed his fist on the desk with the effect of some irrevocable pronouncement. Then another segue of silence hung in the air like hours rather than seconds. Louisette sniffed back sobs as she tried to suppress an anguished whimper.

"Get out," the Beneficent rumbled with finality.

"Excuse me?" Louisette asked, shocked by the abrupt dismissal.

The Beneficent stood up and came at her directly. Louisette did not know what to make of the charge. He grabbed her by the front of the coat, yanked her off of her feet, and pitched her rolling toward the door.

"I said: 'Get out'!" he shouted, seething. "I don't mean just out of this room! I mean out of the Palace! Out of my life...for good! You can take whatever you can carry! I'll arrange a small stipend to be transferred to wherever you decide to settle! But as of now, you have no place here! And certainly you have no father!"

The Beneficent turned and strode back toward his desk.

"What about Victor?" she asked as tears streamed down her face.

"What about him?" the Beneficent answered coldly.

"We're supposed to be...married soon."

"Well, I'm sure he'll be relieved to know that I won't impose that upon him any longer. I thought that having the Champion for a consort would straighten you out, but I see now that it simply isn't possible. I'm not going to have you spreading any more of that...disease you carry around with you, here. Victor will manage quite well without you!"

Louisette closed her eyes for a moment honestly believing that this could be nothing else but the worst of nightmares. But when she opened them again, she was still sitting in a heap on her father's cold marble floor.

"Father..." she cried feebly, "I...I'm sorry. I..."

"You know," the Beneficent cut in, "when a father is told that he has a daughter, his first reaction is one of mild disappointment. Disappointment only in that some egotistical side of himself wants to raise up a man in his own image to seize the reins of the experiences and philosophies that all of us must inevitably set down when we die. But when that father holds that tiny little girl in his arms for the first time and looks into that soft pouting face, its as if unseen forces come to bear on that one magical moment—where he feels himself cradling all the women he has ever truly loved in his entire life. He senses his wife, his mother, his grandmother, his sisters all endowing with their essences the lifeforce of this one beautiful child: his daughter; his princess. And at that moment he vows to keep and protect and nurture her more than he ever imagined he could rationally do for anyone. That's how I felt when you were born, Louisette.

"But soon thereafter, you began thwarting my every attempt to make your life as perfect as I knew how. As a child I gave you everything you asked for, yet still you found a way to be discontented with those things you did not have. I sent you to the finest boarding school in Switzerland, yet I'd get reports of your disappearing into the Duetschland Weeds for weeks at a time. As a teenager, I allowed you to journey on the finest vacations this world could offer, yet in London they found you resupine, incapacitated with narcotics and bare naked in the back of an empty Tube car. And then there were men! Not good men! Not the sons of Committeemen or Blossom bourgeois. No, they had to be the mongrel curs among the hired help impregnating you time and time again like some stray bitch in heat! I'm certain those years were the impetus for your mother's early death!

"At fifteen, you ran off and married that forty-year-old Turkish bead vendor!" the Beneficent winced.

"Dirk." Louisette recounted tearfully. "His name was Dirk. He was a craftsman…"

"He was a bead vendor!" the Beneficent interrupted. "And his name was 'Dirt' as far as I'm concerned! Trash! Trash, like you've always insisted upon being! It took nearly half the Controller's staff to blot out the mess you'd made before the media got wind of it!"

"You had him killed." Louisette whispered.

"So what!" her father justified. "You've been killing this family for years! I should've had you killed! It would have saved me seven more years of grief! And it certainly would have saved Anna Maria's life!"

Louisette looked away and wiped under her eyes with the tips of her fingers.

"I even retained the most brilliant psychiatrists in the world for your counseling," the Beneficent continued. "Yet those you did not deceive, you insulted into resignation.

"And the arranged engagement to Victor cost me a fortune in favors to him and his family."

Louisette's jaw dropped with surprise.

"Yet still you adeptly repulsed him with your insipid, mindless, behaviors.

"And I was foolish enough to hope Anna Maria might have had a positive affect on you as she began to grow up and do all the right things. But instead of elevating yourself to her level, you fought to bring her down to yours until you killed her! Drowned her in the cesspool you call your life!

"I was joyful to have a daughter once upon a time. But now I realize that your birth was the herald of despair or embarrassment for everyone who bothered to care for you. I simply cannot and will not subject myself to the never-ending desolation of spirit that marks your every touch.

"Get out Louise. And make short time of your departure."

The Beneficent turned and slowly walked past his desk, taking up his jeweled wine chalice. He strode toward the balcony, drew wide the satin curtains and stepped out to admire the morning.

Louisette, stunned beyond cognizance, mechanically extracted herself from the floor and trudged out into the corridor, with the bells on her moccasins fiercely deriding her every footfall.

By coincidence she almost staggered into a smiling Victor and Kima fresh from the Champion's dawn workout. But she avoided them, watching closely as the couple headed, arm in arm, for Victor's room.

She closed her eyes and leaned against the wall for a moment trying desperately to make her life disappear. All she could see though, was Anna Maria's smiling face from the day before, suspended above the girl's still corpse.

# XXXI.

On Satellite:

TM:"Good morning, I'm Tom Mourning and welcome to Tomorning.

"Rioting broke out in many Blossom cities last night, which is nothing uncommon to Vogue Day weekend. What made the rioting unique in Rome and in Mecca, however, was that it had little, if anything, to do with Vogue Day festivities in the least.

"The violence erupted outside satellite theatres where Anthony Warwall's 'Mare Cult' premiered. In Rome, patrons standing in line were pelted with chunks of concrete while local constables tried to stave off gangs of disgruntled parents and members of the Psychiatric Union who smashed storefront windows and burned the vehicles of those attending the opening. In Mecca, the Secular Sabres of Man group clashed with members of the Human Civil Liberties Union leaving three HCLU members dead and several others with partially severed hands and/or feet. Another man was blinded when a young woman allegedly sprayed acid on moviegoers with a high-pressured hose.

"The controversial film has been labeled by many right wing activist groups as, and I quote: 'subversive, obscene, and distastefully misanthropic'. While others say it's just art and another expression of the freedom human beings share all over this marvelous planet of ours, including the Moon, Mars and whatever in the name of Asimov lies beyond.

"My guests this morning (or afternoon or evening or whatever it happens to be wherever you are at this moment) are two men with decidedly differing viewpoints on this matter. The gentleman on my right is Dr. Howard Hassani, owner of Sensory Depot, the largest Psychiatry Port chain in the world and chairman of the World Council on Mental Fitness for the better part of the past thirty-five years (though he doesn't look a day over twenty-nine, I must confess). And to my left is Mr. Jesus Noriega, former guitar player for the band 'Paradise Lost', former cultist, former Weed activist, rumored former lover (among others) of the

Beneficent's daughter—Louisette Richelieu whom we saw hosting Vogue Day from Monte Carlo a few hours ago—former mental patient of the Rodham Asylum of Conversion, and currently working as a corporate attorney for Immaculate Pictures, the company which produced the afore-said, 'Mare Cult' film.

"Mr. Hassani, I'd like to start with you since you, in one breath have claimed to deplore the violence that has arisen in Rome and Mecca (some of which has been instigated by your own psychiatrist brethren), yet in the next breath you claim that patrons of the film have brought this down upon themselves and should heed this as a warning to stay away from the movie and its subliminal message altogether. How do you respond to the uproar the release of this film has engendered?"

HH:"Well, first Tom, I'd like to say hello to my teenage son and two daughters who are spending Vogue Day at the Body Plentiful Nude Festival '74 in Havana this weekend which is sponsored by the Sensory Depot Corporation in association with Blusilver Incorporated, owned by my good friend, Dr. Yuri Kihlmen. I'd also like to say that you scumbags in the media—that are trying blame the late great Mr. Morri Gruberstein for what happened at Liberace Gardens—to take a moment and realize that my good friend was to Vogue Day what Santa Claus once was to Christmas. He brought a lot of joy and meaning to a lot of people's lives and that should not be diminished by this unpreventable tragedy."

JN:"But he was to blame, Mr. Hassani. Sources close to the Palace reported that Morri Gruberstein ignored warnings from Operations to evacuate the resort hours before…"

HH: "Tom, as you know, Beneficent Georges and I, or Jorgie as I called him while we were Lambda Ki roommates at UCLA, are great friends. I even got my dad to give him his screen test for 'Lunar Command', the show that made him famous. Anyway, I called him and asked him if all the media reports about Morri were true. He said he never heard anything to that effect!"

JN: "He never hears anything! He's clueless!"

HH: "You need Demerol, son. All your kind need Demerol."

JN: "One more face-lift and your Adam's apple will be blocking your nasal passages!"

TM: "Um, we seem to be drifting from the subject matter, although it may make for a spirited topical debate in and of itself. But what do you guys make of the turmoil in Mecca? Jesus?"

JN: "Clearly this was a case of old-fashioned twentieth century fascism! Some innocent people decided that they wanted to see a movie, 'something new' in the spirit of the holiday, instead of getting together with strangers and gyrating their flesh raw. Then this group of Stalinist butchers attack them, trying to hack off arms and legs!"

HH: "The SSM would not have been there had the HCLU not made a point of showing up in force, dressing up in cultist costumes, and violating civil law by promoting obscene, subversive cult symbolism!"

JN: "They were simply promoting the movie!"

HH: "Singing cult hymns? Quoting cult scriptures? If that's promoting a movie, they deserved to have their damned arms and legs chopped off!"

TM: "So you condone the actions of the SSM, Mr. Hassani?"

HH: "Honestly? No. But when cultist organizations like the HCLU are demonstratively inflammatory, they have to expect that sort of thing to be a consequence."

JN: "I resent your referring to the HCLU as a cultist organization. They represent the true struggle for freedom for the billions of people who live in the E M & M [Earth, Moon, and Mars]."

HH: "How can people struggle for something they already have? At no point in history has mankind been freer to do absolutely anything he pleases within the bounds of basic laws protecting life and property."

JN: "That's not true. The cults are illegal."

HH: "That's because the cults stood in the way of freedom for centuries. Not to mention the psychological damage that was done to generations of vulnerable, insecure human beings who might have enjoyed free and happy lives had they not been systematically brainwashed by utter nonsense."

JN: "How do you know it was nonsense?"

HH: "Because the entire cult experience was based upon shrewd, abstract, delusionism requiring not a shred of concrete evidence from the charlatans who peddled it, other than fail-safe tautological reasonings that preyed upon remote human fears."

JN: "That was not the case at all."

HH: "No? Look at twentieth century televangelism. Look at twenty-first century censorship."

JN: "Look at today's rate of suicide, higher than ever in recorded history."

HH: "A byproduct of the lingering effects of centuries of cultism ingrained in our society. People still have trouble simply believing in their fellow man—giving themselves up and trusting in the body of humanity."

TM: "Gentlemen, if I may interrupt for a moment, we also had rioting in Rome. Members of the Psychiatric Union pelted moviegoers with heavy chunks of concrete as they stood in line to enter the theatre. Any comment on that?"

JN: "Yes. I understand a young mother was paralyzed during the melee and several men, women and children suffered severe head injuries. The arrested leader of the Psychiatric Union described the hurling of concrete as their way of telling people to 'get in touch with reality'! I understand that leader was also a former executive of the Sensory Depot."

HH: "He was. And he was fired for his involvement with the Union."

JN: "Why would he be fired when the Controller's Office has financially linked the Psychiatric Union to the Sensory Depot."

HH: "That's pure speculation, Mr. Noriega. And if you want to engage in speculation, I could speculate that you're a cult revivalist, but I won't."

TM: "Uh, Mr. Hassani, explain to us, what in particular is offensive about the film."

HH: "I, myself have not and will not see the movie. But reportedly, there is a scene in which a woman 'prays' for a miracle and it supposedly happens. There's another scene where that same woman yanks her six-year-old out of school simply because a teacher reads the class a story about two male forest animals who are in love with each other. There's also a gratuitous scene wherein a group of children rebel against their parents by singing cult songs at a social function. And of course, there's the insane protagonist: the lunar scientist who speaks to a 'God', glorifies his sexually repressed monogamy, and castigates mankind for its numerous 'sins'."

TM: "Hmmm. Sounds quite radical. What's the fear of this film though?"

HH: "As the owner of Psychiatry Ports world wide, I'm particularly sensitive to the mental health of human beings everywhere. The biggest crime committed over the centuries by the cults against humanity was the constant demand the cults made on human beings to fight against their natures. People who were poor and uneducated by nature were being told that they had some divine destiny to attain a level equal to those who were genetically more gifted. This resulted in a great deal of mental anguish and frustration among these people when they repeatedly found this 'destiny' was a mirage. The result was either internalized or externalized resentment of themselves, as well as the society in which they lived—which in turn, resulted in many more acts of criminality than we see today."

JN: "That's because the definition of criminality has been relaxed, since the Edict of Separation for Weeds and Blossoms!"

HH: "Can you prove that Mr. Noriega? And likewise, genetically gifted people were overrun with guilt for not helping those who, as we know now, simply cannot and, in fact, do not want to be helped. This resulted in stagnation and ridiculous guilt over reaching one's individual potential. With the cults gone, guilt and repression are eliminated hence, resulting in a psychologically healthier and thriving society for Blossoms and Weeds alike."

JN: "So if humanity is so mentally healthy, why then, do billions of human beings spend trillions of earnings on counselling and assistance in Psychiatry Ports every year?"

TM: "Hawh, Hawh, Hawh, Hawh, Hawh! Yes, why is it that after this show is done, that I'm going to spend the next two hours spilling my guts and my wallet at the local Crankin' Couch next door? (No offense to the Sensory Depot, Howard.)

HH: "That's because as science and science alone unlocks the mysteries of the universe, so too must science be used to unlock the mysteries of the mind. Life is such that people will always have seemingly insurmountable dilemmas to overcome. The Psychiatry Ports help people stay focused and honed in on—pardon the term, Mr. Noriega—concrete, tangible solutions to everyday problems. People are taught to see and feel the answers rather than grope or 'pray', as the cults had us do.

"There's a twenty-first century parable I have on the wall of my office. It goes like this: 'Two men, cast out from their cult are tied to a rail track awaiting their death. One man closes his eyes and prays to be set free, but is killed. The other renounces his faith, struggles loose and lives. Which man then, truly found his salvation?'"

TM: "Uh huh. Interesting."

JN: "I wonder."

# XXXII.

Cannes, France-The Beneficent Palace:

"Albuquerque! Lhasa! Cannes! Anyone!" called a desperate voice over the monitor. "We need help!"

"He can't hear us." Jean-Paul confirmed with agitation.

"Solar flare activity?" Manda questioned.

"I doubt it," Jean-Paul said looking up into the tortured face of the stranded crewman from Mare Nubium on the giant monitor screen. "Our link with Mars cleared up forty-five minutes ago. Reports indicate that solar flare activity is receding. There shouldn't be any interference. Whatever's happening is happening on the Moon."

"They're claiming to have come under attack." Manda frowned.

"Yes. Just like Crisium, Serenitatis, Tranquillitatis, Nectaris, and Imbrium," said Jean-Paul, wrestling with his frustration. "We never even heard from Vaporum or Frigoris; they just cut out."

"Some kind of energized electrical current...shorting out every system on the station." the crewman continued. "Communications restored using auxiliary."

The faint image flickered on: "If there's anybody who can hear me, defend yourselves! Whatever this is..."

A loud crackle of audio distortion cut in on the transmission as the picture blinked off the screen for good.

"Anything?" Manda asked hopelessly.

"No." Jean-Paul resigned. "Nothing. Nothing at all. Just like all the rest."

"Satellites?" Manda requested.

"Satellites indicate no stations remaining on the Moon," a technician responded from his post. "No structures, no debris...nothing. It's as if they never existed."

"Wait!" Jean-Paul interceded. "I'm getting something from Mars."

Jean-Paul reactivated the giant viewscreen, anticipating Manda's request to do so. The grave image of Anthony Denison's assistant, Carmen Yorishu, appeared on screen.

"Good morning, Manda," she began, monotonously droning the amenity. "I know your hands are full, but we picked up what destroyed the Moon bases on our instruments. It just departed the back side of the Moon and is making a direct path for us. At present speed, we estimate it'll be here in about sixty-three hours. We have that long to make whatever preparations we can to avoid…disappearing, I guess."

"What is…It?" queried Manda.

"Your seventh bird-thing or ship-thing or whatever it's suppose to be!" she answered with stress in her voice. "We caught just an image of it as it struck Mare Imbrium. It literally makes entire complexes vanish using huge energy surges. We honestly couldn't tell whether it was some form of absorption or straight old-fashioned disintegration. Details are hard to make out because it emits such intense radioactive levels that imaging from this range is too difficult. That probably explains why getting information from any of the Moon bases was next to impossible and why they couldn't even warn each other as to when or from where the next attack was coming."

"Disintegration as we know it seems improbable." Manda cited. "Even the most destructive form of disintegration we know of would leave some sort of neutrino residue pattern that we'd be able to detect. According to our instruments, there's absolutely nothing there at all…like there never was. Absorption seems possible, but in order to confirm that, we'd have to get a read on the creatures or ships themselves to determine changes in mass or energy input. Unfortunately, like the meteoroid, they seem adept at screening out any sensor readings."

"Dimensional shift?" whispered Jean-Paul aside.

"What?" Manda leaned away from the monitor.

"Just some reading I've done." Jean-Paul theorized. "Complete disappearances of this enormity could be the result of a dimensional shift, and it would explain the totality of the disappearances. It would also require huge amounts of energy which these 'things' apparently have."

"Let's hope to hell not." Yorishu interjected. "If you and I have been reading the same 'comic books' or journals, if you will, that conceivably could lead to imbalances of mass between dimensions, which could result in the ultimate collapse and recreation of our universe as we know it; ergo: the sequel to the original Big Bang! Personally, I don't care much for the odds on even the cockroaches surviving that one!"

"People, we could sit here and guess about this until we drown in our own drivel." Manda asserted. "Our immediate concern has to be defense and/or communication."

"Make that communication," responded Yorishu. "We just don't have the kind of defense out here that Earth has. Obviously, we never thought we'd need it. Aside from the occasional miner's strike, there's been nothing to defend against…until now. We've put out linguistic, harmonic and binary encoded telemetry hoping to make some kind of, I hate to say plea, but contact or warning or something to get it to stop and reconsider. There's no doubt that it probably has in mind for us what it did to the Moon. Unless communication works, in two and a half days, it'll be 'say-onara' Martian colonies!"

Although Yorishu's tone was darkly facetious, Manda grimaced at the prospect of the loss of two million lives on Mars. "Don't you have a backup plan?"

"Actually, we do. It involves nuking half the domed settlements to save the other half. Here's to communication!"

"Understood, Yorishu." Manda shook her head. "Listen, we'll make our technical people here and in Albuquerque available to you and your people for…as long as you need. Maybe together, we can help you come up with a plan C."

"Oh God!" gasped Jean-Paul.

Startled, Manda turned to see Jean-Paul scanning information rapidly scrolling down the face of his computer monitor.

"Hoste, Londonberry, Stewart, Clarence, Diego Ramirez, off the coast of Chile, all gone! Ellesmere Island: gone! Severrnaya, Zemlya, Nordvik, and a good portion of the Taymyr Peninsula—gone! Port Buthelesi, Tutu, all gone!"

"Jean-Paul, what the devil do you mean 'gone'?" Manda snapped. "Gone? Land masses right off the face of the Earth?"

"N-no. No, not really."

"Then what do you mean by 'gone'?"

"Well…" Jean-Paul swallowed hard. "The lands are still there. But…the buildings…the people…they're gone. Gone without a trace…as if they never existed."

Manda stared intently at the scrolling data as reports of disappearances increased by the second. The Operations Center surged into pandemonium as technicians tried to coordinate fragments of urgent data flooding in from all over the world.

Yorishu dismissed herself from the giant monitor, acknowledging that problems on Earth had now taken precedence over her own.

As the Operations crew rushed to scientifically explain and anticipate the human catastrophe unfolding from six points upon the Earth, no one noted that the hideous figure perched ominously atop the giant spire in Santa Cruz had taken its leave.

# XXXIII.

The News:

Tragedy continues to plague this year's Vogue Day weekend—this time on a more personal level for all of us.

Anna Maria Diderot, the niece of Beneficent Georges Richelieu, has died of an apparent neck injury suffered in the Palace gymnasium late last evening. According to Palace sources, Mademoiselle Diderot fell awkwardly onto her neck during a routine gymnastics exercise and was killed instantly. She was thirteen.

Anna Maria can best be remembered for her love and devotion to literature and the performing arts. In her short life, she worked diligently to promote expanded literacy and awareness to the youth of the world, both Blossom and Weed alike.

The Beneficent offered in a brief statement: "Her love of people and the genuine gregariousness of her bright, cheerful smile made her the flower of Cannes and the jewel of humanity. Mankind shall never fully recover from her tragic loss."

From the Champion: "I'm wounded deeply. She was the little sister I never had."

Anna Maria's cousin, Louisette, reportedly in transit from Monte Carlo to Cannes upon the learning of this incident, could not be reached for comment.

Meanwhile, out of the Weeds come reports of alleged cultish rioting in several major cities around the world. The broadcast of events from Santa Cruz has apparently led to a sharp increase in irrational and violent behavior in those provinces. There is no estimate as to the degree of fighting or how long it will continue before it wears itself down. Blossoms vacationing in the Weeds are advised to contact emergency transport services for immediate evacuation.

In other bizarre news, it has been reported that the Lunar Stations on the Moon have vanished without a trace. In addition, there have been unconfirmed reports of the disappearance of large populations of people and structures all over the globe. According to Palace Operations, these reports are thought to be either a hoax or simply a glitch in satellite telemetry due to solar flare activity. Whether these disappearances are related to the preceding events in Santa Cruz remain uncertain at this time. An investigation has been initiated and information will be forthcoming.

Meanwhile, the Beneficent urges all people to continue their holiday festivities until more concrete data can be assembled. We advise that you stay tuned to this station for continuing updates.

We now return you to Lars Larynx at the T. Fonda Hotel and Casino in Monte Carlo as our Vogue Day Party coverage continues after this message.

Tonight on "Growing Up Fast":

Leslie: Hey mom. I was in the locker room after gym class and Katie came up to me and asked me to take a shower with her. Then, two seconds later, Jack Perry asks me to come shower with him? What'll I do? I mean yesterday I was showering alone. Now I've hit the jackpot!

(Studio laughter)

Mom: Well, Leslie, you're eleven years old now. It would be wrong for me to tell you how to think. You've got to start making these kind of decisions on your own. The only thing I hope is, whatever you do, you don't discriminate.

Leslie: But mom, didn't this ever happen to you?

Mom: It still does. But my choice may not be your choice. It would be wrong for me to impose my values on you.

Leslie: Well, fuck you then. I'll figure it out myself! (Exit)

Mom:(to camera) Kids!

(Studio laughter)

Check your local listings.

# XXXIV.

Beaufort, South Carolina:

"Lang!" Mikki yelled to her son's room. "Lang? Lang!"

There was no response. In fact, as she listened carefully, there was not even the slightest hint of rustle emanating from the boy's room. She had told him to pack six days of clothing nearly an hour ago, while she would do likewise and make arrangements for their hastened departure. Now, as she sat by the blinking monitor, on "hold", the sudden quiet of her own home chipped away at her ebbing composure.

She deeply inhaled from another herbal cigarette whose effect had become scarcely perceptible, narrowed her eyes ruefully at the blinking "hold" screen and rose, cursing, to her feet.

"How the fuck can they do this to me?" she spoke through quivering lips and tiny flared nostrils. "They kill my fucking husband, wreck my fucking life, and now they won't even answer my fucking call."

Mikki doused the unfinished cigarette into a nearby ashtray and pulled on her everyday hiking boots. Then she hastily tied back her hair with a new scarf she had planned to unveil during the course of Anthony's vacation, perhaps during a stroll along a hazy dawn-lit beach or during an afternoon picnic in the park preserve.

"The one hundred and sixty-ninth thing he'll never see," she angrily lamented.

She took another look at the flashing monitor screen, attempting to will upon it the helpful face of a Palace Operations officer who would arrange for immediate transportation to Mars. Exasperated with its monotonous ignorance of her, she turned away and stalked toward her son's bedroom.

"Lang, goddamnit!" she yelled as she entered the boy's doorway. "I told you to move! We've got to…"

Looking across the room, Mikki saw the window curtains pushed wide and the panes rolled down. Her son was not in sight.

"Shit!" she screamed running to the open window. "Not now!"

She looked over the green hills which comprised their backyard and out over the narrow stream that ran under the wire fence leading into their neighbor's property.

"Lang!" she called loudly. "Lang, this isn't very goddamn funny! You've got to come back so we can leave together! Lang, we need each other now! Lang!!"

Mikki felt all hope of her future life plummet to the well of her stomach with the maddening, inexplicable disappearance of her son. She grew light-headed as she gripped the window sill, trying to fashion his distant figure moving somewhere amidst the broad landscape. It was as if the final spokes holding her fragile world together were preparing to snap loose.

"Lang!!" She screamed at the top of her voice, which echoed into the hills.

"What?" came a subdued voice from behind.

Mikki spun around and saw Lang sitting, long faced, chin on his knees, in front of his closet wearing his "I Dig Mars Archeology" sweatshirt. His clothes were scattered about the floor leading to an open suitcase which sat against the wall. In his hand, he held a laser penlight refractor, the last gift his father had given him. He waved it about, lazily bending the colors of the daylight around his mother's figure.

"Damn you!" she yelled. "Haven't you listened to a word I've said? We've got to get out of here!"

"When's the shuttle coming?" he said passively, flicking off the penlight and examining it with one eye closed.

"I…don't know yet." Mikki answered, relieved but exasperated. "They keep putting me on fucking hold!"

"What about dad's emergency channel?" her son asked calmly.

"It's not working!" she answered rubbing her forehead.

"That's not right, is it?" Lang observed.

"Well…" she groped. "They probably just discontinued it when your father…passed away."

"Mom, is this the end of the world?" Lang asked, making eye contact for the first time.

Mikki closed her eyes and tried to arrange an answer. The end of the world had been in the forefront of her thoughts since she'd watched Anthony's ship dragged down into the molten crater. But she'd overridden the idea with the singular notion that rescuing herself and Lang from the possibly doomed Earth superceded all perils or concerns. Abandoning rationality, she parried away the persistent reality that the end of Earth must be inclusive of her and her son's mortal demise.

She knelt down and touched her son's cheek. "Even if it is the end of the Earth, I won't let anything keep us apart," she tried to say with assurance.

"Even if we die?" the boy frowned.

"We're not going to die."

"But dad died. You said he wouldn't, but he did."

"We didn't know the danger then. Now we do. And I promise you, you're going to live."

"But what if we do die? We'll be alone then, right?"

"What do you mean?"

"We won't be able to talk or think or move or…anything, right?"

"Hon, I don't think we need to think about this right now. We need to think about getting packed and getting to Mars. Okay?"

Lang looked down and stared at nothing. Then he tossed his pen light into his suitcase and followed it with a handful of wadded-up clothing.

"Hello?" called a voice from the living room.

"That's the Palace!" Mikki said, jumping to her feet. "We'll be fine, now. Wait and see!"

She bolted out of her son's room and slid down in front of the large monitor just as she saw the on-screen attendant reach out to sever the connection.

"Hold it!" she called, putting on her most congenial, albeit harried, demeanor. "This is Mikki Denison! I was calling to arrange immediate transport for my son and myself to Mars…this afternoon, if possible!"

The skinny, slack-jawed attendant on the screen rubbed his large protruding nose and tried unsuccessfully to suppress a sarcastic smirk.

"Excuse me, did I say something funny?" Mikki addressed, quickly becoming perturbed.

"Actually...not at all," spoke the man in a nasally buzzing voice. "It's just that if we could accommodate everyone making that request right about now, the entire planet would be incinerated by the number of thermonuclear lift-offs. We're suggesting as an alternative to flight, that people confer with their Psychiatry Port counselors."

"Now wait just a goddamn minute!" Mikki seethed. "Do you know who the hell I am? I'm Mrs. Mikki Lee Denison! My husband was Anthony Marcus Denison, Chief Coordinator of the Operations-Space Anomalies Division on Mars! We own property out there! He died for you fucking people! Now I demand that you arrange transport right now!"

"I'm sorry ma'am. But that's quite impossible. Please monitor the media and contact your Psychiatry Port counselor for further assistance."

"I don't believe this!" Mikki said, aghast. "I have never been treated this way by any Operations staffer in all my life!"

"Actually...I'm not with Operations, ma'am. I'm with Public Service...actually.

"Public Service?! I sent a civilian priority A encoded assistance request! How in the hell did I get PS?"

"As you can imagine, ma'am, the entire Operations staff is embroiled in combating the threat you're trying to flee. Actually...your request is being handled at the A-level right now."

"Ohhh no! Now you listen to me! What's your name?"

"Julius Kelp, ma'am."

"Well, Mr. Julius Kelp, I want you to put Ms. Manda Martine, Cartel Operations Coordinator, on this line right now or 'actually' there will be hell to pay!"

The attendant appeared only to pity the idle threat. He sighed resignedly and simply recanted what he had been ordered to disseminate to all callers: "The entire Operations staff is embroiled in combating the matter at hand. We suggest that you monitor the media for updates and contact your Psychiatry Port counselor, if you require further assistance. Actually…I'm…sorry."

The monitor screen fell gray as the attendant faded from view.

"Oh shit." Mikki whispered, folding her shaking arms. "Oh shit."

The chill of utter abandonment coldly whisked through her hopes. No rescue was imminent. No assurances were forthcoming. The only option which remained was totally unacceptable: Sit and wait with the rest of humanity to see if and how the end would come.

"Do I still need to pack?" asked Lang standing in the hallway.

She felt like laughing, but couldn't fathom whether it was for desperate sanity's sake or out of appreciation for her son's childish gift for understating the imposition of doom.

"Yeah," she spoke in a low voice. "Just in case."

"Just in case what?" the boy asked.

"Just in case…do what I said, all right?" She spoke tersely.

Lang disappeared back into his room. Mikki fell back onto the couch and stared at the family photographs mounted above the satellite monitor. It seemed as if she and Anthony had only been introduced months ago rather than ten years. Yet the infidelities and addictions which had infected their marriage now seemed to have belonged to some other couple a lifetime ago. But most sadly, the repaired, happy years she'd come to look forward to were now the ashen remnants of another woman's dreams.

"Why?"

Behind her, came a sizzling, crackling sound from the kitchen area emulating the pop of moist meats or vegetables frying in oils. It was accompanied by a thick putrid aroma that accosted her nose like no foul cooking odor she had ever smelled. And she felt a distinctive wall of heat mounting on her shoulders.

Mikki stood and turned to see though, what she must have left burning. But before she could move toward the kitchen, she was shocked frozen by the ghastly appearance of…It: The horrific visage birthed from the crater at Santa Cruz, now standing in the middle of her home. Mikki suppressed a fearful shriek into a muted yelp as her maternal instincts hoped not to alarm her son into immediate danger. Still, it's disgusting hideous presence was decidedly more unsettling in person than it had been on satellite.

The gnarled and twisted, partially decomposed and completely burned body parts it had used to comprise its form still writhed with the seeming involuntary pulsations of their former hosts. Blackened fleshless abdominal muscles in the alien's arms appeared to still be performing respiratory functions. Leg muscles wrapped around its torso moved as if they were in perpetual search for a more comfortable position. And flexing arm muscles in its legs were bound, several together, to support its spindly, mucousy frame. All told, its movements were sickening in the viewing and the listening as it lurched from side to side, even standing in place. Its sinews sought to retrain themselves in their new found lodgings with the sound of bone and tendons sliding in and out of place.

"What…do you want?" She managed, shaking with fear and noting the irony that even her late husband had never been a party to so unearthly an encounter.

The alien's jaw area began moving and shifting unnaturally as if it carried a mouthful of living matter. The dead flesh mask was still matted to its face, but apparently mastery of facial control was still in development. After a few moments of only wet noises, it reached up with a constructed hand and forced its fingers into the mouth opening of the dead face, tearing a jagged pink cavity.

"Your boy," it gurgled in a wet baritone.

"What about him?" Mikki filled, knowing full well what it must have meant.

"Your boy will come with me," it clarified.

"Why?" Mikki asked fearfully.

The alien paused for a moment, leering at her with its bloody eyes and whitened pupils. Then it fashioned its best impression of a grin.

"Why not?"

Mikki blinked at the absurdity of the query. "Was the obvious reason so lost on this inhuman monster?" she wondered.

"He's my son." Mikki stated, probing with her eyes for some humane reaction.

"So?"

"So...he is my son and I...love him." She nodded with emphasis.

"Love." it restated. "You love him as you loved your husband?"

"Yes," she said unbalanced by the scope of its knowledge of her.

"You care for him?"

"Yes. More than anything in this universe."

"This universe...is vast." It informed her. "How can you know this?"

"Because..." Mikki hesitated for a moment. "Because of all I know of the universe, my son is what is most important to me."

"And when he dies?"

"When or if he dies..." She shuddered. "...I will have nothing."

"Nothing in all the universe?" .

"Nothing in all the universe."

"Then you would take his place in death?" It offered.

Mikki glanced at Lang's doorway, hoping the boy would not emerge. Then she looked back into the alien's vile features.

"I would." she answered.

"Then you would die and he would live, and you would still have...nothing in all the universe."

"Yes...I guess," she stammered. "But at least I would have the knowledge that my son was still alive."

"How?"

"Because..." Mikki narrowed her eyes trying to focus on where the alien was leading. "...because I'd know he was alive before I died...I hope."

"But if he died only seconds after you, what good would that 'knowledge' be?"

"I…don't know. I never really thought about it that way. I would assume that he would live a long life."

"How can you assume such a thing?"

"It's…what people do, I guess."

"Sand."

"What?" Mikki asked, thinking she had heard him incorrectly.

"If he died, and you lived, you could still have many other children. Would they be as 'nothing' to you in 'all the universe'?"

"Of course not. I would love them, but I would still carry the sense of loss." Mikki answered confidently.

"Until they died," it continued. "Then you would again have 'nothing in all the universe'?"

"Yes…except more grief and sorrow than any human being should have to endure." Mikki spoke ruefully.

"Why?"

"Because," Mikki felt her ideals coming together, "people build the very foundations of their lives around the people that they love and care for. Our parents, our children, our friends are all part of…a network of love about which humans construct their very essence. Without those bonds, none of us would have anything…in all the universe!"

"Sand." it spoke evenly.

Mikki frowned at the repeat of this word. "What do you mean…?"

"Life is finite?"

"Yes." Mikki answered. "But in the time that we have…"

"Then in the finite terms of your existence, you embrace relationships with other beings such as yourselves as the basis for the very definition of yourself in contrast to all that is in the universe. Relationships who by their very ephemeral, finite definitions do not and cannot endure past the span of the limitations of your own 'lives'. And upon the cessation of that 'life' or the lives of those relationships in which you invest all that you are, you say you have nothing in all the universe. If this is so, then you measure 'all that you have' by your infinitesimal existence on this planet, while the universe measures itself in countless millennia stretching nearly beyond the ken of sentience in distance and dimension. It must then be concluded that such a being does not only have nothing in all the universe by its own accordance, but cannot have, will not have, and never could have had anything of measure in all the universe to begin with."

"What?"

"Sand." It said with its malformed smile.

It walked toward her.

Mikki was cornered in the living room, but tried to move so its back would be turned to Lang's room. When she saw her son pop out into the hallway, she silently motioned for him to go back, hoping this time he really would run away far and fast.

The alien lurched forward slowly, burning its way through the couch. Mikki searched frantically for something that might serve as any type of weapon, although she realized the utter futility of attempting to be physically combative. Desperately, she grabbed an iron sculpture from a table next to the fireplace.

The heat of the alien was upon her as she tried to smash open its head with an overhand lunge. The sculpture stuck to its head, then melted away into its black pores. Her momentum carried her into its chest, and all at once her arms and head were seared away.

The alien thoughtlessly pushed the remains of the body aside, then looked toward Lang's opened doorway. In another instant, the alien disappeared from Beaufort, South Carolina.

The laser penlight refractor toppled to the floor in Lang's empty room.

# XXXV.

Cannes, France-The Beneficent Palace:

"What do you make of all this?" Kima whispered softly, resting her close-cropped head on his expansive chest.

She waited to feel the vibration of his voice overlay the steady beat of his powerful heart muscle, but only felt his stomach rise up like a giant wave, then relax again like an indolent tide receding lazily back into the ocean. She tilted her head slightly to look up at his face. At first, she thought he was looking up at the two of them in the giant ceiling mirror mounted over his bed. But when she did not find his eyes there, she realized he was deeply entranced by the labor of his thoughts.

"Hey." Kima spoke in her naturally husky female voice, which betrayed her physical leanness. "Where are you?"

Victor blinked his eyes clear. "What's that, old woman?"

Kima propped up on her elbow and glared at him with a playful sneer. "Must you call me that?"

"Well, that's what you are." he taunted.

"I'll have you know that the Beneficent's third wife accused him of robbing the cradle when she caught him and me together twenty-five years ago. I was sixteen and he was thirty-five. And to this day he still calls me 'kid' when we pass in the hallways."

"I guess it's all relative," he conceded.

"I guess so," she smiled, arching her eyebrows. "So where were you?"

"When?"

"Just now," she fussed, flicking his cleft chin with her finger. "I thought you were admiring yourself in the mirror, but you were really lost."

"Hmm." Victor groaned. "I guess…I was thinking about Anna Maria."

"It's hard, I know." Kima consoled. "I was her trainer, too. She was a great girl—a little aloof and naive sometimes, but we all loved her."

"But I should have been there," he tensed.

"And been some sort of hero? How could you?" She reasoned. "She was always so bright and optimistic. No one could have foreseen her taking her own life the way she did. No one except probably her cousin. Louise gave her the stuff, after all. But foresight isn't exactly one of Louise's strong suits, is it? Little wonder Georges didn't show her the street years ago. But I guess people always wait for fatality before they take something seriously. Too bad it took Anna Maria's death to show him how worthless his daughter is. Any ideas on where she'll…"

"I don't want to talk about it!" Victor snapped, sitting up on his pillows.

"Fine." Kima abandoned the topic. She rolled over and took up the crystal decanter from the bedside table. She quietly filled two matching crystal juice glasses with protein-enriched apricot liqueur and handed one to the Champion.

"So what do you make of all of this?" She asked again, raising the glass to her lips.

"All of what?" he answered, intent upon being difficult.

"Well, let's see, 'Mr. Dense Today'," Kima poked at his ego. "Meteoroids, earthquakes, mass deaths, rioting, aliens, disappearances, possible annihilation on the horizon, not to mention whispers of cult resurgence, and the Beneficent's daughter telling an E.M. & M. broadcast audience that humanity should just 'fuck off' during this whole crisis!"

"It just shows you what happens when the world subjects itself to the unsteady leadership of elderly men." Victor cited, tossing back the six-ounce glass in one gulp.

"What?" Kima looked up grinning curiously. "What are you talking about?"

"Did you know that Peter the Great became Czar of Russia at the age of seventeen?" he began, irritably.

"I'm afraid my history is a little…"

"And that King Henry V brought France to its knees when he was only twenty-eight? Napoleon was a brigadier general by the time he was twenty-four and had subjugated most of Europe before his thirty-fifth birthday. And

Jesus the Christ became the greatest cult ruler in world history by the age of thirty-two. In fact, his influence still lingers for some reason."

"So...?"

"So, when the world was young, the young men who ruled it did it without interference from their 'experienced' elders. Now, the young are set aside until they become...old and...'wise' (or fearful). Young men, like myself, shaped the foundation of human civilization. But for centuries now, we've allowed ourselves to be manipulated by the machinations of feeble, frightened (albeit shrewd) old men."

"Oh, come on now, Victor! If you haven't shaped the history of world events in your twenty-five years, who has?"

"Georges, that's who," he answered disdainfully. "I do the heavy work, but ask anyone who's held the world together and they'll tell you: Beneficent Georges."

"That's nonsense." Kima said, easing up behind him and massaging his thick and knotted shoulders. "Every arbitration or dispute you've settled has been broadcast on every monitor inside the asteroid belt. Children run through parks playing at some day being you. You're already an icon to billions of people everywhere."

"True." Victor tried to shrug away her hands. "Like a physical oddity...a sideshow freak. 'Master of Arms', 'Master of Combative Arts', but master of no one. To humanity at large, I'm as much a public Cartel servant as the men who work the street sweepers of Berlin. Only worse, they see me as Georges' marionette, jigging to the tug of my strings."

"You're being ridiculous."

"Am I?" Victor glared at her. "Why, just yesterday he as much as said so himself— and dared me to make an issue of it. He even tried to humiliate me in front of...Val. If Val can make fun of me, what about the rest of the world?"

"Your time will come...eventually." Kima kissed his tensed back. "Patience, sweetheart."

"Patience is for cowards." Victor growled. "Patience is for the fatally compassionate. Patience is the virtue of victims. Patience will make beggars and corpses of us all."

"Victor…"

"Did you know that he's a closet cultist?" Victor continued.

"Georges? A cultist?" She grinned, nibbling his lobe. "He's the most renowned humanist the world's ever seen."

"So he'd have us all believe," he spoke, betrayed. "What brought about his little tirade against me was my questioning his embrace of old Christian Mythology. For nearly two hours, he quoted to me from some tattered relic how the meteoroid was the fulfillment of some religious prophecy which foretold the doom of man."

"How silly," she purred on his shoulder. "You must have misunderstood, darling."

"He ranted and raved about our 'imminent' demise. And when I questioned him…he shot at me."

"No." Kima spoke with astonishment.

"Yes." Victor confirmed. "How can we hope to defeat this alien threat when the weak-minded Beneficent, in his heart, believes that doom awaits all of us?"

"Honey, who's to say?" Kima lovingly stroked his golden mane. "I'm sure he'll call you when he feels you're needed."

"I'm to say," he bristled. "I'm the Champion of our Earth. I'm the one who's supposed to ensure man's future, by any and all means. The Beneficent's been like a father to me, but if he chooses to sit, huddled with Val suckling at his bosom, while the alien threat pulverizes our civilization into extinction, then maybe the time has come for me to…take control of matters."

Victor swung to his feet and pulled away from Kima's tender grasp. She admired him as he momentarily inspected himself in a full-length mirror, then stalked up the stairs to his bathing room.

As the door slid closed behind him, Kima drained her glass of liqueur, then fell back into the bed covers, adoring her own modest reflection in the ceiling as she pondered her future as the consort of Beneficent Victor.

# XXXVI.

Cannes, France-The Carlton Luxury Condominiums:

Wesley found the tautness of the sharpened steel wire sufficient for his final experiment. He had lasered the end of it to the chandelier in his bedroom. Now all he needed to do was finish rigging the contractible wire loop. He methodically went about this task, ignoring his bleeding fingers, slivered raw by the wire's fineness.

This work was the only matter that settled his thoughts on beloved Anna Maria…stolen from him by irrevocable death for all time. His unrequited love for her had been severe and unconditional. Though she treated him as little more than a eunuch servant, often confiding in him on matters pertaining to "real men" as she might another female, he knew from the momentous day he met her, that "queen" Anna Maria would always be the center of his universe. Tragically, his only intimate moment with her came upon finding her discolored, lifeless body, as he tearfully stole the kiss for which he had always yearned from her blackened, spattered lips.

He voice activated the lights, licked his finger, and touched the wire coil dangling from above. The moisture crackled and smoked with a flashing "pop". Wesley nodded affirmation of his experiment's readiness.

"Son?" came a voice on the intercom.

Wesley silently cursed the parental interruption. He had never cursed before, he noted. But Anna Maria was gone. Dead forever. What mattered cursing now, in a world angelic Anna Maria could never again grace with her royal, effervescent glory? What mattered the Weed illiteracy? What mattered math or science or history? What mattered the Earth, the Moon or Mars? What mattered friends or family or the dreaded cult resurgence or the damned Beneficent or winged creatures or pernicious aliens? What mattered anything when the heart of life lay cold and still in the Palace bowels to beat or stir no more.

"Son!" the voice repeated sternly.

Wesley wiped his stinging fingertips on the back of his dark trousers and cracked his door open just enough to see his father's sagging jowls.

"Yeah?" Wesley answered with uncharacteristic defiance.

"You okay, son?" his father asked.

"Sure." Wesley responded looking away.

"Look, son," his father continued, speaking through the narrow opening, "I know this girl's death has hit you pretty hard. We all liked her. But I think you need to know that I was very proud of your presentation yesterday. After the Committee Session, a number of my constituents approached me and told me what a fine boy I'd raised."

"The maids deserve some credit in your absences." Wesley cut in with a sobbed whisper.

"I know," his father tried to divert. "What I'm saying is, that you impressed a lot of people today. Important people. People who are going to be able to help you in whatever career you decide to choose. That's something special. And you should be very pleased with yourself. Considering the fact that the Beneficent's niece kind of left you in a lurch, I'd say you did an incredible job! I couldn't have done better myself!"

"Thank you, sir," Wesley spoke looking down.

"Son," his father offered in a caring voice. "This girl...I know she meant a lot to you. But, these things happen. People die. She won't be the last person you lose. One day you'll be lasering my remains. That's life. But if you're...going to be a man, you'll have to deal with it. Hell, the day of my mother's funeral, I had to attend a luncheon honoring the Beneficent instead. It wasn't easy. But in four days, I was presenting an addendum on the Committee floor that needed his support. So I put aside my feelings and did what I had to do. Besides, you can't put all your logs in one fire. What do you think Vogue Day is all about? It's about diversification and the establishment of exciting new relationships with new things and new people! I know she was a nice girl, but frankly she's just the first of many girls who are going to be part of your life. That's just the way it works, trust me! As hard as it may be for you to believe, one day you're going to look back on this moment and laugh at how immature you were. Now…I know maybe my words sound a little cold to you, but I've been around a little longer than you have. Believe me: if you're going to live, you're simply going to have to accept life the way it is!"

Wesley looked up into his father's face with tears welled in his eyes. With the aid of irony, he lifted the sides of his mouth. "Sure, dad," he spoke with assurance.

"Now are you coming?" asked his father, bearing relief. "Lunch is being served."

"I'll be done in a minute." Wesley smiled.

His father smiled back and toddled down the plushly carpeted stairs to feast. Wesley's door slammed tightly shut behind him.

As his father reached the bottom of the staircase, he found himself exceedingly famished by the distasteful dispensing of patriarchal energy. Extra helpings would certainly be in order this afternoon. Lunch smelled wonderful, and he considered whether this afternoon would be the day he would finally persuade his son to share a coca smoke with him.

He stalked into the lavishly decorated dining room, and a maid dutifully pulled an antique, Queen Anne chair out for him to sit. He admired the nine-course spread on ornate, silver dinnerware and wondered aloud, how his boy could remain "so embarrassingly skinny".

"People think there's something wrong with him as it is!" He squatted to sit. "Built like a stork, just like his goddamn mother. And tough as a sheep in a lion's pit! Thank goodness that spaced-out girl won't be leading him around like a pet ostrich anymore."

Just then, the lights dimmed followed by two small concussed explosions emanating from the upstairs which he'd just left behind. Wesley's father scrambled up the spiral staircase in time to smell burning electricity fuming from behind Wesley's door.

"Son!" he called once, expecting no answer. Then he nervously voice coded, flubbing the first time, but gaining access the second. He charged into the room, his eyes and nose stinging with putrid fumes and invisible smoke.

Wesley's twitching, electrified, carrion swayed eerily back and forth, suspended by the thin steel wire which had clearly garotted a quarter of the way through his bloodied, open throat.

A maid entered the room and immediately screeched her shrill terror, causing other servants to trample toward the room from the furthest corners of the luxury condominium.

Wesley's father turned, eyes bulging in horror, and violently struck the screaming maid to the floor to silence her. Though wobbly, he stormed through the wall of servants and barrelled down the stairs falling the last two. As he lay on his back gazing through blurred vision, he tried to focus on how his friends in the Committee would respond to the sudden death of his "promising" young son.

# THE DIARY OF
# ANNA MARIA DIDEROT

## I.

Cannes, France-The Beneficent Palace:

Louisette sat peacefully in the thick white carpeting propped next to Anna Maria's remade bed, clutching its laced, pleated bedskirt in one hand, while counting the blusilver vials piled at her feet with the other.

Anna Maria's room had already been converted into a sterile shrine, starkly cherishing the memory of her short, celebrated life. Books were stacked neatly on the shelves in no meaningful order other than ascending and descending heights. Stuffed animals were noticeably rearranged out of keeping with their "characters". A pink, frilled dress she'd grown out of hung stiffly from a hanger on the closet door. And a two-year-old photograph of Anna Maria and the Beneficent preserving a forgettably staged PR opportunity, sat garishly upon the gold and ivory dresser.

Louisette recalled when her father had ordered her mother's room arranged in a similar fashion. It, no doubt, still stood in peach-toned regal, homage to her mother, just as it had from the day she'd died. In nine years however, Louisette had never once, found the inclination to confirm if it remained so.

After all, she had never been close to Dierdre Paulette Richelieu, the distant, mannequinesque female who had annexed the title of "mother" by right of her unconscious, mechanically-induced child labor. From her earliest memory, Louisette most vividly recalled the word "appearances" pursed on her mother's thin ruby lips as the bane of her existence. It was the word Dierdre chose to live by. And she died by it as well.

Appearances at social functions. Appearances as the Beneficent's devoted, flawless, beauteous queen of the hive. Appearances as the perfect, but unexerted mother to her "princess" daughter. Appearances in perfect form, not a hair, not a skin cell, blemished by the procession of age or the ravages of chronic self-abuse.

"Appearances must be maintained at all times!" she would scold young Louisette. "Appearances are that by which we shall always be judged!"

And so Dierdre Paulette Richelieu always appeared to be contented when she lay on the verge of emotional desolation. She appeared to love her husband though she often, albeit discreetly, stole lovers into her passionless bed chamber. She appeared learned, though she read nothing. She appeared younger as she grew older. She appeared austere, though drugs left her incapacious. She appeared maternal, though she found motherhood utterly repugnant. She even appeared in restful slumber, the evening she inadvertently burned out her 33-year-old life. And everyone with whom she associated appeared to care upon her passing.

"And who'll cry for me when I die?" Louisette somberly pondered aloud. "Would father proclaim a black day of mourning? Would Victor's stone heart shatter with sadness? Would the world be left shocked and speechless at my sudden demise? Or would they all just laugh as my ashed remains were sprinkled into the Cannes streets…my suicidal destiny fulfilled to their expectations? Living up to my…'appearance'".

She stared at the blusilver, glistening beautifully in their compact crystal lodgings. Her veins burned for the cooling sustenance that the drug, again, could restore. She was feeling weak and lost. Something blusilver never allowed her to feel. Since her twelfth birthday party in boarding school, it had become her most reliable ally, and she, its greatest patron. Yet how could this remain so when it had so callously choked off the life of her cousin, like a jealous and demented lover, hell-bent on preserving a madly monogamous relationship? For what the treacherous, murderous, substance had taken from her, how could she ever again embrace it as other than an enemy?

Louisette angrily kicked the vials away (not too far) and slumped covering her head with the silken bedskirt. She closed her eyes tightly, trying to fathom her future away from Cannes, away from her father, without Victor, and without Anna Maria. It was like searching for colors on a blank white wall. She could not even imagine.

Sadly, blusilver appeared the best viable alternative, though there would be no forgiveness in their reconciliation. She resignedly popped open her eyes and lifted her head when she noticed a leather carton, latched closed, underneath the bed. She pulled it out and examined the outside. Though it carried no identifiable markings, it was certainly chosen in her younger cousin's tastes. She unlatched the brass buckle and carefully opened the container. Inside, were three or four dozen cartridges, chronologically labeled and dated in Anna Maria's unmistakably graceful cursive.

Louisette poured them out onto the floor and tried to visually arrange their meaning. All at once, it came to her.

"A diary?" she surmised aloud.

She clicked on the large monitor next to the bed and inserted the earliest cartridge, dating back eleven months. She waited a few moments and then her cousin's familiarly arranged room appeared on the screen. Anna Maria entered the scene, sitting perkily upright on a cushioned, ivory-backed chair, beaming with an excitement Louisette recognized as "discovery". The visual caused her heartbeat to flux. Would that all our fondest pasts could be revisited and preserved in earnest.

"Whenever I do as I shouldn't, I discover what it is I should do." Anna Maria began excitedly. "Last week I decided to partake on an archaeological expedition. And since all good things begin at home, I started in the locked dungeons of the Palace basements. You wouldn't imagine all the old things dating back nearly forty...even fifty years hidden away down there! Why, I could write uncle's entire biography tomorrow if I wanted to. Pictures of him as a little boy with grandmother! Old scripts from his satellite show! Posters from his election campaign! Letters between him and mother when they were sent to different boarding schools as children! Wedding cartridges of him and auntie Dee! Notes on Victor's progress as a schoolboy at survival camp! What an unbelievable vault of family history! Things that happened before you were alive involving people you know are just so…otherworldly in the sense that they happened to people and things that you know, before you existed! And yet, here you are…among those same people…affecting their everyday lives!"

Louisette felt her eyes tear up as Anna Maria's wondrous monologue breathlessly flowed onward. A voice that had been commonplace in her everyday life now played to her as a cherished melody. Her cousin continued on about packed-up photographs and sealed cartridges as treasures never before seen.

Then, not unexpectedly, the girl hoisted up with two hands, a large, dingy, but ornately bound book. As stray animals found some people, books always seemed to find Anna Maria. However, unlike any book Louisette had seen, (though Louisette had seen less than her share) this volume had a foreboding aura of powerful importance, imposed by more than its sheer girth and golden leaf.

"A challenge!" Anna Maria beamed "Looks like a Latin kindred to War and Peace. Actually, the title translated is the definitive documented text of ancient cult Christian Mythology. I've read a couple of excerpted interpretations by scholars and even took a class regarding the fallacy of ancient cults, but I've never…seen the actual…guide people used to mislead themselves for centuries, as it turned out. This may provide excellent insight into how man once came within only a few bombs of actually destroying himself over mere…beliefs! Oh well, tune in tomorrow!"

The screen went blank except for the following date which cued itself up in large block numerals.

Louisette stared at the numbers and recalled Anna Maria's final note, which made reference to "God" and "Heaven". Then she touched her cousin's necklace around her neck.

"Oh, Anna," she sighed. "What the hell did you fall into?"

She pressed a button on the remote, and the second day's date faded away. Again, Anna Maria appeared on the screen, only this time appearing extremely concerned over something.

"I went to see Lou this evening," the young girl began with a tinge of distress. "I wanted to tell her about the basement and all the things I'd uncovered. After all, most of the things bear more directly on her family than mine. But when I got to her room, I heard shouting and glass shattering. She and Victor were fighting again. She sounded…well…inebriated and she was screaming terrible obscenities at him for either being unfaithful to her or the other way around. I'm not sure which. But it was awful! So much rage. So much…anguish. Almost hateful. I love Lou more than anyone in the universe, but the way she gets on about Victor is unnerving. I mean, he's the Champion. The paragon of manhood. And yet to her, he's like some…possession or servant predisposed to service the least of her whims. She parades him like a trophy, but treats him like a pet dog, scolding and berating him with vague complaints. It's not that I haven't seen them happy together. But nights like these make me wonder if it's all worth it. It's too bad. Lou always said that having relationships outside the relationship helped ease the stress in a relationship—but it doesn't seem to be working for them. Oh well. I know how I'd behave if I were dating the Champion of our Earth. I wish them well. They both deserve to be happy. Especially Lou."

The image faded and was again, replaced by the following date. Louisette rebuffed her feelings of guilt.

"She was just too young to understand the work that goes into a meaningful relationship," she justified to herself. "Even one of my analysts said there's no one book on how men and women are supposed to get along. You just have to feel your way through and make the rules as you go."

Louisette pressed forward into the next entry.

"The Nutcracker recital Friday and Saturday!" Anna Maria exclaimed, sitting in her warm-up tights with her hair crudely bound into a pony tail. "Piano recitals Sunday and Tuesday! Why do I do this to myself?"

The image faded away quickly.

"Hmm." Louisette wondered. "I thought she always knew why."

She pressed forward again and the date skipped ahead a week.

"Well, my Amadeus is intact, but I may be growing out of my Clara." Anna Maria grimaced. "My ankles and arches are killing me! Actually, Dr. Canard thinks I have calcium deposits on my heels. Kima says I'm growing so fast, I've probably been overcompensating on my technique causing my feet and ankles added stress. Anyway, that's enough dancing for awhile. Which is good. Now maybe I can catch up on some reading!"

The next date:

"Wesley is really starting to get on my nerves. He doesn't know the first thing about the end of the Hundred Years' War, and yet he insists he wants to work with me on a revival of Bernard Shaw's, *St. Joan.* I think he wants us to go out or something, but he's afraid to say so. He just keeps hanging around pretending to be interested in whatever I'm interested in. I guess I shouldn't be so mean, but it would be a lot easier on both of us if he would simply be up front with me so I could be up front with him. I'm sure lots of other girls would find him okay. He's just not for me.

"Besides, something very interesting happened a couple of days ago. I was working out in the gym with Kima. When I look up, Victor's standing in the doorway just staring at us. I asked Kima if he wanted something, but she said not to mind him. But how could I? Victor…watching my workout? Why would he bother? I must've looked liked a trembling twig to him. But there he stood…for nearly fifteen minutes. Finally, when we were done I took a huge chance and casually waved to him. And he smiled and waved back! It was incredible! Kima must have thought we were both crazy—staring at each other across the gymnasium like silly school children. At that point I ducked into the shower before I fainted right there and tipped my hand. If it weren't for Lou, I'd think he was interested in me. Still, it was just so sweet!"

The muscles in Louisette's jaw tightened as the image on the screen faded.

"Victor…!" was all she could manage as her nostrils flared. What he had done to Anna Maria was sordid enough a tragedy. Now she wondered how long he and Kima had secretly been together as well.

"Shriveling old whore!" she spat as she pressed the monitor remote to forward.

Anna Maria appeared on the screen looking contemplative, mildly fatigued and slightly over studied.

"I read through the first four hundred or so pages of The Holy Bible last night," she began. "I'd have gotten further but my Latin just isn't what it should be. The first thing I can't fathom is why the government has censored such a beautifully written piece of historical literature. I mean, I know that this book, with its mythological licenses, became one of the focal impetuses for the cult domination of humanity for literally thousands of years. But if you ask me, those who take up the banner for the utter condemnation of cult literature and symbols, indeed make much ado about nothing. And, tragically, do so at the peril of diminishing historically documented facts! I took the time to cross reference events chronicled here with my uplink to the world historical database. According to the database, people such as Saul, King David, Solomon, Darius, Amos, and countless others were historically, factually documented living beings. Not fairy tale characters born out of some shepherds' imaginations. And the Phoenicians, the Canaanites, the Hebrews, and many other peoples are also historical bodies based upon proven facts.

"Where I guess everyone has the problem, myself included, is where there are references made to conversations with a great deity—'God' if you will. The text is saturated with not only 'prayer' by leading figures, but the answers they got and the prophecies they were sworn to live by. Like Solomon being told that his kingdom would fall if he broke one of the god's laws. As it's told, he took a large number of lovers and as a result,

'God' frowned upon him and roused the ten tribes of Israel to secede from his kingdom. Well, it's a documented fact that the ten tribes did secede as written, but it seems improbable that it had anything to do with some deity's view of King Solomon's sexual conduct. Also, the creation of the Earth in only six or seven days is a scientific impossibility (unless, of course you take into consideration what would be a 'day' to an entity who didn't measure 'days' as a single revolution of the planet he created). And the foretelling of the great flood. Talking serpents. The timely parting of the Red Sea. All of these things clearly smack of the embellishments of active human imaginations.

"Yet still, the strict codes of morality seemed to carry some weight even if most of them are clearly unattainable. I've often, myself, wondered how humanity would fare if it governed itself with a greater sense of empathy and love, rather than the ethical nihilism that prevails. I mean, irony itself, seems to be built along those lines. You do something bad, something bad eventually happens to you. You do something good, and something good eventually comes your way. And sometimes even things that appear to be good in the short run, or bad in the short run, turn out to be the opposite in the long run. There must, at least, be some principal force behind irony.

"Oh well, I'm babbling. If I can get out of a trip with Uncle Georges to London, I should be finished by tomorrow. Besides, I'd rather do Vienna in a couple of months!"

Anna Maria's image faded.

Louisette found herself strangely entranced by the latest entry. Under common circumstances, anything which vaguely threatened to arouse her dormant conscience, would be instinctively suffocated by her capricious urges to remain in a state of perpetual and constant gratification. But today, with her cousin dead, her estranged engagement evaporated, and the stunted roots of her frivolous station bound up and strangled by her father's condemning pronouncement, her atrophied intellect restlessly stirred.

"She seemed engrossed but hardly moved." Louisette pondered. "How could a book of old stories take her over that way? She was so smart!

Maybe that's what made the cultists so dangerous. If they could take over a strong mind…"

Driven to pursue her supposition, she pressed forward to uncover Anna Maria's conclusions over the cult documents. The next date came up on the screen, but no entry followed. She pressed forward once more and again no entry appeared. She began clicking the remote, searching for the next date under which there was an entry. The dates counted forward on the blank screen for another week…then two…then three.

Finally, in the middle of the fourth week, the date counter stopped and Anna Maria appeared, looking very tired and considerably distraught.

"Why can't everyone just leave me the hell alone!" she shouted uncharacteristically. "I'm not sick! I don't need counseling! I don't need to go away! I just want to be left alone!"

The screen faded to the preceding date.

"I remember that." Louisette recalled, distinctly. "For about a month she was totally not herself. She didn't want to go anywhere. She wouldn't talk to anyone. Even her grades fell into the eighties, like she didn't care. Father was deathly afraid that she'd started using something and had doctors and analysts all over her. I guess he was afraid she'd end up like me. But then, all of a sudden, she was herself again. Even more so. And everyone just let it drop."

Louisette pressed onward. Another week in the diary passed before Anna Maria reappeared.

The girl's face was clearly flushed with consternation as she shook her head with some deeply personal disbelief. The flesh pockets under eyes were pouched and darkened. She looked as if she had aged ten years. This clearly would be an entry like no other.

She tentatively cleared her throat and pensively began to speak just above a whisper: "My life…everything I'd been taught…! A few weeks ago, I finished reading an old book of cult mythology. The book of Christian cult mythology. I did it out of curiosity. Curiosity and the need to know what it was that made the people who embraced this philosophy...this religion (if you will)...so dangerous to our world. As I read, the recurring theme appeared to be the demand of some supreme being that we, as subjugated humans, obey a set of arbitrary laws which suppressed our free wills. Laws governing commerce, laws governing politics, and laws audacious enough to govern even private human...expressions of love. I was astounded by the depth and scope of this philosophy, but was alarmed by the absence of physical, scientific, verifications for acts committed by some omnipresent force referred to as 'God'. It all seemed like some ingenious charlatan's ruse aimed at inhibiting humanity for no other reason than to benefit those who claimed special privilege to disseminate the information passed down from this deity. But then I came upon the telling and retelling of one story which failed to fall neatly into the framework of my hypothesis. It was the story of the 'Son of God'.

"In this story, 'God' allows his son to be born of flesh and blood so that he may walk among humans, suffer among them, and teach them of the focus of their mortal lives and of a glory that awaits all of our...immortal souls. He spoke much about the state of humanity, the temptations of humanity, the ills of humanity, and the laws of 'God'. It was almost frightening how logically he captured mankind's nature at every state of being, every relationship we could ever know, every moral or ethical dilemma we could ever face or struggle against. It was plain to me that this 'Son of God' knew humanity better than any human could ever hope to know himself. And the fact that this knowledge, without fault, transcends our sciences and our progress and our wealth (or lack thereof) and even time itself, was eerily contradictory to what cult scholars have always taught. Here, we cherish our freedom to indulge, rather than our strength to refrain. Here, we embrace the urge to be selfish, rather than the necessity to build our world on the merits of selflessness and true love.

"And strangely, the 'Son of God' spoke of no rewards in life. No riches. No immortal flesh. No fulfillment of earthly avarice. He promised nothing of life at all—but only of a greater joy which would be reaped beyond life, if faith were held in earnest."

A tear ran along the crevice of Anna Maria's nose before she could hastily smear it away.

"And while I'm reading even this," the girl continued, "I'm wondering where and how this all knowing 'Son of God' would reap for himself. It was then that I found that he is betrayed and crucified in defense of his followers. Horribly, callously crucified! And then I asked myself what kind of story is this—of a man who gives up his life for beliefs that yield nothing we can hold in our hands? What kind of 'God' would allow this to happen to his son? In earthly terms, it makes no sense at all. But in heaven…in heavenly terms, it's perfectly, compassionately…logical.

"I read on and was further astonished by the son's resurrection. A prophesied resurrection witnessed by many. A final plea that man cherish life and be assured of life after life."

Anna Maria swallowed with a grimace as if overtaken with some inner pain.

"Yet, in spite of all this, the book ultimately foretells a time when humanity chooses to turn away from these teachings and wallow pathetically in the excrements of his own earthly passions. The result is the destruction of all that is. Death and damnation for all but a few.

"I did a historical cross-reference on Jesus Christ, the Son of God. And like most of the others mentioned in the text, he too is a documented historical figure diminished only by mankind's lack of physical proof of those things documented herein.

"And so for the past month, I've challenged myself with this knowledge, afraid that I may have been seduced by some serpentine philosophy that beckons to poison humanity against itself. Yet, I ask myself, if I am deceived, where is the proof of it? And was it these words which I've read with my own eyes that once poisoned humanity, or was it the human curators of these words who sought corrupted opportunity rather than truth? I love humanity. I always have. And if God made man and Earth and the universe, then I must love him too. And I must live by him. And more importantly help those I love do likewise. It makes sense."

Anna Maria's image faded from the screen.

Louisette fumbled for the remote, as she sought to review the entry once again.

# II.

Operations:

"Satellite defense network is now fully aligned." Jean-Paul reported. "We have a lock on three of the six alien birds or…ships."

"Let's call them ships." Manda spoke as she inspected the defense grid on the giant fifty-meter screen. "Thinking of those things as living creatures makes me nilly!"

"Yes, ma'am." Jean-Paul smiled at her assertion.

Through mid-morning, as continued reports of massive disappearances showered in from all points of the globe, the Operations staff grew frustrated and leery with their seemingly futile fight to rescue the Earth. While large chunks of population were rapidly vanishing, tracking the expansive ships with their bleeding radioactive trails became an arduous task mired in maddening tedium.

Initially stationary, the ships glowed like bright, hovering beacons above what became their primary targets. But as they launched their assaults, the emissions in their wake left blinding trails of inertance which dulled normally clear satellite readings. Compounding matters, the ships systematically crossed each others' paths as they burned their hourly strafes across the lands, disappearing into residual trails until they created for themselves a turbid radioactive cover.

Up until this afternoon, the only way to track the alien ships, at all, was to resignedly chart where they had most recently struck and attempt to forecast where next they would strike. That's when Jean-Paul suggested the launch of longitudinal probes as a net across the Earth in an attempt to detect the movement of their five-kilometer wingspans with what instrumentally translated into an electronic form of "the naked eye".

The first ship was picked up shortly after noon. The second, within forty-five minutes. The third, a half-hour later. The Operations staff was buoyed by this meager success. Now they would at least have the opportunity to die fighting.

"Should I transmit the firing sequence?" Jean-Paul asked. "Or should we confer with the Beneficent?"

"Right about now, I think he'll be willing to live with my decisions." Manda spoke confidently. "If I'm right, he'll get the credit and probably be able to rename the continent of his choice after himself. If I'm wrong…well, there won't be too many people left to spread the blame, one way or another. Go ahead and transmit!"

Jean-Paul spoke the transmission sequence into his computer and reddish-orange lights flashed on the terminals of all of the consoles across the Operations hall. On the giant screen the orbiting defense satellite networks flashed bright green with indication of their readiness.

"G. O'Dowd satellite array is locked onto our friend over India." Jean-Paul relayed. "Lady Stardust array has powered up to strike over Norway. The Reagan array is already firing over Japan!"

The bustling Operations hall silenced immediately as everyone focused on the computer-simulated images on the giant screen. Dark red lines denoting concentrated nuclear powered energy beams streamed down from the satellite networks toward their black-winged targets. "I've got a fourth!" yelled a technician, breaking the impromptu silence. "Hawaiian islands!"

The news was greeted with nervous applause from some of the members of the Operations staff.

"Excellent," responded Manda. "Bring the Kennedy array on line and fire when ready!"

"Yes, Ms. Martine," the technician proudly complied.

A buzzing among the staff, which could have been mistaken for enthusiasm quickly dissipated as the dark red lines continued their descent.

Manda folded her arms and snorted impatiently as she stared intently at the giant screen. It was the only vague indication she would give that she was the least bit unnerved.

Jean-Paul audibly drummed his fingers at his console until a perturbed technician turned to see what the "noise" was about. He then, flexed his fingers and began popping each sweaty knuckle with a press of his thumb. Another technician turned and frowned her disapproval.

Jean-Paul deflected her annoyance by standing up and walking purposefully over to where Manda stood.As he approached her, he noted that the muscles in her jaw tensed intermittently under her rounded cheeks, then seemed to roll back into her neck.

"This is amazing." Jean-Paul spoke as he came up behind her.

"Amazing how?" Manda answered sternly.

Jean-Paul chuckled at the rigidity of her professional response.

As she turned to face him, a portion of the burdensome tension, drained wearily out of her posture.

"Damned amazing," she conceded with a tired smile. "Humanity, brought to its knees…just like this. I tell myself this is some sort of challenge. Like war and bigotry and cultism have been challenges for man to overcome. But this is…scary. Real scary. It feels bigger. Meaner. Relentless. Almost careless of what mankind really thinks—or that we're even worth noticing. It smashed Liberace Gardens in the blink of an eye. And now over a billion people have been wiped out with nary a thought. And it's not even asking for anything. It's like all its decisions are already made."

"No sign of even a challenge." Jean-Paul added. "More like a systematic execution or…judgment."

"Yeah." Manda frowned. "As if these aliens or whatever they are, are judging us not fit to live. But who are they to decide for us one way or the other?"

"There's a cliché." Jean-Paul shook his head. "Almost hypocritical."

"What?" Manda questioned.

"'Who are they to judge?'" Jean-Paul placed a hand on her shoulder. "'Who are we to judge?' Questions as old as the first accusation of wrongdoing. And the human answer has always been: 'Who do they or we have to be?' Or to term it another way, 'might makes right'. The problem is, today, the aliens have the 'might', so they can make 'right' any way they want to."

"Damn them, then!" Manda cursed behind clenched teeth.

"That's why I always liked my grandfather's saying." Jean-Paul reflected. "*'Judge not, that ye be not judged. For with what judgment ye judge, ye shall be judged: and with what measure ye mete, it shall be measured to you again.'.*"

"Hmm." Manda continued to stare at the screen. "Where'd he get that from? Shakespeare?"

"You don't want to know." Jean-Paul answered, massaging Manda's neck with his fingers.

"We have a hit!" yelled an excited technician from her terminal.

The Operations hall burst into a rain of relieved cheers, as if the entire room had been holding its breath.

"Stations!" Manda commanded. A handful of malingering technicians jumped back behind their consoles. Jean-Paul returned to his seat, as well.

On the giant screen, the dark red energy bolt had connected with the traced alien "ship" which was now flashing bright white over Japan.

"Reading a huge electromagnetic disturbance!" Jean-Paul read from his monitor. "Storm activity spreading out over a hundred to one hundred-fifty square kilometers!"

"Any way to tell if there's any effect on that bird?" Manda slipped.

"Oh, we're getting plenty of effect!" Jean-Paul answered. "It's just hard to tell what kind!"

"Moko, tell Albuquerque to maximize our gain!" Manda ordered. "Tell them to reroute forty percent from the other arrays to the Reagan until those others connect with their targets!"

"Yes, ma'am."

The intensity of the flashing vessel deepened.

"Storm activity now at four hundred-square kilometers." Jean-Paul cited as a tiny swirl of turbulence was graphically reproduced on the giant screen. "Increasing steadily. The people we save from the alien ship may die in the hurricane we're about to cause!"

"Understood." Manda spoke flatly, folding her lips.

The dark red bolt of energy widened with the increase in power diversion. The alien ship's bright light flickered as it absorbed the streaming bombardment from the thermonuclear satellite array.

"The storm is now up to seven hundred-square kilometers." Jean-Paul informed, not expecting Manda to waver from her plan of attack.

Suddenly, the energy beam on the screen showed breaks in its stream.

"Satellite array is starting to fail," a technician fretted.

"Can we increase the power to compensate?" Manda asked.

"The increase in power is what's causing the failure." Jean-Paul relayed. "They weren't designed to handle the forty percent boost."

Manda pushed back the tuft of hair that hung over her forehead. No decision could be the right decision now. Cut the power, save the satellite arrays, and the ships continue their annihilation. Maintain the power, cripple the satellite arrays, and the alien vessels still continue their annihilation. She could feel every set of eyes in the Operations hall boring into her, awaiting her next decision.

She closed her eyes for a moment and wondered how, all at once, the fate of the world could come to rest on her narrow shoulders. All she had ever wanted was to become successful at whatever she did. And that immodest aspiration had led her to arguably the most powerful post in the world: Cartel Operations Chief, second to the World Beneficent.

It was not a position of high profile in the eyes of the masses. But profile never mattered to Manda. Control is what mattered. The ability to affect her destiny and the destiny of those around her. It had always been the easiest way for her to ensure that all "things" would be done "correctly". Weighing, balancing and ordering the paradigms of life to a predictable variance of outcomes had been the bane of her existence. Now, the sturdy hub of her personal pride became a seamless vacuum wherein her darkest nightmare held sway. A realm wherein chance or fate held the key to life or death…for billions.

"Manda?" Jean-Paul called to her.

When she looked at him, he saw fear in her eyes for the first time since they'd known each other. Then, as she opened her mouth to speak…

"Got it!" yelled a technician.

Jean-Paul and several others swung around in their chairs to look up at the giant screen. The dark red, now fragmented, energy stream was still there as was the swirling turbulence caused by the strike over the island of Japan. But clearly, miraculously, the giant alien ship had disappeared.

The Operations staff exploded into jubilation. Technicians all around the hall congratulated one another with hardy handshakes and heartfelt embraces.

Relief washed over Manda's face which now glistened with cool perspiration. She righted herself and assumed her command posture.

"Okay, everyone!" she called out to the hall. "That's one down! We still have five on Earth and one on its way to Mars! We've still got a lot of work to do!"

The enthusiasm in the room did not dampen as technicians again, returned to their consoles.

Manda smiled meager satisfaction to herself as she made eye contact with Jean-Paul. Jean-Paul, however, wore desperate pain in his eyes which were still riveted on the giant screen.

When Manda observed the broad map of the Earth, she noted the clearing area just above Japan, as it had been before. Then, to the west, she saw it.

"Korea," she gasped.

A flashing white, winged vessel hovered over Korea. Then it slowly returned to its ominous, unaffected black coloring.

"A different one?" she asked hopefully.

"The same one." Jean-Paul spoke gravely. "It must've…dropped under water to sever contact with the beam and…resurfaced over there."

Stunned, Manda fell back against a nearby console.

The Operations hall went silent.

# III.

Anna Maria's Room:

Louisette found her mood strangely uplifted by the hours she'd spent viewing her late cousin's diaries. Even the increasing references to the cult material Anna Maria had begun to incorporate into her personal philosophy were not as pernicious and destructive as Louisette had expected. Anna Maria, in fact, appeared enlivened, emboldened and fortified with an enviable certainty, that Louisette had previously attributed to mere maturity.

"I've come up with a game." Anna Maria spoke from another entry, with a mischievous smirk on her face. "To challenge myself. There are words in the human vocabulary which, over time, seem to have had their meanings diluted or reconfigured to suit our consciences so that we may continue to warmly justify ourselves and our chronic misdeeds as a people. Words like: 'right', 'wrong', 'good', 'evil' have all had their meanings so haphazardly kneaded and molded over time, that I fear humanity has totally lost the sense of these words altogether.

"For instance, I looked up the word 'right'. My dictionary defines it as 'in conformity with fact, reason, or some standard or principle; correct.' Or 'correct in judgment, opinion or action'. Clear, right? (pardoning my use of the our word in question). Not necessarily. I mean 'conformity with some standard or principle' could make anything right, especially in the absence of clearly defined 'standards or principles'. Why in fact, nowadays, it is perfectly acceptable for people to embrace duplicitous 'standards or principles' purely for the sake of our harmony with others even if those others' values are in complete juxtaposition to our own. A pack of Weed sadists may say that killing is 'in conformity' with their 'standards or principles' for their valuation of life. Whereas in the Blossoms, we've established that murder is not right. Except there is a provision which says you can't kill a Blossom in the Weeds, but you can kill a Weed in the Blossoms if curfew is violated. So is it right for a Weed to kill or not? Is it right for a Blossom to kill or not?

"Well, let's see if the second definition helps us: 'correct in judgment, opinion or principle'. Hmm. That's tidy. But whose 'judgment, opinion or principle' are we talking about? Anyone's?

"Now I admit, I may be stretching it a bit. After all, the principle of Democracy has leant mankind a great hand in dealing with this problem. Therein, whatever the majority of people want is what everyone winds up with. That seems only fair or 'right'. But what about those historical precedences when the majority was wrong? When scientists were put to death by the majority for heresy? When human slaves were bartered about the world by the majority like domesticated farm animals? Or when Nazis killed Jews, or when Catholics killed Protestants? Were they really 'right'? By man's definition, I would say so.

"Which is why I believe that what is truly just, or 'right' must ultimately be something beyond that which is merely humanly arbitrary. It doesn't mean that it must be easy or always pleasant or always fun. It must instead, be something that ensures the freedoms and opportunities for all people at the expense of no one! Because when I look at the beauty and uniqueness of every person I've ever met in my life, Weed or Blossom, I can't believe that God would create any single entity solely to be trod upon and overrun by even a majority. Call it fanaticism or cultism if you like, but when I read the words of God for the first time, I never ever felt so truly close to 'right' in all my life!

"But let's take a simpler word…"

Louisette began to yawn and readied to press forward to skip into the next diary entry.

"…'Whore' for instance." Anna Maria spoke, as Louisette's forefinger suddenly froze above the forward button.

"'Whore' is defined as 'a woman who engages in promiscuous sexual intercourse'. 'Promiscuous' is defined as 'having sexual relations with a number of partners on an informal or casual basis'. Now I know a great number of women, including my cousin Lou, who take great pride and pleasure in the number of 'casual and informal' sexual affairs they've enjoyed. Yet many of them, if not all of them, would bristle if you were to call them whores.

"Of course, the definition is imprecise as to how many sexual relationships with how many number of partners pushes you over the 'threshold'. Which again, leaves this word open for man's liberal interpretation. Does a different man every year make you a whore?"

"It'd make you masturbate like crazy. I know that!" Louisette laughed.

"Does a different man every month make you a whore?" Anna Maria continued. "A different man every week? A different man every weekend? A different man before every meal? More than one man at once?"

"It...depends." Louisette muttered feebly.

"Again, measuring one's morality in man's pliable terms ultimately leaves you confused, uncertain, and groping for flimsy reassurance from peers, Port counselors—even movies on satellite. But when I look at God's design for committed, enduring relationships, the question of being a 'whore' never really enters the picture. I find that comforting.

"Oh, well. More word games later."

Anna Maria's charged, thoughtful image faded from the monitor.

"She just called me a whore...!" Louisette exclaimed. "...I think."

Then the truculent castigation of her angered father faintly echoed in the recesses of her mind. Louisette hastily pressed the forward button, hoping to elude its caustic indictment before it overtook her.

Anna Maria reappeared looking decidedly serious and unsettled.

"It's frightening to think about it, but I think I may have saved Val's life tonight." Anna Maria began with wistful solemnity.

"A storm was rolling in from the sea," she continued. "I don't care much for lightening and thunder, but I have to say I find the warm winds before a Mediterranean storm exhilarating. So after evening class, I decided to go up to the southwest steeple crown where I knew the winds would be strongest. Of course, I didn't tell uncle Georges or anyone else of this excursion because I'm sure they would have discouraged me about being swept off the tower with the first hearty gale. So anyway, I drop my books in the well, and run up the stairs as fast as I can to catch the wind, which I already hear, whistling through the steeple crown. When I reached the top, I saw the darkened clouds angrily chasing away the white ones across the horizon. The wind was, in fact, very powerful, and if I'd worn anything the least bit baggy, I indeed, might have been lifted from the steeple and flown to God knows where!

"Well, anyway, I'm reveling, privately I thought, in the embrace of the air currents when I turn and see Val sitting alone out on the edge of the crown. In fact, sitting isn't a good word. He was dangling. Dangling precariously over the edge as if he were waiting for the first stiff breeze to carry him off into oblivion. I called to him, but he didn't acknowledge me. Thinking he didn't hear me I walked carefully to where he was perched, mindful not to startle him over the edge. When I came within a step, before I could speak his name again, he turned suddenly upon me, almost losing his balance. He tried to fashion his happy smile for me, but I could see from the darkened makeup around his eyes that he'd been crying. When he saw that I saw this, he looked out over the edge again, no longer concerned with hiding whatever was hurting him.

"I was almost certain that he was about to drop himself when I took a foolish chance and reached out to touch his shoulder. It was good that I did. He immediately grabbed my hand, swung back toward me and began bawling like a little child.

"Since Val has come to live with us, or uncle as it were, I've actually come to know less of him than when he'd been a member of my school class. At school, he'd always seemed like a nice but, somewhat fragile boy, in ways no boy should ever be. We had always gotten along cordially, and I noted the odd kinship he cultivated with girls rather than the other boys. But after he left school to become uncle's page, I usually hear more of him than I see, since uncle always leaves him out of official and family functions. If I see him at all, we're either running past each other in the hallways, too busy to more than greet each other, or he's lounged in the background of uncle's private company, seeming impatient for me to disappear.

"When I was finally able to settle him enough to speak clearly, he despairingly sobbed about his future. Not his immediate future, but rather the future of his life. He said that he loved Uncle Georges with all his heart, but could not see them together for more than another year or so, if that. He said he wanted family, but that his parents would not have him any longer. He said that someday, he would like children, but couldn't fathom how they would come. With this, I told him there were many cities full of people like him where many, if not most, had done well for themselves socially and economically. But he surprised me by condemning them as transient-hearted, deluded, and rootless. 'A family, a real family, grows from the love of a man and a woman who become father and mother, and extend that love to their children,' he said to me. This greatest love, he asserted, would be forever denied him by his nature. And he concluded thusly, that he, in effect, had no future of worth.

"There came a slight drizzle as we held hands, and I listened to all of this. I initially had no answer for his dilemma and simply tried to get him to retire with me to shelter. But then, like a forgotten voice, commentary from the book of Christian Mythology surged to the forefront of my brain. I relayed to him how I had read how God views people of his situation. I had been hesitant to embrace this view since it condemned so many, including my own beloved uncle. But to the very well of my heart, in conjunction with all the pain and sadness this depravity seemed to carry with it, I knew that what I had read was right for Val and logical for the ultimate salvation of humanity. I told him that while he shouldered a heavy burden, all people (even those seeming not) battled some vice or ill purported to be insurmountable. And that all of us are bound, by the grace of our existence to combat those ills, rather than indulge them. In effect, I told him that the life he wanted for his future and…his children could be won if he would allow me to share with him all that I'd read and if he would try to be true to it.

"I don't know how much of what I said he actually took to heart. But I do know that I got him off the ledge and down into the kitchen where we stole from the cooks' pots and joked about the prospects of his distant future and mine.

"I've helped children all over the world. Yet it's odd to consider that I may have actually had spiritual influence on someone. But then again, it's not really my influence, is it?

"Tonight, I'll add Val's future to Lou, Georges, and Victor in my prayers. G'night!"

Anna Maria's cheerful smile faded from the monitor.

Louisette leaned back against the bed and skeptically stared at the large numerals on the screen. Val had always been little more than a two-dimensional figurine in the scheme of her father's comfort. The boy had been assigned to her father's disposal and attended him faithfully. For this, he was duly compensated with food, clothing and gifts until such time as his services would no longer be required. That simple, pretty, little Val should have worldly concerns of any depth, even for himself, never entered her mind.

Moreover, the matter of family and future had only recently become any concern of Louisette's. She had always had both, distinctly defined by her prestigious station in life. And she found "love" in singular terms toward a single man or a single woman discouraging by the rigidity of its boundaries. One could have favorite lovers, frequent lovers, and cherished lovers as one chose. She could not comprehend Val's distress over the loss of any one in particular, male or female unless his concerns were purely economic. With the exception of Victor, Louisette usually tired of her relationships shortly after their consummations and rejoiced in the freedom to move on, unencumbered, to exciting, new relationships.

"But Val was worried about the future of…his life." Louisette reflected.

Then she considered the unborn child inside of her, that she might raise alone a world away from its uncaring father. A world devoid of pillars or foundations. A world of perpetual transition and emotional insecurity. Louisette tried to comprehend its future in such a life…should it be allowed to live at all.

# IV.

The Controller's Office:

"So you would have me believe that the Beneficent, unsound in mind, welcomes destruction because he is secretly a closet cultist?" Nikolai summarized, downing a shot of vodka and lifting a cigarette to his lips.

"It's a fact!" stated Victor. "I've heard and seen him with my own ears and eyes."

"And you're telling me that the world is losing its battle with the alien force because of his madness?" Nikolai exhaled a large azure cloud, narrowing his bloodshot blue eyes.

"I do."

"And do you believe that his Operations staff is part of this warped conspiracy?"

"I doubt it." Victor offered. "I think that they're also victims of the Beneficent's crazy, subversive desire to see mankind destroyed. I'm certain he's probably done all he can to stall their efforts."

"Strange." Nikolai stared at the blank computer monitor on his desk. "In all of our...observations, he remains the most steadfast humanist of our time. And his greatest concerns seem to have been with the maintenance and containment of the Weeds, rather than cult activity one way or another. I've even warned the Beneficent of increased grass-root cultism, which he dismissed as 'history's dissipative remnants'. He has emphasized that the genetic class struggles are where our greatest concerns lie. You know: the fear of 'masses over mind and matter'; that even the zoo specimens may overtake their keepers for a time, if left unfed and unchecked. That and the image of his family appear to remain his only concerns."

"Nikolai," Victor began in a sincere voice, "Georges has been like a father to me. And without him, I could never have become the Champion. But yesterday, he called me into his room and shouted cult prophecy at me till he was blue in the face! He called the meteor a 'sign'. He referred to the 'sins' of man as some kind of violation that we would be made to pay for! And when I challenged him, he actually…shot at me, threatened my life!"

"Interesting." Nikolai observed.

"And last night," Victor recounted painfully, "after the Santa Cruz broadcast and the birth of those…things, all he could say is that we were all going to die 'very soon'! This was before the disappearances began! Before we had even started to assess the power of the alien threat! He had resigned all of us to total annihilation."

"Based on what I've seen so far," Nikolai leaned back in his chair and poured himself another half glass of vodka, "he appears to have been prophetic. Masses of people are disappearing by the province. Our thermonuclear armaments are having no effect whatsoever. And all my entire infobase and observation network can do at this point is…report on our demise. I'm not a quitter, though. In my line of work, there's always a new wrinkle in the fabric of politics that allows one to…purvey an old suit to the masses, dyed in a forgotten 'new' color.

"Every few months or so in some corner of the world, the same old question: Can the Weeds trust the World Cartel? No? Then we surreptitiously allow them to have new leaders whom they come to distrust even more. Someone yells 'weren't things better the way they were?'—and then you have uncertainty…doubt. Soon the dissident leaders, themselves, fall on the defensive. And before long, the people are glad to hand over their 'savior' to you on a silver platter because the uncertainty and doubt makes them…less comfortable than their sunken bellies and their dirty streets. I had one Weed assassin in Thailand kill a dissident for nothing, because he said when the man spoke of revolution, it made his head hurt when he inhaled opium. 'Opium isn't suppose to make your head hurt,' he said. 'It's suppose to relax you. Imagine how much I'll hurt if that man comes to power.' Ha!"

Nikolai laughed loudly to himself, careless of Victor seated in front of his desk.

Victor watched the once shadowy and imposing figure of the World Cartel Controller grow dim and remarkably impotent before his very eyes.

"Stalin understood these things." Nikolai spoke to the ceiling as he drained his glass proudly. "So did Nixon."

"Nikolai," Victor attempted to steer the conversation. "I'm going to need your help."

"My help?" Nikolai chuckled, coughing smoke from his cigarette. "What help do you need? I can tell you the name of every cult leader with a constituency of more than ten on the face of the planet! I can name you every revolutionary journalist, singer, scholar and poet…Blossom or Weed. I already have pinpointed where the next six territorial disputes will erupt and even in what order! Hell, in less than a minute, I can describe for you which city officials will die tonight and where and when the bodies will be found. I can even add to the list, if you like!"

Nikolai leaned forward with his eyes slit and whispered: "I can tell you what color underwear your fiancée has worn for the last seven years. That is, on the days she's worn any. I have an entire cartridge listing her sex partners since she was twelve. I can tell you how many moles Val has on his little butt. One night, we even gave each of them names! And I bet you don't know that Kima always fakes her orgasms, unless she's with another woman!"

Victor jumped to his feet, either in shock or anger and grabbed the gaunt, smiling Controller by his black suit jacket.

"Look, Nikolai!" Victor clenched his teeth. "You may be finished, but I'm not!"

"What is it you need, Champion?" Nikolai smirked as he reached behind himself for the vodka bottle, filling his glass without breaking eye contact with Victor.

Victor loosed his powerful grasp on the Controller and apologized with a nod of his head and a softening of his brows. Even in this state, Nikolai was a man to be feared for the shear preponderance of his knowledge of everything and everyone. And a chilling, complicated, conflict with the Controller's office was not what Victor had sought.

"I need your office," Victor looked down then up again, "to look the other way on something."

"On what?" Nikolai grew impatient as he fidgeted with his lighter.

"I'm going to take control from Georges. Then I'm going to try to rescue the Earth before it's too late. But I need your office to look the other way."

"I'll log it in the computer." Nikolai leaned back with a smile. "Let me know what time we shouldn't be watching."

Nikolai lifted his glass to his lips and gestured to Victor as if to ask if there were anything else.

"That's…all." Victor confirmed.

"Good luck!" Nikolai waved to him.

Victor observed the Controller curiously. Then he backed out of the office slowly as the doors opened behind him. Stepping out into the corridor, the office doors slid shut. And as he turned to leave, he could hear Nikolai in his office, loudly singing *Katyousha*!

# V.

Anna Maria's Room:

"Well, I'm back from Tanzania!" announced Anna Maria, looking tanned, but travel weary. "The Weed Literacy Conference went relatively well. The people there seem much less hostile to the idea of the combination of library system resources than they were a year ago. Ben Uhuru, my contact there, and I tried to impress upon them the importance of knowledge regardless of its source, and that it would not be an infringement on their cultural identity at all.

"The highlight of the Conference for me, unquestionably came Saturday evening on the torchlit soccer field at Dar es Salaam Harbor, when Ben, members of his book club, and I took turns reading short stories to the children and teenagers who attended. Ben and his friends are magical storytellers and harmonize the written word into spoken language with enviable virtuosity. Imagine fifteen-thousand kids mesmerized by a single reader! It was an awesome feeling! Although I must admit, I felt plainly inadequate playing diseuse to hold the audience as they did. I think my voice shook through most of Gina Berriault's *Stone Boy*, although Ben thought I'd done it for effect!

"Sadly, Sunday afternoon was marred by violence initiated by right wing groups whom I'm told, protested my reading from *The Lion, the Witch and the Wardrobe*. It was their contention that I was subverting the Conference by reading the works of a renowned cultist fanatic. When the protesters hurled bottles into the crowd, Palace Security assigned by the Controller's office insisted I depart immediately. I bid Ben a hasty farewell, was whisked off to my private transport, and immediately flown home.

"Earlier this evening, I commed Ben to apologize. He told me that a small riot ensued and about thirty people died. A section of the soccer field bleachers were also set afire, and the Conference deteriorated into bedlam. He assured me that I was not to blame, but that Weeds—there and everywhere—had a long way to go in learning to settle their differences without violence. Ben said that the senseless rioting actually underscored points in our favor. Still I can't help but feel responsible since I knew full well what C.S. Lewis stood for and had hoped that placing the spirit of his work in the consciences of those people might do some good. I guess if I'm going to try to be evangelical, I'll have to do so with greater subtlety."

Anna Maria's faintly daunted image faded from the screen, and the following date appeared in its place.

"I could have told her not to bother." Louisette muttered disdainfully. "You can't play 'goody two-shoes' in the Weeds. Father tried to tell her. I'm amazed she was never killed on her little missionary jaunts!"

Louisette could not help but consider that Anna Maria's own innate selflessness in combination with her embrace of Christian Cult Mythology had, in some way, instilled a puritanical martyr complex which ultimately led her to an early death.

"I had no idea what was really going on in that head of hers." Louisette lamented. "If only I'd known—or if only I'd noticed."

She pointed the remote at the monitor, and this time Anna Maria appeared wearing a large mischievous smile.

"Unbelievable!" Anna Maria laughed. "Simply unbelievable! As I said before, Val and I have been spending a lot of time together over the past few weeks trying to get him to understand the Bible and affect repairs on his unhappiness, so that he can build his 'future'. Well, with uncle gone to tour the Lunar Mares, I figured it was time to give Val a sort of masculine makeover. We flew up to Paris for the day, bought him all new clothes, wiped off the makeup, and fixed his hair in better line with his gender. By noon, Val was an all new boy—or man, as it were! As we walked through le place des Victoires and onto le Champs-Elysees, I dare say that Val, himself, was shocked by the number of favorable female glances he received from all directions. He seemed pleased with himself in a way only men can be. On his own he even developed a sort of swaggered gait that even I found somewhat appealing.

"Well, anyway, the day in Paris went beautifully. But when we landed back in Cannes, Wesley was waiting for me at the Palace gate in a very angry disposition. As it turned out, he and I had an appointment to go over *St. Joan* for the umpteenth time (for his benefit, not mine), which I'd forgotten about. In response to being stood up, he yelled at me like a spoiled child. Rather than listen, I was just going to walk past him and into the Palace when he grabbed me! Well, I didn't have a chance to say two words when all of a sudden, Val, who's much smaller, yanked him by the shirt and punched him square in the nose. Wesley fell to the ground and writhed there like a bug stuck on its back. Finally rolling to his feet, he saw the blood running out of his nose and literally ran home crying for everyone to hear. Val looked down at his swelling knuckle as if he'd discovered some newfound power. It's cruel, I know, but we both began laughing as we walked inside the Palace.

"I think when uncle gets home, he'll see the new Val as a much more valuable page than the old one! We're both looking forward to his return in a few days!"

"Doesn't look like the change stuck very well." Louisette noted as her cousin's recorded image faded. "People can't be changed like that. You are who you are."

Louisette froze on that thought for moment.

"And I am who I am," she said with resignation. "I couldn't change who I am or how I am any more than a shoe can change its length or width. I may wear out and die, but who I am will never change...even if I wanted to."

She looked down at the blusilver vials at her feet, scattered about in the thick white carpeting. Though her body had begged for them hours ago, Anna Maria's diaries had warded her from them.

Louisette pressed the forward button once more. Anna Maria reappeared looking challenged by some new dilemma.

"I used to think people listened to me," she began. "But whenever I even broach the topic of morality, let alone Christian Mythology, I get tuned out like you couldn't imagine. This morning, I was helping Lou get dressed for her trip to some three-day party in Chicago. All she talked about was men, men, men. When I asked her what Victor thought of the trip, she said she hadn't asked him. I asked her if she was hoping to meet someone special, and she laughed and said everyone is special! No matter how I tried to steer the conversation to some rational, moral ideal, Lou managed to deflect it in the direction that suited her, regardless of whether my reasoning was right.

"The same thing happened when I tried to talk to Kima the other day. She said I was speculating on repressive nonsense and should consider talking to her Port counselor. And in class yesterday, we were trying to understand why the characters of ancient literature so painfully lamented infidelity. I stated flatly that it was because the human heart, unlike animals, was designed for monogamous relationships. My classmates laughed and my instructor supported them by stating that humans are just another evolutionary form of animal and carry the same innate urges, which cannot be subdued. He said that ancient literary characters were the product of their cult-suppressed societies, and we, as modern people, should learn from the documented errors of our forefathers.

"It's times like these that I come to appreciate the Son of God and his apostles, who stood against the world, even more. I felt so overwhelmed, that I couldn't even stand up to Lou, Kima or my classmates. Yet if I truly believe as I do, I should be prepared to stand against the world and life itself, if need be. But where do I find the will to stand against my friends and family whom I love so much? Where do I find the will to do what's right?"

The entry ended.

Louisette pushed her fingertips into her temples, again trying to make sense of Anna Maria's logic.

Why was she so bent on going against the grain, she thought, with her eyes shut. We had everything. She, even more so! The most basic principle that even I understand is that whatever most people want is what we all have to live by. You don't turn against what everybody wants! But then, she has this 'God' thing mixed in. If he exists at all, should what he supposedly wants be more important than what people want?

She shook her hair as if to clear her head. With no answers in her, she pressed forward once again.

Anna Maria appeared flush and distraught.

"Bad day today," she spoke in a lightly hoarsed voice. "Uncle Georges came home and made Val change back to the way he was. Worse, Val said he can't study with me anymore. He said whatever I was doing was wonderful, but it simply couldn't be for him. He said that whatever God is, this was the life that had been chosen for him. And he simply couldn't afford to defy uncle—or even his immediate future would be placed in jeopardy.

"I was so angry when I heard this that I skipped afternoon class and stormed into uncle's quarters to have it out with him. I was fully prepared to do whatever it took to vouch for Val's independence and ensure that he also remain with us. Unfortunately, when I got there I found Val and uncle, both nude in each other's arms on the sofa. Uncle fiercely glared at me like he'd never done before. It was plain that he was more furious with me at my intrusion than I had been with him before I entered. He was about to get up when Val started laughing and tugged him by the neck, trying to influence him not to leave. Uncle vacillated, then fanned me away with a hand. As I backed out, Val made eye contact, laughing at me as if I'd never known him.

"Later, in the evening, uncle invited me to sup privately with him. He kindly asked me why I had barged in earlier. I told him I was upset with school. After I manufactured the conversation to support that lie, he asked me why I had tried to change Val. I lied again, and told him simply that we had been playing a game. He accepted these answers as I accepted the guilt for shamefully shunting my beliefs. I ask the Lord's forgiveness, but I'm realizing I'm just not strong enough to bear the burden of his truth alone."

# VI.

The Champion's Quarters:

"Are you sure?!" Kima exclaimed, biting her nails.

"Positive." Victor spoke rigidly, as he sharpened the five-foot lance with his laser welder.

"How can you trust Nikolai?" Kima shouted with her arms spread wide. "He's the most untrustworthy sonovabitch on staff! He's probably warned Georges already!"

"I don't think so." Victor said dryly.

"You don't 'think so'?!" Kima yelled doubtfully. "Why, did he give you his 'word'?"

"No."

"Well I should hope not! Nikolai's 'word' is the soonest promise that you'll have a knife between the shoulders come dusk! How can you trust him?"

Victor turned from his smoldering lance, and with a giant hand, snatched Kima by the jaw with his thick palm smothering her mouth. She punched with futility at his massive forearms, having no effect on his tight grip. Finally she just stood there grimacing painfully into his confident face.

"When you start to whine like Louise," he sneered, "I'm going to treat you like her!"

With a flick of his heavy fingers, Victor sent Kima reeling backward into his video cartridge case, where she fell and slumped down holding her jaw. When she assessed that nothing was broken, she defiantly wrinkled her brows at him.

"That's more like it," he smirked and returned to the sharpening of his lance. "At this very moment, Nikolai is toasting himself to the end of the Earth with a bottle of vodka and some old Siberian love song."

"Are you serious?" Kima asked with skepticism.

"It was a thing of beauty to see that gutless little rattler soaking himself with hopelessness," answered Victor, admiring his work. "He doesn't care what I do! As far as he's concerned, the party is already over."

"That means," Kima spoke, jumping to her feet, "that with the Central Operations staff embroiled in combat with those bird-ship things, we can seize the Beneficent office unopposed."

"Unopposed, uncontested, and upon Georges' mysterious death, undisputed," Victor said confidently. "With all of this turmoil, there won't be time for elections. And when I save the Earth this one last time, elections will be a mere formality."

"What's our plan?" asked Kima, unable to contain her excitement.

"Georges doesn't have any private guards." Victor noted. "He only trusts electronics."

"That makes it easy!" Kima smiled.

"It would, except I don't think Georges trusts me anymore. With the world coming apart, I don't think he'd trust a visit from the Champion at this late date. Given his paranoia, he's sure to think I'd be up to no good, as far as he's concerned."

"So?"

"So I think it would do nicely if you showed up at his door, unarmed." Victor offered.

"Me? We barely speak anymore."

"Great." Victor encouraged. "I'm sure he'd be intrigued to be getting a visit from 'the kid' on 'doomsday'.

"I'm not so sure. He and Val…"

"Fuck Val!" Victor raised his voice.

Kima regarded the irrational outburst oddly, but remained outwardly passive.

"Tell him…" Victor began. "Tell him you have information regarding the death of his niece. That way, our plan won't have to ride on the waning appeal of that withered old body of yours."

"Victor…!" Kima became angered.

"Meanwhile, I'll follow you…armed with this." he held up the sharpened metallic lance. "While Georges is occupied with you, I should be able to gain entry unnoticed."

"How will I know when you're there?" Kima asked suspiciously.

"You'll know. All I'll have to do is disable the security grid protecting his room. Once I'm inside, there won't be any need for stealth or pretense. All I ask is that you stay out of the way!"

"No problem." Kima smiled at him adoringly. "But what do we do then?"

"When?" Victor frowned.

"When you become the Beneficent, silly."

"Oh." Victor smiled.

"I mean, the Earth is being gobbled up as we speak. Your term stands to be the shortest in history unless we can stop the invasion."

"True." Victor looked away. "But first things, first."

"So confident, aren't you?" Kima admired.

"Would you have me any other way?"

"No."

"Good." Victor started toward the door. "But when I'm the Beneficent, we're going to have to get something straightened out."

"What's that?"

"Other women."

Kima chuckled nervously, trying to decipher his meaning from his countenance.

"Well…of course darling," she began. "You can have all you want. I understand."

"I'm not talking about me." Victor exited.

# VII.

Operations:

"Two-point-five billion." Jean-Paul reported from his console. "Estimated."

Manda stood at the center of the hall with her head bowed, too numbed by defeat to respond any longer to the escalating death toll. The Operations center was virtually still with only a third of the staff remaining posted at their terminals. The rest had fled to alleged refuges, imagined to be invulnerable to the inevitable.

On the giant screen, the graphic depictions of the shores of the Earth's continents grew red as the regions of death crept their way inland. Jean-Paul's longitudinal "naked eye" still monitored the alien ships' whereabouts, but the exhausted thermonuclear satellite arrays no longer challenged their lethal strafes across the defenseless world.

"This is ridiculous," Manda whispered.

"What?" Jean-Paul looked up at her.

"This is just so totally ridiculous!" Manda repeated. "The Sun isn't scheduled to burn out for another few hundred million years. We've never even made contact with life from other galaxies or had an inkling that such life even exists. How can the end of the world and an alien invasion come to bear on one single solitary day? And why while I'm alive? Why not fifty years from now? Why not fifty years ago? Why today? Why while I have to stand here and watch it happen?"

Jean-Paul felt a powerful sadness in the pit of his stomach as he watched Manda slowly come unhinged under the strain. She had always been his professional pillar. She was the only reason he had not deserted, as most already had. Unfortunately, the grim realization of humanity's imminent destruction had become too much for even his "pillar" to withstand.

Jean-Paul stood up from his post and slowly walked over to the tall, large boned-woman with the rounded face and the tears in her eyes and gently put his arm around her.

"According to the map, everyone in Phillipsburg, Ohio should be gone by now," she spoke through tightened lips as she tried to stabilize her faltering emotions. "Mom, Todd, Bev…everybody."

"I'm sorry." Jean-Paul rubbed her shoulder.

"It was true about A and me." she spoke of Amritraj. "We had planned to get married in about a month and a half. He was going to move to Cap d' Antibes and start a research firm. We were going to have lots of long-winded, control freak, little kids running around in the sand next to our home by the sea. He loved the thought of kids. He'd lost so many siblings in the Weeds growing up in India, I think he wanted to make up for it by taking special care of his own children. When he died I felt guilty at first. I'd just had another pregnancy removed without telling him. Because I wanted to time everything so perfectly, I thought I'd robbed him of at least having an opportunity to leave something behind that was his. But now…I guess I did us all a favor. Young kids, born into this?"

"It doesn't seem fair, I know." Jean-Paul looked up at the screen. "Suddenly, nothing seems as important as it did. Blossoms, Weeds, wealth, poverty, knowledge, ignorance, freedom, oppression. In the face of oblivion, what does any of it matter now? No one will be left to argue anything. No one will be left to even remember anything. Being so absolutely snuffed out is unimaginable. I'd like to think that someone, somewhere, somehow would show mercy to us."

Manda wiped under her eyes. "But there's no such person, is there?"

Loudly, a shrill siren sounded all around the operations hall. Jean-Paul leaped back to his station and quickly called up information pertaining the disturbance. The entire Palace seemed to shake before he could force the words out.

"We have an exterior breach on the Palace itself!" Jean-Paul yelled as remaining staff members ran for the exits.

"One of those ships?" Manda called.

"No!" Jean-Paul responded. "The nearest alien vessel is still over Turkey. This is something else I've never seen!"

# VIII.

The Beneficent's Quarters:

A light string recital of Tchaikovsky filled the air as Val placed the incense bricks upon the grille over the flaming coals, which sat upon the giant porcelain Buddha's hollowed belly.

"Better," the Beneficent inhaled deeply from his velvet chaise lounge. "Much better."

Val observed the Beneficent empty another bottle of Languedoc into his jeweled chalice, filling it only a third of the way. The old man grunted and snapped his fingers. Val quickly came to his side with a new bottle, which the boy skillfully suctioned open with the electronic cork remover. Val prepared to pour, but the Beneficent snatched the bottle from his hand and filled the chalice himself. Val stepped back nervously uncertain of what to say or do next.

The Beneficent drank deeply from his cup, carelessly letting a portion of the burgundy liquid run down the sides of his neck and onto his hairy gray chest. He closed his eyes, smiled satisfaction, and eased back onto the plushly pillowed lounge to immerse himself in the sounds and smells of his privacy.

Val observed the serene pose with worry and concern. After all, he had heard from every corner of the Palace—with the notable exception of this room—that the world was coming to an end. He shuddered at the notion that in the face of this ultimate disaster, his love and liege had recessed into madness. Yet, before his very eyes, the evidence lay mirthfully conducting an imaginary quartet.

The boy considered sneaking off to Operations to escape the oddly deranged vacuum their quarters had become. Even the hostile dissent of Jean-Paul's aversion to him would be a welcomed interlude of reality at this point. But strangely, more than usual, he feared crossing Victor in the corridors. He sensed that the brutal giant might choose to make short work of his promise to avenge himself, with the future of the very Earth mired in doubt.

So Val optioned to remain at the loyal disposal of the Beneficent. And when he weighed the last three years of his life in earnest, this allegiance still seemed to be owed above all sake of reason.

"Sir," the boy spoke aloud.

The Beneficent's eyes flipped open with an initial horror that suggested someone had detonated a grenade in the heart of the London Symphony. Then he sat up rubbing his eyes. As he rolled over, a near full bottle of Languedoc went crashing to the floor.

"What!?" the Beneficent gathered himself. He looked down at the broken glass and spillage, then up at Val with an accusatory scowl.

"How many times have I said 'no wine for you'?" The Beneficent bellowed.

Val knelt down, daintily picked up bits of glass from under the lounge and placed them in an empty wooden bowl.

"Many times, sir," Val answered submissively. "Though I haven't figured out why."

The Beneficent's face went blank with the notion that he had never imparted his reason for refusing his page drug, smoke or alcohol.

"Umm…" the Beneficent fumbled. "you're…too…too young, that's why."

Val paused momentarily, considering the fact that the older man had never before used this particular reason to excuse any other facet of their relationship. Then quickly, he went on about his work.

"The uh, phosphates from the uh…fermentation process," the Beneficent continued, rubbing his beard, "would umm…paste away your lovely complexion. The um…dyes in the grapes would…um…stain your beautiful white teeth. And I've heard that large consumption often results in…um…incurable bacterial…halitosis."

"Halitosis?" Val quizzed. "Is that fatal?"

"Not so often to the carrier," the Beneficent informed. "But considerably deleterious to the recipient...I've been told. Fortunately, I began my imbibing at a proper age. Therefore, you have nothing to fear."

Val smiled warmly as he stood up, in appreciation for the Beneficent's apparent consideration.

Just then, the door chime sounded.

"Should I answer?" Val offered.

"No need," the Beneficent wearily hoisted himself to his feet. "I'm expecting someone. Why don't you go down to our galley and get something to clean the rest of this up."

"Yes, sir." Val gracefully pirouetted, glided out of the room, and pranced down the back stairs to the galley.

The Beneficent quickly scanned the area, searching for his favorite satin fur collared robe. He cursed that he had let his page go without asking him to find it. The chime rang again and the Beneficent swore into the intercom.

"Excuse me?" returned a voice from outside.

Finally, the Beneficent spotted the robe balled up on the seat of his desk chair. He snatched it up, tied the belt around his waist and made sure everything was in place. When he was prepared, he bid his guest to enter.

Kima's angular figure appeared in the doorway. She wore a black camisole, navy leotard and matching navy ankle boots. Her expression was warm and sympathetic.

"Oh, Georges," she began in a quivering voice. "I don't know how to tell you how sorry I am!"

The Beneficent inspected her with distrust, though he appreciated the preservation of her modest beauty.

Kima moved toward him with her arms open to offer an embrace. But the Beneficent stepped cautiously backward with his hands in his pocket, indicating that he would entertain no such informalities this afternoon.

"What is it, Georges?" Kima asked, as if harmed by his rejection.

"What are you doing here, kid?" The Beneficent asked with a straight face.

"Why, I'm here to offer my condolences," she said innocently. "After all, I was Anna Maria's trainer from the day she moved here. I'm so sorry for you. So sorry for all of us, really."

"Is that so," the Beneficent said, doubtfully.

"Why, yes!" Kima implored convincingly. "Next to yourself and Louise, I was probably closer to her than anyone. And she always spoke so highly of her dear uncle Georges."

"So why are you here?" The Beneficent asked sternly.

"Why…" Kima looked nervously over her shoulder. "Why…to tell you how much she loved you."

"Did someone come with you?" the Beneficent inquired.

"No! I mean, I don't think so," she smiled nervously. "Who would come with me?"

"I don't know, kid," the Beneficent's eyes narrowed. "Nikolai, perhaps?"

"Nikolai!?" Kima exclaimed with earnest surprise. "Why would…"

"You worked for him for several years."

"Yes, I know that. You assigned me! But what would Nikolai be do…"

"Victor called me." the Beneficent smiled ruefully, drawing his hand weapon from his robe. "He told me what the two of you were planning."

The complete realization of horrible betrayal suddenly flashed through Kima's mind.

"Now wait just a minute!" Kima pleaded. "I can't hurt you! I wouldn't! Look: I came completely unarmed!"

"You've killed dozens of men with your bare hands, kid. You're armed."

"Georges, wait! I can explain!"

"Victor explained to me. Nikolai wants my chair. You figured yourself in for a share if you did his handiwork. Well…he's already dead. And you can share in that!"

"Georges, it's not Nikolai!" Kima begged, gesturing forward. "It…"

The Beneficent fired his weapon. Kima loosed a gurgled screamed as her chest cavity exploded and her body flew back against the door. Her dead carcass made a terrible, heavy wet sound as it smacked against the marble floor. He looked over at her still, crumpled frame as it lay contorted, blocking the entrance. It had been a long time since he'd killed anyone. The forgotten sensation of moral justification for such an act left him gratified.

He carefully stepped over the bloodied, supine corpse and prepared to signal members of his security staff to the proud scene. But as he reached up for the button, he felt the Palace jolt! Then a heavy wall of warm humidity dampened his flesh. The floors, ceilings and walls of his quarters creaked eerily with the sound of respiratory expansion and contraction. And quickly, a putrid effluvium of befouled and rotted meat stung his nostrils. The odor reminded him of his visits to the Cult Deprogramization Warehouses with his father half a century ago. But here, in the Palace, in this very room, the stench felt frighteningly ill-born.

The Beneficent turned and met the ghastly, imposing visage of the hideous alien which had appeared atop the craggy stalagmite the day before. It stood in the middle of the chaise lounge from which the Beneficent had just arisen, fabric and down smouldering around its gnarled calves.

"So," the Beneficent swallowed hard and thrust out his chest bravely, "you've finally come."

It made a curious noise, then wrinkled the dead flesh it wore over its face.

"I did not know I was expected." It finally spoke in a heavy gurgled voice.

"Why, yes," the Beneficent confirmed. "I have long pondered the coming of a being such as yourself. One who would bring about great destruction and death to us all. One who would threaten the paradise we have striven to build with our hearts and our hands and our minds…"

"…and your souls?" It interceded.

The Beneficent paused for a moment, always put off by having his lines fed to him.

"Our human spirit," the Beneficent finished.

"Sand." It spoke flatly.

This time, it was the Beneficent's turn to appear puzzled, wondering if he had heard correctly.

"You are, what is known among humans as, bald." It addressed evenly.

Still clutching his weapon with one hand, the Beneficent reached up to touch the front of his scalp with the other. He felt only the thick tuft of grey hair which had been there for as long as he could remember.

"You're mistaken," the Beneficent offered cautiously.

"And you are fat." It added without inflection.

The Beneficent looked down and inspected his flattened stomach.

"I say you're mistaken again."

"And you have no liver." It concluded with an elusive tinge of jocularity.

The Beneficent narrowed his eyes and lifted his chin proudly. "Impossible. I would be dead without one."

It almost appeared to smile at the Beneficent with admonishment for having told some childish lie. Then it moved toward him.

Though the Beneficent lifted his weapon warning it to stand in its place, it continued moving methodically forward.

The Beneficent aimed for its chest and fired true. But the alien continued, unimpeded.

A small fragment of blackened muscle did slip from the minor wound left by the weapon's beam. The muscle fell to the ground, twitched in place and then skittered animatedly toward the Beneficent.

The Beneficent fired his weapon twice more trying to strike the muscle as it bounded toward him. But it moved evasively and in another instant, leapt upon his bare foot and burned its way up his leg in a circular pattern. The muscle disappeared under the Beneficent's silk satin shorts, then reappeared as a lump along his rib cage under his robe. The Beneficent wiggled to drop his robe, but before he could free one arm, the muscle appeared on his wrist and then curled around the weapon.

The Beneficent tossed the weapon to the ground and watched as the muscle sat upon it, then slowly melted it into liquid and absorbed it.

The Beneficent gasped.

"Pour yourself a drink," the alien spoke to him.

The Beneficent looked around for his chalice and saw it sitting on his desk where he'd left it when Kima had rang the chime. He cautiously stepped toward it, continuing fearfully to eye the alien. When he reached the cup, he found that it was empty again.

"I appear to be out." The Beneficent smiled nervously.

"Call the boy." It demanded.

"No." The Beneficent defied, hoping Val would secrete himself in the galley remaining away from harm.

"No matter." It said.

It dug its fingers into its chest, slowly withdrawing a glistening fresh bottle familiarly labeled, and sat it on the desk before the Beneficent.

The Beneficent arched an eyebrow in acknowledgment of it's "slight of hand", then searched for his cork remover.

"Now tell me," It began, "how is it that you are not bald?"

As the Beneficent fumbled around in a desk drawer for the cork remover, he looked up at the alien, curiously insulted by the question. In any other company he could have and would have directly refused to answer. Today, however, he sensed that no such luxury would be afforded.

"I am not bald because I have hair," The Beneficent answered sarcastically.

"On your head?" It returned, in a monotone.

"Yes! Are you blind?" the Beneficent answered with irritation, as he dug deeper into his desk.

"Then that is not true." It responded.

"What do you mean 'not true'?" the Beneficent exclaimed as he pulled on the tuft on his head. "I have hair, understand?"

"You have synthetic follicular replacements." It stated flatly. "You do not have hair."

The Beneficent paused his search and looked up at it. He set his jaw for a moment and then asserted. "For all intents and purposes, I have hair. That it is not 'real' hair is immaterial."

"You are fat." It said as the Beneficent resumed his search for the cork remover.

The Beneficent gave a heavy sigh and noted: "I am not, sir!"

"That is not true." It responded.

"Ah!" the Beneficent noted, finding the cork remover at last. "What are you talking about?"

"You inject large quantities of microscopic parasites to consume your mass." It observed.

The Beneficent sighed heavily again. "True. But the end result is that I do not appear fat and therefore I am not fat!"

"You have no liver." It stated firmly.

The Beneficent looked at the alien and offered an almost conciliatory smile. "Very well. My first liver was so badly...diseased, that there wasn't enough of it salvageable for organ replication. Therefore, I have inside of me an organically engineered sponge, which performs my liver's functions. In fact, I dare say it functions better than my real liver. It's been with me for over twenty-five years and only failed once. I think that I not only do have a liver, but own the best which human technology has to offer."

"Pour yourself a drink." It told the Beneficent.

The Beneficent confidently regarded his frightful visitor, certain that in a battle of words he had firmly established his leverage. Though still, its monstrous visage and nauseating stench were difficult, at best, to grow accustomed to.

The Beneficent took up the wine bottle and inspected it. It was a '58, his favorite vintage, though the last had been made extinct from his private hold for several years. He suctioned the cork from the bottle, and expertly sniffed it with his connoisseur's olfactory senses. The aroma was deep and fruitful as it should have been. He then lifted the bottle to his nose and again noted the refined smell of a painstakingly produced, carefully tended, southern wine.

"Well, I will say this for you," the Beneficent smiled at the alien, "you may not be a thing of beauty, but your distillery skills are...admirable."

"'Beauty' is subjective." It stated flatly.

"Or at least a sign of the times," the Beneficent added. "Given current circumstances, perhaps your look will soon be…in vogue."

The Beneficent slid his wine chalice in front of him, and slowly poured the wine. The liquid splashed into the cup, spilled lightly over the sides and began to sizzle. The Beneficent withdrew the bottle and watched as a hole burned into the ornately carved red wood. Then he noted the stem of his chalice wilting. The jewels on its sides slid away. The very shape of the chalice warped and collapsed within itself until finally, it fell over and burned a larger hole into the center of his desk.

"What the hell did you try to do to me?" The Beneficent recoiled, aghast.

"Drink." It said.

"To hell with you!" the Beneficent shouted, and hurled the bottle at the alien.

The bottle shattered against its body. The shards of glass stuck there for an instant, then were absorbed back into its gnarled, mucousy bosom. The liquid, meanwhile, sizzled against its flesh, then steamed releasing the odor of hydrochloric acid. In another moment the acid evaporated into the air and the area of its disgusting black chest appeared as it had before.

"Why did you not drink?" It asked.

"That was not wine!" the Beneficent shouted.

"Was it not bottled properly?" It asked.

"Yes!" growled the Beneficent.

"Was it not labeled properly?"

"Yes!"

"Was it not corked properly?"

"It was!"

"And did it not smell as rich and full as you desired?"

"It did!"

"Then how could it not be wine?"

"Because it burned through my fucking glass, burned through my fucking desk and is probably burning its way through to the goddamn cellar by now, that's why!" the Beneficent shouted with a stomp of his foot.

"But it did adorn itself as wine, smell as wine, and appear as wine, did it not?" It offered evenly. "Then I submit to you that based upon your assertion of 'truth', that while you are not bald, nor fat, nor without a liver, the substance you rejected was indeed, a bottle of wine. The fact that it burned through the table, melted your chalice, and would have killed you if consumed is, as you say 'immaterial'. That it 'appeared' as wine was sufficient enough to confirm that it was."

The Beneficent fell back in his chair and stared away. He tried to measure the alien's reasoning so he could refute it.

"That was not wine…because wine would not have killed me," he snorted.

"Your follicular replacements do not grow as living hair. The parasites which feast on the yellowed pouches of girth about your stomach are not indigenous to your form, but to the frozen riverbeds of another planet. And your liver…your real liver…was murdered by your alcoholic abuses some time ago. Why then, should we mince words upon a wine which burns the flesh swiftly rather than poisons it over time?"

"What matter of mad reasoning…?" the Beneficent probed impatiently.

"The reasoning of man." It answered.

"What do you know of man?" the Beneficent leaned forward in his chair. "But how to kill him en masse, destroy the edifices of his legacy, and extinguish the bright light he lit upon this planet!"

"I know him well enough." It said definitively. "That is why I do as I do. What do you know of man, that you would contest what has been set upon this day?"

"I know the human heart!" pontificated the Beneficent. "And the human spirit!"

"Spirit?" It questioned. "Then tell me of this 'spirit' I have overlooked."

A wistful glint suddenly rose in the Beneficent's eye. It was as if a distant voice from behind some tall stage curtain or some hovering remote driven camera beckoned him to seize his audience.

King Lear, banished by his daughters to the forest? He thought. Or Captain Phil Lander under siege on the black side of the Moon? Don Quixote in full armor setting proudly upon his ass? Or Ronald Reagan leading his fictitious calvary into the sunset of his California ranch?

The Beneficent gracefully arose from his chair, squared his shoulders, expanded his chest and pulled taut the robe about his frame. He took a moment and paced a half circle around his desk to admire the walls and the furniture and the mirrors and the paintings, as if acquainting himself with these belongings for the first time. Then he stopped, lifted his chin and stared down his nose at the hellish creature which observed him. At this moment, Beneficent Georges Richelieu majestically assumed his lead.

"It was..." he began with a powerful pause, stroking the tip of his beard with an index finger. "...the final session of the Cartel Committee, the year 2092 (an election year I believe). A ragged little man, a self-proclaimed curator of the former Vatican, upheld the Committee session for nearly six hours struggling with mad irreverence against the indomitability of the human spirit. He claimed that man owed his existence to...a higher power. A supreme intelligence. 'God' was the term he used to name the assailant of his own rationality. Between sickly coughing and the quivering of his flailing hands, he pitifully (some say bravely) tried to defend the notion that we were created by his 'God'. And that we lived by his 'God's' grace. And that some day (always in the far-flung future, mind you), we would face this 'God's' judgment. And, among the rattling of golf clubs, the blowing of noses, the murmur of chit-chat and giggles of spouses and concubines, he claimed that how we lived and the faith we carried in our hearts would determine not how we died, but how we would live past death in either a kingdom called Heaven or a torturous sphere called Hell!

"And when this little man was asked to provide us with proof, he fumbled for his dated spectacles and produced a giant volume printed full of sayings and poetry and stories and promises and threats. And he said that this, holding up the oversized book with all of his might, and his heart (which ironically failed within hours), was all the proof he needed. And all the proof any of us should ever need!

"Well, as the shaking, deluded feeb was finally escorted back to his seat, Snake Clinden, the World's very first Beneficent, took the podium. I met him once as a young boy, though he was tragically ravaged by the newest strain of immune deficiency by then. But on this day, he was young, vital, handsome, royal in his manner. And his first words were not spoken derisively, but instead with congenial magnanimity for his aged opponent. He then eloquently stated that the old man had all but proven his point. For how could one so frail, so sick with age and illness, he reasoned, stand before his enemies in the face of certain defeat, if he were not so wonderfully imbued with the power of—not the unseen, unheard 'holy' spirit—but with the human spirit which uplifts us all! How could the old man cling so fruitlessly to his fantasies were he not emboldened by the human spirit which told him never to quit, never to capitulate, never admit...when you're wrong. Surely a 'greater', 'higher' force...a 'God'...would have led him to act more wisely than this. And such a being, if it existed, certainly would have acted on the old man's behalf this day, if no other. But the Vatican curator was abandoned to his own devices. Yes, Beneficent Clinden lauded the old man's human spirit before the entire Cartel Committee, and crushed his opposition with the same motion. Beneficent Clinden then pled clemency for his harmless, clearly disturbed nemesis and motioned that the old man live out his days at the Psychiatry Resort on Banks Island, later to become a renowned cult deprogramization facility. Then the Committee finally took its vote. And on that day, the cults, their symbols, their rituals and their abstract idolatry were censored and abolished—recognized as the greatest single source of criminality against the individual right to freedom and our society's free will!

"And since that time, the arts, the sciences, the philosophies, the political structures of the Earth, the Moon and Mars have flourished triumphantly as never before. Flourished under the guiding hand of the human spirit, no longer encumbered by the guilt of myths. The human spirit no longer held itself accountable to angels and demons and ghosts and gods and all matter of invisible sentient inertias born of the mind's insecurities. Instead, man found himself logical enough to accept the flaws of character born in us all without the indictment of our natures and the insistence that we strive against them. This led us to our true glory!

"And history bears this out. Before man knew civilization, he knew only of the wind, the rain, the hunger in his belly, and the lust in his loins. He cared nothing of gods or cults or immortal souls. His carnal flesh cared only that he found shelter, food and companionship. And from that primal foundation sprang invention. And invention begat technology and technology begat philosophy and civilization. And the glory of man's accomplishments came to such prominence that he soon became master of the wind and the water and the earth which spawned him. He became an explorer, a teacher, and most importantly, determiner of his own fate. He was free!

"But note that dark forces have always worked long hours to manacle the human spirit. The weak and the fearful could not conceive of mankind's preeminence. Like raving mimes, they insisted upon the existence of invisible forces beyond Earth, transcending humanity. And these contrivances took root in man's conscience and shackled his inexorable march forward...with piety. Religion smeared its ranked stench upon every aspect of life. For millenniums, billions of people huddled in their temples and their churches and their mosques trying to exorcise guilt for imagined transgressions and reserve favor in some immortal afterworld. They even warred in murderous hypocrisy over such ideals. Tragically, pleasure and caprice became the enemy of life, rather than its virtue. Wealth became known as 'greed'. Sexual diversity became unlawful 'fornication'. Pride became 'vanity'. And any notion of fact outside the bindings of the 'good book' became heresy.

"It's no coincidence that modern man's blackest, least productive days were during the Middle ages wherein Papal preoccupation summoned

centuries of religious inquisitions, crusades, imprisonments and execu-
tions. And the early twenty-first century wherein religious fervor imposed
punitive sanctions and censorship laws in conjunction with agnostic per-
secutions. The result in both instances was a collapse of art, science, technology, economy, and eventually the human spirit itself. Only the
Renaissance, the most remarkable two and a half centuries of human history, and the Power of Man movement of the late twenty-first century
saved humanity from itself. No penitence. No 'God'. Just flesh and bone
and muscle and compassion and intellect synergized into a single irre-
pressible force: the human spirit!"

The Beneficent clenched his fist, triumphantly accentuating his point.
Then he smiled proudly to himself, satisfied with the foundation upon
which he had constructed his discourse. Acquitted to his own satisfaction,
he again lifted his head and stared confidently into its disfigured features.

There was a silence which followed that made the Beneficent feel
assured that even if he died in the next moment, his convictions would
remain undisputed. He was certain the alien creature was far too outdone
to offer argument about "man" in man's arena.

Finally, its mouth puckered and twitched.

"Sand," was the single word it chose to utter.

The Beneficent squinted as if he had caught the glimpse of a mirage.
The word appeared out of context—he could not fathom its relevance.
But before he could request a clarification, it began speaking once more.

"You said you had long pondered the coming of one such as I?" It
questioned.

The Beneficent reached back into their earlier conversation and
recalled having said it.

"Yes," he answered cautiously.

"Why?" It requested.

The Beneficent weighed the question as he played with the ends of his
mustache. Was it that he had always been inwardly fatalistic? Or had
something else planted the seed of foreshadowing doubt over his belief

that the new free world would endure for all time. He sat down for a moment and considered that the true source of his fears would instantly overturn him into a hypocrite before this alien's very eyes. He considered a lie, but refused to fall prey to a lie's entrapment in the face of death. Resolved to whatever fate the truth would bring, he slid open his desk drawer and pulled out the old relic text he had shared with Victor the day before. Hoping the alien would not make the immediate connection between it and the religions he had condemned, he displayed it openly for the alien's perusal.

"Here," the Beneficent spoke resignedly. "It's written here."

The alien paused again as its moist red eyes slid slowly back and forth. Then it's mouth moved again.

"You professed to believe none of this," It began, "yet you truly believe all of it."

The Beneficent felt his blood pressure rise in the sides of his neck. Since no one in this century would ever have brought him to task on this point, he had never prepared to defend it—other than in his own mind. But now he would have to explain himself plainly.

"Not so." He asserted with less conviction than earlier. "This...this book is an effrontery...a sourcebook on the very dismantling of human civilization. It's at the very heart of everything that nearly destroyed us."

"You have read it?" the alien asked.

"I have indeed," the Beneficent answered.

"Then you don't believe in God?"

"I've already answered that!" the Beneficent defended.

"Yet you believe in the Judgment." it observed.

"Not...so." the Beneficent hesitated. "Not really. No wait. I believe...that what is written here may be meant to be true by some malevolent propagandist force who stands opposed to humanity. I believe that for the people who wrote it to have believed what they wrote, that they may have been...manipulated somehow."

"By whom?"

"I don't know! Aliens like yourself! Something we've never seen! Or..."

"God perhaps."

The Beneficent frowned at the inference of his own belief in that entity.

"Not God," the Beneficent spoke.

"Why?"

The Beneficent pushed back his hair and rubbed his neck: "Because...God is something we have never seen. It's foolish and mentally unfit for humans to fear something whose existence cannot be verified."

"Yet you believe in the Judgment."

"I believed that something was going to happen, yes!"

"But herein, it says that the Judgment would be brought about by God. How can you separate the two?"

"I can't."

"Then you must also believe in God."

"No!" the Beneficent shouted. "I've read this damnable thing cover to cover, time and again, and I will never embrace the will he thrusts upon us!"

"Who?"

"God, goddamn you!" the Beneficent yelled before he could measure his words.

"I am confused." it said evenly.

"I'm not surprised," the Beneficent spoke, wearily besieged.

"How can something you do not believe exists, 'thrust' anything upon you?"

The Beneficent dropped heavily into his desk chair and covered his face. Behind his hands he tried to discern an alternate path along a road which had no turns. Disparately, he dragged his hands away from his face and looked up into the alien's eyes.

"I believe that God exists," he confessed in a barely audible tone. "I simply do not believe IN God. He made this world a paradise. Yet he made man incompatible with it. He gave us free will, yet made us choose poorly. He gave us pleasures and desires, yet made them the source of our own undoing. And then he gave us these rules which made us reject ourselves…reject our very natures! And for what? The promise of life after life? What about life here on Earth, today? God created us in his own image, yet like some jealous father, he seeks to truss his children with the swathing of rules and laws that sap the very joy of life. If you know anything of our world, you know the misery religion brought with it! Persecution! Repression! Censorship! Spiritual stagnation! A veritable pestilence for the human spirit! And for what? The sake of his 'glory'? The unverifiable promise of eternal life?

"God says we must quell our own freedom while we live. What horrors we should see if man should ever enjoy freedom of mind and body. He would have us live as Tantalus, bound to the wheel, never to sup on the pleasures of life. But you see, life's pleasure is what man really wants! Not some fantastic journey to some translucent kingdom! Freedom! The most powerful revered word in the human vernacular! The pursuit of freedom is the most impassioned quest upon which man has ever embarked. And in spite of 'God's will', we stand closer to that pinnacle today than thousands of generations ever hoped to! The summit of man's glory! And while I knew, one day he or you or someone like you would come, I made a choice; we made a choice: God be damned! Let man have his day!"

"And what of truth?" It asked. "You espouse one belief yet harbor another."

The Beneficent stood and began pacing again.

"Truth," he said bitterly. "God would have us believe that there is a truth. But the fact of the matter is, that man's truth is whatever he is made to believe. In the Weeds, their truth is that they believe they are impoverished slum dwellers by nature and that no one should take that right from them. In the Blossoms, everyone believes that they are entitled to privilege by their birthrights and do so with a clear conscience. The result is an economically balanced and contented society where everyone is free. And the common belief that religious cult practices stand in opposition to the doctrines of man is also a truth, because that is what everyone believes. The only truth man can ever know is that which he perceives to be true. No more. And those of us who…shape and maintain perceptions are, in a way, the guardians of truth. Truth which ensures the maintenance of our liberties. Nothing else can be tantamount to that!"

The blackened fused muscles of the alien seemed to shift and slide in and out of their lodgings upon the hearing of this. The Beneficent considered it an adverse reaction, which he hoped indicated a strike in his favor.

"Sand," however, was the only retort it considered appropriate.

"Sand!?" the Beneficent scowled in exasperation. "Sand!? What kind of answer is that? How should I know what the hell that means?"

Its eyes filled with more blood until the orbs were bright scarlet. Then the jagged mouth lifted into what almost resembled a frightening jack-o-lantern grin.

"Sand." it repeated. "I would have expected you of all your people to understand its meaning. For I quoth as it was spoken to the denizens of this planet millennia ago: '…*whosoever heareth these sayings of mine, and doeth them, I will liken him unto a wise man, which built his house upon a rock: And the rain descended and the floods came, and the winds blew, and beat upon that house and it fell not; for it was founded upon a rock. And every one that heareth these sayings of mine, and doeth them not, shall be likened unto a foolish man, which built his house upon the* **sand:** *And the rain descended, and the floods came, and the winds blew, and beat upon that house; and it fell: and great was the fall of it.'*.'"

The Beneficent stood in horror as he mouthed the words as the alien quoted them.

"I fear," it spoke with faint sentiment, "that mankind has built his house upon a great dune, that shifts, ebbs, and dissipates upon the ficklest breeze. In gentler climate, this sufficed well enough. But now the rain has come, the flood draws nigh, and the wind is pounding on man's front door. And the loose-grained foundation upon which man has chosen to stake his soul is washing swiftly into oblivion. And great shall be mankind's fall!"

The Beneficent fearfully stepped backward. There was nothing more that could be said. The alien slowly moved toward him. The Beneficent broke into a run, and bolted for the door.

Surprisingly, Kima's body blocked the exit, positioned differently than he recalled. He hastily strained to move it out of the way, but the alien was upon him.

Cornered, the Beneficent swiftly dropped to his knees.

"Lord, forgive us!" he shouted desperately. "We know not what we…"

It reached down with its black, fleshless fingers and clutched the Beneficent by the forehead. It lifted him to his feet as the king of all men begged pitifully for his fragile life. Its fingers slowly began digging and burning into the Beneficent's face. All at once the man's body went limp. A pulse of energy ran down the alien's arm, into its hand and through its victim's head. The Beneficent's limbs became animate for a moment with the jerk and rigidity of involuntary movement. Then finally, the contents of his skull spewed from the orifices of his head. And with a careless motion, the alien flung the Beneficent's dead carcass sliding bloodily across the floor.

The room fell terribly silent save for the perpetual moist lurching and writhing of the alien's metamorphisized structure. It scanned the doorway and then the water cushioned sofa. Then, a faint, shivering sob was heard. And it slowly moved toward the tall balcony draperies.

A sheer white curtain wafted gently with the soft afternoon breeze. And as it filled with air, and settled back to the floor, the shaking, huddled form of Val revealed its impression.

It moved the curtain aside. Val yelped in trembling shock as he felt its heavy, humid aura coat his chilled flesh. The boy, however, remained kneeling, his hands clasped together; his eyes tightly shut…with the whisper of a prayer falling from his shivering lips.

It regarded the boy for several moments.

Val reached as far out of his own heart as he could manage, becoming almost oblivious to the pendulum of the alien's smoldering hot presence as it hovered over his bare shoulders. He felt the rings on his fingers pinch crevices into his hands. His eyes ached as they pushed back into their sockets. His chin mashed into the necklaces on his naked chest. And his bare knees became sweated against the cold marble floor. He felt every tensed muscle painlessly grow numb with conviction. And suddenly, an amazing assuredness whisked the fear out of his soul.

He swallowed hard, and a sharp pain filled his skull and his arms. A cooling breeze through the balcony doorway tickled his soft skin. Then he felt the silk curtain settle gently back upon him. He opened his eyes as he inhaled the air. The vile odor of the hideous alien had begun to dissipate. In a single motion, he hopped onto his feet and pushed the curtain aside.

The creature had gone.

Val loosed a heavy sigh which was the first breath he recounted in the past several tumultuous minutes. Then grief abruptly struck him.

He ran over to where the Beneficent's dead body lay, bloodily defiled. The man's face was twisted and disfigured into a portrait of the horror in which he had died. Brain matter stained his mouth, ears, nose, and empty eye sockets. The boy collapsed to his knees and wept sorrowfully over the only adult who had ever given him affection. For all of the old man's faults which he had come to know well, the Beneficent had been everything to Val another human being could be.

"Bonsoir, mon jeune fille."

Fear jolted Val's heart as he felt Victor's steely vice grip snatch the necklaces tightly around his neck before he could turn.

The Champion jerked him from the Beneficent's body and held him high off of his feet, facing the ceiling, with one hand.

"I always said it would kill him," Victor mockingly lamented, "if he ever tried to spread his brains around."

Val tried to scream, but the sound was squelched by taught jewelry that began to cut into his throat. The boy squirmed and twisted until he was finally able to kick backward marking Victor's expansive chest with the pointed heel of his shoe.

Victor snarled as the playfulness in his eyes flashed to hatred. And he reached back with his fist and smashed the side of Val's rib cage, which shattered and buckled with the echoing sound of splintering wood. Val's flowered pumps slipped from his feet and clattered to the floor. The boy choked and gurgled blood as the Champion held him still.

"Aw, pardon, mademoiselle." Victor chuckled. "I never hit a girl…with my fist before. But then, you're not a girl are you? I mean you smell like a girl. And you talk like a girl. And you even walk like a girl!"

Victor flipped Val over in the air and caught him by the ankle. Val cried out hysterically.

"I always hated that prima ballerina walk!" Victor spoke viciously. "Always fooled the shit out of me from behind!"

The Champion rifled a quick chop to Val's shin and the leg bone snapped and tore through the skin.

"No more of that walk, mon jeune fille!" Victor smiled as he dropped the boy to the ground, convulsing and semi-conscious.

"Have you ever studied much history, mademoiselle or whatever the fuck you think you are?" Victor spoke hatefully, as he walked over to the porcelain Buddha. "Well, about a thousand years ago or so, they had an interesting way of dealing with confused sorts like yourself."

Victor picked up the tongs by the sculpture's feet and began rustling the coals beneath the incense.

"And you'll be happy to know," Victor continued, "that it leaves the outer flesh perfectly intact."

The Champion carefully removed a sizzling orange stone from the base of the fire.

"And I know that it was always important for you and Georges," Victor spoke coldly, "that you always looked your best."

Victor walked slowly toward Val's prone figure which still quivered and twitched with unconscious pain.

The Champion knelt down to the boy's body and strangely petted the back of his neck. Then, he savagely jerked away the boy's hip cloth, revealing

Val's bare buttocks. Victor carefully spread the boy's hind appendages with his fingers, then cruelly jammed the hot coal into Val's rectum.

Val loosed a searing, anguished squeal that shook even Victor's sensibilities. The boy's body began to spasm as his shrieks of agony became ear piercing.

Victor stood over him waiting for the disturbing movements to cease. But it seemed to go on forever until he felt his stomach begin to turn. Finally, he pinned Val's torso with his foot— and with his other, stomped down, crushing the boy's throat with the heel of his boot.

Victor tried to smile, but the emotion to do so was too far recessed.

He picked up the tongs and walked back over to the Buddha. He placed the tongs into the fire until he was certain the metal was hot enough. Then he closed his eyes and began scarring his forearm with burn marks. When he was finished, he appeared to have been in a severe confrontation.

Wincing, he walked over to the comm on the wall and flicked on the switch.

"Operations," he spoke with labored breath. "I'm in the Beneficent's quarters. Something…really awful just happened. I was too late to save them."

# IX.

Anna Maria's room:

"Victor is so sweet!" Anna Maria fawned in her latest diary entry. "We were all gathered in the main dining hall tonight when he arose from his chair and started reciting one of the poems I'd recently had published. This one was specifically entitled 'The Matter of Love', wherein I describe that no matter how some of us try to avoid it, love becomes a 'matter' we must all come to terms with. He even added a satirized verse of his own, which made everyone laugh except Lou. Then he suddenly dropped to one knee and brashly entreated Lou to marry him! With that, she blushed, unable to contain her joy! It was so wonderful to see, because Victor is such a wonderful man! And Lou needs someone like him, I think, to give her a better footing on life. I pray that their love lasts all their lives. And I hope that I'm, someday, so fortunate!"

The entry faded. Louisette blinked back tears. She remembered that evening with distinct clarity. Earlier that day, she had stumbled upon her former best friend, Mary Renee, sneaking out of Victor's room. She confronted Victor with the accusation of infidelity, which he denied and they argued fiercely. By evening, Louisette was certain that their courtship had become unsalvageable. Then, out of nowhere, in front of everyone, came his unexpected proposal. It was the happiest day she could remember.

Little did she know then, that it was part of an "arrangement" her father had made and that Victor was dutifully fulfilling his part in a reluctant obligation. This clearly explained why Victor bristled with irritation on the mention of their marriage thereafter.

Not that she, herself really "cared" for the Champion, she thought. She regarded him mostly as bestial, crude and boorish—but he was a prize by his very station. Living at the very pinnacle of human society required her to have him so that no other woman could. And this required the endurance of all measure of physical torment, humiliation and discontent to make him love her. Reflection upon this added insult to her injuries in that her father still had to clandestinely intercede on her behalf.

She thumbed the forward button on the remote, not wanting to dwell on the matter any further. A groggy, sleepy-eyed Anna Maria appeared on the screen.

"Just got back from Lou's." she yawned, looking at her thin gold watch. "It's four-twenty-three in the morning. We kind of ran into each other in the hallway as she was returning from celebrating her engagement. She seems so happy! Anyway, we sat up in her room and got on about her favorite topic: men! Now I admit, she and I have always had our differences about the nature of what relationships should be. She feels that 'variety is the spice of life' while I prefer to believe that a romance should last a lifetime. But still, her experience with men makes her something of a connoisseur in that area. And I have to admit that with the exception of being around boys like Wesley, or adult friends of uncle Georges, my personal experience is limited.

"She let me sneak my first glass of wine and we talked for hours. Or I should say Lou talked for hours. It seemed every time I offered some pointed observation of my own, Lou quickly laid bare my 'naiveté' with some personal anecdote from her past. She did, however, she talked about how men assert dominant postures to cover up their own insecurities. She said that if men did not have women to give them confidence, they would have no confidence at all. She talked about how Auntie Dee had taught her that a woman's role in a relationship may seem secondary, but is in actuality the support of its entire framework. She noted that men may have destinies, but only women can give those destinies meaning. She laughed when she touched on the notion that men like to think of themselves as great predators, giant cats prowling the plains for their prey—yet in truth, no woman who does not wish to be captured can be. And that while men may be the giant cats hunting and chasing, women are like the concealed snare waiting patiently in coyish brush, to gobble up the suitable victim which stumbles upon her.

"We did get into one area where I feel I struck a valid point, though Lou would not concede. It had to do with people misusing sex as they misuse drugs. That is, drugs were invented to heal illnesses and put the body back in equilibrium. But somehow, people have twisted their use into something recreational just so they can get high, be happy and divorce equilibrium. In the short run, there's nothing wrong with being high and happy, I guess. Especially if you have the means to ensure that the cycle of drug misuse is continuous. But eventually, since we're all just sacks of chemicals ourselves, the preponderance of drug misuse eventually leads to a spiraling set of physiological dysfunctions which invariably lead to premature disablement or even death.

"And such is the case, I feel, with sex. I mean, I'm not so boorish, as many cult leaders have been, to believe that sex is meant purely for reproduction. But I can't help believing that it is something God meant for two people to share as an expression of their love and commitment to each other. I mean, when two people who aren't in love have it off with one another, they're just indulging their sexual infirmity for the sheer joy of getting off on a powerful rush. But when the rush is ended, what do they really have besides crusty private hair and no promise that the person with whom they've shared this experience will ever lay with them again? You've given up your body and emotions and have nothing to show for it. You may even get angry at yourself for having felt something for this other person who used you as a faceless thing. The result is then, that the next time you have it off, you try to harden yourself emotionally so that you don't feel anything for that person you're using. And where does love fit in? It doesn't. It becomes abstract and obscure. Everyone becomes emotionally dysfunctional, uncertain of how to express love because they've always used sex as a selfish means to get themselves high. My point being, sex used properly can save a person's life. But sex, misused, can only create long term confusion, distress and sadness.

"Of course, Lou shook her head and dismissed my thoughts, saying that before I declare myself an expert on drugs and sex, I should try them first.

"This led to her getting into some very gross detail regarding physical things. Some of it was actually very funny, though! In fact, my face hurts from laughing so hard! I think it was the wine. But I never knew there were so many vulgar ways to discuss…sex. And Lou seemed to thrive on it. As if it were the most joyous aspect of her life! All these partners and positions and sizes and aphro-somethings. It was amazing! But not for me, I think.

"I still just want that one…perfect man…wherever he is. So that we can grow together forever until we're swept off the Earth by the hand of God. That's what I really want. I mean…as joyous and wonderful and exciting as sex must be, I can't believe that the creator of the entire universe meant for something so physically and spiritually powerful to be used simply as…a mere toy for our amusement. It must be cherished. And strength must be exercised in our willingness to abstain from its abuse rather than to wallow in our gratuitous self-indulgence! It has to be more…rewarding than a slap on the rear in the morning and a kiss good-bye."

Anna Maria yawned, closing her eyes and winding her neck. "Sometimes I wish I were Lou, though. So free. So beautiful. So without a care. Then I'd have Victor, too."

With a heavy sigh, Anna Maria's image faded.

Louisette frowned.

"'One perfect man'." she muttered. "I'll be damned if there is such a thing. I wonder if her 'God' told her there was. If he did, I wish she'd have told me how to find that needle in the haystack. Because that's what it must be. Even Victor was just another handsome straw. A cold, mean-spirited animal…like all of them. Why didn't I warn her?"

Louisette skipped through entries discussing Anna Maria's vacation, Wesley, her *St. Joan* performance, and her preparation for a presentation to the Cartel Committee. None of it mattered as much as those entries which led her cousin to her fateful meeting with the Champion. She set the monitor into search mode until Victor's name was mentioned again.

The date displayed itself, and Louisette pressed "forward".

"Lou and Victor had another fight in the corridor." Anna Maria began with dismay. "From what I could overhear, it sounded as though Lou had gotten pregnant again and was pressing for a wedding date. They were both very angry and Victor stormed away leaving Lou slumped against the wall in tears. I wanted to help Lou somehow, but I had the feeling that she'd tell me to get lost and that I couldn't understand what she was going through. Sadly, I know it's not for me to say, but she seems to be smothering him as if she's afraid he'll get away, or something. If this continues, she may be right."

The girl's image faded.

Louisette could not even recall which argument the diary referenced, there had been so many. The date, however, was from two months ago—very close to the time Anna Maria had hinted her "passing" interest in Victor.

She scanned for Victor's name again. And it appeared in a week's time.

"I've done some serious thinking." Anna Maria sat on her bed, with her legs pretzeled into a yoga position. "I've done some rereading of the Holy Bible and have noted that probably the most pivotal individual in the entire New Testament, as it's called, (aside from the Son of God) was Saul—or Paul, as he came to be known. In one great miraculous turn, he went from being a religious persecutor to the greatest Christian apostle of them all! No pun intended, but all he needed was to be made to see. And when his sight was returned to him, he became truth's greatest champion. I know that I can't be that person in this 22nd century. But when I think about it, I know there's one who can: Victor!"

"Oh shit!" Louisette exclaimed, loudly. "No, no, no."

"Victor is the key to the world's salvation." Anna Maria heartily proclaimed. "I've studied his extraordinary life for nearly two years. He's noble, loving, caring, charismatic and adored by everyone on the Earth, Moon and Mars. He's also powerful, indomitable, and a force that must be reckoned with. If Victor were made to understand things as I do, no one would dare question him. And everyone would scramble to bask in his illumination. It would be wonderful! Like nothing the Earth has ever seen.

"Now, of course, I know that this sounds like some incredible world-shattering undertaking for a small girl. But I hearken back to St. Joan, Joan D'Arc, a farm girl from a tiny corner of a war-ravaged nation, importuning Charles VII to rise up from the Chinon and set the world aright in the name of God! And as the English were driven to Calais and eventually back into the channel, so too shall iniquity and reprobacy be driven from the hearts of humanity by the Champion. The sadness and confusion of our lost souls will be steered back toward the warm bosom of righteousness. And Victor, like Paul, will herald the most wondrous age for which we could ever hope. An age of true love, rather than one which we try to fabricate with our words and bodies. An age of truth, where free will will be exercised for the all rather than the self. And wherein we can ultimately transcend the limitations of our flesh and blood, and know the truth and beauty of eternal life with God in Heaven.

"I'm pretty sure he's attracted to me. According to Lou, that shouldn't hurt. In fact, a tad of feminine charm should make him much more receptive to what I have to say. And I'll make it so wondrously clear, he'll never even know what hit him!

"With God's grace, I know this may be done. I pray that I'm strong enough to bring his word to light."

Anna Maria's emboldened image faded.

"Why?" Louisette slumped down. "Why didn't she confide in me? I could have told her about him. Warned her…"

Then all of a sudden, Louisette recalled all of the times Anna Maria had tried to confide in her. All of the times she had been off to one party or another, too high upon the crest of a blusilver wave to be dragged down into conversations which gnawed at her inviolable conscience.

# What is Real

The Beneficent's Quarters:

"What did you say happened again?" Jean-Paul questioned as he, Dr. Canard, and a handful of security people from the Controller's office sifted through the sickening abattoir of fresh death which had once housed the most powerful human in the universe.

"Don't crowd me, little man." Victor sneered as Dr. Canard sprayed and wrapped the Champion's injured forearm.

"I don't mean to." Jean-Paul responded with restraint. "It's just that you seem to have gotten away rather easily considering the degree of carnage in this room."

"I said, don't crowd me!" Victor shouted, clenching his good fist.

Everyone in the room halted their investigations momentarily and noted the Champion glaring angrily at Jean-Paul, as Dr. Canard ceased his ministrations.

Victor folded his bottom lip and observed everyone staring at him out of the corner of his eye. Abruptly, his features softened. Then, he rubbed his eyes despondently with his large fingers. "I loved everybody in this room who died tonight!" He spoke in a choked baritone. "Georges…was like a father to me. He helped me find myself…helped me become who and what I am. If it weren't for him, I don't know where I'd be—probably some common professional athlete wasting his talent performing in front of satellite crowds.

"Kima was like…a big sister. Always pushing me to be better than I already was. She's the greatest trainer I ever had. And more importantly, she was a good friend.

"And Val…poor sweet boy. If I'd had a little brother, I'd have wanted him to be like Val. So…tender and full of life. So fun to…tease and…joke with."

Jean-Paul endured the mendaciously mechanical eulogies. Insiders regarded Victor's relationship with the Beneficent as tenuously professional at best, both men symbiotically gleaning stature from the other's popularity. His affair with Kima was also well known to all except Louisette who chose either to accept it or ignore it. And Val. Victor plainly wore his scathing hatred for the young page inside Palace walls. It was rumored that Val had once played some unforgivable prank on Victor—a prank centered upon the boy's frequent transvestitism. But no one was ever certain of the facts.

"I understand how you must be feeling." Jean-Paul offered. "But…we really need to know what happened."

The Champion took a deep breath, then mopped his brow with his bandaged forearm. He looked around the room again and, with a single gaze, ordered all of the security people to carry on with their work. Then he spoke privately to Jean-Paul and Dr. Canard.

"Kima and I had stumbled upon a plot by Nikolai to assassinate Georges and seize armed control of the Palace and Operations." Victor began in a grave tone. "I sent Kima to warn Georges, while I dealt with Nikolai directly."

"We saw." Dr. Canard confirmed dryly. "We found him with his face smashed through the center of his desk."

"Nikolai was not one to whom a smart man shows mercy." Victor spoke assuredly. "Anyway, I arrive here and outside the door, I could hear the Beneficent bravely fighting for his life. I tripped the door electronically…god, it seemed like it took hours…and when I finally entered…! Well, Kima and Val were already dead. The Beneficent was in the clutches of that thing we saw on top of the spire after the crater explosion yesterday. I dove at it, trying to break its hold on poor Georges, but it grabbed me by my arm, burned me like you wouldn't believe, and knocked me back against the door where I almost blacked out. In a blur I saw it toss Georges to the ground. It must've seen me jump to my feet, because it bolted for the balcony window and flew out before I could reach it! I really owe that thing for the three lives it's left on my conscience! I was too late to save them!"

Without a word, Dr. Canard turned and quietly returned to his work of assessing the causes of death. Jean-Paul looked up into the Champion's face, trying to conceal his seething doubt.

"Merci, Victor." Jean-Paul spoke stiffly. "I have to report this to Manda. Technically, she's in charge now."

The Champion's eyes hardened for an instant, then melted to a surly calm.

"No need." Victor said evenly. "I'd like to have a talk with her anyway. I'll break the bad news to her in person."

Alarm struck Jean-Paul's innards. He suddenly feared for Manda's safety.

"All right." Jean-Paul replied, poker-faced. "I'll…let her know you're coming."

Jean-Paul held up his private communicator and smiled benignly.

"You do that." Victor tried to smile back as he exited the room.

Jean-Paul quickly turned to punch up Manda's comm number on his communicator. Dr. Canard, however, delayed him momentarily.

"Got a minute?" the doctor said insistently.

"Sure." Jean-Paul responded, placing his communicator on hold.

"You buy any of that?" the doctor asked with sarcastic skepticism.

"Well.." Jean-Paul hedged, "we don't exactly know what we're dealing with yet."

"True. But while I'm a doctor rather than a detective, it doesn't take Snoopy Glover to figure out that these three people were killed in three distinctly different manners."

Dr. Canard flipped open his medical palm imager. A multicolored, three-dimensional image of a damaged torso appeared above its miniature voice receiver.

"Note." Dr. Canard addressed the grim portrait. "Kima's chest. Sternum split wide open by the shrapnel of a single, bud-nosed shell. Not the cleanest kill, but quick and probably painless.

"Now, look at Georges!" The image shifted into a rotating schematic of the Beneficent's skull. "A pressurized build-up at the heart of the cerebral cortex blew the brain right off its stem, yet with minimal damage to the inside of the case. Not even a surgically-implanted, molecularly engineered explosive used by the Controller's office works that neatly. I'd wager the alien did that.

"But this…" Dr. Canard loudly slapped his medical instrument closed and turned to observe Val's mutilated corpse. "In all my years… It's like the twentieth century war atrocities you used to read about from the old Middle East or Vietnam. Brutal. Sadistic. Angry—but clearly justified in the perpetrator's mind. And I don't think I have to tell you who can and has carried out this kind of handiwork."

Jean-Paul stared down as two security men rolled Val's remains into a mortuary sack. Clearly, the motives and the modus operandi seemed to be in conflict for a single assailant.

"No." his nostrils flared. "You don't. But, unfortunately, the worlds' coming to an end. I don't think a murder trial at this juncture is going to do anyone any good."

"So we just let him walk away?" Dr. Canard exclaimed with a wildly arched eyebrow.

"Why not? The spotlight for mankind is getting smaller by the minute. Soon, even Victor won't have a place to stand. I fear that's the only justice we may be able to count on."

Jean-Paul punched on his communicator to warn Manda.

Dr. Canard tagged the autopsies to be performed tomorrow.

# II.

Bogalusa, Louisiana:

"Satellite signal splice overlay in ten seconds!"

"This is really going to piss off the networks, Pervis."

"Let'em piss! They can't stand in the way a' prosperity, ma' brothers." Pervis Puritan matted down his oily hair one last time. "Om'll die a rich man yet, ya'll watch!"

"Five...four...three...two..."

"Jayyyyzusss!" Pervis screamed into the camera lens. "That's right! Jayzus! Now ya'll know I'm takin' mah very life inta' jayperdy by even spakin' the name a' Jayzus! Aww, but the Baynefisaint says that man has all the answers ta' all our problems. The Baynefisaint says that them satlats was our kay ta' salvation! The Baynefisaint says that the Champeen was our kay ta' salvation! The Baynefisaint says that all we gots ta' do is set in our backyards barbecuin' while the whole dang world's comin' to an end! Well let me tell ya'll sumpin': The onliest way ta' your salvation ta' day my friends, is ta' come ta' Jayzus right now and in a hurra'!

"The satlats done failed! The Champeen ain't nowheres ta' be fount! An' om'll tell ya'll yer friends an' naybers all ova' this great planet a' ours is disappearin' by the barnyards fulls! Om'll tell ya'll that on this dark day a' the lord's reckonin", the onliest way any ya'll gonna' fand salvation is ta' come ta' Jayzus right this minnit!

"Now I know some a' ya'lls is sayin' 'what is Jayzus?' 'How can I get me some a' this Jayzus?' Well, I'm here ta' tell ya' that he, she, or it is the greatest powr in the uny-verse! An' the onliest way ya' gonna' s'vive this world is ta' come ta' Jayzus through me!

"Now I know some a' ya'lls is sayin' 'who is this guy?' 'How can 'e do this?' Well, my brothas an' sisters, whiles ya'lls was goin' the way a' sin, I was talkin' ta' Jayzus. Whiles ya'll was kissin' up ta the Baynefisaint, I was kissin' up ta' Jayzus! Whiles ya'll was throwin' ya'lls money inta' them syco ports, I was throwin' my money ta' Jayzus! An' whiles ya'll was suckin' and fuckin' each otha', havin' a good 'ol tam, I was suckin' and fuckin' Jayzus, know what I mean?

"Now the tam has come, an' me an' Jayzus is fittin' ta' light outta' here! So the question I gots ta' ax myself if I's you is, 'how is I gonna' get out this world with ol' Jayzus an' Pervis Puritan?' 'How is I gonna' miss gettin' ate up by them craychures out there?' Now I could tell ya'll ta' turn ta' scriptcha', but I git the impression that they jus' ain't manna' Bybos out there! But there's still a' chance for those a' ya'll with healthy credit! All ya' got ta' do is comm in yer bank credit numbas, and I can guarantee ya'll a seat right next ta' me and Jayzus on the transport ta' salvation!

"Now what'cha' waitin' for? Ya'lls brothas an' sisters what been ate up by them craychures would'a hopped at the chance ta' save there souls. Now you can! Jus' leave yer bank numba', yer name, yer address, an' yer bank numba' an' anything you want us ta' have, plus yer bank numba' an' Jayzus will be at yer doorstoop, ready ta' take ya'll way from all this misery!

"Now I want all ya'll ta' start sangin' whiles ya' dial this numba' on ya' screens:

Amayyyyyzin grayyyyyz, hmmm hmmm, hmmm hmmm. Hmmm hmmm huhhhh huhhhhh... C'mon, you ain't got ta' know the wordzzz!"

Off camera, the communications junction panel was flurried with droves of desperate calls from the dwindling populaces all over the world. Within mere minutes of pirating the world news satellite signal, Pervis Puritan alias Melvin Johnson, former bootleg heroine merchant, former escort service agent, former political campaign chairman, and most recently an aging New Orleans Weed street hustler, was finally becoming a very wealthy man.

"Yeah, but where's he gonna' spend it all?" Mark spoke as he swung the camera to and fro, frantically keeping pace with Pervis' demonstrative gesticulations.

"Maybe its 'cash only' in the hereafter." Luke joked as he monitored the names and bank numbers as they scrolled across his computer screen. "All I know is that Pervis had it figured that if one tenth of one percent of the people scared out of their wits responded with donations we'd all be filthy rich by sunrise."

"Now the trick is to make it to sunrise," said Mark with his eyes bobbing up and down in the viewfinder.

"You're not really worried about those disappearance reports, are you?" Luke poked at his partner.

"Aren't you?"

"Not a chance. Pervis figures it's some kind of hoax being used by the Beneficent to make himself look like a better leader. You know, like when certain leaders used to pretend there was a threat when there wasn't one. They'd 'crush' the non-existent threat, the media would make it look like the fall of Rome, and that leader becomes a hero—when he actually set up the whole thing."

"You think?"

"Sure. Pervis was in politics for years. Hell, he single-handedly got the Beneficent's autistic brother elected governor of North America. You think he'd go to all this trouble if he didn't think he'd see any of this money?"

"Luke," came a woman's voice from the barn door leading into the makeshift studio.

A tall, naked, young blonde woman stood in the doorway waiting for her cue.

"Yeah! Yeah, Mary! Go! Go! Right now!" Luke motioned her into the camera shot.

"Oh, my lord!" Pervis greeted the jiggling young woman as she bounced into the picture. "What has we got here!"

"Hiiii!" The woman blushed and twirled her long yellow hair with her finger. "I jus' been ta' see Jayzus, an' I want ya'll ta' know he's allllllright! I told him I been bad. That I used ta' love with mens and womens for all the wrong reasons. But when I paid him up, he told me I was allllllright! And now I'm goin' ta' my salvation! I hopes I see as many a' ya'll there' as I can! Jayzus is waitin' for me! An' I'll be waitin' for ya'll! Tee hee!"

"Praise th' lord, chile!" Pervis shouted holding a hand on her firm, copious breasts. "Praise th' lord! Heaven is whateva' ya'll wanit ta' be! If it wernt, it wouldn't be heaven would it? Now ya'll see how easy it is. All ya' have ta' do is come ta' Pervis today an' Jayzus will come ta' you before them craychures does!"

The light fixtures above the stage area began to flicker. Out of the back wall, the blackened, moist, disfiguration of the alien appeared behind Pervis Puritan and with a quick swipe of its bony forearm, swiftly decapitated the upstart preacher before his worldwide audience. It picked up the gushing corpse and hurled it at the camera.

Mark, Luke and Mary bolted for the exit, deserting their posts and their abruptly deposed compatriot.

It departed the empty barn with its host and his audience severed. Though the computer screen continued to scroll the names and bank numbers of those gullibly aimless souls who had allowed Pervis Puritan to die rich, in the absence of prosperity.

# III.

Cannes, France-The Beneficent Palace:

Jean-Paul bounded frantically through the Palace corridors wading against the scores of staff operatives who had gathered up their belongings and were making a hurried exodus toward whatever rumored refuge would sequester their tenuous lives from the inexorable annihilation. Occasionally, a former colleague would cordially bump him as he whisked by, offering to save a place for him at one particular haven or another—if he hurried along.

"Le Chateau Grimaldi is setting up a shield of ultra violet radiation in the cellars!" Renee called to him. "Those birds won't be able to detect us! If you're there in ten minutes, I'll have a spot for you!"

The vision of a mass grave of lethally irradiated corpses flashed through Jean-Paul's mind as he rounded a corner. Desperate times indeed sired desperate, foolhardy measures, he thought.

But his immediate concerns were far removed from the saving of his own skin. He had tried to comm Manda after his brief discussion with Dr. Canard, but had received no response. That Victor could have moved so swiftly against the Operations head, left a nauseated feeling in the pit of Jean-Paul's stomach.

"I can see it now." Jean-Paul morosely predicted as he coded into the private Operations elevator. "I'll get there just in time to see Manda with her head twisted backward on her shoulders. And Victor will have planted a hand weapon on her, even though she loathes the damned things. And he'll say: 'She tried to kill me. I had to defend myself. I had no choice'. Yeah, I can see it now. Then he'll offer me a choice. 'Do what I say, or you'll leave me no choice as well'. Then what do I do?"

The elevator door slid open and Jean-Paul hopped in. As the doors closed, he was ensconced in an eerie vacuum that momentarily left him wondering whether the last two days had only been a mad dream. Part of him actually believed that when the doors opened again, he would see

Operations merely bustling at the height of its routine, with no suggestion of a dark fate looming on the horizon.

Sadly, the vividness of his memory chased away this coveted image. The meteoroid. The exploding crater. The ghastly alien atop the spire. The disappearing multitudes. The horrible, bloodied deaths of the Beneficent and Val. These witnessed events all burned with fierce clarity in his mind— he could not have purged them for madness, even if he'd tried.

Resolutely, he drew his own weapon and turned up its setting. If Manda were dead, he would ensure that one more death would follow.

"Vengeance is mine?" he muttered to himself.

When the elevator door swished open, Jean-Paul hopped through the opening with his weapon drawn. The Operations hall was completely still, save for the light hum of whirring computers and equipment which continued to monitor the movements of the giant birds, and to maintain a descending count of the Earth's population.

He moved slowly down the center pathway toward his own work station near Manda's central command post. Alarmingly, it then dawned on him that the Champion could have already killed him in more than a dozen different ways. After all, weaponry was only a hobby for most Operations staff, like golf or tennis or soccer. World peace and the satellite arrays had rendered armed services obsolete, with the exception of the Police Corps, which operated purely on localized levels, and of course, the members of the Controller's Office.

Victor, by contrast, had been bred for the battle. Bred for the kill. Bred to dole out death like few humans alive. By his scathing vulnerability, Jean-Paul realized that he actually held no control over his life or death. Resignedly, he replaced his weapon on his belt and continued moving forward.

There appeared to be no sign of life whatsoever—only machinery, paper, and turned-over chairs vacated by frightened staffers. Yet as utterly hopeless as everything had become, he could not fathom Manda having deserted voluntarily. Though, whether she had been murdered by Victor or fled of her own accord, he no longer sensed the powerful presence of the woman he had served.

"Jean-Paul," a voice whispered to him.

Jean-Paul snatched his weapon from his belt and spun violently, falling backward against a wall of consoles. As he looked up, he expected to see the blonde, sinewy, giant Champion leering over his prone figure. But instead, what he saw shook him even more.

Manda stood before him, her tall, once sturdy figure rocking unsteadily as if she were about to faint. Her insignia tunic was unbuttoned revealing her heavy, sweat-soaked gray undergarments. She swayed in place barefoot, wearing the haggard look of a victim who had been horribly traumatized.

"Jean-Paul," she repeated in a weakened voice he barely recognized, "do you...do you love me?"

Jean-Paul jumped to his feet to catch her before her imminent collapse. He held her by the waist and shoulder and gently maneuvered her into an empty chair. To his surprise, she was notably lighter and softer than he had ever imagined her to be. She had always worn indomitable strength so convincingly.

"Damn him!" Jean-Paul exclaimed. "What happened to you? Did Victor do this?"

"You didn't answer me," she said, as a sliver of the command tone returned to her voice. "Do you love me?"

The question dumbfounded Jean-Paul. He had admired her, trusted her, respected her, and even hoped to emulate her in every facet of her career pursuits. In his life, she had fallen somewhere between the cracks left by his estranged mother and the elder sister he never had. Yet "love" and his commanding officer had never actually converged upon the same thought.

"You don't have to answer." Manda reached up and touched his face. "No one ever does."

Jean-Paul felt all the strength he had placed in humanity begin to drain through Manda's despair. He didn't want to give up on Earth. But with the source of his professional will slumped into emotional disarray, he found himself finally looking beyond it.

"Manda." Jean-Paul knelt down and took her hand. "What did Victor do to you? Did he hurt you?"

Manda smiled, as if someone had told her an old joke.

"Victor!?" she scoffed. "Hurt me? What...you think he came in here and challenged me to a fist fight? Do I look that bad?"

"Well..." Jean-Paul winced.

"Victor came in here and showed off his bandaged boo-boos." Manda stared up at the giant map screen. "Then he said that under the circumstances, he should be put in charge of the world's affairs. I said 'fine'. I figured with the world turning to shit, who better to be in charge than Earth's biggest asshole."

Jean-Paul managed to smile wryly at her crudely metaphoric analogy.

"I didn't mean to put you on the spot or anything." Manda continued in another direction. "It's just that...well...my family was never into the 'love' thing. I mean, we got along okay. Mom liked dad. Dad liked mom. The kids liked the folks, and the folks liked the kids. And me Bev and Todd all liked each other—but it was never about love. We were just a family and we did what families were suppose to do, y'know?"

"I dated a few guys at O.U. A couple even said they 'loved' me, but I understood what that was about. And then I came to Cannes and got into my work and decided that 'love' whatever it was, must've been meant for other people. Then I met A. He wasn't particularly handsome or extraordinarily brilliant, like a lot of guys I knew. But he was...thoughtful. Not toward me exactly, but toward everything in general. He was interesting, to me, in a personal way no other man had ever been. We hooked up and saw each other sporadically over the years. We even set that wedding date. But do you know that over all that time, he never once said he loved me? I mean...I think he did, but he never actually said it."

"Manda, we both knew Amritraj." Jean-Paul assured. "I'm positive he..."

"No, Jean!" Manda interrupted. "You don't understand! Forty years of life and I've never had anyone say that they love me! Why? Have I been that meaningless to everyone I've ever known? When I die, is everyone going to just yawn and say 'Oh yeah, that's the bitch who used to work for the Beneficent'. I mean, is that it for me?"

Jean-Paul felt her flood of repressed emotions swirl about him as he held her hand gently. For all the years he had known and cared for Manda, he was amazed by how much closer he had come to her in only the past few moments. That she had been so competent a commanding officer suddenly meant very little. That she had become this vulnerable, desperate soul in the face of their imminent deaths seemed to carry far more importance in this blackest hour.

He reached up with a finger, to turn her distressed countenance toward him. He captured her eyes with his sincerest gaze and spoke into her heart: "Manda, I love you. You've been the most important person in my adult life. You've nurtured me and shaped me like no other human being I've known. You took me under your wing and molded me in spite of my arrogance and obstinacy. You helped me take the chip off my shoulder and showed me how to be a total person. For that, I'll always owe you. And for that I'll always love you."

Manda's eyes moistened, so she closed them rather than make a display. She leaned back in the chair and sighed deeply as she locked her long fingers with his.

"Thank you, Jean-Paul," she said with a whisper. "Thank you so much."

"Now this doesn't mean we have to go somewhere and fuck, does it?" Jean-Paul asked sarcastically.

"No." Manda smiled peacefully. "It doesn't."

# IV.

Anna Maria's room:

"If this is Man's Earth, then I cannot share in it!" a battered Anna Maria stressfully lamented. "If this is God's will, then I will not live with it! If Victor is likened to Paul, then who can I be that he should single me, alone, to such horrid abuse! If I am likened to Joan, where is my King who would hear me speak of the Lord? Already fled to asylum with the devil? I came to herald the coronation of a king, but have found my stake already driven...the fires lapping their jowls for my flesh.

"My uncle is deaf, but happy!" her voice cracked. "My cousin is blind, but merry! Everyone is sick, but rueful of a cure that is not quick and sweet. It's as if truth in all its forms must be loathed and shunt if it stands opposed to the pleasures of the moment and the pride of our face. And Uncle Georges knows this! It was his book I read! And Lou could know if she'd only stop killing herself long enough to listen!

"And Victor...beautiful, wonderful Victor. 'Gentle', Lou said. Gentle and loving to everyone, I suppose...but me. I just didn't realize how important the sex would be. But should it have been? It was as if he were the guardian of all secular treasure, and I came upon him, a cankered witch bent to steal away the world's happiness with tasteless piety! Why? Why couldn't he see? Why wouldn't he see? Why must I alone be bred to suffer God's truth, while others can laugh and rejoice the fruits of their scathing ignorance? Why must I comprehend so well? Why must I see so clearly...so alone?"

The girl's face then tightened to the mask of an angry, fitful child.

"*His ways are not your ways. He wills that I go through the fire to His bosom; for I am His child, and you are not fit that I should live among you.*"

Anna Maria weakly craned her head skyward, tiredly resisting the fatigue her crushing questions brought down upon her.

"Why did God forsake him?" she whispered, wearily confounded. "*Why hast thou forsaken me?*"

Anna Maria's pallid, despondent image faded as the final diary entry concluded.

Louisette sat slumped against the bed, staring blurrily at the blank monitor. She clutched a loaded inoculator tightly to her bosom. A flood of anguished tears flowed freely over her cheeks.

"'Alone'!" Louisette shouted closing her eyes tightly. "You weren't 'alone'! Why didn't you talk to me?"

Then she opened her eyes and defiantly shook away the answer that called to her.

"I wonder if she made it." Louisette muttered. "In her note, she seemed to think killing herself destroyed her chances...of making it to Heaven. But I wonder."

Louisette then gazed warily at the inoculator she held tightly in her hand. She had been longer without its sustaining influence over the past several hours than she had been in nearly ten years. More than food or water, blusilver had become the fuel which propelled her empty, sybaritic existence. Her skin seemed so dry now that it felt as if it would split if she did not move gingerly. Her eyes and nose burned like open sores. And the pressure which had built up at the base of her skull under her ears, felt as if an arterial rupture was imminent.

"Well, Anna, I know I'm not going to any Heaven," she spoke, licking the blood which had begun to run from her nose. "But maybe I can go where you went. I've been everywhere else."

She closed her eyes, lifted the golden chain bearing the Latin cross, and pressed the inoculator against the side of her throat. She pushed the release and a full vial emptied slowly into her neck. The cooling substance simultaneously rushed into her brain and down into her shoulders, roaring revitalization through her like a torrid wave washing through dusty, arid basins. Her flesh felt soft again. She sniffed back and could taste blood in her mouth, as her nasal passages came clear. Her comfort and the remnants of her confidence returned as her mind, which had become crowded with ideals and emotions, indolently receded into dimness. She subconsciously threw her head backwards and ran her fingers between her legs. The powerful rush suddenly became more synaptically gratifying than any sexual experience she could remember.

Louisette turned face down into the white carpeting breathing heavily in impassioned coitus with her hallucinogenic lover. She momentarily became totally unconscious of her surroundings, which made her happy. She was cool again. And traveling far...so very far away from sadness. Finally, she opened her eyes, certain she had landed anywhere but where she had been.

She immediately saw the diary cartridges piled in front of the monitor. Then the other blusilver vials sitting just before them.

"No!" she cursed reality.

Louisette clumsily reloaded her inoculator and this time unhooked her blouse. She lifted her right breast and pressed the inoculator directly underneath it. Without hesitation she hit the release and emptied a second full vial directly over her heart.

She began breathing heavily again, but abruptly, a sharp pain shot through her chest. Her limbs went suddenly numb and she felt her head fall back and slam squarely against the bedpost. The side of her head swelled and started to bleed. But oddly, it felt good to her. All she needed was for the twisting contraction in her bosom to cease, but it only tightened, dispersing shards of torment mixed with cool numbness throughout her body.

Her eyes sat open, but she didn't see the ceiling. Instead, she saw her father standing over her, berating and criticizing, and promising to send her away again. She saw Victor reaching toward her wearing his sadistic smile which always preceded the physical brutality he exacted for his reluctant consortium. She felt herself in her limousine, lying naked on the floor with crowds of people staring at her, laughing at her and throwing her drugs that filled her jaws and ran under her skin. A child appeared in front of her with Victor's eyes and the face she once had in her youth. She wanted to love it, but it spat at her with contempt and turned away.

Through all the faces, she strained for a glimpse of Anna Maria but achingly could not find her.

Finally, a putrid rotten odor accosted her nostrils. A powerful, overbearing damp heat crept over her flesh. There was an odd series of lurching, wet sounds that followed. To her, it sounded like an orgy. But strangely, there were no voices.

Louisette tried to lift her head to see what the strange source of these smells and sounds could be. But her neck muscles were frozen rigid.

When the faces which had haunted her faded, she was able to make out a large, black, foreboding silhouette hovering over her.

"Anna!" she cried desperately.

There was no response.

"God?" she asked blearily confused.

Only the sounds of moist movements persisted.

Finally, she blinked her eyes fitfully until they grudgingly cleared themselves.

What Louisette was finally able to discern, was the hideous black alien, wearing the rotted flesh mask standing over her.

She began to laugh.

"Many humans have chosen to destroy their own lives, particularly at this time. For the foundation of their empty lives has been uprooted from the sand upon which they built." It began in a heavy, gurgled baritone. "Why do you?"

Louisette continued to laugh loudly, until she choked and gagged on her drying throat.

"Hold." it commanded.

She felt her throat begin to clear. Her brain began to order itself. Her body, however, remained paralyzed. It still felt as if a boulder sat upon her cold chest and that her limbs were no longer attached.

She momentarily acknowledged the suspension of her imminent death, then chose to immerse herself again in laughter.

"Why do you…laugh?" it finally asked her.

"You…" Louisette began cackling. "You look like Fitz…this guy from Massachusetts I dated."

"How?" It queried doubtfully.

"We…" Louisette tried to suppress her hysterics. "We were all partying in Haifa a few years ago. Right after the Israeli Dissolution. It was so wild! People were cheering, getting drunk, throwing rocks and bottles, shooting off guns! Oh fuck, I was so out of it, I almost shot this fat old lady with a pistol I'd found. The Controller's men were everywhere in their black suits and their rifles rooting out cult terrorists. People were screaming at them, yelling at them. People were screaming at us too. But we were just there to party—and they didn't fuck with us. They knew who I was. I could go anywhere and no one would fuck with me. Well anyway, Fitzgerald…Fitz, my boyfriend, wanted to hit some Palestinian dive…the worst we could find. Said something about Weed prostitutes and their home chemical-based aphrodisiacs. So we found this place called DZ's. Goats and animals and shit running around everywhere. It smelled like a fucking Pakistani petting zoo, but it was just what Fitz wanted. Then some wrinkly, old naked whore came downstairs and Fitz started talking to her. The rest of us just sat on the floor and smoked some homemade this little kid sold us. Everything was real mellow. The music was even pretty nice. Then out of nowhere, Fitz comes tearing down the stairs with no clothes on, eyes bulging, screaming and yelling his head off. We asked him what's wrong? But he was just screaming and waving his arms. And he had this greasy shit all over him! I reached out to touch him and it burned my fingers. Finally, he tried to run outside, but he just ran into the door and fell. His skin burned and sizzled till it started to pucker and turn black! He puked his guts out and died right in front of us. Then the Controller's men came in and kicked us out before we could do anything. It was just so fucking funny…all burnt up like that! You remind me of him! I wonder if he went to Heaven?"

"Heaven." It repeated flatly.

"Yeah." Louisette closed her eyes. "Heaven. Where all the good people go when they die…like my cousin Anna Maria."

Louisette paused regretfully. "Only she didn't seem too sure about where she was going at the end. She just wanted to go. That's kind of how I feel. I just want to go away from here. Wherever Anna Maria went, I hope."

"Why?" It asked.

"Because…everyone is so fucked up! I'm so fucked up! Today I'm beautiful! Tomorrow I'm ugly! Yesterday I was too fat! Tomorrow I'm too skinny! He wants long hair! He wants short hair! He wants big tits! He wants Kima's tits! He wants to fuck me! He doesn't want to fuck me! He wants Kima! Anna Maria wants him! I want a baby! He hates babies! Father loves me! Father kicks me out! Now my cousin's dead! It's just too bloody damned confusing, that's why!"

"You want to escape life." It concluded.

"Yyyes!" Louisette hesitated in a choked voice. "No…I mean…wait. I don't want to escape. I just want to go where I can…just be loved for a change. And where I can love someone else!"

"Have you not 'loved' many here?" It probed. "And have not many 'loved' you?"

"Ha! ha!" Louisette laughed loudly. "'Loved many'? Sure! So many, I can't even remember all their faces! So many, I don't even think I ever stopped to consider whether they cared. In fact, I don't even think I wanted them to care. That would have been too annoying. Too confining. Too complicated. No fun at all. And fun's what it's all about, isn't it? Look good! Feel good! And stay high till you die! That's a song, y'know. A famous ex-boyfriend wrote it for me.

"Only, I can never quite figure…why I still feel so shitty all the time? I've got money!" she recited proudly. "I've got…had position! I'm beautiful, ask anybody! I can go anywhere! I can do everything I want! Who cares if no one likes me. They still want to be around me. In fact their envy and attention is better than being liked. People only 'like' people they're better than. Their jealousy always made me sure I was better than anyone."

"Your cousin did not like you?" It questioned.

Louisette opened her eyes and paused. Her memory flashed through all of the joyous occasions they'd shared, with nary a glimmer of hostility or jealousy between them. All of the years without a single wall…until the end. And then there were the diaries.

"She said…" Louisette frowned, "…she loved me."

"Like the others." It added.

"No!" she asserted. "Not like the others. She really loved me. Cared about me, about how I felt."

"But you did not love her?" It pursued.

"Oh yes! Or at least I tried." Louisette spoke as tears ran to the back of her head. "I really tried. I never even wanted to try for anyone else. But instead, somehow, I managed to…kill her."

"How?"

"I don't know! I tried to show her how to survive! How to be like me! Only it made things worse…and she died."

"What made things 'worse'?" It asked

Louisette closed her eyes again. Her fragmented thoughts had waltzed evasively around a singularly garish transgression from the moment she'd left Anna Maria alone to kill herself. Upon her death, Louisette had still tried to blame Victor and his savage rape of the young girl as the proximate cause of her cousin's tragic suicide. She'd tried to blame Wesley for failing to sustain his usual insipid surveillance of Anna Maria, possessively monitoring her every movement. She'd tried to blame the drug for deploying its mesmerizing, seductive allure as a serpent in the wood entrances a young pup. She'd even tried to blame Anna Maria herself, for attempting to leap forward into an adult forum for which she had been emotionally ill-prepared.

But no manufactured contrivance could sufficiently blot away the scathing epitaph Louisette had emblazoned upon the final panel of their relationship. No diversion of fault or deflection of guilt could salve the indelible scar that seared away all respite for her anguished soul's agony.

"I'd like to go now." Louisette sobbed behind her tightly closed eyes and her clenched white caps.

"What made it 'worse'?" It repeated, without acknowledgment of her distress.

Louisette's face trembled. Large tears now flowed freely toward her ears. The sorrowful burden of pained recrimination finally wrenched its way free.

"I had to keep up…appearances!" she wailed, her voice unrestrainedly reverberating against the silence. "I couldn't let her know…! We were supposed to be in love! The whole world was watching! I couldn't tell her…! I couldn't tell her even when she needed me to tell her…! What Victor was really like! Always hitting and twisting and pulling and biting like a goddamn animal! So full of anger and hate…and himself! I couldn't tell her that! I couldn't tell her I was marrying a man who has no heart! A man that everyone worships, who has no feelings at all! He was going to be my husband! I couldn't let her know that I was taking it and taking it and taking it…! Oh, godddd! Anna…! She thought she was alone! She thought…! She asked me had he…and I said 'no'! I could've saved her! But my face was more important! More important than the truth! More important than her life!"

Louisette's strained voice trailed into loud sobs. She wanted desperately to ward away despair with her cries, but even her enveloping sadness could not fade away the truth.

"What is the truth?" It asked evenly. "What is truth?"

Louisette's contorted features slowly softened. For an instant, she thought it had read her mind. She tried to reach into her tortured thoughts for some answer…any answer. Not for it. But for herself.

She rifled through every stage of her life and found that the definition, as she had only begun to perceive it, had no correlation. It had been as alien a concept to her as the alien itself.

"What people believe?" she thought to affirm momentarily. This had always been a concurrence with all other facets of her life. But Anna Maria had 'believed' that Victor was the most wonderful man on Earth. Yet that 'belief' had segued her life to a premature extinction.

She wrestled with "What people know". But in her diaries Anna Maria clearly stated that there will always be things that are fact that no human may ever know. Which brought her to "Faith"—another concept, equally alien to her in its broadest forms.

"You could have 'faith' in other people," she muddled. "But that never lasts. In time, they always let you down."

Louisette's mind became jumbled as she struggled for the understanding which Anna Maria had seemingly honed with relative ease. Understanding of Truth, of Faith, of God!

She sighed heavily, opened her eyes, and tried to focus on the alien's face.

"I have no idea." she answered in a wavering voice of resignation. "Something about 'Faith' and 'God'. But I have no idea. Anna Maria understood it. I guess that's why I wish I were with her. So she could show me. I mean…I'd like to understand truth…even if it's not what I want. Even it isn't any fun. I want to go where I don't have to be high to feel good. Where I don't have to be beautiful to be…appreciated or listened to. Where when I see things clearly, they don't burst my will to live. Where I don't hurt because I can't understand.

"I mean…it's been like…living in an avalanche. Painful and fun all at one time; falling fast and hard till you finally crash bottom. And then you're buried under all the others who fall over the top of you. And when the dust settles, it's just over. You don't even know what it was all about. It's just over.

"Anna Maria was like this bright light. A…a beacon. Then all of a sudden she dies and that's it. 'Next, please!' There has to be more than that, doesn't there? There has to be more than just living, dying, and having it off as best you can in between."

The alien stood, its muscles and limbs continuing to lurch and writhe. Then its eyes began to glow bright scarlet. And it reached a gnarled, mucousy hand down toward her face.

"You...are exalted." It spoke.

Louisette felt the heavy coagulation in her chest begin to dissipate. Her limbs tingled with the return of normal sensations. But then she felt its searing touch as the disgusting flesh of its palm burned the skin of her face. Her eyes felt as if acid had been poured into them. She could feel her high cheeks split open and melt away. Her tiny nose to flared and stretch outward.

Her lips contracted. Her capped teeth rattled loose. Her rib cage to ached. Her breasts expanded and burst as blood and liquid spurted upward. Sharp pain jabbed at her hips. Her legs felt heavy and thick.

The agony of its fiery intrusions upon her sculpted flesh became ultimately unbearable.

Finally, Louisette could do naught else but scream.

# V.

Palace Operations:

"The coat of arms!"

"'Code of arms.'"

"No, COAT...of arms!"

"'No code of arms'."

"Not 'no' coat of arms! Just the coat...of...arms!"

"'Code...of...arms'."

"No...Coat! Coat!"

"Code?"

"No, you imbecile! Coat! C-O-A-T! Coat! As in: Coat your body with pig's blood and feed you to starving lions, you cretin!"

"Ah." Julius Kelp sucked his protruding overbite as he hastily punched in the correction on his hand computer. "COAT of arms."

Victor stared down from his erected throne with confounded exhaustion. "Better to suffer the loyalties of a fool, lest ye be undone by the treacheries of a genius," he had read somewhere. "Incompetence may impede, but great competence may usurp."

Henceforth, as Victor configured the hierarchy of his fledgling reign, he concluded that the longevity of his Beneficence would be best ensured by the appointment of Julius Kelp, the Public Service career bureaucrat, as the second most powerful human in the known universe rather than Manda Martine, the slick and "too" assertive woman who had previously headed Operations for nearly a decade.

Although witnessing the slackjawed subordinate with the matted oily hair domed over his forehead take dictation, made Victor consider whether a happy medium betwixt genius and utter stupidity might have served his Beneficence best of all.

"Coat...of arms, my lord?" Kelp quivered.

"Yes." Victor tried to regain his train of thought. "Um, the silver fox should be changed to red. And the genitalia should be enlarged to denote...virility. There should also be a golden mane of a lion about its head representing...abundance and...regality."

"'Abundance and legality'." Kelp repeated, keying in the request.

"How about: Redundance and banality." Jean-Paul whispered to Manda.

The deposed woman drew a sharp breath and covered her mouth to conceal a smile.

Victor tilted his head upward and regarded the pair suspiciously as they looked up at him with sudden blankness. He then narrowed his eyes and worked his jaw, trying to utilize an untried restraint.

"Something...funny?" Victor asked the pair.

"No...sir." Jean-Paul responded soberly.

"Good." Victor's nostrils flared. "Ms. Martine, I hope you realize that you remain here due only to your value in assisting Mr. Kelp with his transition into your former slot. Should you become more trouble-some than helpful..."

"Understood." Manda righted herself and met his bright blue eyes.

"Fine, then." Victor looked away. "And finally, those tacky red grapes lodged in the animal's mouth should be removed. Clearly, my predecessor had a certain...predilection for le vin d'rouge, but I found his patronage of Languedoc excessive. In fact, I'm certain his addiction to that region's sour fermentations contributed heavily to his eventual slack in sound judgment."

"Yes. Remove grapes...fermen...slack." Kelp muttered unharmoniously as he continued his input.

"Instead, I'd like to see a large herbal cigar there!" Victor snorted. "And trails of smoke emanating from its snout! After all, 'where there is smoke, there is...um... fire'! And fire shall be essence of my reign!"

"Hell fire," muttered Dr. Canard.

Victor swung around in his chair glared down at the doctor who leaned casually against a vacant console.

The doctor lifted his eyebrows and offered a disarming "who, me?" shrug of his shoulders.

"It's just an expression." Dr. Canard offered. "You know: Hell fire! Kind of like 'Blaze of Glory'!"

"Ah." Victor rubbed his chin and tried to weigh the doctor's veracity.

"Ah," returned Doctor Canard with a plastered grin.

Finally, the Champion began to chuckle lightly until he tossed his head backward and laughed out loud.

Dr. Canard looked across the room at Manda and Jean-Paul giving them the same "innocent" shrug he had offered to Victor.

Julius Kelp spun around in a complete circle trying to ascertain the source of his leader's sudden merriment.

"Outstanding!" Victor roared. "Mr. Kelp, make this additional note. We will depict the fox standing defiantly in a pit of fire. And inscribed above his head in herbal smoke, the words: Blaze of Glory. Have the design commissioned and transmitted to sportswear companies immediately. People in the Weeds will be killing each other for any article of clothing bearing the mark once I'm seen wearing it!"

Manda and Jean-Paul bowed their heads and covered their faces.

Dr. Canard grinned his approval at Victor who smiled back at him.

"Doctor, I think your talents have been wasted on the sick!" Victor laughed. "You'd make a splendid PS head. Think it over."

"Of course." Dr. Canard's eyes brightened facetiously at the inane proposition.

"Blaze...of...Glory." Kelp droned.

The words were quickly abandoned by their luster in Kelp's nasally monotonous voice. Victor repeated them to himself once more to try and restore their original splendor. Somehow it was not the same.

"No matter." Victor dismissed. "Now about my mural portrait on the Rock of Gibraltar..."

"Sir..." Manda interjected.

"One moment, woman!" Victor deflected.

Jean-Paul watched Manda bristle at the careless dismissal.

"My likeness should be painted completely over that of my predecessor, Beneficent Georges," the Champion finished.

"Likeness…over…Georges." Kelp noted.

Victor frowned a moment.

"That is to say that my painting will be…over the painting of Georges." Victor clarified.

"Yes…over Georges." Kelp repeated.

"Not me over him." Victor pointed.

"No?"

"No! The painting over his!"

"His what, my lord?"

"His painting!"

"Yes."

"Not a painting of me over him!"

"Oh."

"My painting of me covering his painting of him!"

"My lord?"

"I mean, I don't want a goddamn painting of me over Georges!"

"But you said…"

"Forget what I said! I mean I want my picture on top of his!"

"You on top of him."

"No! My painting on top of his painting!"

"Of course."

Dr. Canard turned away and paced toward another work station.

Jean-Paul's expression was flush, though he suppressed as much of the hilarity that swelled within him as he could.

Manda, with a broad smile stepped forward to intervene.

"What the Champion means," she began with a placatious smile, "is that he wants the painting of Beneficent Georges covered over with a mural of himself."

"Ahhhh." Kelp nodded with mildly befuddled comprehension.

Victor let loose a sigh. Then he grudgingly eyed Manda Martine.

"Thank you," he spoke, refusing to address her by name. "Only you called me the Champion. I needn't remind you that I am the Beneficent-Champion now."

"My apologies...sir." She intentionally avoided the "my lord" he coveted. "In any event, should we not now be getting on about the business of dealing with the invasion, the worldwide panic...those kinds of things?"

Victor frowned at her, and momentarily regretted not having killed Manda when he'd had the opportunity.

"We tried things your way," he seethed through his teeth. "And look what it's gotten us! The Earth on the verge of total destruction! Georges died trying to do things your way. It cost him his reign. But from this day onward, I will decide what's best for the people of this planet. Me! And there's not a goddamn thing you or anyone else can do about it. The world will be saved! I will save it...as I always have! But first things first."

Jean-Paul observed Manda quake at the inference that she had been at the root of the failings of Beneficent Georges' tenure.

"Mr. Kelp and I have determined that it is in our best interests to restore the confidence of the people during this crisis." Victor announced. "Therefore, I and a small entourage will be paying a visit to the Weed slums of Lyon where we will mingle with the...afflicted. And then I will address the world. Assure them that their...messiah will preserve their lives."

Manda swallowed hard, choosing her words carefully so as not to imply any semblance of dissent.

"Might I inquire as to what purpose this will serve?" she asked with delicate condescendence.

Victor stood up and smiled.

"You may ask," he goaded, staring down his nose. "But I think it better for you to sit back and learn how things are really done. How a king of kings really goes about his business...of earning the trust and 'love' of his subjects. And how I intend to send this alien force reeling back across the void from whence it came. The only hint I WILL give you, is that there was once a man who claimed his kingdom not of this Earth. And by doing so, in effect, ruled this planet for nearly two thousand years after his death! That is power, my dear."

Manda regarded his seamless arrogance, which staggered well beyond the boundaries of rationality, with awed disgust.

"And by the way," the Beneficent-Champion added. "I'll expect you to assist Mr. Kelp with the details of my visit. Should anything go wrong, I'll hold you responsible."

Victor stalked from his perch and strode toward the rear exit.

"Come along, Kelp." Victor motioned. "I must be about…my business."

Kelp turned and waved bashfully at Manda, Jean-Paul and Dr. Canard before he nervously hurried off, lest he be abandoned by the trail of Victor's shadow.

When the door closed behind them, there was a long pause as each of them took a solemn moment to bitterly digest what they'd just witnessed.

"Anybody care to join me for a vodka and tonic?" Dr. Canard offered.

"Only if I get to mix my own." Manda responded.

"He doesn't have any idea." Jean-Paul spoke, shaking his head.

"You mean, about what he's doing?" Dr. Canard clarified. "Of course not! But don't worry. The world's been run like that for centuries. Someone sees someone else sitting on a throne and it looks so prestigious, they decide they'd like to have a crack at being despot for a while. Don't have a clue as to what they're going to do when they get there, mind you! Not that that's even important. The main thing is to get in that chair and sit down as long as the masses are dumb enough to let you. Or until someone with a little more ambition comes along and gives you a run for your money. Meanwhile, you just sit on top of the world and look important. Give a few speeches. Hand out some goodies now and then. Make sure the masses always have a clear conscience and a full belly, and it's smooth sailing! That is, until the planet gets invaded or something."

"And even that won't be a problem for Victor." Manda added. "He'll just remind everyone that the planet was already invaded before he took over."

"And Kelp…!" Jean-Paul exclaimed.

"Don't worry." Dr. Canard smirked. "He's not as smart as he looks."

"I just can't believe it's going to end this way…for all of us." Jean-Paul lamented. It just doesn't seem fair."

"Oh, it's fair all right." Dr. Canard started for the door. "This whole mess has been brewing for a long time. We've all been asking for it."

"What do you mean by that?" Manda questioned.

Suddenly, the far door to the Operations Hall slid open. Manda, Dr. Canard and Jean-Paul quickly snapped around to see who, still remained in the Palace with access to the Operations area.

To their surprise, a short, plain-featured young woman with straight, dark hair stood clutching the door frame. She wore a sheer white night-gown and looked extremely confounded and fatigued.

"Who the devil is that?" Dr. Canard frowned.

Manda and Jean-Paul shook their heads with no recognition of her.

"Um…" the young woman's voice shook. "Does anyone have any pret-zels? I was downstairs…in the uh…kitchen and there weren't any pretzels."

She gazed around the hall for a moment with utter bewilderment. "Where is everyone…anyway?" She frowned…and then collapsed.

Dr. Canard and Manda ran over to assist her. Jean-Paul hesitated a moment, trying to ascertain where he'd heard this voice before.

# VI.

The News:

A shocking story has just been reported to us! As inconceivable as it seems, our sources close to the Palace have confirmed that Louisette Richelieu has been expelled from Mankind's leading family! Apparently, still reeling from the horror of the death of his niece, Anna Maria Diderot, Beneficent Georges Richelieu became enraged by his daughter's exhibition on universal satellite during the Vogue Day festivities broadcast from Monte Carlo yesterday evening.

As seen in these explicit excerpts from last night's program, Mademoiselle Richelieu appeared to be scarcely coherent during the anti-grav plunge which nearly brought her glamourous life to a crushing end. She then recovered well enough to entice a raucous collection of Vogue Day rabble to join with her in a lavatory orgy which sweated and thrust its way into the wee hours of the morning in front of the largest satellite audience in history.

It is not believed, however, that this behavior from Mademoiselle Richelieu (as we've come to expect) was specifically what plummeted her from her father's grace. But rather that she garishly brandished a forbidden cult symbol for most of the evening and, on the steps of the T. Fonda Hotel & Casino, brazenly cursed mankind on its most celebrated and revered holiday. The act is said to have so enraged the Beneficent, that he physically assaulted his daughter, tossed her into her private limousine and sent her speeding on her way without so much as a hug from her beloved Champion or even a change of fresh clothing.

Mademoiselle Richelieu's whereabouts at this hour remain unknown. She has not as yet surfaced at any of her private condominiums or cottages sprinkled across the planet. Nonetheless, we shall keep you posted as to her chosen place of exile the moment any information becomes available to us.

In other news, reports of mass disappearances of people and structures have been confirmed by Palace Operations. Although it is unclear at this hour how many millions—or perhaps even billions—of human beings remain unaccounted for.

Also, sightings of the ghoulish alien creature first seen atop the spire in Santa Cruz have been sporadically reported. But, other than the grisly death of the cult satellite pirate seen on most stations earlier today, subsequent appearances of the creature have not been substantiated.

Well, the big question today is how are people in the E.M. & M. coping with what many are calling "The End of the World". We have three reports coming to you this hour. The first report comes from our Martian correspondent, Christiane Amanpour in Schmidtzenburg.

Video up:

"When biologists, nuclear physicists, geologists, archaeologists, extraterrestrial engineers and astrophysicists settled themselves and their families on the craggy, hostile Martian surfaces almost one hundred years ago, most of us who remained on the Earth and the Moon were skeptical at best as to their prospects for survival. But after some initial failures, notably the decompression of the Sputnik dome which took twenty-five thousand lives in 2102, the quality of life here has flourished, even exceeding the expectations of the original Martian settlers.

"'Rob Hayward and his crew hoped to have one major city established within the first century' noted the son of an original settler. 'Today we have two and a half cities completed and two more under design'.

"Unfortunately, for the better than two million people domiciled in domed settlements across the 'Red Rock', the days of looking ahead have been replaced with mere hours upon which to reflect on their very existence. Early this morning, Governor Kodos Stichenbecker, flanked by his aide, Carmen Yorishu, announced that in order to save half the Martian colonies, half would have to be pulverized by nuclear detonations.

"This drastic measure seems to be the only chance to destroy the giant, winged ship that now hurtles toward Mars. Given the devastation already wrought on the surface of the Moon, and the failure of the satellite arrays on Earth to dissuade its sister ships, this amputative measure appears cruel, but sound. The greatest tragedy, however, lies in the fact that no one will be able to determine which nuclear power stations will be detonated until the alien vessel enters Mars's atmosphere. This will make evacuation of the Planum regions to be sacrificed nearly impossible. To make matters even more grave, even if the alien vessel is destroyed along with half of the population, surface storm activity is likely to contaminate the remaining domed settlements with residual radiation which could damage artificial food and water supplies.

"And ultimately, all of this becomes moot for the Martian colonies, if the Earth itself fails to survive. Mars is still eighty percent dependent upon shuttle supply runs from its mother planet. If the battle on Earth is lost, which now appears probable, the people on Mars face a slow, painful death due to the depletion of essential medical, elemental and mineral supplies.

"Centuries ago, in times of great urgency, people used to pray to 'God' for a miracle. Today, on Mars, everyone is more or less hoping for the best...and crossing their fingers.

"Christiane Amanpour in the capital city of Schmidtzenburg, Sinai Planum on Mars, Satellite News."

Video scene shift:

"Along the Kan River in the south of Weed China has begun one of the most horrible trails of murder and mutilation seen, perhaps, this century. What began as a defiant cult rally staged in the small city of Tayu, mushroomed into a mounting cult crusade up the Kan River, moving toward the Yangtze.

"The cult rally began as a condemnation of the Vogue Day holiday. They called Vogue Day an affront against the laws of their 'God'. But upon receipt of the news of the alien invasion in Santa Cruz, a band of roughly eight thousand cult fanatics quickly swelled to a marching horde of one hundred thousand who have set their destiny on the shores of Shanghai.

"'Repent or die' has been the call from the predominantly young, male pillagers armed with firearms and machetes, who have looted and torched farms and villages marking their sacred trek to the north.

"This farmer and his family were crucified, decapitated and set ablaze when they said they would not join the march. As a result, their crops served as little more than a fast food stopover before all of the farm structures were enthusiastically burned to the ground.

"'We're marching for the glory of God', this young man laughed with his reluctant female companion in tow. 'Anyone who does not join us is going to Hell anyway. We're just giving them a preview of things to come.'

"What the cult plans upon their arrival in Shanghai is anyone's guess. It is, however certain they will arrive virtually unopposed. The Satellite arrays are inoperative. The Controller's Office is preoccupied. And Shanghai constables, who might normally be braced for the rebellious onslaught, have reportedly deserted their posts to seek refuge for themselves and their families.

"'People who fear the alien are fools.,' this young leader shouted during the marchers' brief rest outside the city of Nanchang. 'He is Gabriel heralding the glory of our Lord's return! God will meet us in Shanghai, and no one shall stand between us and Heaven's treasure!'

"Meanwhile, no one will talk about the violent slaughter of the thousands of bodies left in the marchers' wake. When pressed, they will only tell you that this is God's will, that life on Earth no longer matters, and that their divine purpose is beyond human reproach.

"One can only guess what 'holy reward' awaits them when or if they reach Shanghai. At its present pace, the alien or 'Gabriel' if you will, may have already completed its business with the Earth long before the marchers' projected arrival. It's conceivable that Shanghai may not even be there by the time they reach Hangchow Bay. But stranger still is the fact that, assuming 'God' is waiting in Shanghai, according to documented cult lore, they could find that he, she, or it will actually be distressed with the death and mayhem they have left in their wake…and may ultimately exact a horrible vengeance of its own…for the unconscionable crimes committed in its name.

"Noah Nelson in the city of Kingtenchen, for Satellite News."

Video scene shift:

"At the intersection of Regent, Piccadilly and Coventry, young men and women adorn themselves in black plastic sacks at the base of the Bowie statue, attaching broken tree limbs to their bodies and dousing themselves in shiny clear maple syrup. Their aspiration is to win the Music Satellite Channel alien look-alike contest. The winner and three friends are promised a trip to Santa Cruz where they will meet members of the band, Paradise Lost, preceding a benefit concert which will be given for the survivors of those who died at Liberace Gardens. Meanwhile, waftabout musicians continue to crank out their songs in front of holiday tourists as if Vogue Day weekend had only begun hours ago. Teenagers barter amongst themselves, attempting to coax one another into intimate meetings with new acquaintances in St. James Park. And if you are so inclined, you can still catch a heavy buzz if you don't hold your breath when a cloud of smoke drifts from a circle of free basers sitting along the brick outside Old Winnie's Inn. Such is life in the waning hours of Vogue Day at Piccadilly Circus here in London.

"Of course, early yesterday there was a great hush over Trafalgar Square as the disaster in California unfolded on the giant rectangular satellite screen erected in front of the Charles III Gallery. But soon thereafter, the broadcast from Monte Carlo followed. And not to be outdone by the south of France, Piccadilly roiled into a veritable cauldron of human celebration, which has chosen to make light of whatever cloud should soon darken humanity's horizon.

"'The people at Liberace Gardens died happy!' laughed this androgynous threesome headed for St. James Park. 'I don't think any of us can ask for much more than that'! Still one teenage mother lamented the fate of her two children whom she brought to the festivities: 'I've had a chance to party. They haven't. It's not really fair is it?'

"Still, as the Earth's fate will apparently be decided by beings not of this world, some individuals have chosen not to accept death without a final desperate measure. Twenty-five or so London Academy students barricaded themselves in the East Thames Library (formerly St. Paul's Cathedral), where they held candlelight vigil, read scriptures from ancient cult texts, and sang outlawed cult hymns. After three hours inside, the gang was routed out by nerve gas and carted off to prison by local authorities.

"Despite ominous signs of impending doom in the heart of England, Vogue Day's crest seems to remain intact. And it remains clear that while man's arsenal may well be depleted and his life not long for this world, man's spirit…and man's laws shall be upheld to the very end…whenever the end may come.

"Patrick Stewart in London, for Satellite News."

# VII.

Cannes, France-The Beneficent Palace:

Jean-Paul scanned the stark, looted infirmary with distress and amazement. The drug cabinet doors had been forced open and emptied. Mangled wires, wrenched from pillaged diagnostic equipment, twisted outward from their wall moorings. Even the med-lounges were stripped of their bedding; not a pillow or a blanket to be seen anywhere.

"I went to the bathroom this morning," Dr. Canard began, "and when I came back to my desk, my coffee and danish were gone."

"Into thin air?" Jean-Paul questioned.

"Well, not exactly." Dr. Canard answered, fussing with the rolled jacket he had placed under the head of the anonymous young woman who had appeared in Operations earlier. "They left the part of the danish with my teeth marks in it."

"Hmm." Jean-Paul responded, likewise turning his attentions toward the unconscious young woman lying on the only functional med-lounge.

"'Hmm' is right." Dr. Canard commented. "People are a strange lot. They'll screw a perfectly familiar stranger in the blink of an eye. But God forbid they should eat after the Palace physician."

"I just can't believe Palace staff people would clean out all the common areas. Weeds, maybe." Jean-Paul commented. "I mean, what do they think they're going to do with all those things?"

"Get off on giving each other prostate laser surgery, maybe?" Canard deadpanned bitterly. "Or perhaps just enjoy one last rush of material gain before the end comes. And don't be surprised by the actions of 'Palace staff people', by the way. We're all Weeds when times get desperate enough. You, me, Victor, Georges…everybody. Barbarism isn't just a state of economics. Its a state of mind. Take away the education and the clean living, and I can be just as smelly and nasty as the next guy."

Jean-Paul managed to smirk just a little.

"You too, I'll bet," the doctor added, as he flipped on the med-lounge switch. A flat fourteen inch monitor rose out of the lounge's side near the head of the patient.

"You don't have to sell me on the fallacies of the caste system, doctor." Jean-Paul smiled. "I've hated it for years."

Dr. Canard frowned at the readings that scrolled up on the lounge screen, then momentarily turned to Jean-Paul. "Then why the hell haven't your people ever tried to do anything about it?" Canard snapped with an angry glare.

"Now wait a minute..." Jean-Paul started.

"And don't hand me all that cockamamy B.S. about the Cartel Charter and the Edict of Separation and the 'right to ignorant bliss'. You're right at the top. If you knew something was wrong, why didn't you do some-thing...say something? You had the Beneficent's ear!"

"It's not that simple..."

"Isn't it?" Dr. Canard cut in. "Unless shedding light on the inequality means that eventually, your own comfort will be threatened. Yeah. History is chock-full of Manda Martines and Jean-Paul Vendemiaires—apathetic, empowered bystanders who let kings and chancellors and presidents and beneficents strut the countrysides espousing to pimp the entire world for its own best interests! And all the while people like you, who know better, fret and despair in whispers. But when it comes down to doing what's right, your conscience doesn't have the backbone..."

"Are you finished?" Jean-Paul finally shouted.

Dr. Canard angrily folded his lips, fighting mightily to check himself. Finally he looked away and began reading the lounge monitor again.

"Look," Jean-Paul started. "The system was in place long before I was born. I grew up in it; it allowed my father to take care of his family. As I got older, I saw how messed up the whole Blossom-Weed thing seemed to be. I even wrote articles about it in school news journals, and got repri-manded pretty severely by some scary people in some high places. I tried to get backing in the Weeds, but they seemed like they didn't really care.

After awhile, I decided being a dissident wasn't worth it. So I went about my business of simply trying to graduate on time. When I got out of college, all the job slots for my major were filled. Fortunately, I minored in Public Operations and miraculously landed a job in Cannes. Eventually I was able to get back into physics and combine my two areas of interests into a pretty decent career. I've been happy ever since. And that's all I can care about! It'd be nice to change the world the way we want it, but I've found that there are greater factions who have a vested interest in keeping things just the way they are."

"'Greater' factions?" Canard questioned. "Or simply stronger in their convictions."

Jean-Paul instinctively poised his retort. But as the doctor returned to his business with the lounge monitor, somehow the ideological debate at this belated juncture cast itself into a sphere of tragic irrelevance. Instead, while Dr. Canard continued, Jean-Paul seized the reprieve to pace to the foot of the med-lounge and admire the young woman who lay there.

She bore the unspectacular simplicity of a forest maiden, like those drawn with fine ink in children's storybooks. Artlessly beautiful in the utter absence of synthetic beauty. Her cheeks were of a rich and natural coloring. Her nose, long but stately in its narrowed elegance. Her lips were small, soft and pink as the day they were birthed. Her dark brows and thin lashes rested carelessly in their indolent slumber.

Her body beneath the gown shewed equally appealing in its modesty. Her breasts were small, her waist narrow enough, and her hips were broad, but firm in the mold of Renaissance sculptures of goddesses or queens.

"And the voice." Jean-Paul mulled over again. He had never seen the like of her, but the voice whispered faintly to his memories.

"You'd think we'd have seen her before." Jean-Paul said aloud.

"Not necessarily." Dr. Canard winced at the information scrolling on the monitor. "You've been locked away in Ops for the last forty-eight hours. Since the disaster and the subsequent lapse in security, I've been watching people wander in and out of here all day. She's probably just a local who got trampled and dinged on the head by the hordes of people lighting out of here this afternoon!"

"She's beautiful." Jean-Paul muttered aloud.

"What?" Dr. Canard cupped his ear.

"Nothing."

"I'll say this for her." Dr. Canard shook his head. "Either this girl was just born yesterday, or she's got the cleanest, healthiest anatomy for a girl her age I've ever seen."

"How old is she?" Jean-Paul asked.

"Scan says 8,142 days, plus or minus twelve hours." Dr. Canard frowned. "That works out to twenty-two and a few months. But her condition is…unreal! Not one microbe of carbon monoxide, in her lungs which is impossible if she's been anywhere on Earth for more than a day. Heart beats like store-bought new, which is unheard of—even the best of us have signature irregularities. Liver couldn't be cleaner if you boiled it for an hour. Red cell/white cell count is perfect. Veins and arterial networks are perfectly clear. Muscle development is perfect. In fact, I'd say she exercises with some regularity. Teeth are perfect. Bone structure, perfect. Hair has so much protein you could string a harp with it. And most unbelievable of all, not one molecule of scar tissue…anywhere!"

"You mean she's never even been…scratched?" Jean-Paul continued to stare at her.

"This baby's never even been bruised." Dr. Canard spoke, with both brows raised to the center of his forehead.

"Then why did she pass out?" Jean-Paul questioned.

"Well, according to what I'm seeing," Canard noted, "her tank's on empty. She hasn't eaten a thing in I don't know how long."

"Any chance you could be getting false readings?" Jean-Paul asked as he lightly ran his palm along the outside of her leg. "It could have been damaged during the looting."

"I thought so." Canard scratched his head. "I hoped so! Three diagnostics say it's supposedly working fine, though. I even ran a scan on my own

hand to make sure. Arthritis, the knuckle I shattered sixteen years ago, and
some lousy circulation all show up as they should…I guess."

"Then she's perfect." Jean-Paul marveled, kneeling down and taking
her by the hand. "She really is perfect."

"Now hold on there." Dr. Canard chuckled. "Before you decide to
break into song and serenade her into the valley, you need to know something."

"What's that?" Jean-Paul whispered as he tenderly brushed her hair
away from her forehead.

"She's also pregnant." Dr. Canard smiled.

"Pregnant!?" Jean-Paul snapped out of his trance and rose to his feet.

"Yeah. About seven weeks."

"How?"

Dr. Canard smirked, shook his head, and returned his gaze to the monitor.

Embarrassed by his own question, Jean-Paul struggled to clarify, "What
I meant was, how could she be so totally…inviolate, but be seven weeks
pregnant?"

"Tender loving?" Canard cracked.

Unamused, Jean-Paul's face wrinkled with perplexedness. Then her
voice came back to him again.

"Do we know who she is?" Jean-Paul ushered her face through his
memory of acquaintances.

"Good question. I've ordered a DNA trace. Assuming global disappearances haven't damaged the information net, we should have an answer in…"

Dr. Canard's eyes jumped with surprise. Then he frowned and re-input
the identification request.

"What is it?" Jean-Paul asked.

"Nothing." Dr. Canard said straight faced. "Maybe this thing is damaged."

"Why?"

"Damnit!" Dr. Canard exclaimed. "There it is again!"

"What?"

Dr. Canard loosed a heavy sigh, then looked out at Jean-Paul, mildly despondent. "Well…I'd like to tell you who this young lady is, but…"

"But what?"

"But according to the DNA match, the infobase is telling me…this is Louisette Richelieu."

# VIII.

Over Grenoble, France:

"I presume the media was advised of my visit." Victor spoke, glaring at the cloud configurations passing carelessly beneath his transport window.

A look of worry immediately crept over Kelp's long face as his color visibly drained to a pestilent, grayish-white. He quickly looked over to Manda who sat on the cabin floor with her eyes closed and her head resting comfortably on her fist. Kelp needed her again, but she appeared to be napping peacefully against the bulkhead, unaware of his latest crisis.

"Kelp!" Victor raised his voice with impatience. "I said the media has been advised of my visit, correct?"

Kelp swallowed hard. His mouth went dry. His stomach churned until he felt himself growing nervously sick. In following the Champion all about the Palace for the past several hours, he had repeatedly heard him mention the media and the importance of their coverage of this momentous event. Yet it never occurred to him that the duty to ensure their attendance rested squarely upon his station. Now it was too late.

"I um..." Kelp began to stammer, dreading the repercussions of the admission of his omission. "Well...N..."

Out of the corner of his eye, Kelp suddenly caught a glimpse of Manda lightly stirring. Turning toward her, he saw her wide awake, arms folded, smiling at him with a mocking grin of pity.

Kelp bulged his eyes, silently cajoling an answer from her. Manda inaudibly snickered through her nose, nodded her head in the affirmative, then lazily closed her eyes and returned to her nap.

"Yes, my lord!" Kelp hastily called out loud to Victor.

Victor turned his head from the window and ruefully chastised Kelp's delayed, then overzealous response with a harsh scowl.

When the Champion returned his attentions to the snow-coifed alpine mountains to the east, Kelp melted back into his seat, relieved to have narrowly averted yet another blunder.

Victor, meanwhile, continued to absorb the rolling landscapes and their immaculate enormity as they passed beneath him. White mountains, brown hills, and finally the lush green fields of farms and vineyards. And then the spires of small towns and larger cities. And the people, the subjects who dwelt therein.

"If I shall make ye free, ye shall be free indeed," he spoke to his faint reflection, etched across the lands below.

"Do you know those words, Kelp?" Victor asked, transfixed on the image in the window.

"Uh…yes." Kelp fumbled. "I mean…no.

I…mean…actually…uh…only as I just heard you say them…just then…my lord."

"I'm not surprised." Victor smiled at himself. "They are ancient words spoken by a king of kings, a ruler of rulers. A man who called himself Jesus Christ."

Manda's eyes suddenly popped open.

"This man," Victor continued, "and of course, he was only a man, was able to…manipulate the human conscience in a way no human ever has. Not Socrates. Not Aristotle or Plato. Not Mohammed. Not Buddha. Not even Marx. He told a world of God-fearing people that he, in effect, was God. And while he was crucified for his 'blasphemous' indiscretions, his martyrdom enshrined his memory into the very marrow of civilization throughout history. Even today, we measure the passage of time by his life—A.D.: 'the year of our lord'. Most of us don't even stop to think about it anymore, except for the smattering of cultists hidden away in their lamp-lit caves waiting for his 'second coming'.

"Yes, they've waited for centuries; watching statues 'bleed' wine; watching paintings 'cry' with condensation; watching his image appear in the clouds or the stars or on pealing tree bark or rusted oil drums…because he said he'd return…some day.

"And in the meantime, wars were fought for him; against him; about him; but rarely without him. Billions gave up their lives to defend this martyr's image. And in the end, all so his followers who survived could continue to sit and wait for the fulfillment of his…'prophecy'.

"But how could he fulfill his 'prophecy'? He was dead! But then again, he was supposed to be 'God', wasn't he? And if he said it would be so, then to his followers, it would be. No time limit. No restrictions. Just his alleged divinity, his legend and his promise."

"Turning cult monger on us, are we?" Manda acidly accused sitting up against the bulkhead.

Kelp slumped further into his seat, cringing at the tone of her voice directed at the Beneficent Champion.

Victor, however, only smiled arrogantly, turning slowly to meet her charge.

"Really woman, if you want me to kill you, why don't you just ask." Victor spoke nonchalantly.

Manda shook for an instant in anticipation of a possible assault. But when he did not move, she flared her nostrils, took a deep breath and leaned backward, abdicating her challenge, but holding his eyes.

"Actually, I'm not going to monger any cult," he said, returning his gaze to the window. "I'm going to let the cult monger me. Jesus gave his subjects love. So will I. Jesus gave his subjects humility. So will I. Jesus healed the sick. I'll heal the sick. Jesus fed five thousand. Hell, I'll feed five million. Jesus promised life after life. In the wake of the invasion, I'll promise them their mortal lives…which, I'm sure will suffice. Jesus battled 'Satan'. I'll battle the alien. And win, lose or draw, I'll have what Jesus had. Immortality etched upon the face of human history. A king of kings for all time."

Kelp smiled nervously, first at Victor, then at Manda, then at Victor again. Neither looked in his direction.

Manda stared blankly at the floor trying to make sense of the Champion's claim.

Victor continued to stare over the landscape, with his indelible dominion over all things fixed in his mind.

# IX.

Cannes, France-The Beneficent Palace:

"Louisette?" Jean-Paul exclaimed. "This girl?"

"That's what the DNA trace says." Dr. Canard confirmed. "But like I said before, the entire information net is probably messed up because of all the worldwide disappearances of hardware."

"But it almost makes sense." Jean-Paul frowned. "Her voice…I thought I recognized it. And when you mentioned Louisette…it's her voice I thought I was hearing."

Dr. Canard looked at Jean-Paul, smiled, and shook his head in total disagreement.

"Look, Jean-Paul. Maybe you know what you think you heard," the doctor began. "But I brought Louisette Richelieu into this world. I've been her doctor since day one. I know more about her physiology than I care to know. I've supervised every surgery, prescription, and therapy (this side of pumping her stomach every nine months), she's had from the day she was born. There's no way this woman here on the med-lounge is her!"

"But…" Jean-Paul mildly offered protest.

"Uh, uh." Dr. Canard waggled a finger. "I'll show you."

The doctor ordered the computer to bring up Louisette's medical history.

A long scroll appeared with the notation "please say 'continue' for next screen".

The log read as follows:

Louisette Antoinette Richelieu
Born: May 19, 2152
Sex: Female
Mother: Dierdre Paulette Richelieu
Father: Georges Louis Richelieu II
Height: 9.213 cm
Weight: .9847 kg

5/20/52-Placed on full incubatory respiratory assistance. Lungs, cranium, drained of excess fluids.
5/21/52-Treated for jaundice.
5/25/52-Treated for pneumonia.
6/12/52-Taken off of incubatory respiratory assistance.
6/27/52-Discharged.
8/30/52-Treated for dehydration, pneumonia.
9/8/52-Discharged.

"She was premature." Jean-Paul noted.

"Yes, she was." Canard confirmed. "Her mother had had some extensive cosmetic abdominal and pelvic reduction surgery done in her early twenties to prolong her modeling career. Her muscles were so weak there, it really screwed up her pregnancies. That and the fact that she was a pretty bad pill junkie. Personally, I was fairly certain she was going to miscarry again. But when she finally hit the seventh month, everyone was ecstatic."

"I understand most of this, but what's with the dehydration and the second bout of pneumonia?" Jean-Paul asked.

"Well," Canard sighed, "motherhood just wasn't Dierdre's thing. She'd take off and leave Louise for days at a time to 'clear her head' without telling anybody. Maids would find Louise half frozen with a full diaper all the time. We finally assigned a full-time nurse which suited Dierdre just fine. I don't think the poor kid knew who her mother was until she was five."

Jean-Paul could only shake his head.

Dr. Canard ordered "continue".

9/27/52-Vaccination-Measles. Mumps. Rubella.
10/21/52-Vaccination-Whooping Cough.
11/19/52-Vaccination-Cancer series I.
12/10/52-Vaccination-Neuromuscular spinal.
12/25/52-Vaccination-Polio.
1/15/53-Vaccination-Tuberculosis.

2/16/53-Vaccination-Cancer series II.

2/30/53-Vaccination-Hepatitis.

3/30/53-Vaccination-HIV A

4/9/53-Vaccination-HIV B

4/22/53-Vaccination-Cancer series III.

7/3/53-Concussion (mother fell holding child). Treated and released.

1/4/54-Pneumonia. Discharged 1/12/54.

"Pneumonia again?" Jean-Paul frowned.

"Dierdre didn't want the nurse on a public family vacation." Dr. Canard clarified. Said it made her look like an unfit mother. Imagine that."

6/17/54-Laser seal of knee gash (running). Treated and released.

10/11/54-Left eye infection. Treated and released.

2/3/55-Laser seal of right ankle gash (fell from grav-cycle). Treated and released.

6/1/55-Tetanus booster.

7/7/55-Overdose of mother's tranquilizer prescription. Stomach pump. Enema. Discharged 7/11/55.

12/5/55-Forehead contusion (cause undisclosed). Treated and released.

8/7/56-Crayon stuck in nose. Treated and released.

11/13/56-HIV booster.

1/4/57-Begin Counsel/Therapy for hyperactivity (at mother's request). Weekly.

5/28/57-Aptitude tested. Upper fourth percentile.

9/9/57-Prescribed pediatric tranquilizer (at mother's request. Medical opinion is that Louise is a perfectly normal five-year-old.)

10/1/57-Hyperactivity Counsel/Therapy discontinued.

11/30/57-Treated for lethargy and depression (due to parental misuse of child prescription). Tranquilizer prescription discontinued. Released.

5/27/58-Aptitude tested. Upper third percentile.

8/28/58-Enrolled at Helga Buehner School in Switzerland.

9/17/58-Compound fracture of the left tibia (ski lesson accident). Surgery. Electrostimulus splint fitted. Discharged 9/25/58.

10/27/58-Begin Counsel/Therapy for depression. Bi-weekly.

12/10/58-Electrostimulus splint removed.

3/12/59-Counsel/Therapy for depression discontinued.

5/22/59-Aptitude tested. Upper fourth percentile.

10/8/59-Left ankle sprain (field hockey). Treated and released.

11/20/59-HIV booster.

9/23/60-Laser seal of chin laceration (field hockey). Treated and released.

1/2/61-Upset stomach. Treated and released.

5/26/61-Aptitude tested. Upper ninth percentile.

10/3/61-Shin splints (field hockey). Treated and released.

4/17/62-Upset stomach, severe headache. (School physician noted that it appeared to be the result of excess alcohol intake). Treated and released.

12/9/62-HIV booster.

3/11/63-Teeth mark abrasion (fighting). Treated and released.

5/24/63-Aptitude tested. Upper twenty-second percentile.

8/29/63-Constant nose bleed. (School physician noted cocaine in urine specimen. Louise denied usage. No action taken.) Treated and released.

11/6/63-Right knee surgery to repair torn medial collateral and anterior cruciate ligaments (field hockey). Fitted with electrostimulus splint. Discharged 11/21/63.

12/27/63-Overdose of pain pills. (Determined by school physician and authorities to have been a suicide attempt.) Discharged 1/7/64.

12/29/63-Begin Counsel/Therapy for depression. Weekly.

3/2/64-Begin Therapy/Rehabilitation of right knee. Four days/week.

3/30/64-Re-injury of right knee. (During fight at an unauthorized music concert in Berlin.) Surgery. Re-fitted with electrostimulus splint. Discharged 4/8/64.

5/1/64-Begin Counsel/Therapy for alcohol abuse. (School physician noted Louise admitted usage began two years prior to counseling.)

5/20/64-Blusilver poisoning (at birthday party). Treated and released.

5/23/64-Begin Counsel/Therapy for general substance abuse. Weekly.

5/24/64-Begin Therapy/Rehabilitation of right knee. Four days/week.

6/16/64-Therapy/Rehabilitation of right knee discontinued (at patient's request).

6/22/64-Minor abrasions, bruises (from alleged sexual assault by field hockey coach. Physician believes injuries may have been self-inflicted. See legal for details.)

7/1/64-Counsel/Therapy for alcohol and general substance abuse suspended (at mother's request).

7/1/64-Counsel/Therapy for depression discontinued (at mother's request).

7/17/64-Cosmetic surgery (at mother's request). Nose reduction.

7/19/64-Prescription. Micro-organic fat digestors. (at mother's request. Physician noted normal height/weight distribution already present.)

7/31/64-Cosmetic surgery (at mother's request). Chin reduction.

8/21/64-Cosmetic surgery (at mother's request). Cheek implantation.

8/28/64-Cosmetic surgery (at mother's request). Ear taper.

10/12/64-Fractured vertebrae, broken right tibia. (high-speed hover quad-public transport collision in Germany). Fitted with electrostimulus cervical collar and leg brace. Discharged 10/27/64.

12/16/64-Begin Counsel/Therapy for Bulimia. Weekly.

12/19/64-Cocaine poisoning (on winter holiday in South America). Comatose for 37 days. Discharged 2/5/65.

2/4/65-Resume Counsel/Therapy for alcohol/general substance abuse (at Beneficent request).

5/29/65-Aptitude tested. Upper sixty-first percentile.

6/18/65-Cosmetic surgery (at mother's request). Double hip replacement. Pelvic bone reduction. Discharged 7/3/65.

6/18/65-Counsel/Therapy for Bulimia, alcohol/general substance abuse suspended (at mother's request).

6/25/65-Begin Rehabilitation/Therapy for walking.

8/1/65-Cut wrists, blood loss (suicide attempt). Discharged 8/3/65.

8/3/65-Begin Counsel/Therapy for depression.

9/25/65-Rehabilitation/Therapy for walking completed.

11/6/65-Broken rib (kicked during fight outside bar during unauthorized trip to Hamburg). Treated and released.

1/17/66-Pregnancy removal.

1/17/66-HIV boost. Prescribed non-fertility medicine.

2/27/66-Collapsed nose (cocaine usage). Surgery. Discharged 3/1/66.

5/10/66-Cosmetic surgery (at patient's request). Lip enhancement.

5/20/66-Pregnancy removal.

7/1/66-Cosmetic surgery (at patient's request). Breast enlargement (polymer cellulose injections).

9/2/66-Pregnancy removal.

9/10/66-Resume Counsel/Rehabilitation for alcohol/general substance abuse (at Beneficent request). Weekly.

9/20/66-Cosmetic surgery (at patient's request). Nose reduction.

10/2/66-Complete dental recaps (at patient's request). Intravenous diet prescribed.

12/3/66-Pregnancy removal.

12/6/66-Counsel for sex behaviors assigned. Weekly.

12/21/66-Counsel for recurrence of Bulimia assigned. Weekly.

1/2/67-Full-time psychiatric analysis staff assigned (at Beneficent request).

4/15/67-Cheek and nose reconstruction (beating from boyfriend. Also see legal.) Pregnancy removed. Discharged 5/3/67.

5/3/67-Prescribed pregnancy termination medicine.

5/23/67-Aptitude tested. Upper forty-second percentile.

6/27/67-Cosmetic surgery (at patient's request). Breast enlargement (polymer cellulose injections).

9/6/67-Cosmetic surgery (at patient's request). Chin cleft.

10/1/67-Commissioned private cosmetic surgical equipment (at Beneficent request).

2/9/68-Barbiturate poisoning. Stomach pumped. Treated and released.

3/4/68-HIV boost.

5/20/68-Alcohol poisoning (birthday party in Milan). Discharged 5/22/68.

10/14/68-Severe vaginal infection. Treated and released.

1/31/69-Fainting spells. Blood detoxification prescribed.

5/20/69-Aptitude tested (Incomplete. Louise slept through examination.)

2/27/70-HIV boost.

5/20/70-Blusilver/heroine poisoning. Heart failure (birthday party in Cuba). Surgery. Discharged 6/13/70.

1/18/71-Dislocated left shoulder. Cracked left collarbone. (cause undisclosed. Louise claims fall.) Treated and released.

6/11/71-Broken jawbone. Fractured right eye socket (causes undisclosed. Louise claims fall.) Optical laser surgery correcting nerve/lens damage. Discharged 6/19/71.

12/13/71-Torn rib cartilage (cause undisclosed. Louise claims exercise). Treated and released.

2/14/72-Internal hemorrhaging (from apparent beating. Louise had no explanation). Discharged 2/24/72.

3/1/72-HIV boost.

5/8/72-Broken left thumb. Four fractured fingers on left hand (causes undisclosed. Louise claims moving furniture). Fitted electrostimulus cast. Released.

6/21/72-Sent to Delhi resort for weight gain/eating disorder (at Beneficent request). Returned 8/16/72.

8/18/72-Cosmetic surgery (at patient's request). Lower rib removal.

11/3/72-Mild skull fracture. Hematoma (from apparent beating. Louise claims fall). Discharged 11/7/72.

5/20/73-Severe cell damage of legs and lower back (abuse of cosmetic equipment. Possible suicide attempt). Discharged 6/4/73.

10/6/73-Neck sprain (cause undisclosed. Louise claims sleeping awkwardly). Treated and Released.

2/19/74-HIV boost.

End

"My god." Jean-Paul shuddered. "I never liked her. But I had no idea…"

"Lucky to be born," Dr. Canard sighed, "lucky to still be alive."

"And nothing but misery all in between." Jean-Paul finished.

"Oh, don't say that." Dr. Canard shook his head. "In between, she's become the toast of the world. A 'Pop Icon', they used to say in the late twentieth century. Beautiful, wealthy and famous! When you live that high, your personal lows are just pit stops between the parties and the adulation. After all, people adore style over substance. Substance makes you think too hard. With 'style', you can just look at it and sum it up by saying 'wow'.

"Now, of course, when Louise was a kid I felt sorry for her. To her parents she was more like a forgotten pet that needed to be boarded, groomed, and shown off to friends every now and then. But as she got older, neither I nor my entire staff of counselors and psychiatrists could get through to her. She was like a hollow mannequin without a soul to touch. Whatever I'd seen in her as a little girl had evolved into something cold and spiritless. Finally I resigned myself to the fact that she was truly destined to be the hybrid of her mother and father's union. So I just started patching up the holes and pushing her back onto the track until I was needed again. Basically, I said to hell with her salvation."

"'Salvation'?" Jean-Paul glanced up.

"Whatever." Canard dismissed with a wave of his hand.

"How did she react to her cousin's death?" Jean-Paul asked.

"Now there's one I didn't see coming." Canard rubbed his forehead. "Really broke my heart, if you want to know the truth. I thought little Anna Maria was an angel when she moved into the Palace. Couldn't have been related to Georges or Louise in any way possible, I thought. Then I get the call that night and find her the way I always expected Louise to end up. I don't mind telling you I went back to my office and cried after that. I should have known better."

"But how did Louise react? Wasn't she there?"

"Oh, she popped in for a hot moment. Cried a few crocodile tears. Then she ran off to Monte Carlo, partied her brains out, and probably forgot all about it. That's how her mother was. Her father too."

Dr. Canard waited for a response. But Jean-Paul sustained his enchanted gaze upon the unconscious young woman's face.

"In any event," the doctor continued, "as you can plainly see, while this girl lying here may be approximately the same age as Louise, they look nothing alike and their medical histories are about as similar as night and day."

"But her voice, didn't you hear it?" Jean-Paul insisted. "The inflections, the enunciations…"

Dr. Canard smiled. "If you ask me, I think you've got a little Louise fixation. You know: 'Every little breeze…'"

"Forget it!" Jean-Paul cut in. "I couldn't stand the girl."

"Then why must this girl be Louise?" Dr. Canard asked with mild exasperation. "Unless you want her to be."

"I don't know." Jean-Paul's eyes narrowed.

"All right." Canard sounded conciliatory. "For your benefit, let's do this. Louise is probably still obliviously hunkered down in the palace somewhere, so I'll have the computer locate her.

"Computer," he ordered. "Scan the upper floors for Mademoiselle Louisette Richelieu."

"Not present." the computer spoke back.

"Hmm". Dr. Canard rubbed his chin. "When did Mademoiselle Richelieu depart the palace."

"Mademoiselle Richelieu returned to the palace yesterday morning at 07:42:36," the computer answered. "She has not departed."

"Then if she's not in the upper levels, and she hasn't left the palace, where is she?"

The computer paused momentarily, conducting a comprehensive scan of the entire palace grounds.

Finally, it confirmed: "Mademoiselle Richelieu is in the Infirmary."

Dr. Canard looked around over both shoulders to see where someone else could be concealed. Then again, he looked down at the young woman on the med-lounge. Finally, slowly, with some reluctance, he looked up at Jean-Paul who was simultaneously looking up at him with the same stumped and confounded expression.

"Doesn't she have all that surgical cosmetic equipment?" Jean-Paul asked doubtfully. "This could be another change."

"Yes." Dr. Canard spoke as if in a trance. "But you're talking about more than a year's worth of changes. The human body couldn't accept all that cellular restructuring in a matter of a just a few hours."

The infirmary fell silent, except for the low hum of the med-lounge and the almost imperceptible rolling of ventilation through the ceiling ducts.

Dr. Canard grudgingly resigned himself to the improbable premise which hauntingly refused his scientific denial. With a surgeon's eye, he traced the contours of the young woman's body; methodically inspected every pore, every crevice, the pattern of her hair line, the vein network under her chin, the shape of her skull.

"I think I know." the doctor finally spoke.

"Computer, display last recorded complete visual of Mademoiselle Louisette Richelieu.

The full body image of Louisette on the steps of the T. Fonda Hotel in Monte Carlo appeared on the computer monitor.

"Augment face." Canard ordered.

The screen panned in on Louisette's face with her black curled bangs hanging over her brows. Her heavily dark-lashed eyes were light blue slits. Her incoherent, but ebullient white smile lifted her oversized, implanted cheeks. Her small nose was turned up and pointed like a tiny triangular button above her large red lips.

"Yeesh," commented Jean-Paul.

"Now show me Mademoiselle Richelieu from January, 2164." Canard requested.

The screen split and displayed an eleven and a half year-old girl standing by field bleachers, wearing a full leg splint.

"Augment face," the doctor ordered again.

The half-screen filled with the sad, plain face of a very ordinary young girl. Her small mouth almost pouted. Her short hair was braided back across the crown of her head. Nothing about her even faintly resembled the other image next to it.

"Very cute. Jean-Paul noted. "Looks a tad like Anna Maria. Except I never saw Anna Maria look that sad…that lost."

"'Forsaken' was the word I always used." Canard added. "Like a lonely puppy you see wandering the streets in the Weeds. That's how she was a lot of the time. Here, she had just ripped up her knee playing field hockey, and was undergoing therapy for a suicide attempt. I chose this time because it's right before her mother started the barrage of cosmetic surgery.

"Now computer, take the image on the right and age it about eleven years using all the genetic coding information we have on file, but excluding the account of known chemical substances abused by the subject."

The day counter in the bottom of the right screen rapidly rolled through time as the face of eleven-year-old Louisette gradually, electronically matured. Both men awaited that particular moment when the computer-enhanced image would resemble, even slightly, the Louisette they had come to know. But, as the day count continued to escalate past five thousand, then six thousand, then seven thousand, the artificially-enhanced face on the right, which continued to evolve, never even vaguely matched the "reality" frozen on the left.

Finally, the counter rolled to 8,150 days and stopped.

"Age enhancement complete," the computer informed.

"My god." Dr. Canard gasped. "Computer, recede augmentation."

The two men glared at the computer time-lapsed figure of Louisette displayed on the right side of the screen. Then they turned once more, and marveled at the pristine form of its living breathing doppleganger who laid peacefully detached from their miraculous discovery.

"It's her, isn't doctor?" Jean-Paul spoke above a whisper. "It really is...Louisette."

# X.

Lyon, France-Place Bellecour:

Kelp froze frightfully before the sprawling Weed multitudes who had gathered amidst the giant tree stumps of Place Bellecour, awaiting the Beneficent Champion's appearance on the wide, circular platform stage.

He decided to sit. Then he decided to stand. Then he decided to step forward. Then he changed his mind again. Finally, the grungy huddled maw of humanity grew restlessly impatient with his blatant indecisions and decided to pass the time jeering his helpless, inhibited presence.

"Sit down!" Manda called to him. "You're only making it worse for yourself!"

Kelp abruptly sat down several meters in front of his chair, fueling greater verbal derision from the expectant throng.

"Get up!" Manda called.

Kelp looked at her with utter bewilderment. Then others in the crowd began shouting "Get up!" until it became a mirthful chant.

Manda covered her face and listened closely for the transport signal in her earpiece. She could hear the crowd cheer loudly as Kelp, the reluctantly comical "opening act", had apparently obliged the audience by staggering to his feet. Finally, through the heavy crowd noise, she heard the transport signal come through. She frantically signaled to a knock-kneed Kelp that Victor was finally on his way.

Kelp, adjusted his trousers, which had twisted sideways around his thin waist and gingerly approached the crude, outdated, wired microphone. As he drew closer, a deafening whine began to emanate from the equally dated sound system. Finally, as he clutched the microphone, an ear-piercing whistle shrieked harshly throughout the square.

Kelp stepped back from the microphone, and the whistle died down. He stepped forward again and the shrill noise intensified. He stepped back and the sound receded. Then he jumped forward and grabbed the microphone stand and the distorted sound screeched out its mangled, head-splitting feedback.

Manda ran over to Kelp who spun around twice, entangling himself in the wiring. She reached into his jacket pocket, ripped out his wireless transmitter and all at once the air echoed and fell silent.

Some of the crowd cheered the cessation of the noise. But others screamed obscenities at the pair, who vulnerably stood with only a hundred media personnel and two dozen armed police constables between them and the hostile mob.

"Tell them!" Manda implored Kelp, who was still tangling himself further into the microphone wire, while attempting to untangle himself.

Finally, thoroughly wrapped in black cord, Kelp again lifted the microphone.

"Ladies and gentleman...and everyone," his voice buzzed from the amplifiers. "I...uh..."

Kelp looked up at the skies, momentarily distracted by the sound of the approaching transport from behind the distant spires.

"Go!" Manda whispered.

"I uh..." Kelp continued. "...would like to now introduce the uh..."

"...'most decorated'." Manda fed to him.

"...most decorated..." Kelp paused again.

"Read the card!" Manda pleaded.

Kelp fumbled for the card in his front pocket as his other hand was pinned by the tangled microphone wire. As he clumsily extracted it, the card tumbled to the stage floor then wafted away in a gentle breeze.

"I uh..." Kelp continued.

Manda finally pushed the microphone away from his mouth and motioned the crowd to observe the transport's descent.

As the sleek, gleaming silver vessel drew nearer over head, the low frequency hum of its concussed engines vibrated the spectators' eardrums.

Manda seized the opportunity to untangle Kelp from the microphone cord and escort him back to his seat. Though she was not certain whether this placed his clumsiness out of harm's way—or harm out of his clumsy way.

Despite the oppressive thunder emanating from the transport engines, the Lyonnais Weeds who crammed Place Bellecour, surged noisily with enthusiasm as the bottom door of the Beneficent-Champion's vessel slid open.

"I see him!" yelled one boy from well out of visible range of the transport's under-belly. Everyone near him either craned their necks further above their shoulders or howled blindly into the air, mindlessly ecstatic in anticipation of this momentous occasion.

The crowd suddenly roared with a dense and synergistic power that seemed to cause the very ground to rumble. Manda looked up into the bottom of the transport and saw the heels of Victor's boots as he embarked upon his regal descent, suspended in the air by an anti-gravitational field.

His boots were tan, mid-calf leather with gold and blue tassels swishing down to his ankles. His pants were solid black leather, tightly bound to his heavy, muscular legs. Over his thickly squared torso was draped a sleeveless silk tabard quartered in two panels of gold fleurs-de-lys on frosted black background (representing the flag of Weed France) and the upgraded coat of arms bearing the red fox with the lion's mane, the herbal cigar, the enlarged genitals, and the pit of fire dancing about its feet.

His massive, sinewy arms were stretched out toward the throng as if he were welcoming them all into his private den. Draped around his broad shoulders, across his wide chest were the gold, ornate Beneficent links. He plucked a giant herbal cigar from his lips as his charismatic bright white smile engaged the cameras. The lightning crisp azure eyes seemed to capture every gaze with genuine personal affection. And his glistening golden hair was modestly capped by a sixteenth century nobleman's toque. It bore a golden "V" (expropriated from Val's jewelry chest), set to one side to appropriately accentuate his stately accouterments.

From all directions the fanatical throng pushed against the constables protecting the stage area, who in turn were pushed up against the media people, who were nearly crushed against the stage itself.

As Victor's boots finally touched down, another resurgent cheer swelled up to deafening decibel levels.

Yet, if Victor was at all overwhelmed at being the heart of this spectacle, it did not show. He flipped his cigar butt toward a satellite reporter causing him to jump into a constable, who elbowed him across the nose. When Victor pointed and laughed, the enormous crowd eagerly joined him in his moment of mischievous merriment.

He stepped forward toward the microphone stand and shook his head at the tangled, knotted wiring wrapped sloppily in disarray.

Leaning forward he took the microphone and spoke for the first time.

"Who the fuck is responsible for this?" He bellowed through the sound system which echoed across the square.

Laughter filled the air as Victor mockingly turned and stared at Kelp and Manda sitting behind him. Kelp began to stand, ready to offer assistance, but Manda grabbed his arm and wisely re-seated him.

"How am I going to save the world with people like this working for me?" Victor asked the wild gathering.

Many whistled their derisive contempt for the pair that had seemed to delay the Beneficent-Champion's arrival by their very precedence. Manda felt much like a human sacrifice as she and Kelp became the target of vulgar obscenities.

"Stupid cunt!" one mangy toothless patron spat from behind her seat at the side of the stage. "Get over there and suck his cock!"

Manda inhaled and clutched the sides of her chair, impassively staring off into the distance. She wanted desperately to lash out in retaliation, but she knew it would only serve to exponentially heighten the painfully, ignorant contempt already mounted against her. She considered how this public ridicule might, in some roundabout way, be her penance for having been sequestered behind Georges' impermeable cloak of deceit for so long.

After all, she had not only been dutifully complicitous in his regime, but had been in many ways, its most ardent proponent for the sake of world stability. For this, she almost felt justification for Victor impugning her competence to a world audience. Then she was almost relieved that her relatives in Ohio were already dead, rather than witness her publicly shamed. An oddly selfish thought for an oddly confusing condemnation of her life's work.

"Ich bein ein Unkraut!" Victor shouted into the microphone. "I am one of you!"

The crowd exploded into another minutes long roar of approval for the most important man in the universe. A handkerchief conveniently appeared in Victor's hand and he feigned to wipe tears from his dry tear ducts.

"However…" he continued, motioning for quiet with his bandaged arm. "I do not come here today to celebrate with you. For today is a day of grave circumstances. Today is the day we all may die."

There was a smattering of mindless applause and several maddened yelps of celebration for even death's anticipated arrival. But the majority of the crowd fell to eerie quietness upon reflection of what this meant.

"First of all," Victor strained to add emotion to the monotonous cadence of his voice, "I must confirm for you that Beneficent Georges Richelieu is dead."

The Weed assemblage greeted the news with applause and shouts devoid of any remorse.

"Shitty fucking show!" one vagrant shouted. "Shitty fucking satellite actor!"

A handful of people near the vagrant laughed.

"I'm sorry you all feel that way." Victor woodenly scolded. "He was like a father to me. And he always cared so much for all of you. His primary concern was to always ensure the continuance of your way of life: Freedom without restriction. Recreation without restraint. He was proud of the fact that his Beneficence allowed you to live without Blossom politicians meddling in your affairs. He firmly believed in the creed: 'Weed, do as thou wilt'.

"Without him, I would not be standing before you today. He took me aside when I was a little boy and said that one day, I would be a great Champion. The greatest Champion. And while I had my doubts, I worked hard every day to ensure that his words came true. And you know something, when I was the Germanic Regional and was called upon to fight the man who was Champion, I realized that Georges' words were destined to come true that day. And when I drove that lance through the former Champion's throat on E.M. & M. satellite and became Champion of our Earth, I knew I could never again doubt his prophetic words.

"Ironically he and I were only talking a few days ago about destiny. He seemed tired and disillusioned with having been Beneficent for so many years. He felt that he had failed all of you in some way that he couldn't put into words—but I told him not to feel that way. Because he had been the greatest Beneficent the universe had ever seen. He put his arm around me and he looked at me and, (I'll never forget it), he had a tear in his eye, and said 'My son, I have done well. But there shall be one greater than even myself. A…Messiah. And that messiah will be you'. Little did I realize that in two short days, he would be dead, and his prophetic words would ring true once more.

"Yet I stand before you not in celebration. For my time is premature. Our leader, our king of kings, was murdered by the evil alien who has threatened to destroy our great paradise. And the murdering continues as the alien's giant ships are now responsible for the disappearances of over six billion people, Weed and Blossom alike. I wept for those lives most of the way here. But now, the time for tears is over."

Victor paused for a moment, his bandaged arm extended toward the crowd. His eyes were lifted skyward as they alarmingly shifted from side to side. Then he broke from the momentary lapse, as his forgotten lines trickled back to him.

"But now the time for tears is over!" he recanted with emphasis. "You see, Beneficent Georges was much more than a great leader. He was a learned scholar. On occasion, he and I would discuss the cults."

The crowd immediately became uneasy as a few loudly whistled their disapproval of the cult inference.

"Now of course he knew that there were no gods." Victor smirked confidently. "He knew that the Cult scribblings were nothing more than an amalgamation of words designed to oppress the free will of mankind and keep him from his glorious destiny on Earth. But Georges believed that while the content of the Christian Mythological writings were false, they were not written without intent. Near the back of the book called the 'Bible', there is a story that foretells the destruction of this planet and a great struggle between good and evil—man and the unknown. Georges hypothesized that these predictions were no less than a timetable set millennia ago by aliens determined to see humanity destroyed. And that the great battle foretold in those pages would be brought about by the aliens themselves to determine whether humanity lives...or dies. In the end, the evil aliens would choose their champion. I believe we have already seen him. And likewise, the forces of good—man, would choose his champion, the savior of the human race, the messiah: me!

"Needless to say, I find my place, my destiny somewhat unsettling. All I've ever wanted was simply to be a common person, like all of you. I love my wine, my herbal smokes, my...friends and all the women I can get my hands on...like any normal man. But in light of recent events, I see now that life is much more than that for me. I have been called upon through the eons to save the human race. I bear the entire burden of the universe upon my humble shoulders."

"Ha! Ha!" laughed a fat, wart-faced woman being held unsteadily by one of the constables. "Humble!?"

Many, near her chuckled.

"Put me not to the test, dear lady". Victor pasted the warmest smile he could smear across his angry lips in response to the woman's ridicule.

"Now I can hear some of you questioning my sincerity," the Beneficent-Champion stiffly improvised. "But as I stated earlier, Georges saw something of greatness in me that could not be denied. But Georges also taught me that the greatest way to lead the people is to serve the people. Georges prided himself on being able to provide people with everything they ever wanted. As Georges was your provider, I shall be your greatest provider. As Georges was your healer, I shall be your greatest healer. His only regret was that his schedule rarely permitted him to walk among his masters…you people."

"He always managed ta' get two weeks on Maui on 'is schedule!" A voice yelled.

"That is why I have chosen the great Weed city of Lyon to offer the humble symbol of my love and adoration of all my people all over my great world." Victor finished reciting.

Manda tried not to focus too clearly on the Beneficent-Champion's address. Of what she could hear, its content had become oddly disquieting. She stood and motioned to the constables. The constables broke ranks just long enough to allow a dozen or so children to line up at the foot of the stage.

Meanwhile, Kelp was handed a small wash basin and cloth from another constable which he sloshed awkwardly to where Victor stood leaving small puddles of water in his wake.

"Today I lay down my gauntlet!" Victor smiled. "I challenge the evil, murderous alien to combat in the Dome of Madrid tomorrow at noon to decide the fate of mankind! I am not blind to his power. I have seen the destruction and death he has brought with him. I have seen his terrible disregard for life. I know that he is capable of perhaps wiping out all of us with the aid of his creatures. But I stand upon the good ground…the ground of the planet Earth. And that ugly evil alien is trying to take over our home playing field!

"When I was a Regional, I never let anyone beat me on my home soil. And when I won on someone else's home soil that meant…that meant that they deserved to die. I know no one on Earth deserves to die. We are a great people. And I know I don't deserve to die because I am the greatest of people. I…am the Champion of our Earth! Champion of our Earth as none have ever been before. King of kings. Leader of leaders. The best that has ever been. The Messiah. And, of course, I serve the best as well! Georges made me see that man has never been better. And as the greatest servant of the greatest of mankind, I dare the alien to kill me! I dare him to come down off his mountaintop or wherever he's hiding and stand toe to toe and take me on…like a man!

Less enthusiastic cheers than those which had greeted him lifted themselves up in response to the Beneficent-Champion's challenge.

"For you see," Victor raggedly segued. "I fight not for myself, for I am only one man of great destiny. I fight for our children—the children of tomorrow who shall inherit the Earth!"

The tattered and filthy children of the Weeds, ranging from ages five to nine, single filed their way up the side stairs and onto the stage. The leader, a younger girl marched toward the Beneficent-Champion, then stopped the procession directly in front of him and looked up at the cold, hulking figure of Victor.

To the surprise of everyone, without hesitation, Victor dropped to one knee, took up the damp cloth in the basin and began washing the girl's feet.

"What the fuck is this supposed to prove?" wondered one man aloud.

"What's a mess…messiah?" another questioned.

As Victor smeared the dirt from the tops of the girl's feet, the rank odor emanating from the line of children stung his nose and coated his tongue. He was not certain whether it was the smell of uncleaned bodies or soiled clothing, but its unpleasantness was unexpected, making his staged performance less bearable.

He looked up and manufactured a smile for the smudge-faced child as he worked quickly to rid himself of her. The girl read something cruel in his eye and suddenly began to sob.

When Victor looked up at Manda, she immediately stepped over and escorted the crying girl off of the stage.

The next child was an older boy who held reverence in his eyes at the wonderful opportunity to meet his hero.

"Hi!" the boy spoke enthusiastically. "I'm Robert!"

"Hello." Victor spoke with a restored smile as he resoaked the cloth and began wringing it dry.

"You kick ass!" Robert beamed.

Victor smiled to himself as he began to wipe the boy's feet.

"Thank you." Victor returned.

"I saw you disembowel the Brazilian Regional on satellite last year!" Robert recalled cheerfully. "His guts went splat! You were great!"

"Thank you." Victor continued to work.

"And I saw you yank off the Martian Mining Champion's testicles right before you cut open his chest and pulled out his lungs!" Robert recalled.

"That's…right." Victor had almost forgotten, as Val's mutilated image returned to plague him instead.

"You're great!" Robert continued to babble on. "I'm going to do the things you do some day!"

Victor felt his stomach cringe at the notion.

"All done," he spoke to the boy. "Nice meeting you."

"Champ?" Robert asked as he turned to leave.

"Yes?" Victor began soaking the cloth for the next child.

"Are you really going to kick the alien's ass tomorrow? I mean…you're awesome and all, but look what he's done."

"Don't worry." Victor tried to smile reassurance to the boy. But as Robert turned and excitedly ran off the stage, Victor felt a droplet of sweat trickle down the center of his spinal column.

"My mother told me to tell you," began a young girl of nine or ten, "that you can have it off with me if you get some 'silver for her. I'm still a virgin."

Victor hastily wiped the girl's feet without showing any response whatsoever.

"Don't you like virgins?" the girl asked curiously.

"You seem very nice." Victor worked quickly.

"Then it's a deal?" the girl tried to close the sale.

"I'm sorry." Victor grimaced. "I'm…engaged. Engaged to Louisette Richelieu."

"So?" the girl frowned. "We saw her having it off in Monte Carlo. If she can, why can't you?"

"All finished." Victor looked up and smiled at the girl.

"I know," the girl pouted. "You like boys, don't you? I have a younger brother."

Victor, this time signaled to Kelp who timidly approached the girl to take her by the hand. But as Kelp reached to her, the girl punched him in the groin leaving him doubled over as he toppled back into becoming the crowd's object of ridicule.

The girl skipped off the stage. Seeming embarrassed, Victor motioned for Manda to escort Kelp back to his seat.

A grimy boy, five or six, stood before Victor with a runny nose and his tiny belly hanging out from his undersized shirt.

"Hello." Victor mechanically greeted the boy.

Abruptly, the child sneezed loudly, spraying the Beneficent-Champion directly in the face. Victor tried to blink his eyes open but the thick saliva refused to cooperate with his eyelids. He lifted up the cloth in his hand, but expressed reluctance at using it.

Manda quickly appeared at his side, handing him a fresh damp towel. He snatched it from her and wiped his face. The crowd chuckled mildly, but most could barely make out what had happened.

As Victor washed the child's feet, the boy coughed severely in Victor's hair. Victor looked up and noted the bluish discoloration in the child's face. Then lowering his eyes he spoke "all done". And Manda stepped out and escorted the sick child off the stage.

"How many fucking more!" Victor hatefully whispered.

"Eight." Manda whispered back, ignoring his ill-temper.

Several more children followed without incident. Though Victor began feeling sick that all of them, at the least, smelled horribly or were covered with some caked matter of filth. In the back of his mind, he regretted this course of his strategy. But he knew Christ had done much more before smaller audiences, to earn much less than he would ultimately reap for himself.

The strong smell of child's urine stung Victor's nose as another small girl, perhaps the youngest of all, appeared before him. She closely held a tattered doll, and her face and hands were smeared with melted brown chocolate.

Victor bowed his head to begin working, when her hand appeared near his face. Victor snapped backward.

"No." Victor spoke sternly. "You don't want to do that."

Victor tried to apply the cloth again, but again the girl reached toward him with her dirty wet hands.

"I said 'no'." Victor spoke louder.

The girl smiled. Victor bowed his head once more.

This time, the girl snared a lock of golden hair that swung from the side of his head. He tried to pull back, but the girl held on tightly. Finally Victor reached out with his own hand and tried to pry the girl's fingers loose.

"No!" the girl began to whine.

Victor finally pulled her filthy hand free.

"No!" the girl shouted loudly as she smacked him across the face with a smudgy open hand.

Victor snatched the child by the arm and pushed her down, away from him.

The girl fitfully began sobbing on her stomach—and immediately the enormous Weed crowd swelled into anger.

Full and empty bottles flew up onto the stage as the mob whistled their disapproval.

Manda briskly swept up the fallen girl and shielded her from flying debris with her body, while leading the child safely off of the stage.

Victor leered angrily at the violently hostile Weed crowd, while Kelp, who had contemplated this move nearly an hour ago, signaled the transport to come pull them out.

Manda reappeared at the Beneficent-Champion's side hoping his hulking muscular frame would shield her. But Victor jerked her from his shoulder and held her in front of him as shattered glass and liquids splattered everywhere.

Kelp nudged Victor's shoulder and pointed skyward as the transport hummed slowly into position.

Manda struggled against Victor's iron hold as a small empty bottle shattered against her knee and several others whizzed past her head.

"Let me go, damn you!" Manda yelled at Victor.

Then suddenly, a large bottle exploded against her forehead, spraying the three of them with rancid alcohol.

Manda's body went limp and Victor dropped her uselessly, at his feet. He reached for Kelp as her replacement, but the transport finally crawled directly overhead.

"Farewell," he waved to the jeering crowd. "*I must be about my father's business*!"

Kelp quickly knelt down and hoisted the tall woman's body awkwardly over his stooped shoulders.

Slowly, the threesome were drawn up into the transport by the antigravitational field emanating from its bottom door.

As he disappeared from view, Victor obscenely gestured at the crowd's ignorance and signaled for the pilot to pull away at maximum speed.

Meanwhile, Kelp searched for a first aid kit, hopeful to curtail the bleeding from Manda's gaping head wound.

# XI.

Cannes, France-The Beneficent Palace:

As she laid in silence, Louisette vividly recalled the searing agony which had torridly burned its cruelty through every cell of her body. The unsettling visage of the gnarled, twisted black alien remained etched upon the forefront of her cognizance. The fetid stench of its crackling, rotted flesh remained potent in her nostrils' memory.

As she gradually became aware of the sensations of consciousness, she braced herself instinctively for the pain which was certain to follow. After all, her awakenings had always been accompanied by some measure of discomfort or another for as long as she could remember. At this particular moment, she expected the excruciation to be even more so.

But to her utter amazement, there were no stabbing pains in her temples or sinuses. No debilitating nausea swirling unevenly through her organs. No sting of bruises or scrapes from some forgotten melee or lascivious contortion. As she slowly raised her knees, flexed her fingers, and pried open her eyelids, her muddled subconscious reveled in the unfamiliar comfort of feeling perfectly fine.

Yet the enveloping alien horror visited upon her while she lay numb in Anna Maria's carpeted floor still felt present and threatening. I feel well, but not safe, she thought.

As she finally opened her eyes, frighteningly, her greatest fear was visualized. An eerie heart-shaped brown configuration hovered mere inches from her face. Louisette let loose a loud scream and unwittingly rolled off of the med-lounge, crashing awkwardly onto the floor.

Dr. Canard spun around from his desk, saw the empty lounge and witnessed Jean-Paul hastening to assist the fallen patient.

"What in the world is going on!" Canard shouted, sounding almost parental in his address of the sudden ruckus.

When Jean-Paul knelt down to assist Louisette to her feet, she began swinging wildly with her arms, smacking him, twice loudly, across the face with open hands. She jumped up and backed against a wall, frightened and disoriented, trying desperately to absorb her surroundings all at once.

In another instant, Dr. Canard pushed between them and tried to capture Louisette's attention.

"You're okay!" the doctor spoke with a steadying gesture. "Nobody's going to do anything to you. Now do you know who I am?"

Louisette paused for a moment, eyes wide, mouth quivering. The alien still seemed so close.

"Dr. ...Retard," she finally blurted the nickname dubbed from her early, rebellious teens.

Canard's brows jumped with a look of embarrassment.

"Dr. ...Canard." she corrected.

"Yes." Canard maintained his eye contact. "That's right. Now how do you feel?"

Louisette hesitated again, uncertain of how to interpret feeling so different. She was neither chilled nor feverish. She was neither numbed nor aggravated by phantom itches or irritants. The clarity of everything around her brought a new disorientation with the vividness of their intricacies. It was as if someone had chiseled away a dull coat of translucent plaster to which she had become accustomed and showered away the scratchy granules leaving her cleansed, but uncomfortably bare.

"Fine...I guess," she stammered. "A little heavy, maybe. I'm not sure. Just not myself."Dr. Canard offered her a truce with his outstretched hand, but Louisette regarded it warily. The last hand which had extended itself thusly, caustically seared through the core of her sensibilities. It was the alien. But then she blinked and realized that this was only Dr. Canard.

"Come on." Dr. Canard spoke soothingly. "You and I have done this before."

Finally, something familiar did hearken Louisette's recollections. Distant recollections. Recollections of childhood and adolescence...and Dr. Canard always trying to bargain through her reluctance, for her own well being. She had always been ashamed at seeing him time and again—yet usually thankful that she had.

She reached out to his hand and the warm touch of his long fingers grounded her. Thoughts of the black alien slowly receded into grey as the foundation of her life crept back to her. Dr. Canard gently led her out of the corner and back toward the med-lounge. Louisette clutched his arm, resting her head on his shoulder.

"Plunk! Right onto the floor!" Canard whispered aside to Jean-Paul. "So much for 'never been bruised'! I can see why they gave you one of those desk jobs. What the blazes were you trying to do to her anyway?"

Jean-Paul was still flustered with humility. He had hoped Dr. Canard would have been too preoccupied to ask. Sheepishly, without a word he opened his hand and revealed brown and white crumbs.

"What's that?" Canard eyed the mess.

"A pretzel." Jean-Paul mumbled.

"A pretzel?!" Canard laughed.

"Um, yeah." Jean-Paul looked away.

"What for?" Canard asked.

"Well, remember when she showed up in Ops?" Jean-Paul sighed his confession. "She asked about pretzels."

"So you brought her some." Canard mocked. "How romantic."

"Only when she woke up," Jean-Paul avoided the doctor's eyes, "she wasn't all the way awake and she…got a little scared."

"Smitten by the kitten, eh?" Canard smirked. "Good thing she didn't ask for caviar."

Jean-Paul shook his head, scolding himself as he wiped his hand on the side of his pants.

As Dr. Canard concluded his light-hearted teasing, he suddenly felt Louisette slip from his arm. He turned his head quickly and caught her stopping in front of a tall mirror with a look of confusion and astonishment.

"I don't think you're ready for that." Canard addressed her feebly, lacking adequate words.

But Louisette recognized herself immediately. Or at least she recognized the woman in the reflection. It was more as if she had come upon a former schoolmate: taller, fuller, and mature in an odd sort of way that still allowed for her most distinctive features to remain easily distinguishable. For a few strange moments she mimed herself in the mirror, moving an arm, turning a leg, then twitching her nose and mouth and eyebrows. Nothing was as it recently had been. But everything was as she remembered it from another time in her turbulent life. She wanted to smile at the forgotten friend in the mirror and almost did. But then she was not certain whether this was really a good thing or not.

"How did this happen?" she continued to stare, running her hand along her neck and across her chest.

"We were hoping maybe you could tell us." Dr. Canard stepped next to her.

"You mean, you didn't do this?" Louisette spoke to his reflection.

"I couldn't have." Canard spoke softly.

"You just showed up like this a few of hours ago." Jean-Paul added.

"Showed up?" Louisette tried to recall.

"Yes." Dr. Canard took her shoulders. "You came up to Operations. Jean-Paul, Manda, Victor and I were there."

"Victor?" she spoke.

"That's right." Canard led. "But where were you before then?"

Louisette paused. She wrestled to separate perceived dreams from perceived reality.

"I was…" her forehead wrinkled. "I was…in Anna Maria's room. I was…watching her diaries. It was so…sad. I mean, not all of it. But at the end…"

"I can only imagine." Dr. Canard spoke downcast.

"Then I tried to O.D. myself." Louisette continued unsteadily. "Really kill myself! For what I'd done to Anna Maria…and everyone else. I felt myself going. And it felt so good…so good to finally be leaving. But then…God came.

Dr. Canard's head jumped back with surprise at this turn in Louisette's reconstruction of events. He darted his eyes toward Jean-Paul, who looked equally dumbfounded by the odd cult reference.

"God?" Dr. Canard asked carefully. "What makes you think it was...God?"

"Because...I called to him by name." she focused into space. "And he spoke to me, made me see inside myself, stopped me from dying."

A momentary hush fell over the infirmary as Canard tried to figure what he should ask next.

"What did 'God' look like?" Jean-Paul threw in with immaculate simplicity.

Louisette's eyes began to tear. Canard could feel her shoulder muscles tensing and shaking.

"Come sit down, Louise." Canard offered.

Louisette stood still.

"He...it...was black," she untangled the memory. "Black and large...and twisted. And he smelled..."

"Jesus." Canard exclaimed.

"The alien." Jean-Paul confirmed.

"Alien?" Louisette turned to them.

"What did it say to you?" Canard held her gently by the arms.

"Questions." Louisette shook her head. "I just remember...questions."

"About what?"

"About..." she pushed her hand to her forehead. "About...love and...truth and..."

"No wonder he dusted the Beneficent!" Jean-Paul concluded. "Can you see Georges answering those kind of questions?"

"Father?" Louisette asked with sudden concern.

Dr. Canard shot Jean-Paul an angry glare. Jean-Paul shrugged, as if to say that "it had to come out some time."

Canard tenderly took Louisette by the hand and led her to the edge of the med-lounge where he carefully seated her. Then, with heavy sadness, he looked her directly in the eye.

"Louise...sweetheart," his lip quivered just a little. "There's a lot you seemed to have missed. Your father...died yesterday. In fact...a lot of people have died. Billions."

"God killed father?" Louisette's voice shook.

"Louise." Dr. Canard tried to steady her. "That thing is not God. It's some kind of alien that landed here a couple of days ago and is responsible for the loss of billions of lives."

"No." Louisette fussed. "That's not right. He came to me—and I was already dying. And he saved my life. He couldn't kill father. He wouldn't have!"

"Louise." Canard pressed to get through to her. "I'm sorry. But...the way your father died, nothing on Earth we know could have caused his death in just that way. It was that thing all right."

"Then why didn't it kill me? I wanted to die!" Louisette sobbed.

"We don't know."

"We don't even know why the damn thing is here!" Jean-Paul added. "It just began systematically wiping us out all over the globe."

"Victor?" Louisette wiped under her eyes.

Jean-Paul suddenly dropped his arms and momentarily looked away.

"Victor is...fine." Dr. Canard confirmed. "Said he had a little run-in with that alien thing right after it murdered Georges. But he's fine. He's Beneficent now."

Louisette was not certain how to take the news. She instinctively wanted to smile and say it was "wonderful", but her new face retained no skill in sculpting mendacious illusions. Instead, her eyes grew hard, and her lips budged indecisively.

"That's nice," was all she could conjure.

"So what's with all this 'God' stuff?" Jean-Paul asked pointedly, trying to fight down his accusatory tone. "What do you think the alien has to do with the cults?"

Louisette's eyes receded into another search through her turbid memories. She pushed past the acceptance of her father's death. She struggled mightily through the grotesque face of the alien's dead-fleshed mask. Finally she came upon the despondent, ravaged visage of Anna Maria in her final diary entry. The words: "Why hast thou forsaken me?" echoed resoundingly in her thoughts.

She urgently clutched the front of her lace gown and began pinching down the center of it. She felt the tiny object nestled warmly between her breasts. She then, reached inside the open neck of the gown and pulled out the gold chain with the tiny diamond studded Latin cross dangling brightly from it.

"This was Anna Maria's," she said softly. "She was wearing it the night she died."

Dr. Canard's eyes fixed on the glimmering symbol.

"I don't remember seeing this," he sounded betrayed by his apparent oversight.

"Wesley gave it to me...with a letter." Louisette answered.

"A letter?" Canard questioned with piqued interest. "What'd it say?"

Louisette fought down the sorrowful emotions which accompanied thoughts of her cousin's suicide. It became amazingly clear to her, that she might never be able to truthfully absolve her hand in the girl's tragic death; she would simply have to teach herself to live with it.

"It made no sense to me at the time." Louisette cleared her throat. "It said things about 'the Lord' and 'Heaven' and asked for forgiveness. But when I got back from Monte Carlo, I found her diaries. Months of them. She found a...Bible. She read it. And it changed her. Made her so...incredibly sure about...so many things."

"It made her kill herself." Jean-Paul presumed.

"No!" Louisette raised her voice. "Victor did! I did! She loved us! Loved us both! And we betrayed her!"

"Louise, what are you talking about?" Canard took her hands.

"Victor…raped her." Louisette spoke through clenched teeth. "You saw all the bruises."

Dr. Canard lowered his eyes.

"And I gave her the blusilver," she somberly continued. "I thought it would help her…like it'd helped me."

Both men fell silent.

"He used to rape me too, you know." Louisette reflected. "Or maybe because I always came back, maybe it wasn't rape. At times he could be so dear. But other times he used to punch me and kick me and break bones every now and then. But you knew that, didn't you doctor. You used to try to get me to admit it, but I wouldn't. After all, he was the Champion. I should have been honored. And besides, what could you have really done if I'd told you? Tell father? Make him choose between his dumb, drugged daughter and his prized Champion? Father had enough to worry about without my causing another scandal."

"Louise…" Dr. Canard wanted to console.

"Anna wasn't weak minded." Louisette glared at Jean-Paul. "She was young, but she wasn't weak. In fact, she was stronger than any of us. She wasn't worried about what people thought. In fact, she detested what we've become. If she had been weak, she'd have been like me. Happy and high every day of her life. No one would have questioned that. She'd have fit in just fine with all the rest of us. But she wanted the truth. And she was willing to sacrifice every measure of comfort and convenience to have it. She couldn't see the world in terms of Blossom or Weed. She could only see people. She could only see souls. Souls, drowning in the man-made…bullshit; lies scrawled into law on government toilet paper. Lies telling us that there is no God and that we should have as much 'fun' as we can until we die, with no idea of what our lives were all about!

"Anna's only mistake was that in her heart she loved people so damn much. She loved God. But she loved her uncle and Victor and me, also. And we betrayed her! For her, that was the most unbearable thing. I mean...everything she tried to do was FOR us. Yet we abandoned her like...St. Joan.

"I only hope now (and I have no idea what Heaven is or what the rules are supposed to be), that she made it to Heaven...made it to God. More than any of us left on Earth, she deserved it. It's what she wanted most, I think."

Jean-Paul shook his head in disbelief as he stared in awe of the flustered young woman of conviction, who still answered to the name of Louise.

"'Different as night and day', I think I said." Dr. Canard fancied. "I guess the only real difference between night and day is illumination."

Louisette gave them both a quizzical look as if suddenly detached from her charged discourse.

"So Anna Maria made herself a Christian?" Dr. Canard probed. "Jesus, Paul, John, Matthew, the Tribulation...all of that?"

"I...think so." Louisette answered, not terribly certain.

"So what do you believe?" the doctor asked.

"I think she was probably right." Louisette responded defensively.

"No. I didn't ask you that." Dr. Canard looked into her eyes. "What do you believe?"

Louisette stared into his kind blue eyes. The eyes of the only man, the only person other than her younger cousin, who had ever shown her more than an obligatory measure of care or concern. But even removed from the conventional boundaries of legality, she was well aware of the inviolate sanctions levied by law against cult symbols, cult rhetoric and cult beliefs. She had even seen a schoolmate or two shuttled off to Banks Island for deprogramization. Though at the time, she could not conceive of a cult's lure, when drugs, sex and travel were in abundance. She carelessly dismissed their punishments as a fool's fate for a fool's folly. And even though she had earlier brandished the Latin cross at the T. Fonda Hotel, those actions were more attributable to a complete absence of sobriety, rather than any residing truth in her heart.

But now, the Palace physician was pointedly asking her about her beliefs. And in her sobered state of mind, she wondered if trusting this person could bring down upon her some disturbing secular indictment of her reason, her sanity and her freedom.

"I believe in God." Louisette stated flatly.

"Why?" Dr. Canard challenged.

"Because…" Louisette swallowed hard. "Because every time I have tried to take my own life, he stopped me. He stopped me because he wanted me to live…wanted me to see or do something."

"How do you know?"

"Because…"

"I saved you all those times, didn't I?" Dr. Canard pushed. "They brought you to me and I saved you, treated you. I'm a man of science. I'm a man of medicine. I'm your doctor, isn't that right?"

"Yes." Louisette answered.

"Then how can you say that God stopped you from killing yourself?" Canard cornered her.

"Because…" Louisette spoke softly. "Because you weren't in Monte Carlo."

"Excuse me…?" Canard shook his head.

"The Anti-Grav Plunge." Louisette finally focused on the incident. "I tried to kill myself then. I pretended like I didn't know what I was doing, but I'd been 'Plunging' for years all over the world. The instructor put the belt on my waist, and I…pulled off the battery pack and dropped it in his pocket. Then I fell…and waited to hit the floor. I was so doped up I knew I wouldn't feel much, but I wanted to be sure to hit that floor because I knew that would be it. I heard the signal go off and I didn't touch anything, not that the field button could have worked without the battery. I heard people screaming and I just shut my eyes. Then after what felt like a ten thousand-meter drop, I just stopped in mid-air. I knew it wasn't the field. It felt totally different. It was something else. And then it just dropped me to the floor. I was angry for an instant, but then I just laughed. I just went with it. I was so high, it was just something new. But the next morning, I realized what happened was impossible. Then I watched Anna's diaries. And realized…God must have been holding me out for…something…all along."

Jean-Paul sat in stunned silence.

With a heavy sigh, Dr. Canard rose to his feet.

"Anna Maria…was right," the doctor consoled. "I only wish she'd confided in me. Or I had confided in her."

"Then the alien is God?" Louisette wondered.

"I doubt it." Canard rebuffed. "But based on what you've told me, it fits in some kind of way."

"Then what now?" Louisette pushed her hand through her hair.

"I haven't the foggiest." Canard confessed. "Maybe we should just…pray."

Dr. Canard closed his eyes and took Louisette's hand.

Jean-Paul stood away, arms folded.

# XII.

On Satellite:

Announcer: Hello everyone. And now to tell all of you what you just saw, it's time for political analysis from…the Disseminators. And here's your host, Tom Mourning.

TM: Good morning, afternoon, or evening or whatever hour it happens to be in your part of the world. We have just seen an extraordinary event; Champion Victor Esel Hausmeister acceding to the title of Beneficent, making his first public address before a humongous crowd at Place Bellecour in Lyon, not to mention an even humongouser (haw, is humongouser even a word?), humongouser crowd on E.M. & M. satellite (although, as you well know, the second "M" in E.M. & M. is no longer with us since the Moon bases were completely destroyed yesterday).

We are honored to have with us today, our esteemed panel of political experts to tell all of us exactly what it was we just saw happen in Lyon and what it means to the survival of mankind. On the far left (for no particular reason, I assure you), is Mr. Judd Lupica, editor of the North American Wire. In the middle, we have the lovely Ms. Magenta Ferguson, Cannes Correspondent to the Beneficent Palace for the London E-Sheet. And on the right, we have Freddie Edlestein, Palace affairs analyst and columnist for the Syrian Sun Terminals.

Folks, what I saw was very big, very spectacular, very emotional, but at times somewhat confusing. What can we tell our audience out there about what they just saw?

JL: Tom, you and I watched most of this together across the hall and I said at the time (and you heard me), I have never seen the Champion look more resolved, more confident, more determined than he did today in Lyon. Here's a man who's inherited such a horrible burden—what with the alien invasion decimating the population of the Earth and soon Mars, as we speak. His mentor, his father figure, is murdered right there in the Palace. In fact, a source close to me said it happened right in front of him.

And he shows up in Lyon, and he's resolved and confident and determined to take over the reigns of leadership and see if he can't do something about this alien problem that's tearing up the world! I have to tell you, you had to be extremely impressed. I mean we're talking about a guy, who has physically accomplished more as Champion of our Earth, than any of his predecessors. And while everybody loves him, behind closed doors people are wondering whether he has what it takes to be Beneficent. You have to think he answered a lot of those critics with his performance today.

MF: I have to agree with Judd, Tom. You had to be extremely impressed with how Victor came across today. He was witty, he was resolved, he was charming. I was almost moved to tears when he began talking about his relationship with Georges. I mean, that was something he did not have to do. You could tell it was painful for him, but he's the kind of person who's going to bare his soul if he feels something needs to be said. And one thing that also stood out for me, besides those gorgeous muscles, was the fact that he really came across as a great teacher today— something no one had ever really given him credit for when he was merely the Champion.

TM: Yeah, well, he taught some Regionals a thing or two when he was ripping their arms off and shoving them down their throats!

MF: Yes, but I think that's what's worked against him up until now. I mean, we all knew he could beat up anybody who stood in his way. But the thing with the children was so darling. He was so gentle and caring.

FE: Gentle and caring for the cameras, maybe. But you can't ignore the rumors that have pursued this man all the way back to the days when he was a Germanic regional. Allegations of murders of classmates during his survival training in Serboslovia. For almost a decade, allegations of rapes and beatings of young women have followed him all over the world. I know at least one woman who was coerced by the Controller's Office to drop charges against Victor for pulling out her teeth with a pair of vice-pliers because she refused him oral sex in the middle of a bar.

JL: Now that's exactly the kind of talk that dampens the enthusiasms people have for their leaders. That pliers incident happened almost four years ago. Nothing was ever proven. Once the media got wind of it and pursued it, the woman backed down and retracted the entire story!

FE: Well, what about all the other murder and rape allegations that still persist to this day?

MF: What you've got to realize is that Victor is one of the greatest celebrities humanity has ever seen. He's far and away the greatest Champion we've ever had—and people are drawn to that. A man in his position is bound to be the target of rumors, innuendoes and plots to ruin him. Fortunately, people as a whole are very smart and see through most of it. But it can still be very damaging and hurtful. Case in point: Victor didn't even make plans to leave the Palace for Vogue Day weekend because of all the scrutiny and attention he gets.

JL: And you can't knock the fact that he went to one of the worst Weed slums in this part of the world to give that speech, when he could have done it from the Palace, or Milan or southern California or any safe Blossom area where he knew he'd be well received. What he did today took a lot of courage, a lot of guts, and we should all be behind him!

FE: Look, I never said Victor wasn't smart. Going to Lyon was just another shrewd move to win the confidence of the general public. If he had broadcast from the Palace, it would have simply roused more suspicion about his ascent to the Beneficence, and no one would have bought it. This way he looks like he cares.

MF: I think he does care. Did you see him with those children?

FE: Did you see the one girl start crying as soon she got near him?

MF: She was only a toddler.

FE: And did you see the brand new, expensive tabard with the Weed coat-of-arms! I'm sure Weed parents were thrilled to see that. Weed kids will be killing each other in the streets to steal one just like it, since they won't be able to afford one.

JL: Oh, that's just nonsense, Freddie! You just don't like Victor! What, did he turn you down for a date or something?

FE: I hear he never turned Maggy down.

MF: I resent that! I co-authored his book last year and got to know the man very well, but your inference is slanderous!

TM: Y'know, maybe it's just me, but was anyone else here disturbed by the image of the Beneficent's assistant being hit in the face by that bottle? I don't know about you, but it gave me a pain right in the noggin just watching it!

MF: Don't worry. That was just Manda Martine—and she's not really an assistant anymore, not that she ever was. She's been retained purely to aid Julius Kelp in his transition from Public Service Head to Head of Central Operations. In my dealings with the woman, she always had a bit of a hard head anyway. I'd be more worried about the bottle of wine.

TM: Ooooooo! Are those fingernails or cat's claws I see over there?

MF: Well, I just hope it wasn't a very particular vintage.

JL: Y'see. This lady is tough [pointing to Magenta]! When I'm doing a story in Cannes, I stay the hell out of her way!

[All laugh]

MF: But seriously, you saw what I would describe as a typical domineering Manda Martine performance today. She was trying to boss Kelp. She was trying to boss Victor. She was trying to boss the children, the constables, the media! I mean, no wonder this woman isn't married. Unless a person loves to be nagged to death, who could stand it?

I'll share with you a little inside scoop on the inner workings of the Palace under Georges. Georges had to limit this woman's inter-office communiqués to one page. Otherwise, she'd swamp him under with reams and reams of extemporaneous badgering. He told me when she first came on, she had him reading two text books worth of inter-office memos a day! You can't run a planetary system that way! And I won't even get into the abuses of power, because it's a moot point. But most people saw her as the ultimate sneering spinster/bureaucrat who probably did more harm to

Georges' term, and brought more tension and animosity to every aspect of Palace life than anyone else.

TM: So what about this Kelp guy? He seemed kind of lost up there today, to put it mildly. Is he competent? Is he a boob? What?

MF: When you're following Martine, you'll always look lost! I can't tell you how many times she almost made Georges look like a fool.

FE: The guy's a comedian!

JL: You know something, if you talk to anyone around Cannes or anyone who had regular dealings with the Public Service division of Palace Operations, they will tell you that Victor could not have chosen a better person than Julius Kelp to assume the post as Head of Central Operations. The man is bright. The man is witty. The man is engaging and very funny! You'll notice that the crowd in Lyon was so at ease with him on stage before Victor arrived. They loved him! How can you not?

FE: His experience is a question mark.

JL: But what's better: no experience or bad experience? I think he'll be a breath of fresh air and bring much needed unity and cohesion back to the Palace.

TM: That's assuming there's even going to be a Palace a week from now. Haw haw haw haw haw haw!

FE: That's something to think about.

MF: I think that's what the cultists and the nay-sayers are worried about.

JL: Oh, please! Of course there's still going to be a Palace. And there's still going to be Blossoms. And there's still going to be Weeds. And there's still going to be reruns of the "Flintstones" and "LAPD 2000".

[All laugh]

But it's clear that this alien definitely is going to set us back a little bit. How far, is up to how soon the Beneficent-Champion can bring down the alien in this challenge of his.

FE: I wouldn't be so sure. I mean what we've seen of what the alien can do clearly surpasses anything we've seen Victor do. How do we know the alien won't just continue about his business and ignore the challenge altogether? I mean, Victor has done his share of arbitration and killing, but the alien commands those giant birds, too.

MF: Well, Victor didn't challenge the ships, he challenged the alien. If the alien has any sense of fair play, he won't bring his whole fighter squadron.

TM: Hell, I would! Haw haw haw haw haw! He may need to!

JL: I think we all just need to settle down, cross our fingers and trust that Victor's going to handle it. There's no sense getting into a panic over something we have no control over.

TM: So what, does Victor come out on top in this one? Or is this the end of civilization?

MF: I couldn't get hold of my hairdresser this morning. Civilization's already ended for me!

[All laugh]

TM: Freddie?

FE: I think we wait and see. If it's one on one, I go with Victor. But if the ships get involved, forget it.

TM: Judd?

JL: You have to believe that Victor has got something up his sleeve to pull this out. Ships or no ships, you've got to believe that Victor's going to pull us through.

MF: I agree.

TM: Well, okay. We're going to take a break for a commercial and when we come back, we're going to get into how Louisette Richelieu is going to perform as Beneficent Consort, assuming she returns from exile (and assuming that the wedding is still on).

MF: Oh, it is! She'll go cold turkey long enough to make sure the papers get signed. She parties a lot, but she's not stupid.

TM: And later on this evening, I'll be narrating a tribute to Beneficent Georges Louis Richelieu: At the Heart of the Human Heart. We'll be right back!

# XXIII.

Cannes, France-The Beneficent Palace:

Louisette sat up on the med-lounge headrest feeding herself a pretzel with one hand, while the other rummaged deeply through the plastic sack until it snared two more. Her eyes were riveted on the small monitor screen next to the bed. Reports of death, desperation, and Victor in Lyon continued to dominate the broadcasts. Occasionally, she would flip to a music station still broadcasting the remains of Vogue Day festivities from different corners of the globe—days old festivities which now seemed to her, from a past lifetime.

Meanwhile, Dr. Canard and Jean-Paul momentarily sequestered themselves into Canard's private office at the rear of the infirmary.

"God?" Jean-Paul raised his voice. "God? Are you out of your fucking mind? God? Louise, I can see! With her mental history and all the trauma she's been through, I can understand her need to submerge herself into some...psychological cult sanctuary! But you, Canard! You're a doctor, for god sake!"

Canard smiled and shook his head.

"You're a man of medicine and science and logic!" Jean-Paul paced angrily. "An intelligent, rational, thinking human being! How the hell can you justify giving any merit to such anti-humanist, anti-freedom, unfounded, mythological, groundless tripe!"

"Do you consider the creation of the universe, the galaxy, the stars, the planets, human beings and all the beasts that dwell herein 'mythological and groundless?" Dr. Canard leaned back in his chair

"No!" Jean-Paul shot back. "They're a matter of fact! We see them, we touch them! They're absolutely positively indisputably proven to exist! There's nothing mythological about them!"

"That's right!" Canard agreed. "But when did we know for sure? Were the cavemen in their loincloths, sitting around their 'miraculous' campfires so sure?"

"Of course not." Jean-Paul frowned.

"Why?" Canard asked.

"Because the technology did not yet exist to verify those things." Jean-Paul calmly conceded.

"Indeed. So how do you think the most 'intelligent', 'rational' thinkers of that time regarded the lights in the sky?" Canard questioned "Street lights from the far yonder?"

"Who knows." Jean-Paul considered. "I guess they were limited to their imaginations by their ignorance."

"What if one of them had stood up and pointed toward the sky and said: 'Ugh! Plan-ets!'?" Canard gestured.

"He'd have been ridiculed."

"Why?"

"Because he'd have had nothing to substantiate his hypothesis."

"But he'd have been right!"

"True. But without any verifiable proof, they'd have made him out to be a fool."

"But he'd have been right!" Canard repeated.

"Yes."

"And because of that, they should have listened to him." Canard pressed.

"No."

"Why?"

"Because they had no way of knowing he was right."

"But they would be wrong," Canard stated flatly.

"That's true." Jean-Paul again acquiesced with irritation. "What's your point?"

"My point is, that we, in our ignorance, govern matters of fact purely by the summit of our verifiable knowledge. We limit our ken, only to those things we can 'prove'!" Canard pounded his forefinger into his desk. "To live and think that way, with no acknowledgment of those things beyond our ability to conceive is to presume that our present knowledge is all the knowledge that will ever be—wallowing in our ignorance, like the cavemen who couldn't comprehend planets and stars, when we know full well there is so much more to learn and understand. There are a billion things in this universe we can't verify by the limitations of our technology. But it would be foolish to insist that because we can't prove it, those things can't happen or don't exist! Hell, if those cavemen were to walk our streets today, they'd see wonders beyond their wildest imaginings. Vehicles that fly, boxes with people's voices and faces coming out of them, people floating in anti-grav fields. I'd be willing to bet they'd give their right arm just to understand what happens to shit when they flush their first toilet. And those are just commonplace facets of our everyday lives now. At the exponential rate of technological advancements, how do you think the thirtieth or fortieth century will look to us? Unimaginable, isn't it? It would probably blind us into insanity! Yet there it would be! Hell, they may have even met the being who created all this by then. And the people of that time will look back on us and say 'how the hell did they ever live that way? How could they have been so ignorant of everything around them?' Meanwhile, we'd probably look at them with our mouths hanging open, thinking we'd died and…gone to Heaven!

"I don't know about you, but I just don't consider myself smart enough to discount the existence of God! Not when I look at how incredibly intricate, complex and remarkable the fabric of our universe is."

"Well, there's always been 'Theory'." Jean-Paul noted. "Without that, there could be no advancement."

"And thank God for 'theory'!" Canard's face lit up. "If it weren't for 'theory', my Bible would still be sitting in my basement in the bottom of a box with my fraternity sweaters and my beer bongs!"

"You were a cultist in college?" Jean-Paul surmised.

"No." Canard smirked. "Hardly! The book was just a prop from a play I was in. I kept it on the shelf in my room afterward because it made girls think I was 'radical'."

Jean-Paul lapsed into a momentary grin. "So what 'theory' made you turn."

"Neutrinos." Canard offered.

"Neutrinos?" Jean-Paul frowned.

"Yeah." Canard confirmed. "Neutrinos. Know what they are?"

"Of course." Jean-Paul answered, almost indignant. "They're uncharged, often massless particles that carry away energy from the thermonuclear process in which protons are converted to neutrons. As an undergrad, I studied under the guy who had determined that neutrinos probably hold enough of the hidden mass in the universe to reconfirm the old 'Big Bang' theory. But what do they have to do with…"

"'Massless', did you say?" Canard steepled his fingers. "That makes them pretty light, doesn't it?"

"Weightless, in fact." Jean-Paul folded his arms.

"And what color are they?" Canard frowned as if he had forgotten.

"There is no 'color' as we know it."

"Okay, it's coming back to me now." Canard thumped the side of his head. "About twenty years ago, my wife had told me to, once and for all, pare down the number of magazines I was subscribed to. My study was just littered with journals and periodicals I was interested in, but never had time to read. When I'd thought I had a chance to be stationed on Mars, I subscribed to this astrophysics periodical just to bone up on how I would get from point A to point B. Well, the job offer fell through, but of course, I kept the subscription (never read a one of 'em mind you). But on that fateful day when my wife threatened to set my study on fire, I figured I'd at least page through one before I carted the whole mess out to the disposal.

"The first article was about neutrinos! They were commemorating the two hundredth anniversary of the Cowan and Reines discovery of Pauli's missing energy link. They described these things as being without mass, capable of achieving the speed of light, and so small, they generally passed through planets without touching anything at all. Amazing, I thought. That something no one had ever seen or smelled or touched—something less tangible than even the air we breathe, could be used to help explain our very existence. My first thought was: sounds like something right out of the damn cults. But these weren't cultists. These were scientists writing about scientists! Writing with reverence about the discovery of something a man, with no physical proof, simply postulated out of thin air because his calculations couldn't make sense without them. Pauli, in effect, circumvented every basic law governing science and built his entire model around something he couldn't prove, but was absolutely certain existed. And of course, twenty-five years later, Cowan and Reines came along and snared the lion's share of the credit because they finally found proof—but without Pauli's positive belief, none of what followed could have been possible.

"So soon after that, I started wading through a lot of philosophical brush that my own profession had dragged me through. Like how the human body, constructed like a piece of complex, organic machinery could simply be the result of some cosmic series of improbable coincidences. How a human brain can independently process and access information faster than any computer we know? And moreover, how does that brain create and organize abstract principles? What's responsible for DNA encoding? Why do humans and animals have to reproduce specifically the way they do? Why do we have feelings and emotions? Why must we experience pleasure and sadness and love and regret and anger and loneliness and happiness and all the other feelings we have to govern? Why do we smell and hear and see and taste? Why is food our fuel? Why are there life spans? Why do we sense moral and ethical dilemmas?

"Believe me, I went on like that for months, questioning and extrapolating until I arrived at the one conclusion I'd been taught all my life to reject. That there could be... No, probably was something out there so big, so powerful, so omniscient, so boundless by our measurement of boundaries and knowledge that it could have created all of it...with a specific purpose in mind. I bounced this idea off a colleague of mine over chess one night. And he told me I sounded like I was ready to go join a cult. We laughed and didn't say another word about it. But when I went home that night, I dug through all my old junk from undergrad, remembering that old cult book that used to get me laid like nobody should. And

I started reading it…the history, the philosophy and the prophecies that came to pass. And over time, I came to realize the exhilaration Pauli must have felt on that fateful evening in 1931 when he solved his equation. I was totally astonished by my revelation of the truth."

"Look doctor," Jean-Paul sounded conciliatory, "I respect your beliefs…"

"Oh hell!" Canard fanned his hand. "You don't have to respect my beliefs! What kind of fool sense does it make to say you 'respect' the beliefs of someone when you think they're dead wrong? That's a cop out! I'd just as soon have you say I'm crazy, than have you pretend to 'respect' my belief in something you have no respect for! There was a time in human history where it became very much the rage to settle every argument by saying: 'I respect your beliefs'. And do you know what usually happened the next time those 'respectful' partisans bumped heads? They went to war! Cut each others throats! Why? Because they didn't really 'respect' anything but their own myopic viewpoints. And because they copped out on the argument, copped out on the pursuit of the truth, the only thing they ever resolved was to shed each others' blood!"

"Well, then I'm afraid I have to disagree with you." Jean-Paul asserted.

"You don't 'have to'." Canard observed.

"Well, I do!" Jean-Paul sneered. "I do because all cult philosophy did was stand in the direct path of mankind's rational thinking!"

"Oh, bravo, Beneficent Jean-Paul!" Canard mocked. "I'm sure Georges would be moved to know that you were listening after all."

"This has nothing to do with Georges!" Jean-Paul spat.

"Doesn't it? Sounds to me that you, the Beneficents and Cartel Charter are in perfect accord."

Jean-Paul turned away from Dr. Canard as the resolution of his countenance began to falter.

"This has nothing to do with Beneficents or Cartel Charters or Committeemen or any of it." Jean-Paul spoke in a low voice. "My grandfather was one of the last cultists before the cults became outlawed. When he retired from teaching, he used to sit out on street corners and preach to passersby about…'God'. And the neighbors and my schoolmates used to make fun of my parents and me because he lived with us. I mean, we all loved the old man. He was the best philosopher I ever knew; full of sayings and axioms that just dissolved problems in the wink of an eye. But he made us the object of complete ridicule. None of us had a clue how to defend him and my mother couldn't get him to stop. Then one day, the constables just came and took him away. Had him shipped to Banks Island. My mother went and visited him once there and came back a total wreck. So much so that my father forbid her go back again. A couple of years later, we heard that he died. They shipped us the body and we buried him. That was it."

"I'm sorry." Canard offered.

"Don't be sorry." Jean-Paul looked up. "He was crazy. He was wrong."

"He wasn't wrong…" Canard tried to console.

"Of course he was wrong!" Jean-Paul raised his voice. "People laughing at him…calling him names! Taken away in a rubber suit and lobotomized with a laser scalpel! How does something like that happen to a gentle old man if he's right, doctor? I ask you!"

"They did it to Socrates for defying 'the gods'." Canard spoke softly. "They did it to a monk named Bruno for preaching about an infinite universe full of planets and suns. They did it to King for demanding equality by birthright for every human being despite their so-called 'ethnicity'. They even did it to Christ for being their savior. Sometimes, a single person can be right. And a whole planet full of people can be wrong. That doesn't mean that the person who's right is going to win—but it doesn't change the fact that he was right, nonetheless."

"So you and Louise and everyone'else like you is supposed to be right?" Jean-Paul diverted from his grandfather.

"I wouldn't say 'supposed'." Canard leaned back in his chair. "It's more like…convinced."

"By what?" Jean-Paul exclaimed. "A confrontation with an alien creature? Louise's foggy recollection of an anti-grav plunge?

"You don't believe her?" Canard questioned.

"Do you?" Jean-Paul protested. "Do you really? She probably doesn't know what she did up there. She probably just fancied the whole thing because she couldn't stand to live with herself anymore. So she contrives some personal experience that no one can confirm or deny."

"Nothing like that's ever happened to you?" Canard asked.

Jean-Paul stared at him defiantly and said nothing.

"I won't even bore you with all my experiences from surgeries where I've closed somebody up, guessed them to have about an hour to live on full life support, only to have them defy incalculable odds and walk out of here on the road to full recovery in a matter of weeks. Louise was one of those people...a couple of times. And I won't bore you with the miracle of how the homeliest, simplest woman I ever dated, somehow stole into my heart and became my wife.

"Instead, let me tell you about how my cat suggested a surgical procedure to me that saved a man's life."

"Oh, come on." Jean-Paul chuckled ruefully.

"No, seriously." Canard smiled. "This foreman is supervising some renovation work on one of the Palace crowns about ten years ago. Suddenly a gust of wind comes along and a few seconds later, splat! He falls ten stories down onto solid concrete face first! He's dead! Or going to die for all intents and purposes. Severed spinal cord, brain damage, massive internal hemorrhaging...a mess. Well, staff council and I get together and confer over when to cut the stasis life support machinery and let him go! I mean it was clear this guy wasn't going to make it. But I said I wanted to go home and sleep on it. So they said 'fine'. I go home, go into my study, pour myself a brandy, and then ask myself what the devil I was trying to prove by keeping that poor bastard alive overnight.

"Well then, my cat walks in, hops up on my desk, and stares at me like I'm supposed to ask him a question. For the sheer lunacy of it, I ask him what I'm supposed to do and he utters one word. I blink, and I look at him. Then I look around. Then I ask him again. Same word. I access my dictionary and look it up. The word was an ancient Italian synonym for trauma. I toggle to my desk reference, and it turns out to be this outmoded 19th century battlefield method for treating head and spinal trauma. I call up the staff neurologist and ask him about it. He says he'll call me back. About 25 minutes later he calls me back and tells me to get back to the Palace because he wants to try something. Well, to make a long story short, it turned out this outmoded, outdated technique helped us maintain the patient's brain activity long enough for us to go in and repair the internal injuries. In another month and a half, the guy was talking (albeit with a pronounced drawl) and walking with the aid of bone graft prosthetics. When the neurologist asked where I had heard of the procedure that prolonged the patient's brain activity, I laughed in his face and walked away. He got mad at me, but he'd have gotten even madder if I'd told him to talk to my cat."

"And I'm supposed to believe this." Jean-Paul shook his head.

"No." Canard drummed his fingers on his desk top. "I think the point was, that I was supposed to believe it."

Suddenly, both men heard a commotion erupt in the infirmary. Canard bounced to his feet just as his office door slid open. Louisette was standing right in the doorway, looking very distressed.

"I think you'd better come, doctor," she spoke, still clinging to the pretzel bag as if it were a sacred sack.

She stepped backward as Dr. Canard and Jean-Paul hastened into the infirmary area. To their surprise, giant Victor filled the room with Kelp and two Operations assistants at their sides.

Victor and Kelp looked worn out, as if they'd just been through a brisk and harrowing ordeal. The two Operations assistants meanwhile, were busy setting someone down on the functioning med-lounge.

"Manda!" Jean-Paul shouted.

"All right! Out of the way!" Canard pushed between the two assistants.

Canard looked down into the swollen, lacerated, unconscious face of Manda Martine.

"What the devil happened?" the doctor asked as he activated the lounge and began analyzing the head wound.

"You mean you weren't watching?" Kelp asked.

Canard and Jean-Paul both glared at the man with naked contempt.

Kelp lowered his eyes and backed away.

"I was trying to shield her from the angry crowd." Victor stared at Manda's still body. "She was struck by a bottle of some liquor. I was too late to save her."

"Too late?" Jean-Paul fumed. "Again? Funny how you always manage to be 'too late' for people who stand in your way!"

"Really, little man," Victor regarded him mildly, "you have no idea. You didn't even watch. Don't put me to the test."

"Test?" Jean-Paul moved forward aggressively. "I'll test you and fail you right here and now!"

The two Operations assistants intercepted Jean-Paul one step in front of Victor. Jean-Paul struggled against them as all three pushed and tumbled to the floor.

"Let him loose." Victor smiled calmly. "I'll finish him."

"That's enough, Victor!" shouted Canard. "I'm shorthanded, as it is and I don't need another mess to clean up!"

Jean-Paul ceased his struggle against the Operations assistants as they hoisted him to his feet and held him there.

"Release him." Victor commanded. "He knows he's no threat."

Jean-Paul jerked his arms away from their loosened holds then glared angrily at Victor.

The Beneficent-Champion shook his head and motioned for Kelp and his charges to make their departure.

"We have work to do." Victor spoke coldly. "Preparations. It's too bad, though. She was an interesting woman."

The Beneficent-Champion turned to exit the infirmary when he felt a small hand alight on his giant forearm. He turned and looked down to regard a diminutive young woman in a white lace gown. After a hasty inspection, his face became a disdainful sneer.

"Hands off." Victor jerked his arm away.

Louisette jumped back, startled by his careless dismissal.

He turned again to exit.

"Victor," she called to his back.

He froze in the open doorway and turned back toward her with a look of perplexedness.

"It's me," she began. "It's Louise."

Victor stared at her for several moments in utter disbelief.

"That's…impossible." Victor squinted. "Really? How?"

Louisette shook her head and smiled. "I asked myself the same thing a couple of hours ago. But you see…"

"Oh, I get it!" Victor shook a finger at her. "More surgery."

He began to laugh.

Louisette looked down and away from him.

"What, Louise? Did you think I would go for the plain sow, Weed look?" He scoffed. "I mean, no tits, big sloppy ass, pinched up, sickly little face? Ha! Did you really think I'd go for this? You're such a pathetically fucked-up little cunt!"

Victor laughed loudly until Dr. Canard and Jean-Paul both looked up at him. When the Beneficent-Champion finally noticed that he had become an annoyance, he dumped his countenance back into an authoritative scowl.

"If you weren't sickening before, Louise," he whispered to her, "you sure are sickening now. Good luck with your new look, stupid."

He turned and strode out into the corridor.

Louisette stood, clenching her fists around the pretzel bag, feeling momentarily heavy in her heart. Then, at the moment when she normally would have broken down into tears, she noted that Victor's cruel castigation failed to pierce her as it might have only days ago. In fact, she found this particular, contemptuous, verbal assault, remarkably liberating.

Meanwhile, Dr. Canard continued his ministrations to Manda Martine.
"She's very lucky." Canard noted.

"Lucky!?" Jean-Paul winced at the sight of her swollen forehead, black-ened eyes and various cuts.

"Yes. Very." Canard confirmed. "These chunks of glass in her cheek could easily have found her eyes. Also, there's no brain swelling. Usually, with skull damage like this, you can count on some cerebral complications."

"You're talking as if she's fine!" Jean-Paul became irritated.

"Well, she is." Canard concluded. "Sorry to deflate your worry warts, but she's fine.

"What about her head?" exclaimed Jean-Paul. "It's like a melon!"

"Considering she got her head split open with a large unopened bottle thrown from some distance, hematoma of this degree is perfectly under-standable." Canard stepped back from the med-lounge. "Now she does have quite a concussion, but the actual damage is quite superficial. I'm going to drain the swelling so I can close the wound. Then I'll apply an electro-stimulus coolant to keep the swelling down and heal the outer skull. Other than that, she'll probably get to sleep in tomorrow...unlike the rest of us. If she's lucky, she may even miss the end of the world all together!"

Canard peered into his looted instrument case to determine which tool could best be adapted to perform the task of the tool which was missing.

"How is she?" Louisette appeared at Jean-Paul's shoulder.

"Um...okay I guess." Jean-Paul tried to capture her eyes. "How are you?"

"Fine," she smiled to herself.

"Good." Jean-Paul stared at her. "I was...worried."

"Well, you needn't be." she spoke confidently, "Victor and I just need to talk, that's all."

A cool chill struck Jean-Paul as Victor's name fell from her lips. Then he looked once more at Manda's injured face and stormed angrily out of the infirmary, unnoticed.

# XIV.

Atalanta Planitia:

Ellsworth Pocklington felt a ragged irritation in his throat and nostrils as he grew lightheaded. The incandescent blue light which had seemingly enveloped everything around him was gone. The droning hum which had ached the cavities behind his ears had ceased. But now, the membranes of his eyes began to dry and sting. His flesh began to sweat and burn. With all of his might, he forced himself to stagger to his feet and amble blearily out of his private library, where the leather and wood had begun to stink pungently.

He heard the anguished yowls of Billy and Hilly, his pedigreed Afghans, from the open window at the end of the hallway. As he stepped onto the strangely hot floor, he felt his numbed bare feet begin to slide. He looked down and cringed at the sight of red smears on the white marble tile marking the slips of his bloodied footfalls. It was disturbing, but a sense of urgency quickened his paces to the window.

He looked out to see his lavishly manicured green lawn and beyond it, his coveted garden of rare and imported perennials. But instead, there was only cracked, barren rock that disappeared into the harsh yellow mist, which obscured the distant horizons.

Far off, he thought he heard horrible yells and painful screams, but before he could interpret them, they seemed to die away beneath the faint rumblings of seismic instability and collapsing man-made structures. Then the effluvium of sulfur dioxide burned into his nostrils causing his inner organs to wrench.

Feeling sick and wanting to vomit, he fell forward and clutched the window sill. Just then, something wet, hairy and deformed leaped up and bit away three of his finger tips.

He fell backward and his flesh sizzled against the floor like cold meat on a broiling skillet. He struggled back to his feet as the skin on his thighs, forearms and shoulders peeled away and remained there, shriveling and crackling into nothing.

He staggered forward again to peer out at what had attacked him. Cautiously he poked his head out of the window and felt the burning mist singe away the hair on the side of his scalp. He looked down quickly and glimpsed the eight-legged, hairy coagulation that lay dead on the craggy, dried ground. Billy and Hilly were scarcely recognizable, but Ellsworth knew it was them.

He pulled away from the gruesome sight and wobbled instinctively to a cooler, safer room in the mansion. He stumbled almost blindly into the gallery, where the fireplace smoked without benefit of flame and where the Rembrandts and LaCroixs had begun to pucker and pit. The fibers from the long carpeting, stuck to the bottoms of his bloody feet. The feeling was oddly relieving.

He thought about the rare wines stored in the basement along with souvenirs and artifacts from his extensive, expensive travels. But sadly, he could now fathom them ruined by the prevailing, acidic atmosphere without needing to witness their destruction.

He swung toward the kitchen searching desperately for something cool. With every labored breath, his lungs felt like filled with acid. Each muscle movement felt like the tearing and shredding of soft tissue.

He looked across the kitchen area and felt that if he could reach the refrigerator, he might gain some momentary respite to discern how he had maddeningly come to so painfully grim a fate.

He stiffly tried to shuffle forward. The carpet fibers shifted from the bottoms of his feet and he slid unsteadily, again. Then he stumbled and fell across the body of young Eleanor, his Vogue Day companion from the evening just past.

Her pretty youthful face was a blistered, ghastly, eyeless blue mask as it melted into the floor. Her long blonde hair fanned out into the sizzling blood that deserted her peeling dried flesh. The polymer-cellulose sacks from her surgically enlarged bosom had melted through their fatty moorings and bubbled inorganically against her embroidered silk camisole.

Ellsworth could feel his pelvis and torso begin to soften and liquefy, merging with Eleanor's already collapsed form. He tried straining and screaming against the agony of this horrible death as he gnashed and ground his loose teeth that soon slipped from their lodgings and into the disgusting lump of organic matter.

His last thoughts were of things lost, friends he never trusted, family he never loved, and lovers he would never again be able to exploit for his personal gratification.

He did not live long enough to feel the wood and stone of his mansion come crashing down upon him.

And he might have been astounded to learn that his smouldering, ashen remnants were not committed to the earth of the Earth as had been customary in the deaths of all of humanity's forebears, but rather to the caustic, rocky acidic surface of planet Venus, second sphere to the Sun.

# THE LAST CHAMPION

## I.

Cannes, France-The Beneficent Palace:

11:50 p.m.

Amber, Fleurette and Jezzie giggled heartily, champagne sloshing from their gold stemmed goblets as they rocked and kicked among Victor's pillows and bedsheets. Music blared loudly, echoing noisily down the corridor in defiance of death, disappearances, and all other matters of import that would keep until morning. Victor stood oiled and naked, before the three nude women shaking a long, curved necked bottle of Dom Perignon in one hand, and his oversized, engineered organ in the other.

"Okay ladies!" he smiled tautly through clenched teeth that made the veins in his thickly muscled neck writhe. "Which one spews first?"

"The bottle!" Amber yelled. "The bottle!"

"I want to see how high the cock spews!" Fleurette craned her neck back opening her mouth as a yawning receptacle.

"Same time!" bounced Jezzie. "Same time!"

"Can't be the same time!" Victor continued to smile.

"Why?" Jezzie pouted her fat drooping lips.

"Because I said so, you stupid bovine!" Victor frowned momentarily.

"Hey, I have a degree!" Jezzie tooted her mouth. "I'm not stupid!"

"You are, if you keep whining like this." Fleurette warned in her ear.

"Okay." Jezzie fanned her hand. "Bottle!"

The tight, confident grin returned to Victor's face. He continued to shake both objects with vehement alacrity. The women giggled tensely, gleefully covering and uncovering their faces in anticipation of the momentous outcome. Finally, Victor loosed a mischievously maniacal laugh as white foam spouted into the air toward the threesome on the bed.

Amber cheered loudly as she shook the raining champagne from her large blonde mane like a soaked canine. Fleurette closed her eyes and tried unsuccessfully to catch the streams of fluid in the back of her mouth.

Jezzie, however, suddenly cried out, grabbing her face and rolled off the king-sized bed and onto the floor.

The mindlessly festive air immediately deflated from the room. Amber and Fleurette hopped off of the bed to see what had happened to their fallen companion. Jezzie was curled up kneeling at the side of the bed continuing to hold her face. Fleurette knelt down next to Jezzie putting her arm around her.

Victor impatiently scowled at the scene as his bottle grew sticky and his mood fell flaccid.

"Hey honey," Fleurette comforted, "what's wrong?"

Jezzie was audibly sobbing behind her hands.

"Hey Jez, we're supposed to be having a good time." Amber's voice trembled slightly. "You don't want to be a bad guest. What's wrong?"

Jezzie finally, slowly, lifted up her head and looked into Fleurette's face.

"He got some of that shit in my eye." Jezzie whined.

Fleurette's face jolted for a moment, shocked that it was not anything more. Then she hastily tried to fill in the expanding void between themselves and the Beneficent-Champion before the evening fell apart completely.

"Well, that's cool!" Fleurette laughed nervously. "So did I! That stuff stings, huh?"

"Fuck!" Jezzie screamed and began sobbing more.

"Oh c'mon, Jez!" Amber forced a smile. "It's okay."

"Oh yeah?" Jezzie cried. "Well get some in your eye and see how you like it!"

Victor sighed heavily as he plainly bore his irritation.

"What the fuck's wrong with her?" Victor sneered.

"She's just stung, that's all." Fleurette fought the defensive tone in her voice.

"No." Victor growled. "More like she's a stupid cunt! I thought you bitches were supposed to be professionals."

"Well, we are." Amber shook her hair. "But you got something in her eye."

"Yeah, well I'm about to put my fist in her eye if she doesn't straighten up!" Victor threatened.

"Hey, asshole!" Jezzie stood up holding her face. "You better hope your aim is a little better tomorrow than it is tonight or you're finished!"

An irrevocable pall suddenly cast itself between the naked females and the naked Beneficent-Champion. Amber and Fleurette fearfully searched the sheets, the comforter and the floor for their few articles of clothing.

Cold detest filled Victor's angry eyes.

"Sorry." Jezzie feebly tried to apologize.

"C'mon hon." Fleurette tugged at Jezzie's arm. "Get your stuff. We have to go."

Jezzie still tried to apologize, babbling to Victor's seething countenance. Then, without warning, the Beneficent-Champion burst into a horrific rage.

"Get…OUT!!" he shouted charging the threesome like a mad rhinoceros.

Victor lifted up the foot of the bed, wrenching it from the headboard and turned the mattress and boxspring over onto the three women.

Still naked, they struggled out from under the cushioned wreckage and stumbled through the vestibule of trophies and placards and finally out into the corridor where all three broke into a full sprint.

Victor gave a half-hearted chase, finally flinging the empty champagne bottle after them, which smacked against Jezzie's jiggling bare buttock and bounced without breaking against the marble floor.

"There's my aim, whore!!" Victor yelled madly. "Fucking whores! After tomorrow, I'll see the three of you staked and whipped! Whores!!"

He spun around wildly and thrust his giant fist through the dark wooden wall, causing the placards to rattle loosely against their mountings. Then he smashed his forehead against the wall and held it there until the peak of his fury subsided.

When the fire in his brain began to recede, Victor pulled his arm from the wall and stepped back to admire the trophies which honored his life of accomplishments.

Every moment of his life had been another pinnacle of greatness, another testament to his unrivaled glory. Men from every corner of the globe respected and feared him, if not revered him for his well-chronicled achievements as World Champion Arbiter. He was the living embodiment of what every man who'd ever lived should have aspired to become. Yet chillingly, he measured all of this against the displayed might of the alien—and found himself such a tiny, wanting little thing in the vastness of what the universe had conjured against him.

Victor growled away the probability that tomorrow he would be slaughtered in front of a universal satellite audience and along with it, his coveted secular immortality. He stalked back into his bedroom, snatched up a large towel, wrapped it around his narrow, muscular abdomen and stormed angrily out into the corridor.

Louisette yawned and stretched in her bed as she turned over the large book Dr. Canard had given to her. She had waded unsteadily through all of two pages of it.

"Lights out," she ordered as the room went black.

She turned on her side to sleep, but her new body protested against the familiar position. So she turned on her back and heard her stomach growl in rebellion against the enormous pretzel supper she had scarfed down in the infirmary.

"How did Anna Maria ever get through that whole damn book in a few days?" Louisette muttered to herself. "Of course, I haven't read much besides shopping catalogues the past few years.

"Still. In the beginning…could it have really been that way? Just the way it's written?"

A thunderous crash against her door shook her upright.

"Lights!" she called.

Her first thoughts were of the alien returning for a second round of conversation and to inflict a more severe pronouncement upon her, as it had apparently done with her father. But the smell was absent as was the wall of moist heat. And from all accounts she had witnessed through the media, it never made use of conventional entrances or exits.

And as she pondered it, the pounding at the door bore a familiar ilk.

"Who is it?" she called.

Another smash against the door was her answer. This time it buckled part of the way. A large hand reached through and tore the remainder of the door away. Victor's glistening muscular body then filled the entrance.

Louisette instinctively tensed her body for a physical assault—she'd seen him this way many times before: Drunk. Angry. Vindictive. The aggregate of his unhappy circumstance always boded poorly for her mental and physical well being.

"I know why you did it!" he grumbled lowly.

"Did what?" Louisette responded lifting her knees up to her chest.

"You think you can do it to get rid of me!" Victor growled through his teeth.

"What are you talking about?" Louisette pleaded. "Get rid of you how?"

Victor's face flushed with snarling rage. He charged her bed, snatching away the covers. Louisette jumped to her feet to run away, but he easily cornered her.

"I'm talking about this!" he growled, ripping open her night gown. "This! You think you can just fuck yourself up so bad that I'll just go away, right? Look at you! No tits! Big ass! Your face looks like a…an unfed collie! You think that'll do it? You think that'll get rid of me? Well, you're wrong!"

"Victor, I didn't do this." Louisette fought to reason through the alcoholic odor billowing from his breath. "The alien did it! Against my will!"

"Lying fucking bitch!" Victor punched through the wall by her head. "The alien doesn't go around doing makeovers! You know what the alien does?"

Victor pronged two of his giant fingers and pressed them against Louisette's forehead.

"He takes his fingers, see?" Victor demonstrated. "And he jabs them into your eye sockets. Then your brains go flying all over the fucking place! That's what he does! That's what he did to your fucking father!"

"Dr. Canard said you didn't see what happened to father." Louisette trembled. "He said that you said you arrived just after…"

"Fuck Dr. Canard!" Victor shouted, pushing her to the floor. "And fuck you, too! I saw it!"

Victor turned away, grabbed his hair at the roots and let loose a loud snarl of anguish. It was a sound Louisette had never heard from him, and it's pitch chilled her to the marrow.

"Victor…" she spoke softly.

"Oh god, I messed her up." Victor began chuckling ruefully.

"Messed who up?" Louisette asked.

"Anna Maria!" Victor frowned. "Who do you think, Louise!"

"We both messed her up." Louisette closed her eyes trying to cope with the tragedy. "We all messed her up."

"No, no." Victor shook his head. "Not like I did. I mean, you had her looking so good. So nice. But she wasn't ready. And I knew she wasn't ready. But I had to…"

Louisette shivered as she grappled with the troubling memory once more.

"You know how it is, Louise." Victor wavered slightly. "You know how I am. How men are in general, you know. I mean, she was there and I had to. A man doesn't just turn something like that away! But it went too far. Way too far. I should have known better. But she wanted it…"

Louisette could barely stand to listen. She had seen the aftermath of his handiwork which had been horrid enough. She did not care to hear the particulars.

"Victor." Louisette interrupted. "It's done. We can't do a damn thing about it now, can we?"

Victor's shoulders respired heavily, but he said nothing.

Louisette reached out to touch him, but he pulled away.

"You." Victor dropped into a baritone of reflection. "Me. Everyone. This planet. This galaxy. All the ideas and philosophies and history. What is it all supposed to be about? I mean, tomorrow it all ends…and we don't even know. Don't even have a clue."

"Victor…" Louisette wanted to offer some insight.

"Shut the fuck up!" Victor gestured as if to strike her. "You don't have any idea what's going on! You never did! Well, tomorrow the curtain comes calling."

He glared down at her until finally she lowered her eyes, as he'd trained her to do. He flinched his raised hand, feigning to slap her. Louisette anticipated the blunt impact of his solid knuckles, but did not move. Finally, he snorted his disapproval of her and swaggered unsteadily toward the door.

"'The curtain comes calling'." Victor snickered more to himself than to her. "Sounds like something your goddamned father would have said."

The Beneficent-Champion then stepped through the crumpled door and lumbered back out into the corridor.

## II.

Jean-Paul sat at the desk in his study staring intently at the quartered panels on his flat computer monitor.

Top left, was the map of the Earth where ninety-five percent of the land masses glowed malignantly crimson, as the giant bird/ships continued to blot away all evidence of man's existence. He fought not to dwell upon why Cannes had been spared thus far. Though somehow, he had it fixed in his mind that when the population finally struck zero, he, Manda, Dr. Canard, Louisette, and everyone in the Palace would be the final beads on the abacus.

Top right, was the cooling crater site at Santa Cruz, with its jutting rocky spire still pointed eerily skyward. Probes, dispatched in the wake of the destroyed science vessels continued to transmit spurious analytical information which scrolled across the crater's dark orange image.

Bottom right, was a formula calculation he had initiated on a hunch regarding the nature of the disappearances.

"Dimensional shift," he had mentioned in passing to Manda and Yorishu while trying to combat the giant ships and quell worldwide panic; it was only a theory from a journal he'd read. But when the satellite arrays failed, he opted to muddle his idle fear by inputting the parameters for the postulation of such an occurrence: Energy output/intake levels of the bird/ships, mass of matter displaced or absorbed, new gravitational fluxes between Earth and any other astronomical bodies, solar wind variances, radio emissions, spectro emissions, electro emissions, etc. Though, what could be gained by this information now seemed immaterial, perhaps the mere knowledge of how the alien had destroyed them would be consolation enough when the end finally came.

And bottom left, least relevant of all, were file images of Louisette making public appearances at various banquets, parties and concerts. Emerging from either hovering stretch limousines or red carpeted canopies with celebrity escorts in tow and the clamorous public fighting for the faintest glimpse of her. Always sauntering with aloof royal arrogance, pointed nose in the air, narrow hips swishing provocatively past the commoners. And always so high, everything, either comic or tragic, prompting her to laugh superciliously—and her glazed eyes never really holding contact with anything or anyone for more than a gracious instant.

Jean-Paul had always hated her so much. Her perfect form. Her shallow conceit. Her unbridled enthusiasm for making squandered blight of every moment of every luxuriously pampered day. She had been the paragon of Blossom rot. The epitome of opulent, glutinous, hedonistic ideals devoid of substance or reason. Queen of the sybarites. Over the years, he had never seen even a vaguely redeemable quality about this sickening, contemptible woman.

But now, he was in love with her. ·

"And she's carrying his child." he ruefully reflected. "But why do I care? She's still messed up in the head. Gone from a Blossom slut to a cultist cloud worshipper. Is one any worse than the other? Lost is lost! Why should I feel any different about her now? And she still wants Victor! He's beaten her, raped her, raped her cousin, probably killed her father (or let him be killed), scoffed at her real appearance not more than a couple of hours ago, and she still wants him! She's insane! But...now...for some crazy, twisted reason, I care. I care very much. And I know I should know better.

"She's praying with Canard. She thinks that alien is 'God'. I'm a fool. As big a fool as my grandfather was! He'd sure like her now. She'd have been the perfect granddaughter for him. They could have preached and prayed together all the way to Banks Island!"

Jean-Paul stood abruptly and walked away from the monitor, hoping with futility to elude the dilemma imposed upon his heart. He stepped slowly to the window which overlooked the nervous bustle of the Cannes city streets. He noted an odd number of children, seemingly abandoned, darting in and out of storefronts and alleyways.

"What would grandfather say to me now?" Jean-Paul whispered. "What would he tell me to say to her? What would he tell me to do?"

# III.

Golgotha:

Just east of the stone cranium of Golgotha, the cracked, uneven, concrete roadways were gone. The sagging, dirty, pitted, overcrowded, tenement chapels which had housed all matter of filthy human squalor and deprivation had disappeared. Even the frequent sounds of automatic gunfire and the putrid effluvium of child urine no longer lingered in the early morning air.

The sickly, emaciated prostitutes with their thin, scarred legs and their bony, sunken rib cages had vanished along with their dimly lit lamp post perches. The illegal homemade pharmaceutical outlets left no trace of their purveyance of grandiose delusions. Nor did the grimy subterranean nightclubs and the depraved sidewalk musicians who pandered the affections of young children for the profitable satiation of adult perversions.

The quivering, cankered addicts who littered the downtown service doorways with their festering, shaking carcasses and the fat self-righteous old women who nagged and cursed them into the night, collaboratively departed their stage, leaving no sets, props or costumes to mark their hastened departure.

Only a smattering of mangy, bewildered stray pets and startled, suddenly homeless broods of rodent vermin remained to scurry about the cool, sandy, moonlit landscape.

Then an ominous rumbling swelled up from just beneath the starry blue horizon. The dogs yelped and howled as the pressure in their ears pushed down into the bases of their skulls. The felines yowled and hissed at the dark skies, sensing the imminent betrayal of nature's indiscriminately temperamental force. The rats and mice frantically burrowed into the ground to conceal themselves from the danger that tickled their snouts.

Then the blue horizon went black, as the Moon was eclipsed by the expanse of a giant winged shape whose pulsing scarlet vein network strobed its hauntingly methodical approach. The droning of its engine/organs asphyxiated all other sounds beneath it, as it slowly initiated its awesome descent.

As it neared the ground, the glow of its red veins and the red eyes on its bulbous head were so powerfully incandescent that it created a disorienting vertiginous effect for the few four-legged onlookers left to witness the event.

Finally, the ship/creature touched down upon the sandy surface, lightly for its near kilometer height, but still with enough impact to cause mild tremors across the entire region. It then retracted its mammoth wing span which spread out over the distant, receding dunes. The glowing eyes and veins also dimmed gradually, as it retracted its bulbous, flat-topped head toward its bosom.

When all of its movements ceased, it appeared as a black, mountainous monument of a great bird of prey, roosting restfully after an exhaustive and fruitful hunt.

As it settled motionless, an identical winged shape appeared on the horizon. Then a third and a fourth until there were six. And they nestled quietly into the sand forming a steep, walled valley with no passages leading in.

And inside, at the center, the alien appeared: standing black, quiet and still.

# IV.

Elsewhere:

Victor stared across the green and brown synthetic surface of the Dome of Madrid. The crowd around him cheered loudly, some tossing Iris bouquets onto the field of battle to symbolize their faith and devotion.

But there was a sudden, loud noise and the crowd's adulation turned to shrieks and screams of horror. The dome roof crumbled and collapsed inward. The grandstands quaked and buckled as the partisans madly trampled over one another to reach the exits.

Victor dodged several alloy girders as they toppled from above, embedding themselves into the ground, jaggedly protruding like metal stalagmites. The warm Spanish sun pushed down upon him, glaring his vision, and coating his skin with wringing perspiration. The walls of the dome dramatically collapsed in deafening dusty heaps of steel and concrete. But more startling still, was that looking out into the distance, whatever remained of the once, enormous city, had been covered over by grassy hills and earthen plains...totally devoid of human life.

At this point, the Beneficent-Champion did not wait for the ranked stench of rotted flesh or the wall of burning humidity to inform him. He knew the alien was near. He turned quickly about, and saw the black, mucousy, writhing alien admiring him with a hideous jagged grin torn into its dried, dead flesh mask. Victor shuddered for an instant as he felt warm urine run down the inside of his leg. After a startled hesitation, he reached to his holster and removed his club. He fumbled with the controls on the handle momentarily, unable to read the labeling. Then he just pushed any button and a bolt of energy shot out and staggered the alien where it stood.

It swayed unsteadily in its tracks appearing ready to fall. "Could victory be won so easily?" Victor considered. Unfortunately, it recovered itself sufficiently enough to fashion another disturbing smile. Then its eyes filled with blood. It dug the fingers of both hands into its blackened, fused chest and pulled open its sternum. Victor lurched at the gory, unearthly sight of self-mutilation. Then, before he could react, a gnarled black extremity shot out of the alien and painlessly pierced Victor's chest.

Victor looked down in amazement at the twisted tendons and charred muscles of the grotesque limb that impaled him. He tried clutching the dreaded extremity, but its touch burned the tips of his fingers. Then suddenly, the limb withdrew from him, wrenching out his bleeding, pulsing, oversized heart muscle. At this moment, Victor knew he should have died, but oddly, he felt no pain. He fumbled with the club again, and had no idea what setting he pushed. But another bright beam shot out toward the alien. A flickering ball of energy encompassed its lean angular figure. Then slowly, miraculously, it began melting downward creating a dark hole in the middle of the synthetic turf. Lightning and bolts of energy flew out from the flickering ball as it dragged the alien into the earth. Its struggles against the spherical prison seemed to be in vain. Finally, the ball of energy disappeared from view. Victor stepped cautiously to the edge of the hole to see how far down it had descended. He carefully looked down over the edge of his feet, and the hole was dark and silent.

He breathed a heavy sigh of relief. His mind jumped to thoughts of how he would embark upon reshaping his inherited Earth. But, there was a sudden numbness in his chest. He looked down and saw the wound over his missing heart spewing blood profusely. He reached up with his giant hands fighting with futility to halt the massive spillage. He should have at least been faint by now, but for some reason he was not.

The Beneficent-Champion tried to step backward from the hole, but his legs would not move. He looked down and saw thick black tentacles from the hole wrapped around his ankles. He tried to pull back with more alacrity against the hellish bonds, but they jerked and pulled him downward. He screamed out loud begging for aid as he clutched the rim of the hole with his massive arms. Then, thankfully, out of the corner of his eye he saw a white-gowned figure slowly approaching.

"Oh God!" Victor cried. "Louise! Thank God! Help me!"

But as the figure came nearer, he recognized that it was not Louisette at all. The body was taller, thinner and slight. The length of the auburn hair was comparable, but the purple, swollen eyes and the badly bruised young flesh was unmistakable. He tried to squint so as not to see the dried blood which had run down the insides of the girl's bare legs. Yet still, what he had left of Anna Maria remained all too vivid in his memory.

"Oh God, Anna!" Victor began sobbing. "I'm sorry, baby! You know it was a mistake! But you've got to help me!"

The innocence he remembered in her eyes peered out from under the bulbous swelling. Anguish contorted her soft, bruised cheeks.

"I love you, Victor," the girl spoke in a delicate whisper.

"Then help me!" Victor smiled desperately.

"No." Anna Maria stated flatly.

The girl continued to approach him. It was only as she moved within a few feet that Victor noticed the object clutched in her tiny hand: a leather whip bound with spiked metal barbs.

"Anna…!" Victor called. But before he could fashion another plea, the whip was around his face, tearing at his nose, ripping at the artery beneath his ear. He reached for the whip, but felt his hold slip on the hole's rim. He turned his head away from the assault and tried to crawl to the other side of the hole and gain respite from this unimaginable torture.

But then he saw another figure approach. Through the sweat, blood and dirt that filled his eyes, he recognized Georges, scarlet tears running from his empty eye sockets. Before Victor could beg, his once-mentor drew his whip and launched into a savage assault of his own.

Victor crawled around the rim again, feeling the flesh on his back, shoulders and arms shred to the nerves. Then he heard a horrible scream— a shrill, anguished death scream, he'd heard before. He looked up to see naked Val, dragging his broken leg which hung by the skin, blood cascading over his chin, and down the front of his nude body.

With the first lash, Victor felt his sight halved as the raking metal barb tore out his eye. As the vicious whips continued to sting mercilessly upon his skinless back and shoulders, the Beneficent-Champion begged for death. But it would not come. He incoherently crawled around the rim until he saw the tops of Kima's black boots. He glanced up just long enough to see the irrevocable judgment of betrayal in her eyes, and the ragged bloody chest cavity which revealed her shrapnel pitted heart, lungs and breasts. She lifted her whip to flog him, but before the lash could strike, Victor loosed his grip on the rim of the hole and hoped that he would die soon, so that his searing agony would end quickly.

When he awoke, he was almost disappointed to be alive.

"Fuck! Fuck! Fuck!" Victor shrieked as he crashed to his bedroom floor.

He nervously ran his shaking hands over his perfectly smooth (albeit sweat-soaked) skin. He jumped to his feet and cautiously inspected his moonlit surroundings. No Anna Maria. No Georges. No Val. No Kima. No whips. But the alien was yet to be dealt with.

The comm by his bed buzzed loudly, and he jumped before he realized that this was the sound which had rescued him from his tormentors.

Victor sighed heavily, then tried to mask his distress with regal perturbation as he punched on his monitor by remote.

The back of Kelp's head appeared.

"He must uh…be asleep." Kelp's voice buzzed aside from his monitor.

"What!!" Victor yelled into the comm.

"Oh!" Kelp turned and blinked. "You're awake…my lord. Actually…I uh….didn't think you would be, my lord."

Victor pushed his giant fingers through his rumpled golden mane. "Neither did I," he huffed. "What the hell do you want?"

"I uh…actually, my lord, if you were sleeping…" Kelp fumbled. "…it can keep until morning."

"Kelp, if you don't tell me what it is you called me about, right now," Victor snarled, "I'm going to come down there and pound it through your nose!"

Kelp cringed at the unveiled threat. "Well, actually…a young man showed up in the palace tonight. He asked to speak to you."

"I'm not his father." Victor yawned. "I'm very careful."

"Ah...well," Kelp continued. "He's uh...not implying that...my lord. He uh...says he's from South Carolina, North America...actually."

"So what?" Victor grew impatient. "I'm from Wiesbaden, Hesse. Who gives a goddamn!"

"Well, actually..." Kelp cleared his throat and lowered his eyes, "...the young man in question says that his father worked for us and died recently and was wondering if you could help..."

"Kelp, can't you handle this?" Victor closed his eyes and sighed.

"Um, well...actually if you insist...my lord." Kelp scratched his head. "But there are several other children..."

"Thank you!" Victor chopped, severing the communication.

"Thank you...my lord." Kelp spoke to his empty gray monitor screen. Then he turned and looked at the sad-faced boy standing next to him.

"Hmmm". Kelp rubbed his long chin.

"You're not going to make me go back out with the others, are you?" the boy pleaded. "My dad was in charge of Mars."

Something about Mars suddenly struck a chord in Kelp's brain. He had spoken to a frantically distressed woman from South Carolina only a day or so past. She had mentioned that her husband had been someone important on Mars, and that he was dead, and that she needed urgent transport there. At the time, it was only one of a dense bevy of pleas he had handled from his Public Service post. But now this boy seemed oddly linked to the distraught woman he had been unable to assist.

"Um, no young man." Kelp spoke compassionately. "You wait right here."

Then Kelp looked out over sea of yelling, crying disorderly young children that filled the large palace reception area.

"But the rest of you," Kelp tried to assert in an authoritative tone, "you're just going to have to go back outside with the rest and wait until daylight!"

The crowd of children groaned their unanimous dissent. But then, the few remaining palace assistants ushered the small children back through the entrances, down the stairs and out into the Cannes streets.

Lang Denison admonishingly looked up at Kelp, who refused to meet the boy's eyes.

# V.

Turner Satellite Station 4, orbiting Earth:

"Jerusalem?" Al Arledge shouted into his headset. "Where the hell is that?

"Oh. Part of the Israeli Dissolution settlement. Yeah, yeah. Weed territory. I get it. But what the hell is that alien doing there?

"Right. Right. But Victor said Madrid. The whole world heard him say Madrid. I got twenty transmission drones sitting in Madrid.

"What do you mean there is no Madrid? No dome? Well, what the hell happened to 'em? They were there, last time I checked!

"When is the last time I checked? Three hours ago!

"Check again? Hold on."

Arledge swung around in his chair and punched his intercom.

"Chet?" Arledge called. "I've got Gene on the line from TSS-12. Could you bring up the visuals on Madrid?"

"Sure, Al." a voice on the intercom responded.

Arledge leaned back in his chair. "Yeah, they're coming up right now," he spoke into his headset.

The small screens in the narrow control room all blinked on until panning multiple images appeared across the four walls. Beautiful images of dawn lit, pillowy green hills meeting a rich blue sky were shown from twenty different angles. Conspicuously, there were no signs of a sprawling, modern metropolis lazily awakening from its slumber. No signs of hovering, darting traffic amid the contemporary 22nd century architecture of a hazy skyline. No sounds of people or vehicles or loud, animated billboards. There was only the sound of a indolent breeze across the drones' directional microphones...and the braying of the grazing sheep who feasted ravenously on the fresh grass beneath their feet.

"What's this?" Arledge frowned.

"Madrid, my ass! What the hell is this?

"All right, all right. Hold on a minute. Chet!"

"Yes," the voice on the intercom responded.

"What the hell are these pictures you're sending me?" Arledge demanded.

"Madrid."

"Are you out of your mind?" Arledge raised his voice. "I got twenty pictures of goddamn farm animals out in a field somewhere!"

"Just a moment."

"He's checking something." Arledge spoke into the headset as he drummed his fingers along the seams of his leather chair.

Two sheep calves ambled across one of the screens. Then one turned on the other and began pushing its sibling with the front of its head. Then two larger ones trotted into the picture and guided the wayward youths back toward the security of the herd.

Arledge stared at the image then covered his eyes with his fingers.

"Okay," the businesslike voice returned over the intercom.

"'Okay' what?" Arledge's eyes popped open.

"Okay, it's Madrid all right." Chet confirmed.

"That's impossible!" Arledge fretted. "Those drones must have been thrown off coordinance!"

"I'm afraid not." Chet responded. "They're at the same coordinance we've been using for the Dome of Madrid for the past eight years. It's gone. Just like everything else."

"Okay, fine Chet." Arledge drew himself up. "I'll get back to you."

"That's right." Arledge returned to the headset. "He said it's gone.

"How the hell should I know where? It's just gone!

"No, Don and Pomp are still here. They were about to leave for Madrid, but...

"Yeah. I agree. Looks like this Jerusawhatever is going to be the spot.

"Yeah. Yeah. Well, I've still got two, maybe three transmission drones I can send. We'll have to use orbitals for the rest.

"You bet your ass I'm still running the ads. A contract's a contract. If there's even one goddamn lawyer left on Earth, they'll try to clean us out for breach of contract!

"No, I don't think so. Once the buildings and people disappear, they don't seem to go after anything else.

"No. Cannes is the only ground station still transmitting.

"Yeah, I'm glad they missed us too…I guess. All I know is this will be the smallest audience we've ever had. I don't think there are any monitors left on Earth to bother watching it.

"Yeah, I know. Biggest goddamn Arbitration in the history of the planet and no ratings to show for it. Well, at least we'll be able to say we were here to see it. That's something.

"Yeah, I agree. Who's left to give a shit what we saw. Oh well, maybe this is just some kind of nightmare and everyone will just reappear if Victor wins.

"Nah, I don't think so either. But it was a nice thought. Sure would like to get an interview with that alien though. Did you see what he did to that sorry cult satellite pirate?

"Yeah. No shit. We'll let Pomp interview him then. People would love seeing him get the shit kicked out of him right on the air. Oh well, I got work to do. Good luck with that seance. I hope that Jesus guy likes space stations. Cross your fingers. Happy Vogue.

"Yeah. Thanks."

# VI.

Cannes, France-The Beneficent Palace:

"Damnit, Kelp! This is an infirmary, not a nursery!" Dr. Canard snapped as he slammed his palm scanner onto a nearby table.

"Yes. Well...actually..." Kelp started.

"Don't you see I've got an injured woman here, whom your Beneficent-Champion so 'valiantly' failed to protect from that Lyonnais mob!" Canard gestured toward Manda who was lying on the med-lounge. "I mean she's not in any immediate danger, but the last thing she or I need is a little kid running around here!"

Lang, feeling rejected, turned his back on the two adults and wondered what would become of himself.

Kelp read the dismay in the boy's posture. As Lang's shoulders stooped with resignation to abject abandonment, oddly, upon the sight of it, something angry jumped up the sides of Kelp's neck, ran through his temples and leapt out of his shaking, wet lips.

"Now just a minute...doctor!" Kelp raised his voice, causing Dr. Canard to double take. "I know damn well where I am...actually! And this young man is not just some...'kid' as you like to say! This is Lang Denison. His...his father was Anthony M. Denison, Chief Coordinator of the Operations-Space Anomalies Division on Mars! Now actually...I think that makes this young man a pretty special person. Now I've got hundreds of thousands more children to think about outside. I'm only asking you to look after one! And come to think of it, you have to do as I say since I'm in charge of Operations anyway. So here he is! And if anything happens to him, I'll make sure that the Beneficent comes down here and...pounds it through your nose!"

Kelp petted Lang on the head and stormed into the closet door. Then, with a flustered huff, he altered his errant path and strode through the exit with as much authority as he could ever hope to summon.

Dr. Canard, rarely at a loss for oratorical rebuttal, stood speechless in the middle of the infirmary floor as the doors slid shut. Then he looked down at the nervous little boy who had been left to his lean paternal care.

Lang looked nothing like Canard's own sons. Though estranged through a twenty-year-old marriage termination, he recalled their mannerisms of uncertainty, as this youngster eyed him warily. For just a moment, Canard pondered what had become of his grown children and their children in the midst of humanity's total annihilation. He tried to imagine Val-d'Or without the sounds of any youngsters scraping across iced ponds, artfully wielding their hockey sticks come the Fall. Then he quickly smothered the thoughts, caring not to become overly preoccupied with matters he could not change.

Dr. Canard glanced over at Manda who continued to rest, peacefully sedated on the med-lounge. Then he took two steps toward Lang and knelt down.

"So." Canard began unsteadily. "How are you?"

Lang looked the doctor straight in the eye and conveyed with a childish stare: "What an utterly ridiculous question."

Canard immediately sensed that he had badly insulted the boy's preadolescent intellect. So he re-tooled his approach, endeavoring to dilute his condescending address.

"Um," Canard began carefully, "I know it's tough. I didn't know your dad. But by reputation, he was quite a man. You have to know, he died doing what he loved to do. Which was trying to help as many people as he could."

Lang looked away. He appeared unable to find the emotions for the occasion. Dr. Canard was equally confused by the awkward situation.

"But uh..." Canard continued, "what happened to your mother? I mean...you didn't come all the way to Cannes by yourself, did you?"

Canard observed the boy fold his lip, as if some sensitive personal bruise had been brushed upon. Lang's brows wrinkled as if he were still wrestling with whatever issues remained unresolved in his mind.

"Son…" Canard touched the boy's elbow. "Did something happen to your mother?"

Lang stared out into the open as if the events were replaying themselves in front of his very eyes. Dr. Canard had seen many people, young and old, in varied degrees of sorrow and anguish, but could not wager upon this child's expressions with any manner of speculation.

"I think she…" Lang finally spoke. "…died too."

"Where?" Canard asked just above a whisper. "How?"

"Home." Lang answered.

"Home?" Canard frowned. "You mean, where you're staying in Cannes?"

Lang's eyes narrowed.

"No," the boy spoke again. "In Carolina. At home. I heard her cry. And then I was here, outside…with all the other kids."

Canard's eyebrow nearly shot up over his forehead. What might have sounded like the fabrication of an active imagination from most children, rang through this child's lips like a regretfully astonishing truth— as if Lang would have willed it all not to be if he could have.

"Lang," the doctor began in a gentle voice. "Tell me as best you can, exactly how you got to Cannes."

Lang looked up into Canard's face with an innocent yearning that wished that someone else could answer that most puzzling question for him. He grew nearly distraught over the realization that the mystery which had capsized the comfort of his youth would remain a mystery…perhaps forever.

"I don't know." Lang acknowledged dejectedly. "Just all of a sudden. I was in my room, and then all of a sudden…"

Lang closed his mouth and flared his nostrils. His head tremored against the stress of trying to stay as strong as he knew how. Dr. Canard could see that the boy's strength had neared its end and decided that a postponement of this interrogation was in order. He stood up and guided Lang toward a desk and flipped on the wall monitor in front of it.

"Well, I guess there's not much we can do right now." Canard sighed. "But in the meantime, I'm really going to need your help. This screen is showing me that woman's life signs."

Canard gestured toward Manda on the med-lounge.

"If these arrows drop below the green and into the red, she's in trouble."

"Right now she's stable." Lang offered.

Canard looked down at the boy with a shocked expression.

"Um…that's right," the doctor hesitantly confirmed.

"Just kidding." Lang shook his head. "I didn't know that."

"Oh." Dr. Canard sounded relieved. "For a minute, I thought my career had missed a short cut somewhere. Anyway, she is stable. But that could change at any time. So I need you to watch these levels so that she doesn't fall into any danger."

Lang skeptically looked up at Dr. Canard, then over at the inanimate readings, and back to Dr. Canard again.

"Really." Canard offered. "It's important."

Lang regarded the frozen readings again, sighed heavily and began working his jaw with impatience.

"Don't ever go into selling used medical equipment, doctor," a voice groaned from across the infirmary. "You'd starve."

Dr. Canard turned around to witness Manda unsteadily trying to sit up on the lounge.

"Oh, no you don't!" Canard scolded as he started toward her. "Back to bed, missy!"

"Missy?" Manda winced reaching up to touch her forehead.

"Whatever." Dr. Canard answered. "I was about to administer another sedative. You need at least a day's rest."

"Oh shit." Manda blinked her darkened eyes. "What the hell day is it anyway?"

"It's Monday." Canard confirmed. "Monday morning."

"Damnit," she swung her legs around. "I slept through the whole night!"

"For a change," the doctor noted. "Took a cheap bottle of Beaujolais across the noggin, but you finally slept a whole night."

Manda wanted to laugh, but her aching head wouldn't let her.

"Now we can either wrist wrestle for the next half-hour," Canard continued. "Or you can lie back down like a good patient and do as I tell you."

"I can't." Manda frowned, as she slid to the edge of the lounge. "I have to go to Operations."

"And do what?" Canard tried to reason.

"And do my job, doctor." Manda winced again as she tried to support some weight on her feet. "Or what's left of it."

"Have you forgotten Kelp's doing your job?" Canard reminded.

"That'll be the day." Manda groaned as she stood carefully with her hand on the doctor's shoulders. "Now where the hell are my clothes? My ass is freezing."

"Manda," Canard became serious, "you really do need to stay. Your concussion was pretty severe. I'm surprised you haven't had memory loss."

"I wish to hell I had." Manda grimaced. "Then I could forget the name of the asshole who used me as a shield after he pissed off that crowd by pushing down that little girl. And maybe I could just forget about the end of the world too."

"Yeah, I know." Canard shook his head.

"Hi Manda." a young voice spoke from behind Canard.

Manda looked down and saw Lang standing at the doctor's elbow, squinting at the purplish-blue mask marking the woman's injury.

"Lang!" Manda broke into a painful half-smile. "Lang, what are you doing here? I thought you were…long gone by now. How in the world did you get here? Did you and Mikki…?"

"Mom's dead."

Manda glanced at Dr. Canard, who encouraged her to continue the conversation with his eyes.

"Oh." Manda groped momentarily. "I'm so sorry, honey."

"I miss my friends." Lang suddenly blurted.

"Y—Your friends?" Manda didn't know what to make of the remark.

"Yeah." Lang stared into his memories. "I miss them…the most."

There was a pause as the two adults digested the unexpected trail of remorse. Neither could conceive of the emotional priorities arranged in this eight-year-old boy's heart. Yet here it was.

"Lang." Manda started again. "Did Mikki put you on a transport and send you here?"

"No," he answered immediately, appearing nervous again.

"He says he was in his room," Canard filled in, "then all of a sudden, he was here. That almost stands to reason. According to Kelp, there's thousands of children, from God knows where, running the streets outside."

Manda shook her head and managed a stiff smile.

"Par for the course," she sighed. "In lieu of recent events, I'll believe anything.

"Lang," she addressed the boy again. "Since I won't need to be monitored any more, would you like to come up to Operations and help me?"

The boy's eyes refilled with interest.

"Sure," he answered softly.

"Fine." Manda rubbed his head. "Now doctor, if you don't mind getting my clothes, we can get out of your hair."

Dr. Canard inspected Manda's injuries again and resigned himself to the fact that if they were not serious enough to keep her unconscious, she could not be content to remain bedridden.

"When the blazes did I lose control of this place, anyway?" he grumbled and turned toward the closet.

Manda petted Lang on the shoulder. Surprisingly, he reached up and took hold of her hand.

# VII.

Louisette's Room:

Nothing fit anymore. The dresses snagged her hips uncomfortably. The blouses and halters drooped sloppily over her chest. Even her stylishly hand-tailored lingerie had become estranged to the contours of her reconstructed figure.

"Merci, 'God'." Louisette fussed in front of her closets. "Or whatever you were. I can't even dress myself. And I can't imagine any shoppes being open today."

She looked away from the sea of racks bearing custom-designed clothing that were no longer of any use to her and considered where else she might search for anything to wear.

"Anna was way too thin," she considered borrowing. "And mother was thinner still."

Louisette was disgustedly resigned to pulling out another nightgown, when the door to a recessed memory suddenly swung open as a possibility.

"The locker!" she snapped her fingers.

She hurriedly pulled on another gown, an interim solution, then hastily barefooted out into the corridor and trotted two doors down. Unlike the other outer doors, the locker door was colored to match the walls so as to remain discreetly inconspicuous and not disrupt the glamour of everything else with its meniality.

Louisette voice coded and the painted doors slid open. A musty staleness greeted her senses as she entered the room, lit in a dim fluorescent white. With the exception of a thin layer of dust which coated nearly every surface, the room was rendered practically sterile by scathing disinterest. For this was solely a place where things old were stored for no remembrance and things new, but never used, were preserved as unsullied discards born of the overflowing opulence which she'd long ago been taught to indulge. Scores of faded, store-sealed garment bags from le place des Victoires to the Michigan Mile hung on tarnished silver hooks. A collection of unopened birthday gifts in their elaborate wrappings were stacked in a corner next to absurdly gauche artifacts ceremoniously awarded to her by one region or another for the grace of her mere presence. And several ornately hand-tooled cedar chests were huddled together in a corner, all but one unable to jog her memory.

The familiar chest, which she'd always regarded as a "junk box", became an immediate object of curiosity. Louisette had never been one for nostalgia since it threatened to stall her from exciting new experiences, but lately, she had reflected upon so much of her past. With the future appearing only as an epilogue to a long novel, relevance now seemed securely affixed to the rear.

She walked over to the chest, which had been her going-away gift to boarding school. At the time, she'd regarded the detailed Elk Hound carving on the front as her only friend; she'd hated her parents fiercely for sending her away. Opening the lid, she saw dated copies of nude men magazines she and her friends had secretly collected like censured contraband. She found her old knee brace from her athletic career-ending injury, along with her first cocaine pipe—given to her at a party in Hamburg when she was eleven.

There was a poster of her mother, filled with dart holes, posing in chic golden tassels draped about her lean, angular figure, entitled: "Dierdre Richelieu, Woman of the Year". Her heavily painted countenance bore such arrogance, elegance and unwavering certainty. It was hard to picture this woman dead three months after the award, the victim of severe blusilver poisoning. For the first time, Louisette could detect a glimmer of tragedy in her mother's expression which she'd missed as a child. Though she quickly replaced the poster among the belongings, she sadly regretted not having seen her mother's manacled plight with such clarity before today.

After a heavy sigh, she pulled out a baggy pair of pin-striped knickers, unfolded them, and laughed.

"Little, fat Mr. Mettleton, always chasing after the young girls," she shook her head. "How did you sneak all the way back to the Instructors Chateau without your trousers?"

She stood and held them against herself. Then she sniffed them and they smelled only of cedar. Finally, she raised her gown and stepped into them. To her embarrassment, they fit rather well.

"And we used to call him bell bottom." Louisette teased herself. "What does that make me?"

When she reached back inside the chest, her fingers hooked the straps of something soft and leathery.

"Oh no." Louisette smiled. With an easy tug, she pulled free a pair of barely worn, ugly dark brown sandals. "Hah! 'Death to Dress Code Day'! The old ladies hated me so much for thinking up those things! The only shoe style forbidden at Helga Buehner, and I get the whole campus to wear them! Must've been because they were comfortable. No one was allowed to be comfortable at H.B.'s. 'That would be unladylike!'"

She dropped them onto the floor and slipped her feet into them with ease. She paced sloppily to and fro once. Then, to her feet she asked: "Where have you been my whole life?"

As she continued to rummage through the chest, she pulled out several plaid skirts, a pair of white, high-topped spikes, and two of her old field hockey sticks.

"Those were the days," she sighed. "Till I started playing drunk."

At the very bottom, she saw a folded white sweater trimmed in the green and gold school colors, with her name and number stenciled on the front pocket and the word "Thylacines" sewn across the stomach. She had always remembered the jersey as being ugly, oversized and unseemly. But when she pulled on the sweater, it too, fit quite neatly now.

"Vive la Thylacines!" she laughed to herself.

Feeling fully clothed and comfortable for the first time in a while, she shuffled over to a dusty mirror which leaned next to the doorway and took in her plain, washed face, her tied-back hair, and her make-shift accouterments.

"If my outfitters in Milan could see me now," she smirked, noting not only the irony of her appearance, but how little "appearances" seemed to matter any longer.

# VIII.

Operations:

The glowing red continents of the planet Earth were no longer visible on the giant fifty meter viewscreen above the vacant Central Operations hall. In its place was a wild, animated schematic of the terrestrial planets with annotations and arrows and sparkling trails and pulsating outlines. All together, it best resembled the academic regurgitation of an enthusiastic science professor, who could not physically push together, fast enough, the pieces of a great puzzle his mind had already solved.

"What the hell is this?" Manda squinted as she approached her former station, with her arm around Lang.

"Manda, my god!" Jean-Paul popped up from behind a row of terminals which had been haphazardly pushed together. "Look at you!"

"What?" Manda froze, momentarily startled by his sudden appearance. "Oh. I know. I look like shit. Sorry, but it couldn't be helped."

"No!" Jean-Paul energetically hopped over the terminals and started toward her. "That's not it. I mean you do, but that's beside the point. You're up!"

Manda was taken aback by Jean-Paul's surge of near hyperactivity. All around her, everything and everyone had seemed to be grinding down toward some resigned conclusion. But now, here was Jean-Paul, worked up about something that had to be incredible.

"Um...yeah." Manda tried to smile through her injured face as Jean-Paul patted her on the shoulder. "I told Dr. Canard I'd make him look like me if he didn't let me out. What....?"

"Hey kid!" Jean-Paul bent over and smiled at Lang. "Manda, who's the kid?"

"Um...Lang Denison..." Manda started.

"Anthony Denison's kid?" Jean-Paul continued to beam.

"Yeah. He..."

"How'd he get here?" Jean-Paul interrupted again.

"It's a long story, Jean." Manda held up her hands. "And you're acting like a humming bird on speeders. Now will you take a deep breath, relax, and tell me exactly what the devil you've been doing in here?"

Jean-Paul could feel his own pulse racing. He'd been working at a fevered pace ever since the answer to his hypotheses had rung up on the terminal in his quarters. From that moment, all other matters of imminent disaster had been suppressed in favor of solving the frustrating riddle that had eaten at his intellect from the moment the disappearances had begun. He leaned back, took a short sigh, then shook his head in both disbelief and accomplished satisfaction. Finally he ran his hand through his hair and smiled again at his friend and former superior.

"Okay." Jean-Paul sat down at the nearest terminal. "Remember when we were talking to Yorishu and trying to figure out how those ships were making everything disappear?"

"Um…yeah." Manda found her memory not as sharp as she'd thought. "Right. We figured…"

"We figured 'disintegration'." Jean-Paul filled in. "But we weren't getting any kind of residue pattern to substantiate it. We figured 'absorption'. Only as huge as those ships were, even they couldn't account for the mass of every human being and man-made structure on the face of the planet. It would have defied every physical law we know!"

"So?" Manda beckoned his conclusion.

"So, I said: 'Dimensional Shift'." Jean-Paul's eyebrows rose. "To wit, you guys had some serious doubts."

"So you mean, you were right?"

"Well…not exactly." Jean-Paul tapped his fingers on the console. "But close. You see, my feeling was that since it couldn't be disintegration and it couldn't be absorption, it had to be some sort of…matter transfer. Based upon my reading, I figured possibly a transference of matter and/or energy to another dimension of some sort. Well, as it turns out, I was wrong about the dimensions (not that they don't exist), but I was right about the transfer of matter!

"Look at Mars! What do you see? What is that white dot, there?"

"Based upon our calculations, that must be the seventh ship, arriving on Mars," Manda recalled.

"Right! Now look at Earth…towards the Middle East. What do you see there?"

"A large white cluster."

"That's right! The other ships have converged there! They must be having a meeting or slapping wings, patting each other on the beaks or whatever the hell, but there they are…all six of them!"

"Okay." Manda followed.

"Now look at Venus!" Jean-Paul urged.

When Manda inspected the murky golden planet surrounded by its chevron-patterned cloud cover, her mouth hung open in amazement as she noted seven flashing white specks distributed across its face.

"Seven more?" Manda surmised.

"Nope!" Jean-Paul grinned. "I thought the same thing at first. For a few minutes, I concocted this elaborate Venusian invasion theory. I'd dubbed the alien as some kind of advanced scout and figured they were cleaning off the Earth so that they could move their own inhabitants here and enjoy Caribbean vacations without being bothered by the UFO police— or something. Wrong! Turns out…those are the same seven!"

"The same seven?"

"No doubt about it." Jean-Paul shook his head. "I knew those damn things were gobbling up huge amounts of mass, but there was no way it could be stored. I also knew that we never got clear readings on the composition of those ships; we thought, because of huge emissions of some sort of radioactivity, alien to our system, wouldn't allow it. But we weren't getting the whole story. The ships that rose up out of the crater at Liberace Gardens are only a small part of an entire matter transference system. The other part is on Venus! And in between the ships is a long mini-dimensional corridor through which everything and everyone…is being funneled to Venus."

"Like a bloody incinerator." Manda frowned. "Nothing could survive there. Unprotected organic matter would be broken down in seconds because of the acid and heat."

"And the metals and minerals, a little bit longer." Jean-Paul added. "But essentially, everything would wind up breaking down and either evaporating into the atmosphere, or melting away into the surface of the planet."

"What's this mini-dimensional corridor?" Manda asked.

"Um…I'm not sure exactly." Jean-Paul confessed. "Aside from heavy ionic disruptions in the solar wind currents between here and Venus, I really can't be sure. But the proof is in the measurements of matter disappearing at the ships' points of contact on Earth and its reappearance at the 'twin' ships' locations on Venus. In fact, this is a wild guess, but I'm willing to bet the 'twins' are actually one life form coexisting in two places at once, which explains why our readings never meant anything—and why the thermonuclear energy from the arrays was absorbed so easily. When we hit those things with everything we had, it just channeled all of it straight to Venus. It was like trying to shoot a doughnut by aiming right through the middle of it. We were probably just incinerating part of some mountain on Venus the whole time!"

"Jean-Paul," Manda shook her head. "How did you even begin to figure this out?"

"Well, like I said, there were heavy ionic disturbances in the solar winds. I set the computers to monitor any additional anomalies that might fall outside normal measurements. We missed the change in Earth's magnetospheric activity because of all the constant satellite radio telemetry. The fluctuations were camouflaged within our normal parameters. And if I'd been smart, I would have noted that there should have been a large drop in telemetry due to all the disappearances in transmission equipment on the Earth's surface. But it evened out, and I missed it!"

"Shame on you." Manda teased.

"But look at Venus!" Jean-Paul continued. "It's magnetospheric measurements are out of hand. Because Venus's magnetic properties are about twenty-five thousand times less than Earth's, all that matter transference at the point of entry that went pretty much undetected leaving the Earth, caused a huge magnetic disturbance upon entry into Venus's atmosphere. Once I saw that, the answers started screaming at me!"

"So what do we do?" Manda rubbed Lang's shoulder.

"Do?" Jean-Paul's expression filled with irony. "Well…we don't do anything. I mean, there's nothing we can do. What little weaponry we had has been either disabled or disappeared by now. I guess we just have to sit and…wait for it all to end."

"On Venus." Lang pouted.

"Not necessarily." Manda comforted.

"Maybe I shouldn't have been so excited, after all." Jean-Paul leaned back slowly, in front of the humming terminals. "I guess…I just needed to know…how in the hell this was all happening before we died. I mean, man's body of knowledge at least deserves to look into the eyes of its executioner. That's some consolation, isn't it?"

"Of course, there's the other question." Manda offered. "'Why'?"

Jean-Paul looked out over the open hall and shook his head, smiling ironically once more.

"Yeah," he said just above a whisper. "'Why'? It could be anything. We'll probably never have any idea…unless maybe you talk to Canard or Louise."

"What do you mean?" Manda stepped over and took a chair.

"It's crazy." Jean-Paul clasped his hands together. "They seem to think…that this all has to do with cult lore. Christian cult lore. Lore that speaks of a collapse in morality, the wrath of 'God', and the ultimate destruction of the Earth. All the good people go to 'Heaven' and all the bad go to 'Hell'—or maybe Venus, as it turns out."

"That sounds a little desperate." Manda speculated.

"I agree. But it's funny though. My mother's father used to talk the same way. Tell us about getting our acts in order before God came and did away with everyone who was screwing up. He talked about 'fire and brimstone' and 'gnashing of teeth' and 'searing of souls'. And we'd all just say 'okay grandpa' and go on about our business wishing he'd…shut up…or something. Funny thing is…on Venus…I bet that's exactly what's going on right now. Gnashing teeth, seared souls. Hell."

Manda drifted into remembrances of her lost family. She could conceive of nothing they'd ever done to deserve so horrible a fate. Like herself, they were quite decent, normal people, abiding within the boundaries of planetary law. She rubbed Lang's soft hair once more to insulate herself from the images of her family dying in utter agony.

"So why are we still here?" Manda asked hopelessly. "I mean, I'm no great person. I worked right along side Georges in everything he did. And he got an alien house call!"

"And I worked right alongside you." Jean-Paul noted. "And Victor and Nikolai. It doesn't make sense."

The threesome fell silent, Manda with her arms draped over Lang's shoulders. Jean-Paul, meanwhile, reached into his memories for something his grandfather might have said to somehow, make their final hours seem meaningful.

# XIX.

Three floors below:

"…my alloy gauntlets, my club," Victor recited his combat inventory, as he purposefully strode down the hallway, "my lance, my belt, my knife, my bearing grenades, my pulse rifle, thirty magazines…"

"Maga…zines, my lord?" Kelp stammered as he skipped to keep pace with Victor's long strides. "Any uh…particular editions, my lord?"

"Editions?" The Beneficent-Champion's eyes darted back and forth. "Editions? What editions? What are you talking about?"

"Editions of uh…magazines, my lord." Kelp timidly clarified.

Victor's powerful strides came to a sudden halt. He closed his eyes and appeared to be counting to some unspecified number. Then he clenched his fists and his massive arms began to tremble.

Kelp nervously shrunk from the Beneficent-Champion's shadow as the giant turned a seething gaze of utter contempt upon him.

"Magazines, you quivering imbecile!" Victor growled through his teeth. "Magazines, as in: clips! Ammunition! You know. So I can riddle your skinny carcass with holes, you incompetent little monkey spanker!"

"Ah!" Kelp hastily entered the clarification into his hand computer. "I wasn't sure what magazines you were talking about, especially given the long flight to the Middle East. You might have simply been requisitioning some light reading, actually. Of course, I should have known that you were talking about weapons, since weapons were actually what we were talking about. But then again…"

"Kelp!" Victor roared.

"Yes, my lord." Kelp jumped.

"Where's that…Manda Martine who was supposed to be helping you?" Victor sneered.

"Still, uh, in the infirmary I believe, my lord."

"Well get her up here, now!" Victor demanded.

"Uh…" Kelp dreaded giving an adverse answer, "she is still pretty heavily sedated…uh recovering from her injuries in Lyon."

"Is Dr. Canard with her?"

"I believe so, my lord."

"Then send him to meet me in the transport bay, on the double!" Victor commanded.

"But what for…my lord?" Kelp continued to cringe. "The crew complement was to consist of the pilot, myself and you…"

"'Was', Kelp!" Victor snarled. "You're fired! Now get the fuck out my sight before I kill you!"

Kelp backed away from the Beneficent-Champion slowly. Some instinct informed him that he was lucky he had not been killed already and that a hasty departure would best serve the preservation of his life. As he finally reached a corner in the hallway, he gave Victor one last servile glance of fear. When Victor leaned forward, Kelp bolted out of sight, the sound of his footfalls, scattering clumsily down the corridor.

When the noise of Kelp's departure finally died away, Victor fell back against a wall and closed his eyes for a moment. He wished he had dealt with Kima in a different manner. He knew full well that the older woman had her own ulterior motives veiled behind their "romance", but she'd been his personal trainer and assistant through every arbitration he'd fought as Champion. And now his preparation for the greatest challenge of his life was collapsing into jumbled disarray. He never before had to worry about inventories. He would simply reach for what he needed and find it carefully lodged where it should have been. Now he'd have to try to do it all by himself. And that, among many things this morning, frightened him.

"Are you all right?" a familiar voice gently inquired.

Victor, quickly straightened himself and remounted his powerful, impassive demeanor. He then, looked down over his shoulder and saw Louisette looking concerned.

"What the fuck are you dressed as?" he disdainfully turned up his nose.

"I'm not dressed as anything." Louisette gestured. "These are just…clothes."

"'Thylacines'?" Victor read across her jersey. "They're extinct."

"So are we." Louisette answered. "Almost."

"Not at all!" Victor scoffed. "Today is the beginning of a new age for humanity. Once I eliminate the alien, I'll be the most revered man in human history. I'll have literally saved the Earth…and all mankind."

"Or what's left of it." Louisette added.

"So much the better." Victor parried. "A clean slate for me to etch my own immortality into the face of history."

"Do you really believe that?" Louisette became annoyed.

"Of course." Victor stiffened. "Why shouldn't…"

"Where's the frightened little child who came barging into my room last night?" Louisette met his eyes. "I thought he was going to wet his pants."

"What are you…?"

"You know what I'm talking about!" Louisette pressed on. "Last night! You came staggering into my room like a frightened little boy, chased from under his blanket by bad dreams!"

Victor quaked imperceptibly as the piercing terror from his real nightmare, shot through his body.

"Whining and clawing at his mommy, afraid that he'll be left alone!" Louisette continued.

"That's not what happened!" Victor raised his voice.

"Isn't it?" Louisette charged. "You ridiculed me in the infirmary like you could barely stand the sight of me. But in the middle of the night when you were lonely and scared you came crawling to my room like a baby…"

Victor violently snatched her up by the hair and jerked her toward him, nearly breaking her neck. Louisette, momentarily startled, continued to look directly into his eyes.

"What you saw…" Victor growled lowly, "…was me drunk. I was up with dumb whores all night…"

"Really? Well paid, I hope." Louisette spat as she tried to push away.

Victor's rage rippled through his body. He snarled loudly, but pushed her to the floor doing relatively little harm.

"Oh, come on Victor!" Louisette shouted. "You can do better than that! I'm just some little woman! I've seen you kill grown men over beers, for less! Or has a full stomach of killing made you tame? Or maybe this alien has just made you a coward."

"I'm not afraid." Victor declared.

"Good!" Louisette answered. "Because neither was I. And maybe that's why it let me live."

"Let you live?" Victor's eyes narrowed.

"Yes." Louisette climbed to her feet. "Made me live! When I wanted to die more than anything in the world. When I cared less for my life than I'd ever cared, it insisted that I live."

"No." Victor whispered. "You're lying. I saw it kill! It killed Kima and Val and your father. They never had a chance!"

"I didn't even want a chance, Victor." Louisette confessed. "My whole life had been one big fat fucking shallow travesty. And I'd had enough. But instead of letting me go…it took away all the…lies I was living, and gave me my life."

"That doesn't make sense." Victor clung to his doubt. "You were probably just high, again."

"Look at me, Victor!" She grabbed his tabard. "Do I look like I'm lying? Do I look high to you? My whole body's been reconstructed! No technology in the world could have done that over night!"

Victor looked down at her desperate attempt to convey the truth. Gently, he touched her hand and pried her fingers away.

"I've got this all figured out," he said sternly. "I can't let you confuse me, now. If I hesitate out there, I'm dead—and so is everyone else who's left."

Louisette dropped to her knees in total frustration. The logic she had begun to construct in her own mind was so exhilarating. She was vaguely coming to understand how so much of what Anna Maria had learned had buoyed the girl's spirit. Yet, like her young cousin, she too was now exasperated with the unwillingness of an intelligent mind to hear her out.

Victor looked down at her one last time.

"I've got to go," he said softly. "Wish me luck."

Louisette looked up at him with her mouth shaking, her tiny nostrils flared.

"No," she closed her eyes. "Take me with you."

"What?"

"Take me with you," she repeated soberly. "You're going to need me."

Victor smirked with feigned divertive annoyance.

"It didn't kill me, Victor." Louisette pleaded. "It's killed most of civilization, billions of people, but it wouldn't kill me. Don't you wonder why? Don't you wonder why it let a drugged out wretch like me live? Don't you think it's just possible that I may have some say in whether you and everyone left may live? I mean it's possible that after you have a talk with it, it could spare your miserable life, too! Then again, maybe not. Care to make a wager on it?" For just an instant, Victor's assertive countenance threatened to melt away.

"Either way, it makes sense to take me." Louisette insisted. "Unless you're really willing to gamble away your life on your arrogance."

Victor stared down at her with his face hardened.

"Very well," he finally answered. "Suit yourself."

# X.

Outside, on the Palace rear stairs:

"My god, Lang." Manda stood with her mouth open. "You put it mildly. There's a helluva a lot of kids out here!"

Manda, Jean-Paul and Lang stood at the top of the palace stairs gazing out over the palace north yard and beyond the palace gate where tens of thousands of children, ranging from infants to near adolescents noisily meandered about.

Some tried to squeeze through the narrow iron bars and were poked back by Operations assistants. Others simply clung to the barricade, looking bewildered and lost, hoping for some guidance to fill the void of their fearful uncertainty.

By their dress, they appeared to have randomly been displaced from all parts of the globe: Weed Southern Africans, Russians, North Indians, and South Americans stood alongside Blossom North Americans, East Asians, Arabians and West Europeans. Though ultimately, as a collection, they appeared amazingly homogeneous in the common virtue of their youth.

Even stranger was the manner in which the elder children looked after the young. While there was no small measure of crying and screaming, no child under the age of six was not tended to by an older child. These intrinsic displays of care and nurture could have easily been less genuinely expressed by most adults. But here, assurance was selflessly provided as needed.

Farther off, up the narrow roadways leading into the city, were greater crowds of children, some playing, most wandering about, trying to become familiar with their surroundings.

"There must be hundreds of thousands." Jean-Paul guessed. "Maybe over a million."

"There weren't this many before." Lang seemed almost as surprised.

"And how are they all getting here?" Manda shook her head.

"Thin air!" a man in a Controller's office suit appeared. "Thin air!"

The man hurriedly trotted down the stairs to assist others in trying to control the swelling mob.

"Hey, wait!" Manda called, gingerly taking the steps two at a time. "Did you say: 'thin air'?"

"That's right ma...Ms. Martine." the man suddenly recognized her through her blackened eyes and nose. "Out of nowhere! Twelve hours ago, the city was nearly vacant! Everyone fled to the farmlands thinking the city would be a magnet for those bird-things. Then a few kids showed up here and there. For a while, we thought they were just some abandoned orphans. But then we got Weed kids with southern African accents, North American kids, and now they're popping in from all over the place! I'd put one over the gate, and three more pulled on the back of my coat from nowhere!"

Manda was impressed to learn Lang had been telling the truth all along.

"I don't know what we can do!" the man continued. "But we better get on about doing something awfully fast, otherwise they're going to be one on top another!"

The man then, ran off to assist a woman in an Operations jacket hoist an overweight boy over the gate whose shirt had snared a post. The boy finally rolled over the top and crashed onto two girls who were already distraught and unsettled. The trio, tangled and sprawled on the outer walk, mournfully to cried in "traumatized" unison.

"This is bad." Manda spoke aloud.

"An understatement." Jean-Paul appeared at her shoulder.

Manda's eyes flickered as her brain formulated some solution which would diffuse the chaos that might soon boil into a life-threatening catastrophe.

"We've got to get them to think we're doing something besides not listening to them," Manda spoke without looking at him.

"Like what?" Jean-Paul shook his head.

"Well, first, let them tell us who they are." Manda decided. "I mean, that's what Lang wanted to do most—tell us who he was and where he came from. They're all far from home, cut off from everyone they know.

They need someone to know who they are! Even as an adult, my first impulse would be to identify myself to someone."

She turned to Jean-Paul and took him by the arm.

"So you want me to go get…" Jean-Paul grinned, recognizing her "sending you on an errand" look.

Manda could not help but smile, albeit painfully, herself. "Go get, assuming it hasn't been stolen, that PA-3000 unit so I can make an announcement to the city. And also bring whatever hand computers Kelp hasn't dropped."

"Oui, mon commandant!" Jean-Paul playfully saluted.

"S'il vous plait, smartass." Manda shook her head.

Smiling, Jean-Paul bounded up the palace stairs to search out the requisitioned items.

Despite her injuries, for the first time since the meteoroid struck, Manda was beginning to feel like herself again—perhaps even more so.

"So what's going on?" Lang asked, hoping for the simplest answer.

Manda sighed and took in the nearly overwhelming sight of hundreds of thousands of children seeming to fill every visible surface.

"Son," she affectionately rubbed his shoulder, "it's finally dawned on me that I don't have a clue 'what's going on'. Today. Yesterday. The day before. Maybe all my life. But it sure feels good to know what I have to do now."

Manda and Lang walked toward the gate as she gathered together what remained of the palace personnel for her instructions.

# XI.

Inside the Beneficent Transport, above the Mediterranean Sea:

Victor reclined on his leather chaise lounge and drank deeply from the wine bottle clutched in his giant fingers. When he finished, he loosed a resounding belch that echoed throughout the luxury transport.

"Sauvignon Blanc!" He smiled at Dr. Canard and Louisette sitting across the way. "The breakfast of...victors!"

Dr. Canard and Louisette eyed him wearily. They had not been in the air for more than twenty minutes and already the journey (or more specifically, the company) had begun to drain on them both.

"Shouldn't you be checking your gear?" Dr. Canard tried to advise.

"My gear?" Victor snickered. "It's all there. Checked it in myself. First time. What the fuck did I ever need Kima for? I can do it all!"

"That's all well and good." Canard continued. "But don't you think you should at least, ease off the wine a little bit? I imagine you'll need optimum reflexes when we reach the...battle site."

"True!" Victor wrinkled his forehead and smiled. "But you forget I have duel responsibilities now. I'm Champion AND Beneficent. I've got to do the Champion's fighting, but I've also got to do the Beneficent's drinking. I wouldn't want the office palate to slack under my administration. That wouldn't be right, would it?"

Dr. Canard leaned back in his chair and looked away.

"Would it?" Victor repeated as he sat up and turned toward Louisette. "Would it, mon amour?"

Louisette sat with her legs crossed in her seat, arms folded, staring out of a side window.

"Hey!" Victor called. "Hey, bitch! I'm talking to you!"

Louisette cringed a moment, then melted it into a sigh, and continued to ignore him.

"Hey!" Victor leaned forward and hissed a stream of wine through his teeth. "I said, I'm talking to you!"

Louisette finally turned and brushed off the Operations jacket she'd taken from the palace hangar, then glared at him admonishingly.

Victor forced himself to chuckle.

"Hmh," he snorted. "That alien sure did make you ugly. Not that you were any great prize before. All that polymer and silicon and reconstituted cellulose. Shit, it was like trying to fuck wet clay. But now…you look like one of those Vietnamese Weed whores. You know, the fat, pale ones, who work the curbs right up until they get their labor pains…"

"Sir!" Canard interceded. "Haven't you said enough?"

"Doctor!" the Beneficent-Champion mocked. "I'm talking to my fucking fiancée. So mind your own goddamn business!"

Dr. Canard folded his mouth, restraining the desire to speak his mind. Here, he knew his veracity held little sway. Victor was not rational. And agitating the Beneficent-Champion at this point, would only bode poorly for everyone on board.

Victor, meanwhile, once again, turned his attentions to Louisette. But she chose to sever her interaction with him, gazing thoughtfully out over the mildly turbulent blue water. Her indifference to him, was a new tactic no woman had ever employed. After a moment, Victor probed for something that would draw her back out.

"Did you get rid of it as I asked you to?" He finally asked in a cold commanding tone.

Louisette rustled in her chair, then turned slowly toward him, unable to allow this particular topic to pass unaddressed.

"I haven't had time."

"Oh." Victor answered with an emotion she could not read.

There was a tense pause that hung in the transport cabin as the monotonous drone of the engine hummed through the prolonged silence.

When Louisette looked up at Victor, he was staring blankly into nothing.

"I don't want your baby anymore, if that's what you're asking." Louisette said spitefully.

"Just shut up!" Victor broke from his trance. "I've already said all I have to say about it. You do what you want!"

Victor leaned back on his chaise lounge and poured another large swig down his throat.

Louisette, again, tried to read some emotion from him, but could not.

"So, what about the alien?" Louisette asked.

"What about it?" Victor responded staring at himself in a mirror at the foot of his lounge.

"How are you going to beat it?"

"I'm going to rip its head off and shove my club-mace up its ass! Real simple," he sneered at her.

Louisette closed her eyes and shook her head.

"I mean, really," she spoke with exasperation. "Are you going to try and talk?"

"What, beg?" Victor scoffed. "Beg for my life? Is that what you did?"

"I told you what happened to me."

"Oh, I see." He sipped from his bottle. "So if I tell it to kill me, it'll 'let me' live. Maybe even give me a makeover. Make me short and skinny, maybe. Fuck you."

"It wasn't like that." Louisette became frustrated. "It was much more complicated than that. I'm not sure I totally understand it myself."

"Then spare me, Louise!" Victor raised his voice. "You didn't have a choice. Neither did Georges."

"Or Kima, or Val." Dr. Canard added.

"Or Kima, or Val." Victor confirmed. "But I can fight. And I can kill just as brutally as it can."

"There's no question of that." Dr. Canard agreed.

"But..." Louisette sounded stressed, "...how do we know that's going to save the world...even if you win?"

"It will." Victor stood and smiled confidently. "If it were going to kill all of us, you'd be dead already. And if I didn't have a chance, it wouldn't have accepted my challenge."

Louisette ran her hand through her hair.

"There's some silver in the cabinet if you need it." Victor looked down at her.

"No." Louisette perked up alertly. "That's all right."

"Well," Victor crashed his bottle into a receptacle. "I'm going to check on our ETA."

"Victor." Louisette spoke softly.

"What!" Victor paused impatiently.

"I'll pray for you." She tried to capture his eyes.

For a moment, Victor was not sure how to respond. Then his face brightened as he began to laugh loudly with hopeless defiance. His heavy voice vibrated against the metal of the inner hull, but it remained a pitiable attempt to remount his flagging confidence, which had clearly collapsed from within. Though still, he instinctively summoned the habit of lifting his squared chin and glaring down the slopes of his flared nostrils.

"No Louise," The Beneficent-Champion snarled through his teeth. "You've got it wrong. You'd better start praying to me. Like I told those smelly, grimy savages in Lyon, I'm the messiah—and I'm the only thing that can save the human race."

Victor departed through the cabin door and made his way toward the cockpit.

Louisette followed him sadly with her eyes until the door quietly closed behind him.

"I don't believe it." Louisette rubbed her temples. "I see him so differently now."

"You thought you loved him, didn't you?" Canard moved to the liquor cabinet.

Louisette shook her head, again confronted by the discomfort of her clarity.

"I didn't even know what love was."

# XII.

Cannes, France-Outside the Palace:

"Please sit down and wait for a palace representative to come around and identify you." Manda's voice echoed over the omni-directional public address flyer which hovered over the city. "We want to help you. And the only way we can do that is to find out who you are!"

Manda, Jean-Paul and Lang stood at the top of the north palace stairs as they watched a dozen and a half adults equipped with hand computers (some Operations staffers, some Control staff, some palace maintenance) foray into the noisy channel of children.

"This could take hours." Jean-Paul noted the overwhelmingly disproportionate ratio of children to adults.

"Years." Lang chimed in.

Manda rubbed the boy's head affectionately and regarded Jean-Paul with calm.

"Were you in a hurry, Jean-Paul?" she spoke sarcastically.

"Now that you mention it," Jean-Paul folded his arms, "not particularly."

"Good." Manda turned her gaze back to the crowded streets of Cannes. "No one should be. Not now."

"Manda, is there something I've missed?" Jean-Paul asked with a slight frown.

"No, I don't think so. Why do you ask?"

"Well," Jean-Paul wasn't sure how to begin, "are you sure that wine bottle didn't knock something askew?"

"Excuse me?"

"I mean," Jean-Paul continued, "the closer we get to death, the calmer you seem to be about this entire affair. When the meteoroid struck, you were frenzied with determination. When the crater exploded, you were alarmed and braced for anything. And when those ships began absorbing everything and everyone, you were positively combative. But now, you seem…almost content. I mean, we've all lost family and friends, and it's hard. And coming to terms with one's own death is the most difficult thing any of us can face. But…am I wrong or are you confident about the outcome of Victor's challenge?"

"Victor's challenge?!" Manda chuckled. "I don't think so, Jean. I think Victor's going to get his ass kicked."

"Then you think we're doomed." Jean-Paul concluded.

"Not necessarily." Manda put her hand on Jean-Paul's shoulder. "Didn't you say that Louise claimed to have survived a confrontation with that alien?"

"Yes, but you know Louise. She's so strung out all the time, she could have been having a conversation with her bedpost."

"Dr. Canard didn't seem to think so."

"True. But I told you, they're both caught up in this cult stuff. They're desperate! They're just contriving some half rational…"

"So what are all these kids doing here?" Manda met his eyes. "From all over the world. What are they doing here?"

Jean-Paul watched as crowds of children gathered around each adult logging names, birth dates and places of origin.

"Besides making a load of racket, I have no idea." he confessed.

"Exactly." Manda nodded. "Neither do I. But I do know they're here because someone put them here. And we're here because someone left us here. Twelve and a half billion people have died in the past few days, including our beloved Beneficent. Yet here we are…and all these kids. I don't know the reason. I won't even speculate, at this point. But if we wait…"

The communicator on Manda's belt beeped. She pulled it from her waist and spoke.

"Yes, this is Martine." She answered authoritatively. "Is there a problem?"

"No ma'am," the Irish accent of the Control officer came back to her. "I just thought ya' should know that we been gettin' these kids from all over world like ya' said."

"Yes." Manda answered "We know that. What's your point?"

"Well I just thought ya' should know, we got some out here from Mars as well."

"Is that confirmed?" Manda asked.

"Aye," the officer answered. "Three from Chen-Cho, complete with Viking jackets and red dust smeared across their faces. I ran their names and they're confirmed; born and raised there. I thought ya'd want ta' know."

"Understood." Manda spoke with a painful smile. "Thanks."

"Great!" Lang smiled.

"Yeah. Great." Jean-Paul frowned.

"Maybe they came through one of your corridors, Jean." Manda offered.

"Unlikely," he assured. "Those corridors were linked to Venus. This must be something else."

"Unquestionably." Manda answered. "Something…else."

"Like 'God'?" Jean-Paul spoke in an accusatory tone.

"Oh no." Manda shook her head. "That was a dirty word in our house unless the word 'damn' followed closely behind. But there's a plan in the works. I'm sure of it. And while I'm not quite ready to concede to unseen forces, I'm willing to bet that alien has everything to do with us still being alive and everything to do with these children being dropped in our laps—and not just any children, either."

"Why do you say that?" Jean-Paul asked.

"Well, I'm no child expert, but wouldn't you think that with so many children concentrated in one place under these circumstances, there'd be a little more…bedlam?"

Jean-Paul's brows jumped, struck by this pointed observation.

"Hmmm." Jean-Paul rubbed his chin. "Come to think of it, it is a rather tame gathering. You'd think there'd be utter chaos out there."

"But there isn't." Manda focused. "Crying, dismay, concern, yes! But not the kind of mindless, hyperactive, aggression you associate with normal children. I'm wondering if that isn't why they were selected."

"Sheep." Jean-Paul concluded. "Maybe the alien is harvesting sheep. Those prone to being easy followers."

"Like you and me?"

"Not exactly what I meant." Jean-Paul looked away.

"Nor I." Manda clarified. "You were as stubborn as they come when you started working for me. Still are. For you, seeing is believing. Otherwise, it's 'fuck you, sir'."

Jean-Paul fought down a grin.

"And me," she continued, "I followed orders, but there were many times when I had to make it up as I went along because Georges didn't have any orders. I worked within the general framework, yes. But if I was a sheep, I don't think I ever relied too much on the shepherd."

"Then what?" Jean-Paul asked.

"Maybe..." Manda narrowed her eyes, "...they're just bright. Insightful."

"Oh come on, Manda! That's a big guess."

"Could be." She pulled a hand computer from her belt. "But I aim to find out."

Manda gingerly walked down the stairs, then turned and looked up at Lang.

"Come on, Lang," she called to the boy.

Lang folded his arms and sternly frowned down at her.

"I'm no sheep!" the boy defied her.

"I know." Manda smiled painfully again. "I was going to follow you."

Lang bounded down the staircase two steps at a time, then took Manda by the hand and led her toward the palace gate.

Jean-Paul watched them and wondered if his commander was losing her mind. Then, his thoughts ran over the Beneficent-Champion's challenge. Were there any stations remaining which might broadcast the conflict on satellite? Suddenly, his thoughts flashed to Louisette— he hadn't seen her all morning.

He headed inside the palace to initiate a search for the woman who continued to uncomfortably frequent his thoughts. But as he turned, he was almost jolted backward by the unexpected presence of Kelp, standing directly behind him.

"Whoa!" Jean-Paul jumped.

"My apologies." Kelp groped to steady Jean-Paul's balance.

"Where did you come from?" Jean-Paul pushed Kelp's hands away. "Aren't you supposed to be with the Beneficent?"

"Well, actually…" Kelp began explaining more to himself than to Jean-Paul, "…it was decided that my services in the capacity of Operations head would no longer be required…at this juncture, actually."

"You mean, Victor went by himself?"

"Well, there was the pilot, actually."

"Of course there was the pilot!"

"And Dr. Canard."

"Canard?!"

"To take my place." Kelp clarified.

"I can see that."

"And Mademoiselle Richelieu."

"Madem…" Jean-Paul stammered. "Louise? With Victor? Why? That doesn't make sense! She could be killed!"

"Well, I…"

"How could that bastard make her go?"

"Well, actually." Kelp cleared his throat. "It was my understanding that um…Mademoiselle asked to go. Demanded…actually."

Jean-Paul felt a heavy plunge somewhere between his stomach and his heart. He wanted to believe that Victor had violently abducted Louisette and forced her onto the transport against her will. But there was no hint of it in Kelp's conveyance. Maybe she had simply dosed herself into mindless complicity with her drugs. But he could not envision the lucid beauty who had awakened to him in the infirmary, resorting back to such careless recreation.

So he resolved that, for whatever reason, Louisette had voluntarily become a passenger on a suicide mission. And oddly, the prospect of her death, among twelve billion, was the one he could least accept.

# XIII.

On Satellite:

(Roll ominous, foreboding music. Panning close-up of the alien.)

"Dark. Ugly. Murderous. Not of this world. It invaded our planet four days ago and brought death and mayhem down upon the intrepid brow of humanity. With little regard for the young or the old; the strong or the sick; the beautiful or the cosmetically challenged; the Blossom or the Weed, it has accomplished in days what no famine, disease, war, or cult could: brought humanity to its knees. On this, the most celebrated holiday in man's history—the celebration of peace, love and diversity, this horrible creature has exterminated virtually the entire population of the planet Earth. The art is gone. The music is gone. The sound of children playing is gone. The wonder of scientists discovering new means of ensuring our comfort is gone. The joy of young teens discovering their burgeoning sexual orientation is gone. The films are gone. The books are gone. The parties are gone. And so too is Vogue Day gone…perhaps forever.

"But cross your fingers. There may be hope.

(Orchestral flourish. Aerial file footage of the Champion perched atop Mount Kilimanjaro.)

"For five years, he has been the symbol of man's integrity, justice, courageousness, and moral conscience. '*In action how like an angel! In apprehension how like a god*'. Time and again he has battled brilliantly to uphold man's freedoms. He has been dumped but never daunted. He has been bloodied but never beaten. He has been vicious but equally as gracious in victory. He is the backbone of man. The pillar of our lives. He is the Champion of our Earth. And today, he determines whether mankind has smoked his last pipe!"

(Sudden fade to black)

"TSS presents, in association with D'King promotions: The Final Challenge live from Jerusalem. Today, the Beneficent-Champion, Victor

Esel Hausmeister faces the alien from beyond in an epic battle for the survival of mankind.

"Today's arbitration is brought to you by Sens-U All, the leaders in Home Sensory Depravation Entertainment.

"And by the Midnight Show with Denny Lemming.

"Also by, the Sensory Depot, Psychiatry Ports that help free you to Conform to the Norm!

"And by Smack Jack! Serving two billion subscribers last year! You can't be a 'More Fiend' until you've done Smack…jack! And remember: please be sane. Change veins!

"Hello, everyone. This is Pomp Kustas along with my colleague, Donald Ubu, former southern African arbiter. And today we have a dandy for you! Literally, this will be the arbitration to end all arbitrations! And what better matchup could we bring to you than, perhaps the greatest Champion of all time, not to mention our current reigning Beneficent, Victor Hausmeister, against an absolutely awesome force in the gruesome, grim-faced alien. A true confrontation between good and evil! Victor, the golden Adonis bearing the fate of all mankind, pitted against the alien monster, poised to snuff out what little life remains on the planet Earth! Don, you've got to be excited about this one!"

"Well, Pomp, actually I'm excited about just being alive right now. Twelve billion people dead, and yet we are lucky enough to be here calling the action. The thing that has to concern us though, is that none of us have really seen the alien perform one on one. Most of what we've witnessed has been the bird/creatures disintegrating buildings and people. We have one clip of the alien attacking that cult satellite pirate, but that's it.

"Here, if you watch in slow motion, he uses a broad swiping motion with what looks like an arm and sends the pirate's head flying, end over end, into a bail of hay. Then we see another arm impale the pirate's body and hurl it toward the camera. That's pretty impressive stuff! But again, that's all we've seen. Victor could be in for a lot of surprises today."

"As could we all, Donald, my friend. As could we all! But right now, we have an interview with the Champion I conducted some months ago in the Beneficent Palace courtyard during which I asked him how he came to value life and truth so much. Let's watch."

# XIV.

Golgotha:

Victor, Dr. Canard, and Louisette stared tensely across the sandy windswept landscape as an unseasonably chilled gust mournfully moaned through the darkened valley. It had been a bright and sunlit journey to the Mid-Eastern territory. But now, as if cautioned away by the ominous imminent proceedings, even the daylight above, seemed to bend itself away from the rim of the kilometer-wide pit fashioned by the tall, monstrous still forms of the roosting creatures.

In the distance, the faint, distorted silhouette of the alien was visible, shadowed against a white stone hill. Its gnarled, lurching presence conspired with the cool shaded air, causing Louisette to tremble with memories of the searing agony its acidic touch had burned through her flesh. Dr. Canard squinted intently, trying to capture his first live glimpse of it, while he pondered why the theatrics of this meeting were even necessary. Victor, meanwhile, began unloading his battle gear from the hovering transport, appearing eager to settle matters quickly, one way or another.

"I'm too damn old for this mysterious rendezvous crap." Canard groused. "Either say what you want, kill me, or leave me the hell alone so I can go home and sleep with both eyes closed!"

"I—I'm freezing." Louisette shivered, folding her arms and huddling her neck beneath the collar of her jacket.

"I told you, you should've had a few shots with me." Canard smiled as he briskly rubbed her back and shoulders. "There's still some brandy in the transport, if you want."

"No." Louisette's voice quaked bitterly. "None of that shit for me. It's better to feel things as they are! I'm through lying to myself!"

Dr. Canard's brows rose with surprise.

Louisette caught herself as her words echoed back to her and apologetically softened her furled countenance. "No offense, doctor. I didn't mean to be overly serious. It's just well…maybe I should…"

"No, no!" Canard held up his hand. "Far be it from me to be a…corrupting influence. After all, '*Woe to that man by whom the offence cometh!*'. But I do think I saw some blankets in the overhead cabinet. Why don't you go grab one while we wait to see what the devil is supposed to happen."

Louisette smiled appreciatively, then trudged toward the transport through the cool, dry sand.

She saw Victor fumbling to assemble a sleek, metallic, six-barreled apparatus mounted on a narrow-trunked alloy platform. With his giant forefingers he spun the treaded seals until they tightened around the base of the long barrels. Then one of the seals slipped out of its housing, bounced off the base of the platform, and disappeared into the sand. Victor dropped to his knees and frantically searched for it.

"Shit!" Victor bellowed in frustration.

"Too much Sauvignon?" Louisette taunted as she prepared to climb aboard the transport.

"Just shut up!" Victor sounded exasperated. "You came to 'talk'. But don't talk to me. I'm busy!"

"Well, good luck." she turned up her nose facetiously as she continued her ascent.

"Fuck off, Louise!" Victor spat.

"Here it is." Canard knelt down next to Victor.

The Beneficent-Champion snatched the seal from the doctor's hand, stood, and hastily continued his work. Dr. Canard sighed quietly as he rose and walked away to inspect the empty landscape.

For the first time, the doctor saw satellite transmission drones hovering just above the animate ridges of the valley walls. He counted three, surveying the transport site. Off in the distance, he could vaguely distinguish two more, prudently circling the hill by the alien, trying to maintain as unobtrusive a distance from their subject as possible.

"Who's left to broadcast this?" Canard muttered to himself. "Who's left to watch?"

Louisette heard music blaring from the cockpit area as she headed for the luxury cabin of the Beneficent Transport. It sounded very much like the Vogue Day theme which had been branded into her brain by the past weekend's festivities. She tried to shut it out as she moved toward the overhead cabinets.

Punching the cabinet release, the door slid open and at eye level were several choices of cashmere coverings in all colors imaginable. Near the middle, however, she saw a cranberry-colored fold bearing a familiar golden fleur-de-lys pattern. It was unmistakably her father's, now deposed amongst the guest linen. She pulled it out, admiring the few fond memories it stirred, then slung it around her shoulders and imagined herself as a toddler, held securely in her father's loving arms.

In the background, the music grew louder momentarily, then she heard someone approach. As she turned around, a thin, pale young woman about her age, holding a Palace Services helmet, stood in the doorway.

"Yes?" Louisette addressed her.

"Hello," the woman blushed a bluish-pink and lowered her eyes. "I'm...the pilot."

"Oh." Louisette responded unsure of how to respond.

"I hope I didn't interrupt you," the woman fidgeted with her helmet.

"No. Not at all." Louisette smiled. "It's just cold outside."

"I can fix you a drink!" the woman obsequiously jumped forward. "You'll be warm before you know what hit you. I used to fix them for the Beneficent all the time."

"That's all right." Louisette noted the light blue haze in the woman's eyes.

"Sorry," the woman looked down again. "I shouldn't have bothered you."

"It's okay." Louisette tried to settle her.

The woman looked up and nervously fixed a smile on her face again.

"What's your name?" Louisette asked her.

"Anna," the pilot answered proudly. "Anna Alexandriev."

"That's pretty." Louisette spoke softly.

The pilot tried to read the shift in Louisette's expression, but it disappeared before she could grasp it.

"So you knew my father?" Louisette recovered herself quickly.

"Yes!" the woman's face brightened. "He was the nicest man! I met him in Moscow during the reapportionment. I was doing some chauffeuring to put myself through school. Then one night, the Russian Governor and the Beneficent hopped in my limousine, just like that! I couldn't believe it! And of course, most celebrities just tell you where to take them and then carry on with themselves, but your father was so nice to me. I was studying political science at the time, and he even asked me for some political advice...I think. Well, when I got off shift, he invited me up to his hotel. Then, before he left, he said he could get me transport work if I wanted. It was the chance of a lifetime! I've flown and partied with so many famous people since then. I'm so thankful!"

"That's wonderful." Louisette masked her condescendence.

"But it's funny," the woman continued, "in four years, I've never, ever met you before. I mean, I've seen you on satellite and read about you in the media, but I never met you. In fact I didn't even recognize you when you came aboard today! You look different on a monitor. I keep getting cosmetic surgery to look a little like you, but you keep changing on me."

"Well, I'm done with that, for awhile." Louisette noted. "And my father and I rarely traveled together."

"I can see that." The woman smiled. "He was business. You were pleasure. It makes sense. I envy you."

"Why?" Louisette wondered now, more than ever.

"I saw you on satellite in Monte Carlo this weekend," the woman's gaunt cheeks flushed bluish red. "You were so happy and free! Not a care in the world! Everyone wanting to make love to you! I can't imagine!"

"It wasn't all it was cracked up to be, actually." Louisette reflected upon her specious existence.

"It didn't appear that way." The woman looked puzzled.

"It never does."

"Well, I know you're very busy," the woman smiled nervously again, "but I was hoping that you'd…autograph my helmet for me?"

Louisette noted all of the different names in different colors scrawled across the top and sides of the woman's helmet.

"You've been around, haven't you?" Louisette commented.

"That's the idea isn't it?" the pilot smiled, handing Louisette a pen.

"I used to think so." Louisette searched for a clear spot to sign.

"You almost sound burned out," the woman pointed to a white sliver along the helmet crown.

"I hope not." Louisette considered. "I'd like to think I'm only getting started."

"Well," the pilot hesitated for a moment, "if you don't mind, I'd love to hang out with you next Vogue Day…assuming there is one."

Louisette smiled broadly. "I'll tell you what, Anna. How about if we just say we'll hang out whether there's a Vogue Day or not?"

"Sure," the woman looked at her curiously. Then she looked down at her autograph and folded her lips. "Thanks. I'd better get back now."

Louisette watched the pilot scamper back toward the cockpit station. She then tightened her father's blanket around her and headed for the exit.

Outside:

"So what makes you so sure this cockamamy bazooka of yours is going to do the trick?" Dr. Canard questioned.

"Well," Victor began, as he loaded the bearing grenades into the launcher barrels, "I do my homework before every confrontation. That's why I never lose. Fortunately, that Manda woman and her flunkies were very efficient in amassing detailed information about my adversary. From that, I was able to extract the chemical heat signature it emits. Then, I programmed that signature into the detonation ignition programs of these plasma ball-bearing grenades."

"So they'll act like seekers." Canard concluded.

"Yes, but even more so." Victor affirmed. "Having dealt with this thing once already, and seen how it moves about, my biggest concern is its ability to teleport or instantly move from place to place. If I fired a single grenade or missile, it would be able to outrun it from now until doomsday. But if I lay down a wide pattern…try to box it in, then as long as it stays within the boundaries of this valley, it should run out of places to run."

"What makes you so sure this thing is going to play by the rules?"

"I issued a challenge." The Beneficent-Champion folded his massive arms. "It answered. You don't answer a challenge unless you plan to play by the rules. Otherwise, it could have wiped us all out by now. I'm willing to gamble that there's a reason it's let some of us live—and that there's a chance that those of us who remain may survive."

"That has a familiar ring to it." Louisette chimed in as she approached the pair. "Think it up all by yourself?"

"I told you to leave me alone, and stay the hell out of my way!" Victor snorted down at her.

"The pilot's a nice girl." Louisette carried on. "Why didn't you introduce her to us."

"The pilot's a whore!" Victor asserted.

"How dare you say that!" said Louisette, appalled. "She's got a bit of a silver problem, but she's very nice. Kind of shy, actually."

"Funny," Victor squinted, "she didn't seem so shy when she was tearing open my underwear in the cockpit. Did the 'nice girl' tell you she begged to suck my penis? I'm surprised you didn't hear her choking on it through the air vents!"

Louisette was too startled to respond.

"She's a whore with a pilot's license, Louise." Victor sneered. "Another piece of stray Weed trash that happened to follow your father home from the sewers. That's another thing I never understood about him. I always believed in a 'scorched earth' policy, myself."

Louisette clenched her fists angrily but could not verbalize a response.

Victor smirked at how the depth of his cruel assessment of Anna Alexandriev stung the righteousness of his fiancée.

"Before I die today, will someone tell me who the hell made you two get engaged?" Dr. Canard frowned. "It took my wife and I twelve years of burned meals and broken china to almost hate each other as much as you do!"

Louisette stalked away, almost tripping over her dragging blanket tail.

Victor raked the back of his throat and spat a large ball of white and yellow phlegm into the sand. Then he ducked his head into the infrared site and began setting up his target.

"Fine." Dr. Canard threw up his hands.

A sudden, brisk wind yawned eerily through the valley whisking parcels of sand upward into miniature funnels. Victor reached down into a canvas bag and pulled out a pair of protective lenses and pushed them over his eye sockets. Then he reached down again, pulled out two more pair and tossed them to Dr. Canard.

"Maybe it's sick of waiting." Dr. Canard spoke above the wind as he pushed in his lenses, then assisted Louisette with hers.

"Maybe you're right," the Beneficent-Champion's expression hardened. He again, placed his face against the weapon's site. One last time, Victor quickly ran through his firing pattern options. This was something else over which he would have conferred with Kima, days in advance. But he had not had days, and Kima had been a costly game piece sacrificed, perhaps too early, in the pursuit of his coveted title. And in spite of the chilled air, Victor felt the return of that damp stream of moisture trickling down the crevice of his broad back. An undaunted reminder of the stark fear which blasted cleanly through the thin veil of toughness which protected his rootless ideal of manhood.

"Stand clear," he commanded without checking to see where either stood.

Dr. Canard took Louisette by the hand and guided her several feet behind the Beneficent-Champion. A staccato beeping sound emanated from the multi-barreled weapon which seemed to herald the beginning of the end. Louisette heard Dr. Canard whisper a brief prayer, but she could not follow its meaning well enough. So she simply asked God to make manifest the truth, however humanly unpleasant it might be.

The weapon fired with a concussed explosion followed by a bright orange flash. Dr. Canard was braced for the burst's heavy eruption, but Louisette loosed an inaudible scream as he held her close. Victor stepped back and looked across the sandy arena to admire the execution of the glowing red grenades' mission as they harmoniously whistled along their destructive paths.

The pattern appeared almost perfectly symmetrical from behind, forming the shape of a six-pointed star. Though in reality, some lagged several meters behind the others to form an inescapable net around the adversary.

For the first time, the alien showed some semblance of response to the events which surrounded it. Though with seemingly meager interest, it lethargically lifted its malformed head and observed the devices which had been sent to destroy it.

"Is it just going to stand there?" Canard asked aloud.

Victor either did not hear the question or could not fathom an answer as the grenades bore down on their angular humanoid target. The Beneficent-Champion literally licked his dried lips in anticipation of an early and easily won victory. Then suddenly, the alien disappeared.

"You've got to be kidding!" Canard's voice shook with dread.

"It's all right!" Victor spoke with a nervous steadying motion. "It's all right. I planned for this."

The ball-bearing grenades swung skyward, maintaining the perfect integrity of their formation. They hung in the air momentarily as if the invisible strings guiding their homing mechanisms had been momentarily severed from their quarry. But then, they rotated above the white stone hill and darted eastward along the base of the valley walls. Gathering speed, they descended rapidly with a high-pitched whine that was painful to the ear.

The alien reappeared five hundred meters in the grenades' path as they expanded their proximities forming an enveloping, explosive net about its position. Strangely, the alien again sluggishly tilted its head, appearing almost delusional in the face of its certain annihilation. The sound of the grenades' torrid approach became positively ear-piercing as they swiftly bore down on their target. Three hundred meters. Two hundred meters. One hundred meters.

The formation tightened.

Fifty meters.

Twenty meters.

The alien disappeared.

"Goddamnit!" Victor yelled as he wiped the sweat away from his face.

"Now what?" Canard called.

"No, no." Victor quivered a smile as he watched the star formation ascend to the sky once more. "It's all right. It's all right. It's playing by the rules. It's only a matter of time now."

"Do you really think you've got that sonovabitch on the run?" Dr. Canard questioned doubtfully.

"I know I have." Victor responded, wildly surveying the swirling dunes. "I know I have."

The ball-bearing grenade formation hung in the air for several minutes, flinching toward the west, then back toward the east and then retrenching due north a few meters before it returned to its original position.

The wind groaned once more in accompaniment with the whine of the indecisive star formation. Nothing beneath it stirred at all, save the top layers of sand, which indolently rippled to the intermittent currents of the intemperate desert breezes. The scene became maddeningly monotonous in the postponement of something spectacularly climactic.

Victor licked his lips barely able to contain the anticipation which left his mouth dry. Canard felt himself shake unsteadily as his heart pounded heavily in his chest. Louisette locked her arms around the doctor's waist as if he were the only thing left to anchor her in this surrealistic cauldron of cosmic conflict.

Then a loud shrill voice shattered the stillness.

"It's here!" screamed a voice from the transport. "Oh fuck! It's here!"

Victor whirled around to see frantic movement inside the cockpit window of the transport.

"The pilot!?" Louisette yelled. "Why is it after the pilot?"

"That doesn't make sense." Victor muttered to himself. "She's nobody."

There was another horrible scream from inside the transport that gurgled the sound of death. Splatters of crimson blood colored the inside of the windshield.

The Beneficent-Champion quickly pulled his club from the canvas bag, then broke into a full sprint toward the transport as a spiked mace formed on the club's head. A final, physical confrontation with the alien drew nigh. He could smell it. The cry, "warrior to warrior" rang inside his head. If he and the Earth were to die this day, this is how he would have willed it to pass.

As his foot hit the transport ladder's third stair, he heard Louisette yell to him from the ground. He turned and saw her diminutive form framed by a blinding red incandescence. It was the ball-bearing grenades—locked on the alien's chemical heat signature, screaming down toward the transport.

"Get down!" he read on Louisette's lips as the roar of the ball-bearing grenades drowned out her voice.

He leaped from the transport as he saw the bright star formation of the grenades contract around him. Then there was a deafening explosion and he felt a concussed swell of searing heat jettison his momentum from the epicenter of the blast. Flung head-over-heels through the air, he landed awkwardly, sprawled in the Golgotha sand.

Victor was shocked to be alive. Two hundred meters away, he saw the fiery, pulverized husk of what remained of the Beneficent Transport. Then he ducked as burning wreckage and debris landed all around him.

When the sky finally cleared, save the black smoke billowing from the site of the detonation, he took inventory of his aching body and struggled mightily to his feet. He growled as he felt that the thin tabard had been partially scorched from his blistered back. He tore away the remainder of the garment and winced at the raw sting that tortured his numbing muscles. Still, a proud smile crept over his split lips when he ascertained that he had just survived the greatest challenge of his life. Then he looked up at the transmission drones that were scrutinizing the burning wreckage.

"They should be focusing on me," he thought. "Unless they're looking for charred alien body parts!"

Then something secondary invaded his personal revelry.

"Louise?" he whispered, squinting over the desolation.

He slowly began retracing the path over which he had been hurled by the massive explosion. An almost debilitating dread labored his footfalls as he searched for a gruesome first sign of human debris.

"Louise!" he called out loud. The crackle of fire and the swirling winds were the only answers which he received.

Then he happened upon a tuft of dark hair embedded in the sand. Fearfully, he reached down and pulled it up until he held a freshly severed skull in his hand. Most of the flesh had been burned away with dried blood cauterized into the bone causing a sickening, brownish-red discoloration. The expression of a horrific death remained charred into its terrified, skinless features. Oddly, one side of the nose and a dead eye remained disturbingly unmarked. The dangling jawbone disgustingly peeled loose and fell to the ground. Then Victor noted the ciliary pigmentation in the eye. A darkened chemical blue melted away from a natural dead hazel.

"Pilot." Victor uncaringly flung the skull away.

He trudged onward wondering how he should perform for the cameras when he found his dead fiancée. After several meters, he came upon the half-submerged figure of a man lying face down in the sand.

"Canard!" Victor knelt down. He shook the motionless body but it did not stir. Then he gently rolled the body over and looked into Dr. Canard's dirt-covered face. The doctor slowly flickered open his eyes. "So how do we get home now?" The doctor asked, trying to the blink away the confusion.

Victor frowned and gently grasped the doctor by the back of the head.

"Louise?" he questioned Dr. Canard. "Did you see...?"

.

The doctor groaned as the slightest movement seemed to invoke discomfort. He held up a finger asking for a moment's respite. Then he began brushing away the sand beneath him, revealing the pattern of Beneficent Georges' cranberry cashmere blanket.

Victor pushed the doctor to the side and dug away the sand until he found the back of Louisette's shoulders and head. Then, gingerly, he lifted the young woman out and rolled her onto her back. She immediately coughed, lifting her hands to cover her face.

"They call me the human shield." Dr. Canard shook his head as he struggled wearily to gain his feet unassisted.

"Hmh." Victor responded still fixed upon Louisette's recovery.

The Beneficent-Champion tenderly reached out his hand to assist her. But as her eyes cleared and she gathered her wits, she disdainfully pushed his help aside.

Victor frowned, stood, and glared down at her. She turned and reached toward Dr. Canard, who sighed, gazed at Victor, then wearily aided her to her feet.

"I did it!" Victor stared up at the walls of the dark valley. "I did it! We're free!"

He smiled and spread his arms out toward the sky. "Free! Do you hear me you overgrown pterodactyls? Free! What are you waiting for? Shoo! Get lost!"

"Maybe they're waiting for orders from their master." Dr. Canard squinted toward the white stone hill.

"Master!?" Victor laughed. "I'm their master now! And I say, away with them! A pox on them! Get the fuck out of here! It's my world now!"

Victor spun around and almost lost his balance with self-indulged glee. But Dr. Canard and Louisette quietly continued to stare across the windswept valley. When Victor finally followed their gaze, to his horror, he saw that the alien stood vigilant—as impassive and unmoved as the moment they had arrived.

The air haunted them with yet another sorrowful wail as if to bemoan the Earth's impending bereavement of all human life. The aura of anticipated struggle evaporated into that of a dreaded march to a poised and sharpened guillotine. Louisette looked over at Victor and saw what she had sensed for the past twenty-four hours. His bottom lip quivered. His eyes, always ablaze with the crispness of lightning were now hopeless and empty. The Beneficent-Champion still stood tall, but in doing so, now trembled with fear.

"M—maybe we should…" Louisette broke the silence.

"Shut up, Louise!" Victor interrupted instinctively. "I swear I'm not finished yet."

Victor anxiously scoured the littered landscape for a weapon, or even the fragment of a weapon with which he might confront the alien with his last breath.

"The rifle…" Victor mumbled to himself. "…the rifle."

Dr. Canard looked out over the strewn wreckage, then back at the Beneficent-Champion. If there had been a rifle, it could not be found now. But Victor's eyes remained madly focused as if to raise one from the smouldering transport fragments.

"Victor?" Canard finally spoke aloud. "Are you all right?"

The Beneficent-Champion clenched his fists as the thick muscles in his hulking biceps swelled and tightened. The network of veins in his neck protruded from his tanned skin. Canard wondered whether Victor would try to crush the alien with his bare hands or collapse into an aneurysmal seizure.

"No!" Louisette jumped in front of him. "You're not going quit like this!"

"Get out of the way." Victor snarled down at her.

"No, damn you!" Louisette yelled. "You can kill me! You can kill yourself! But that…thing isn't going anywhere! The whole world is dead! Everyone except for us! You said it yourself! There has to be a reason! Talk!"

"I can't." Victor looked away.

"You won't!" Louisette accused. "You won't because you're afraid of what you may hear!"

"No." Victor whispered.

"You're afraid!" Louisette pushed against his barreled chest. "I can see it all over you! So can Dr. Canard! So can the bloody cameras! You're scared!"

"Shut up, Louise." Victor threatened.

"Or what?" Louisette challenged. "You'll hit me? You'll cry? What? What do I have to fear from you now? What does anyone? Can't you see what's happened? There is no fight! There's just it…and us…and the truth!"

"Truth?" Victor shook his head. "Truth that we're all about to die? Or maybe, become some race of slaves?"

"No." Louisette dropped her shoulders with exasperation. "What about the truth of our lives. The truth about ourselves that we've been covering up and pretending doesn't exist for so long. The truth that lasts for more than years, decades or even centuries."

"The cults have taken over your mind, Louise." Victor offered with pity.

"No." Louisette met his eyes. "God has."

The Beneficent-Champion recoiled from the woman as if some unspeakable arcane curse had spewed from her lips. He then looked over at Dr. Canard, who had heard all of this. The doctor simply stared back, waiting to see what the Beneficent-Champion would do next.

Victor slowly looked once more at the distant black form of the gnarled, twisted alien figure. Then, resignedly, he put one foot in front of another and trudged purposefully toward it.

Dr. Canard started on behind him, but then noticed that Louisette remained frozen in her tracks. Despite the strength of her own words she appeared famished, frightened and unsteady. When Canard extended his hand to her, she took it—and together they followed the Beneficent-Champion's path.

# XV.

For the first time since their arrival, the winds had almost unnoticeably died down. The air gradually warmed to a normal temperature as they neared the stone hill where the alien stood motionless.

Dr. Canard noticed the reddened, skinless burns in Victor's hulking bloodied back as they plodded onward.

"Victor!" Canard called. "I'm carrying something that could help your back."

The Beneficent-Champion pushed on, never breaking stride. Never acknowledging whether he'd heard the doctor's offer.

"Don't mind him." Louisette spoke between labored breaths.

"How are you doing?" Canard saw perspiration forming on her forehead.

"I've felt worse," she offered candidly. "It's just getting a little warm."

"Need a break?" Canard stopped for a moment.

"No," she blinked and nearly fainted.

Canard held her steady.

"Okay," she relented. "Take the jacket. I'll hold the blanket."

Dr. Canard removed his own jacket and tossed it to the ground. Then he did the same with Louisette's.

"I don't think anyone's going to steal them." Canard winked.

Louisette smiled weakly as she tied her father's blanket around her waist. Then she reached for the doctor's hand to continue on.

As Victor approached it, he felt his innards churn. In earnest, he had never confronted the alien face to face. He had heard much of its debate with Georges before it took the Beneficent's life. And he had caught a glimpse of its backside as it stood over Val and judged, "disturbingly", to spare the boy's life. But he had never looked into its decomposing face. Never gazed into its blood red, orbless eyes. Never observed closely the disgusting involuntary movements of the fused, blackened body parts which comprised its lean, lurching, mucousy form.

Victor finally felt the wall of moist heat which enveloped it—the odor of rotted human meat stung his nostrils and caused his eyes to tear. With this, he stopped and stood, awaiting the sound of its heavy, gurgled voice.

He could hear the labored breathing of Dr. Canard and Louisette as they struggled up behind him and stopped. But as he tensed his reflexes, prepared for anything, he never moved his eyes away from the alien's hideous face.

Its jagged mouth began to slide with an odd wet sound and it finally spoke: "You are the first whom I address a second time. You are well?"

Louisette dropped her blanket where she stood, and struggled against her exhaustion. She felt Canard nudge her arm. That the alien had addressed her, suddenly registered in her mind.

"Oui!" Louisette blurted out, thanking her fatigue for curtailing her fear.

"And the faithful physician." It addressed Dr. Canard.

Canard penitently dropped to one knee and lowered his head: "'*Go your ways and pour out the vials of the wrath of God upon the Earth*'," he quoted.

"Well said." the alien responded with what appeared to be its attempt at a grin. "But I am not He."

Canard lifted his head slowly, wearing a mildly embarrassed expression. "Just checking," he said as he climbed back to his feet.

The alien nodded and turned it's head to Victor.

"And he who crouches behind couches and calls himself…'messiah'." It recalled with a bite of disdain. "Heir to…the actor."

Victor swallowed hard and trembled as he fought to remain impassive before the hovering cameras. Awed by his remembrance of its resounding conquest of Beneficent Georges in rhetorical joust, he was unable to configure a verbal retort.

"A mute?" the alien mocked. "A mime?"

Victor's jaw set as his mind raced for a response that might allow him to maintain his face. He searched through its conversation with Georges (which he'd witnessed from behind a sofa). He searched through the Cartel

Charter. He searched everywhere he could for some ideological ground upon which to build, but found slippage and uncertainty at every turn.

"What is all of this about?" Louisette finally pleaded. "Why did so many have to die?"

The alien again fashioned an odd, jagged grin as he gestured a broad, sluggish circular motion above its head. Victor, Canard and Louisette looked skyward. As they did so, they saw the six heads of the giant creatures who formed the valley, change into magnificent, colorful spheres. Spheres, which by their swirling marbled patterns, appeared as planets.

"Worlds." it murmured drearily. "Seven worlds in this universe, currently supporting sentient life. All life bases, unique. All physical laws dissimilar and distinct. All traditions and rituals and pastimes and political structures, specific to the needs of those who dwell therein.

"On Methanos, there is no dry land. And the sentient oceanic species perennially wars on itself. Billions upon billions die each one of their years. They are brutal, savage, and the most ruthless murdering sentients presently living in all the universe. The crimes and atrocities they commit on one another's persons are unspeakable amongst themselves. Yet it continues unabated."

"Hopeless." Victor frowned with feigned indignation.

"Hopeless?" it scoffed and lurched with what sounded like a chuckle. "'Hopeless' did you say? I should think to see a billion eons of history through time and space and ne'er see any life form as hopeless as man!"

Victor's eyes narrowed, fruitlessly groping for the alien's line of reason.

"But we have peace," the Beneficent-Champion gestured defensively.

"You have peace...of mind," it responded evenly.

Victor looked to Dr. Canard to see if he was following the alien any better. The doctor's eyes were fixed on the alien, though neither confusion nor clear understanding were registered on his face. He also glimpsed at Louisette who was still taking in the sight of the six planets.

"On Heliosol, the intelligent life forms are all gaseous," It continued. "Completely incorporeal, they are devoid of sight, sound, taste, touch, smell, or even…sex as it is interpreted on this world. They have an ever-lasting peace. An everlasting bliss. They have no science, no technology—for they have no need."

"That's barely life at all." Victor frowned. "No bodies? No sensations? No things? Sounds like the poorest existence imaginable."

"And man is rich in bodies and sensations and things," it answered, "and yet, I can think of no life form so poor and destitute and blighted as the human being."

The Beneficent-Champion looked again at Dr. Canard, who remained totally impassive. Louisette held the doctor's arm as she now stared intently at the black, writhing alien.

"On Meddox, the geological-based sentient life-span can last a thousand years," the alien continued. "The thin atmosphere on the surface requires that the inhabitants live underground amidst the inhospitable seismic, volcanic activity. Every few years, hundreds of thousands are wiped out at a moment's notice due to sudden shifts in the flow of subterranean molten rivers. And no inhabitant has ever seen its own daylight."

"Life in perpetual darkness, with unpredictable disaster striking at any time?" Victor's nostrils flared. "We live in the light of our days. We avert our planet's natural disasters through our own technological controls."

The alien's flesh mask wrinkled slightly. "Yet, I know of no life form, as ignorant of the blackness in which it dwells, so recklessly devoid of control over matters of the gravest consequence, as the generations of groping, near-sighted, slack-jawed humans, content to feast upon the excrement of their own feculent ignorance."

Louisette tugged at Dr. Canard's elbow. He looked down and read the confusion in the woman's face.

"You'll see," he whispered to her.

She sighed and trustfully rested her head against his shoulder.

"On Shakir," the alien continued. "The carbo-nitrogen life forms send their young into the frozen wilderness to fend for themselves shortly after they master rudimentary verbal communication. Mortality is high. And no parent ever sees their offspring into adulthood. It is considered demeaning to remain in the shadow of one's family."

"Our children are usually raised by at least one parent." Victor defended. "Sometimes, both. And they're never abandoned by the family unless the child exercises their right to leave."

"Yet I know of no life form in all the cosmos," it gestured with the expanse of its gnarled arms, "which abandons its youth at birth, condemning them to certain death by the omission of the teachings of eternal life."

"But life is not eternal." Victor spewed with impatience.

"Indeed," the alien's voice fell an octave lower. "For one such as you, would that this were so. For you will come to pray that it were thus, when your soul is bared naked and judged a festering cankerous irredeemable thing."

"My soul…is mine." Victor weakly asserted. "What I do with it and what it becomes is my business. That's my right…"

"Your 'right' is nil but by the grace of the creator of all things," it interrupted. "Like a drifting creditless wayfarer, you seek to claim dominion over that upon which you squat, but can never hold title to. Your logic is that of a plant life which disdains the ground that spawns it and severs its own root; and dries and withers to nothing but woe and want."

"But I'm a man…!" Victor challenged.

"Yes," it concurred. "And in this infinite expanse known as our great universe, that is all that you are. Yet, even more distressing, is that this is all you aspire to be. Sacks of bone and blood mired in the hedonistic, arbitrary pursuit of secular pleasure—only with a style and sophistication that narrowly elevates you above the four legged creatures you dare call animals."

"Animals have no morality," the Beneficent-Champion countered.

"And man does?" it questioned. "What is the basis for this 'morality'?"

"Our philosophy." Victor added. "Our ideals. Our history."

"And if these things have produced the morality of mankind, then the animals have done well to live without them," it condemned. "For what is truly the morality of man, but the banter of convenience and the salve which soothes a selfish, troubled conscience. What is the morality of man other than the hollow justification for gratification absent of accountability or commitments. What is the morality of man other than the fluid interpretations of 'good', 'evil' and 'indifference'."

"The times change!" Victor grew annoyed. "And man with it!"

The alien's eyes filled with blood. It allowed the echo of the Beneficent-Champion's statement to vie for its claim to reason.

"Fool." It coldly assessed with chilling finality.

Louisette could see Victor's certainty unhinge. His giant hands shook at his sides. His large, cleft chin quivered with deserting confidence.

"So what do all these worlds have to do with what you've done to us?" Louisette intervened.

"On Crilen, the carbon-based mammals have built the most technologically efficient society in the universe. They have colonized neighboring planets and moons and are prepared to journey beyond their galaxy in the next century. They have overcome the scarcity of resources as well as the repression of free will. Virtually every facet of their existence is wholly dependent upon electrical power, transit and communication. Without these things, every aspect of their society would falter. Every aspect, but one: their knowledge of and their faith in a grander, more immaculate power which guides the destiny and fate of all things. That which lies beyond the ken of mere sentience. That which creates, preserves, illuminates, and destroys on an omnipotent and cosmic scale. That, of which we may comprehend but a fraction on this plane of existence. That which mankind has denied and forsaken: God."

"'*But unto him that blasphemeth against the Holy Ghost it shall not be forgiven*,'" Dr. Canard recited.

"Indeed," the alien's face softened. "For on Methanos, Heliosol, Meddox, Shakir, Crilen, and Tutis, where life is spent to game and sport, none but the lowliest of whelps amongst them have denied God's will. Yes, they war and murder, even in God's name. Others tarry about accomplishing nothing tangible with their forms or their trappings. Some struggle fruitlessly against the cruelties of their environments never certain of how soon or late life will be struck from them. Still, others revel in the exhilaration of their intellectual achievements and inventions. Yet ALL, ultimately found the common question and the common answer which ensured the salvation of their living souls. The acknowledgment of forces greater than their own to which they must all be held accountable. Not just a force of creation, but a force of logic, reason and compassion which constructed life, not for the mere myopic musings of its denizens in this 'life', but for something inconceivably grand and immaculate for the future of the universe.

"And the pity is that Earth had the greatest potential of all. It was given the greatest teachers. Provided the most diverse, yet easily digested lessons: that freedom is a means, not an end; that complicity for the sake of conformity is a travesty of truth, not a virtue; that blindness is an affliction, not a privilege; that love and life are, by grace, a responsibility, not a selfish matter of choice.

"But in the end mankind became sick with vanity, narcissistically enamored and demented by its own pale, ephemeral reflection. And tragically, concluded that it could fare better, incestuously ignorant of nothing but itself.

"And in so doing, man has made a bastard of himself. He masturbates blindly to the poetry of a bastard's ideals. He gropes and clutches fruitlessly at a bastard's idle dreams. He muses to the delusions of his bastard's house of smoke and dust. And in the end he dies alone—fatherless, motherless, forsaken to a misbegotten bastard's death."

Another silence drifted between the three humans and the lurching alien. Victor's eyes darted about, struggling to rig one last salvo that could rescue the human race from it's final pronouncement.

"So you mean to just close us down like a badly run franchise?" Dr. Canard questioned. "Hand us our walking papers, then set up shop somewhere else? How about new management?"

"It has been tried here," the alien spoke with some regret. "Was it not in vain?"

"Yes!" Victor stepped forward. "It was in vain!"

Louisette lifted her head as she watched Victor take two steps toward the writhing black figure. She glanced at Dr. Canard who returned her look of uncertainty.

"It was in vain." Victor continued. "Because the Christ didn't...stay around long enough. His remembrance was long but his reign was short. As a messiah, his work was good, but he didn't finish. He was killed before he could!"

To this, the alien remained silent and weighed the Beneficent-Champion's plea.

"I've read about the good he tried to do," Victor offered with an acquiescent gesture. "But there's so much more left to be done. That's...why I sought control of the Cartel. Control of this planet. I saw the wrongs. I saw the need for change. I realized that I was the only man who could bring those changes to...fruition. That's why I called myself...the messiah. Because I care the way Jesus cared. And I'm...strong enough to finish what he started!"

The alien's eyes boiled bright scarlet again. Then it took the bony, twisted talons of its own fingers, and tore open a large cavity in the middle of its lurching sternum. From inside the self inflicted wound could already be heard the sounds of unearthly hissing and insect-like buzzing that caused the humans' flesh to pimple and shiver. A wretched effluvium wafted out and dankly polluted the humid air. It reached its malformed appendage into the fresh tear and slowly withdrew a tall, bloody object near its equal in stature.

"Dear God," Dr. Canard gasped.

"The cross." Louisette touched the necklace around her neck.

The giant cross gripped by the alien may have been even more horrible an image than the alien itself. For the cross was alive, squirming and twisting amidst the slithering bloody snakes and eels and maggots which grotesquely comprised and defiled its once, hallowed symbol.

"What..." Victor recoiled, clutching for his missing belt of weaponry, "...is that?"

"The crucifix," it answered. "The crucifix consumed by the sins of man."

The Beneficent-Champion, sickened by the sights and smells before him, swallowed hard so as not to vomit. Then he dashed through his memories for an understanding of the brandished cult object.

"So...what?" Victor stammered defiantly.

"So you claim to be as Christ," it stated flatly.

"Yes." Victor answered, seizing the distinction without hesitation. "Yes. A great man, prepared to do great things for his people!"

"And you know that in so doing, Christ bore the sins of mankind so that man could continue," it stated.

"I...had heard..." Victor began.

"Then you will do as he did, 'messiah'," its voice gurgled low and almost taunting. "You will also bear the sins of man."

"But you're not God!" the Beneficent-Champion cried out in defense.

"And you're not Christ," it responded.

The alien slowly moved toward him. Victor thought to stand his ground, but then recalled Beneficent Georges' horrible execution. In a panic, he consciously disdained the restrictions placed on him by the cameras which had recorded his every prideful movement. Instead, he turned to run. But, the sandy foundation mired his footfalls and the Beneficent-Champion fell hard.

"No!" Louisette screamed as Dr. Canard held her from attempting to intercede.

In another moment it was upon him. It raised the sickening, infested cross high above its head as if wielding a heavy battle axe. Then, in one powerfully swift motion, it brought the animate cross crashing down upon the Beneficent-Champion's body.

Victor growled, then shrieked with blind despair. At first he appeared uninjured, but simply covered in the fowl nest of snakes and eels and maggots. But as he clawed at them with his fingers, the true horror was revealed. For they adhered and bored into his flesh like starving piranha aroused to a ravenous frenzy. They tunneled into his massive thighs and came out through the backs of his kicking legs. They chewed through the flesh and muscle of his giant arms until tendons and bone showed through. They tore at his shoulders and chest. He tried scratching them away, but instead, ripped away clumps of meat from his own bosom. His golden mane fell away in small patches, bloodily severed from the fresh scars chewed across his scalp. And his face became a mask of crimson wounds as the maggots filled his cursing mouth and ate through his bloating jaws.

Most cruelly, the Beneficent-Champion never suffered a mortal injury that could have rescued him from the unimaginable measure of suffering he was forced to endure.

"No!" Louisette cried out again. "This is wrong!"

"There's nothing we can do." Dr. Canard fought to restrain her.

"Then let me go!" she hissed angrily.

Dr. Canard loosed his grip on her wrist and watched her slip away.

She ran over to Victor, who convulsed painfully in the sand as the slithering ravagers continued their work. A hideous pink and brown eel lurched at her feet and she jumped backward in revulsion. Finally she exchanged one horrific sight for another and faced the horrible visage of the blackened alien creature.

"This is wrong!" she repeated as tears ran down her face.

"Why?" it asked casually.

"I don't know why, you fucking foul, monstrous..." Louisette shook angrily, and tried to restrain herself. "I don't know why. But stop it...please!"

It motioned to Victor's quivering body and immediately, the snakes, eels and maggots departed his remains and disappeared into the sand. Dr.

Canard ran over to Victor who resembled a corpse torn asunder by disputing carnivores.

The doctor hurriedly began taking life readings with his medical palm imager.

"Why?" it repeated.

"No!" she became flushed. "Let me ask you the same question. Why? Why are you doing all of this?"

"I answered you," it spoke coldly.

"No. You only answered part of it. You explained why so many people died. But you didn't explain why some of us are still alive. You never explained why you let me live!"

The alien's eyes drained to a softer reddish hue and its jagged mouth slid shut, then pulled itself open. "You asked for the truth. You did not ask it to be hidden from you. You did not even ask for your mortal life. You elevated the truth of living, the truth of the universe above all other things."

"Oh." Louisette sounded surprised at herself.

"Without truth, there can be no morality. And without morality, there can be no life. An advanced race is not advanced in its technology, but in its spirituality. That is the heart of wisdom. God never intended for a Godless, amoral race to procreate, anarchically cannibalizing itself for the sheer 'joy' of brief secular life. Such a pathetically arrested race can only spread its stagnating pestilence to the stars and eventually infect all that comes into contact with it."

"So we die?" Louisette concluded.

"So you start again."

"'Remedial Earth 101'?" Canard spoke as he administered to Victor's living remains. "Like setting us back a grade?"

"Several, in fact." It acknowledged.

"But how will we know where to start?" Louisette shook her head.

"You will know." It assured her.

"And if we fail…again?" she fretted.

"Earth has seen the last of lenity," it groaned. "If you fail again, my gentle hand will have no part in the punishment. That finality will be meted out by another."

"'Gentle hand'?!" Dr. Canard stood up. "Killing billions in the blink of an eye may pass as gentle somewhere in the universe, but what you've done to Victor is downright vicious. You've destroyed every regenerative element in his body. You've mutilated a perfectly healthy man and left him half dead! Where's the gentleness in that?"

"You are correct, physician," it nodded. "I will finish him."

"Wait!" Louisette spoke up. "Don't."

"Louise," the doctor stood and stepped toward her. "He's...in very bad shape. At best, he may be an invalid. Horribly scarred. Nothing like he was before. At this point, maybe it would be better..."

"He's going to be my husband." Louisette stared at the large prone figure in the sand. "He's going to be the father of our child."

"Louise," the doctor gently took her by the shoulders, "keeping him alive at this point isn't going to do anybody any good. I know you're trying to be...noble. But do you really love him?"

"I'm...not sure," she answered with tears in her eyes.

"Then why are you doing this?" Canard spoke softly.

Louisette wiped the tears from her face with the side of her hand. Then she stared off into the distance.

"When Anna Maria and I would have our talks, she'd always try to force the idea of love on me as meaning 'commitment'—sometimes joyful, sometimes miserable, but something that made you whole if you and the other person were determined to work at it. She used to recite the old cultist wedding vows to me: 'for richer or poorer, in sickness and in health', etc. And I used to laugh. But now...I see what a tragic farce the absence of commitment has made of my life. Transience has made me...transient. And I can't stand how that feels anymore."

"But you know what he is." Canard warned.

"By now, better than anyone," she met his eyes.

Louisette and Dr. Canard looked over to the gnarled alien figure.

It nodded its malformed head slightly. Then it gradually faded into the white stone hill until the sight of its blackened hideous form and the sound of its unsettling movements had vanished.

When Victor groaned in anguish, Dr. Canard walked back to him with Louisette following closely behind.

His bright blue eyes bulged from his dried bloodied face. His tongue thrashed about, slapping against the sides of his teeth where his jaws had been eaten away. His arms trembled slightly as he tried to move them, but all he could manage was the movement of three fingers. Finally his eyes moistened as he looked up at Louisette.

"Why didn't you…let it…finish me?" He slurred badly. "Why would you…want to…marry me now? I'm…not even a man anymore."

Louisette's eyes narrowed as her nostrils flared slightly. "You never were a man, Victor. But you still can be."

Suddenly, the valley quaked. The giant creatures which formed its steep walls stirred. One by one, each lifted its bulbous, flat-topped head, spread apart its mammoth wings, and launched itself skyward. As the final creature lifted off, the distant empty duned horizons were almost a welcomed sight.

"So what the devil do we do now?" Canard asked no one in particular.

Then the final bird/creature paused above them. And in a flash of crackling blue energy, Victor, Louisette and Dr. Canard disappeared.

# XVI.

Cannes, France:

The city streets were nearly filled to the lamp posts with displaced young children, who had grown restless under the dim, early afternoon cloud cover. Some, who had displayed inordinate patience in the morning hours, took to shattering storefront windows with bricks and loose chunks of concrete to while away their idleness. And policing this vandalism was clearly impossible, since the adult population was outnumbered nearly ten thousand to one.

"I'll be right back." Lang patted Manda on the rear end. "I'm going to smash a window."

"What?" Manda spun around from the group of children who had lined up to have their names tallied. "Hey! Just a minute, mister!"

Lang skidded in his tracks and looked over his shoulder, pausing for his cue to continue onward.

"You are not going off to break any windows!" she scowled at the boy.

At that moment, another large plate window abruptly collapsed into giant glass shards which shattered on the concrete sidewalk.

"Then why do they get to?" Lang pointed at a group of boys who laughingly chased each other away from the mangled crime scene.

"They don't 'get to'!" Manda scolded. "They're just being bad!"

"They're just being bored." Lang countered. "And so am I."

Lang resumed his gait toward the other children who were searching for something to throw and something to throw at.

Manda prepared to stalk after him, when the children waiting next to her tugged at her jacket. Then her communicator beeped.

"This is ridiculous!" she sighed in frustration. "This is Martine!" she answered with mild disgust.

"How's the babysitting?" Jean-Paul's voice came back to her. "Sound's like the novelty's wearing thin."

"I get the feeling this isn't going to be a novelty, Jean." Manda shook her head, struggling to hold impatient children at bay. "Anyway, what's going on?"

"Kelp and I just got through watching the challenge." Jean-Paul sounded as if he had just spent the afternoon in front of a monitor, watching a soccer match with his best friend. "We were waiting for 'post-game' interviews, but all of a sudden our connection got severed. I think our alien friend took out the last of the satellites."

"Victor lost?" Manda inquired.

"He wasn't even close."

"Dead?" Manda asked.

"Worse than dead." Jean-Paul informed.

"The others?"

"Okay, the last I saw." Jean-Paul became serious. "But Louise is stranded out there..."

"...and Dr. Canard." Manda added.

"Right." Jean-Paul caught himself. "That monster left them in the middle of nowhere. There isn't another soul from there to...Cannes. They'll die unless we get a rescue transport out there to find them."

"And you're volunteering?" Manda followed his lead.

"Oui, mon commandant!" Jean-Paul concluded.

"Forget it." Manda doused his enthusiasm.

"What?!" Jean-Paul raised his voice.

"I said 'forget it'."

"Manda, how can you say that?" Jean-Paul sounded hurt. "Dr. Canard's been more than a friend to all of us. He may have saved our lives from what I saw of the confrontation..."

"And all of a sudden, you're in love with Louise." Manda interrupted.

The communicator fell silent for a moment. Then Jean-Paul's composed voice came back: "That's not an issue, Manda."

"That's right," she concluded in an authoritative voice. "This isn't an issue at all. We've got a couple of hundred thousand kids that have been dumped in our laps and only a handful of adults to look after them. At this point, I'm not even willing to risk Kelp's life on a foolhardy rescue mission, let alone yours. You're needed here!"

"So we just leave them to die?" Jean-Paul indignantly protested.

"No, Jean." Manda answered. "The alien left them to die. Just like it left twelve billion people on Venus to die. In the meantime, I'd rather save the lives I know we can save, rather than take any risky chances."

"Well," Jean-Paul's voice became testy, "I'd rather not!"

Manda heard the communication pop closed. She considered dropping everything to chase down her irrational "right hand", but the children began to tug at her sleeves again. So with a heavy sigh, she resumed logging their names into her hand computer—and privately wished Jean-Paul all the best.

There came, however, a faint rumbling in the distance. At first, Manda presumed it was Jean-Paul's transport preparing for departure to the Middle Eastern Region. But as it grew heavier, shingled store signs vibrated and the broken glass on the sidewalks rattled. The children looked at each other with nervous bewilderment, then searched for the adults as beacons—though the adults were equally confounded.

Manda saw Lang and two other boys standing at the top of a brick staircase looking skyward with their mouths gaping in awe. Manda followed their gazes to the modest Cannes skyline and gasped in horror at the foreboding sight which approached the city.

Its wingspan spread across the entire western sky. Its pulsing red veins perniciously conveyed the presence of an irresistible power. As it neared, the light-gray clouds darkened as the expanse of its sprawling silhouette absorbed the very daylight from the skies above it. This would be the final deliverance of the ship/creatures, which had nearly exterminated all mankind from the face of the Earth.

The shrill, despairing cries of children filled the air, swelling to an unnerving crescendo of terrified young innocence. Manda grabbed the nearest children and held them closely in her arms. She wanted to extend her embrace to the hundreds of thousands of frightened children who had no cognition of what would follow. But sadly, she was helpless to do so.

Then it began.

Pulsing branches of blue energy rained down upon the city, crawling down the sides of buildings and systematically wrapping themselves around every lamp post and statue. The children dashed from the streams of light that crackled dangerously low above their heads. Manda knelt down, holding the children closest to her and the other adults did the same.

Through the strobing flashes which enveloped the very atmosphere, Manda could see buildings begin to disappear in the distance.

"This is how it was in Phillipsburg." the faces of Manda's family flashed through her mind. "This is how they died."

She braced herself to be taken at any moment by a bolt of light which would carry her to a torturously horrible death on Venus. But as she inventoried the incredible vanishings of large and small structures, she noted that the number of children remained constant. She held that thought for a moment as she looked up at the giant Beneficent Palace and wondered when it would go. Yet, the wild light that was striking all about them, allowed the palace to remain intact.

Then, just as suddenly as the incomprehensible assault had begun, it all blinked to a sudden halt. Manda and the children slowly rose to their feet. In front of them, the Beneficent Palace stood as solid and firm as it ever had. But behind them, all around them, where once had stood a beautiful old city with opulent buildings and crowded narrow streets, only craggy, red hills of rocks and intermittently dispersed tufts of dark green grass remained.

The ship/creature's red veins flashed a bright incandescent scarlet, then rotated slowly in the air and with a sudden burst darted swiftly up toward the overcast sky. Soon it became only an eerie faint flickering light under the dense gray cloud cover. As, it disappeared into the distance, there fell an amazing segue of silence.

When Manda sighed heavily, she was nearly breathless. Had she breathed at all during the past several minutes? Then there was a loud cry as one of the younger children began to sob. Several other sobs followed, while the older children began to talk and mill about in dazed astonishment.

Infirmity churned in the pit of Manda's stomach, as she reached for her communicator to call the remaining adults. "This is Martine. I think we need to get the children moving toward the palace— no one should be wandering off right now."

She placed the communicator back on her belt and wondered whether her instructions were more for her own assertion, than for the benefit of the children.

Manda slowly waded toward the palace gates. She groped for relief in sensing that the overwhelming horror which had begun days ago was finally over, but it was difficult to come to terms with the tumult, the fear, and the genocide of the past several days. It would take years for her to understand why forces from beyond had determined that this all needed to come to pass. But for now, she was simply determined to ensure that the survivors would not survive in vain.

All around her, the air buzzed with mounting questions and fears which built upon one another exponentially—and to her dismay, every panicked concern carried a distressing measure of validity. The issue of "where to begin" vexed her most of all.

As Manda pushed through the crowded gate entrance, she noticed a sudden commotion drawing onlookers to the center of the courtyard.

"Oh great," she thought. "Someone's hurt. Question number 313: Who's going to play doctor?"

The children who were gathered around the periphery of the "spectacle" saw Manda approach and slowly pulled back, fashioning a narrow passage to the center of the disturbance. Just as she reached the edge of the small clearing, a weary young woman wrapped in a blanket, stood up and look out over the crowd. Manda's mouth fell open with surprise.

"The girl who staggered into ops." she whispered, failing to recognize the "new" Louisette.

The young woman knelt back down. Manda burst through the wall of cluttered children and beheld a most unexpected sight;Dr. Canard was administering to the severe and horrific injuries to the Beneficent-Champion's bloodied carcass. Helplessly, Louisette held the unconscious Victor's hand as if desperately trying to heal him empathically.

"What..." Manda stammered, "...are you guys doing here?"

"I need a stretcher, a third-degree laser, and about six liters of AB negative!" Dr. Canard shouted, immersed in Victor's condition.

Manda instinctively pulled out her communicator to fill the doctor's request before she realized that the infirmary was no longer manned. Therefore, her first post-alien era improvisation was to order the older children and few adults nearby to hoist the Beneficent-Champion's giant frame onto their shoulders and haul him into the palace.

Louisette continued to hold Victor's heavy, listless fingers as the small crew wrestled to convey him toward the staircase.

Just then, Jean-Paul appeared at the top of the stairs and without hesitation, bounded down two steps at a time to greet them.

"Louise!" Jean-Paul moved toward her, shouting above the din of young voices.

Louisette either did not hear him, or elected not to respond. Her serious and concerned gaze remained focused upon Victor's mutilated features.

"Louise!" Jean-Paul unceremoniously grabbed her by the shoulders. Her hand separated from Victor's fingers, as the crew of children and adults carefully hoisted him up the staircase.

She was jolted by the sudden severance of her contact with Victor. Without acknowledging Jean-Paul, she struggled weakly against his grasp.

"Louise!" Jean-Paul tried to capture her eyes. "It's me! Jean-Paul!"

Too worn to resist him, she finally looked up into his handsome, excited features.

"Bon jour, Jean-Paul," she greeted him with impatient fatigue.

"Bon jour?" Jean-Paul smiled brightly. "Is that all you have to say? I was worried out of my mind about you! When I'd heard you left, I almost died!

I was about to fly out looking for you when the transports disappeared right out of the hangar. I thought you were lost! But you're all right!"

"I'm glad to see you too," her sad eyes met his, "but I have to go."

"'Go'?" Jean-Paul shook his head. "'Go'? There's nowhere to go, now. Nowhere except here. The bloody alien destroyed everything everywhere!"

"You don't understand," she tried to pull away. "I have to be with my husband."

Jean-Paul's excitement collapsed into an expression of hurt.

"Husband?" he said just above a whisper. "Did I miss the wedding ceremony?"

"No." Louisette swallowed. "No, you didn't. But we're going to be married."

"Married?" Jean-Paul fretted. "After everything he's done to you? Done to Anna Maria? Louise, he doesn't even love you!"

"You don't know that." Louisette snapped defensively.

"Do you?" Jean-Paul challenged.

Louisette remained silent.

"Louise." Jean-Paul's expression softened. "I know this is going to sound insane. Every time I say it to myself, I wonder if I've lost my mind. But ever since I saw you in the infirmary...the way you really are...well...I realized that...I'm in love with you. In fact, I think I've been fixated for quite some time. I just never really knew why."

His numbing admission tingled Louisette's skin. She looked deeply into the man's eyes and felt a depth of adoration she'd never experienced through a myriad passionless liaisons. She had heard of "love" as fictionalized through poetry and song, and even refuted its alleged merits to her cousin in spirited debate. Yet she'd never experienced even a vague remnant of it through any of her twenty-two years. Now, amongst all the other confusing matters she'd been forced to ingest over the past several days, here was "love", true love funneling nakedly into her heart. It could not have come at a worse time.

Louisette fought to hold back the tears. The muscles in her gaunt cheeks worked indecisively.

"Then where were you when I needed someone?" she spewed coldly and jerked out of his grasp. "Where were you when I needed…anyone?"

Jean-Paul felt his soul shatter against her sharp dismissal. Then, before he could say anything, Louisette ran up the stairs following the procession to the infirmary. He felt children start to push and tug at him as he watched her burgundy-blanketed figure disappear into the palace's north entrance.

"What's supposed to happen now?" a young boy in an African tunic asked him. "What are we supposed to do?"

"I…I don't really know," Jean-Paul admitted as he looked out over the waves of children being herded toward the palace gate.

"Of course, he does!" Manda interceded smiling down at the boy. "Its clearer to all of us than it's ever been. We need to stop looking down at the ground, minding our own feet— they can only carry us so far. Let's look up and out past the stars, past our galaxy. Let's build an understanding of…what the powers of the universe expect from us, rather than what we expect for ourselves."

The boy's face contorted with a total lack of understanding.

Jean-Paul gave Manda's bruised face a quizzical glance.

"Mon commandant, what in the world was in that bottle that hit you?"

"Clarity." Manda's eyes froze on reflection of that moment.

"What does she mean?" a young girl pulled at Jean-Paul's trousers.

"Um…" Jean-Paul's eyes darted about as if pushed onto a stage without a script. "I'm not totally certain. But my grandfather used to speak of a being up in the sky who created all things, including us. And that being hoped that we would love him and cherish the things that he gave us and would strive to be as much like him as our human weaknesses would allow. And if we did as he asked, we would one day return to his side and so that we could live forever in total happiness."

The boy stared blankly at Jean-Paul, then at Manda, then back to Jean-Paul once more. "How?" the boy finally spoke with a youthful glint of puzzlement.

"'How'." Jean-Paul guiltily rolled his eyes and nodded in agreement. "That's...a very good question. One that I think, bears some study on all of our parts."

"What if we don't do as the being asks?" the young girl smiled mischievously.

"Then I imagine," Jean-Paul grimaced, "that it will be a lot like the past few days, for as long as you exist."

"No," the girl pouted.

"I'm afraid so." Jean-Paul confirmed.

"Then we should try to do whatever we can to keep that from happening," the boy asserted.

"Yes," Jean-Paul smiled. "Yes we should."

Manda's communicator beeped and she pulled it from her belt once more. "This is Martine."

"I know we're supposed ta' be watchin' out for the young'ns." the distressed Irish Control officer answered. "But if they're gonna start kickin' an' punchin' an' directin' all matter a' foul language my way, I'm gonna' feel obliged ta'..."

"Smack 'em." Manda finished his sentence.

"I beg your pardon, ma'am?"

"Smack 'em." Manda repeated in earnest. "You're authorized to use whatever force you feel is necessary to keep them in line. If these kids don't learn to respect us, they'll never learn to listen to us. So smack 'em."

"Uh...aye, Ms. Martine." the voice sounded hesitantly relieved.

Manda replaced her communicator and with a heavy sigh, folded her arms looking toward the clouded gray sky. She wondered if she would ever see the sun again. Then she heard another commotion break out among the children, and silently conceded that if the sun should return, she would scarcely have time to notice.

# XVII.

Two days passed as dormitories and campsites were organized for Earth's surviving generation. Food and clothing were scarce. And it had been discovered that every source of power or energy had been extracted by the final alien strafe. The adults had been so busy, there had barely been time to consider sleep, let alone hunger or the loss of loved ones abroad. There was, however, a sense of renewed invigoration for the survivors. A strange and more powerful appreciation for the frailty of life and the necessity of enhancing a more spiritual understanding of it—to guide them through the dawn of humanity's dusk.

Louisette had spent the past forty-eight hours in the infirmary assisting Dr. Canard with scraped chins, bruised foreheads, and all manner of cuts which only children seem to create on their persons. She also was able to monitor Victor, who remained painfully conscious and much farther from death's grasp.

As nightfall approached, and the food lines in the palace courtyard dwindled (where massive quantities of Irish gruel were doled out to disquieted youth), Louisette finally stole a moment to slip away from her exhausting duties.

She barefooted down the torchlit back stairs of the infirmary into the catacombs of an area that bore the antiseptic smell of a mortuary. Just yesterday, she'd helped Dr. Canard carry two young children here, who had fallen from a palace window during room assignments. In the middle of the cellar, she had noted three concrete coffins sealed and tagged with the names of casualties recently departed. This evening marked her first opportunity to return.

She lightly touched upon Val's coffin, the young boy she had never really known, but had come to respect through her cousin's generous assessment of him.

She continued onward and froze in front of her father's coffin. A man she had wanted to love all her life. Keeper of the "toy chest". Blood of her blood. A stranger.

Finally, Louisette knelt down to Anna Maria's coffin. She closed her eyes tightly, trembled and began to weep. She tried with all the emotion in her to purge any regrets. She gently touched the Latin cross warmly nestled between her breasts. Then she looked up and ran her fingers along the inscription of Anna Maria's name and dates. For a moment, she was able to reconcile her nagging sorrow.

"I miss you," She spoke in a trembling whisper. "I need you. Especially these past few days. I mean, you wouldn't believe all that's happened unless you'd seen it with your own eyes. I really wish we could've shared it together. But…I guess that wasn't possible since I let you down so badly. I mean, I don't know why, but I know you always trusted me. But I let you down. And I don't know if I'll ever be able to forgive myself for that. I hope God can." Louisette paused and smiled at the irony. "Yes, God. Like I said you wouldn't believe all that's happened in the last few days. I found your diaries…right after father told me he never wanted to see me again. I didn't know what I was going to do or where I was going to go at the time—frankly, I just wanted to die.

"But seeing you alive again, listening to you without my interrupting, showed me how much I'd ignored; that God had been trying to save my life all along, without my help. It made me wish you'd confided in me more…or that I could have been a better listener. I mean, I always accused you of living in this storybook little world of yours. A fantasy land. You were always insisting upon the way people 'should' live rather than how they do. Always talking about people as if they were obliged to reach for some absurd moral plane that was clearly unattainable. Always taking joy in wrestling with some new ethical dilemma that never had a clear answer. Taking pleasure in the pursuit of knowledge and…truth, as if it were fun. I mean, what I've seen of truth so far is that it's the hardest thing for a person to accept. It usually isn't even something you want to deal with. But when it's made known to you, what then? Do you ignore it? Do you pretend you didn't see it?

"The strangest thing I've noticed is that ever since I started dabbling in the truth, my conscience has been…more settled. I don't feel guilty. I barely second-guess myself. I just do what I…should…even if I don't want to. It's an odd feeling. A clean feeling. Like nothing I've ever felt before. Like maybe pleasing God is actually the most meaningful satisfying thing a person can do. Almost like the people I used to think, came from storybooks. Storybook people looking over their storybook shoulders fretting over their storybook morality. It all seemed so ridiculous until a few days ago, when I thought my life was over and the world was coming to an end. But now…I see it all so differently."

Louisette rose to her feet and swept her fingers under her eyes. "The Earth is still here…and so are some of the people…and so am I. I only pray that you're in Heaven, Anna Maria. And I pray that some day I see you again…my love."

She slowly backed away until she could turn and resume the balance of her life. Then purposefully, she climbed up the backstairs, appearing in the infirmary just in time to see Dr. Canard wrestling with an angry boy with a bloodied nose.

"When are the damn school buses coming to take these kids home?" He groused, wiping the unrepentant combatant's face with a wet towel.

Louisette smiled and with a friendly wave of her fingers, bid the doctor a good night. She considered returning to her room, which she now shared with four five-year-old girls. But she detoured instead, to the beach for one last dose…of privacy.

Along the shore, in the near distance she could hear the restless campsites reluctantly settling in for the evening. As she drew near the Mediterranean, however, the human noises grew faint. She inhaled the smell of the sea, while reveling in the indolent breeze which caressed the aching muscles beneath her soft cotton gown. It was a welcomed, restful interlude as the beach was made a shadowy, corrugated tableau by the ebb of twilight from across the horizon.

She walked slowly in the cool, soothing waters which periodically swept over her tired feet, until she came upon the "great" sand village the children had labored to construct during the late morning hours. It was a proud accomplishment for the girls and boys who had sculpted their imaginary castles and trails and marketplaces and soccer stadiums with such fine and meticulous detail. She recalled the tiny little windows on the steepled towers, the kids-only playground with its network of curving slides, the "two-hundred thousand" seat amphitheater where the bands would always compete in the "loudest music contest", and the labyrinth of connected roadways which led conveniently to all such places. Truly a beautiful, compelling achievement for such young, creative minds.

But alas, the mid-afternoon tide had come and raged through the village streets. The vaunted towers were toppled as their supports were washed away. The amphitheater became more a muddied lake as its capacity now brimmed with water and debris. Pebbles and sticks, like boulders and trees, had smashed buildings and littered the roadways. In reality, there was very little which even hinted at the remains of a once, expectant civilization.

"Sand." Louisette whispered on the wind. They would have to learn to build their foundations upon sturdier ground than this. Foundations that could withstand the tests of inclemency…and eternity.

Louisette smiled to herself and thought of the hideous alien. Then she made her way back toward the palace, pondering the destiny of her immortal soul and all of those that remained on the planet Earth.

# EPILOGUE

2184 A.D. (Ten years later)

Cannes, France:
"Go ahead. Have it off with whoever you choose. Lie, steal, cheat, hate. Love only yourself and your things. Because if you don't believe in God; if you don't believe in the salvation of your soul, then it's only logical to live for the edification of your flesh. Why be good just for goodness sake if you never have to answer for it? That's stupid! Look out only for yourself. But be wary. Because someone just like you will be doing the very same thing.

"Break the rules? If there's no God, then I submit to you that there are no rules to break. There's just the good times. The good times, which last for maybe an hour, or a day, or maybe even a whole month, if you're lucky. But of course there are the bad times too, which always have a way of lasting just a little longer than the good times. Sickness, loneliness, hunger and despair never make a short stay. And then you die. And what was it all for? On Earth, they'll barely remember that you were ever here.

"In fact, I was paging through the dictionary the other day. And I was amazed by the thousands of names of once renowned poets, writers, military leaders, scientists, diplomats, musicians, philosophers, and dictators. Men and women whose impact on our culture was so profound that their very names became integrated into the foundation of our language. Ironically, I only recognized maybe a couple—and I profess to a reasonable knowledge of our history. Some of the names sounded like or resembled other names. Often, I couldn't even tell whether the person was a male or female. And I certainly couldn't get a handle on their body of work, nor did I really care to. They were simply names, titles and dates. That's it. Their legacy to the planet Earth. A few decades of fame amidst the millennia. If that's all you think you're worth, then I submit to you that you are worth LESS. Because in this life, of all the things we covet, nothing endures except our souls. Not wealth. Not beauty. Not even the love of a loved one. Those things must be put into their proper perspective so that you may invest in the most important possession you have: your immortal soul!

"You can be a productive person. You can become a famous person. You can even be a 'good' person. But unless you understand the logic of God's commandments; unless you build a bond with Heaven, then your goodness has no root! No foundation! And in difficult times, your so-called goodness will be swept away with the adversity. And then you'll be hard pressed to recover yourself even when things do get better, because you'll have discovered that your empty morality and beliefs are fluid, translucent and meaningless.

"As I read to you from Luke 12:16 please follow along: '*The ground of a certain rich man brought forth plentifully: And he thought within himself, saying, What shall I do, because I have no room where to bestow my fruits? And he said, This will I do: I will pull down my barns, and build greater; and there will I bestow all my fruits and my goods. And I will say to my soul, Soul, thou hast much goods laid up for many years; take thine ease, eat drink and be merry. But God said unto him, Thou fool, this night thy soul shall be required of thee: then whose shall those things be, which thou hast provided? So is he that layeth up treasure for himself, and is not rich toward God…Therefore I say unto you, Take no thought for your life, what ye shall eat; neither for the body, what ye shall put on. The life is more than meat, and the body is more than raiment*'.

"I'm not some divine puritan who professes to know all and does no wrong. For a very long time, my life was nothing but wrong. All I cared about was looking immaculate, feeling no pain and…having sex with people I didn't care about—people who didn't care about me either, by the way. That's what I thought life was about. And as a result, deep down, I really hated life. At times I thought it might have even been easier to die than to continue to struggle to maintain all the empty facades I thought were so important. But now I know I have only one person to please. And it's not any of you. He's told me clearly and concisely what he expects of me. Now, all I have to do is work my ass off everyday to be "rich toward" him. And that "him" is God almighty!"

Louisette stacked her notes at the podium and turned to the last page.

"Next week," she addressed the gathering flatly. "I'll have expected all of you to have gotten through the first ten chapters of the book of Ezekiel."

The young adults groaned disappointedly.

"I'm sorry," Louisette raised her hand. "But there's more to the Holy Bible than Matthew, Romans, and the book of Revelation. If Jesus could memorize the entire Old Testament, the least you can do is study it now and again. Now that's all. God keep you. Amen."

"Amen." the congregation spoke in unison.

All at once, the chairs in the former Central Operations hall squeaked and rolled to the shuffling of papers and feet and the murmur of young voices. The mostly teenage congregation, with some relief, exited out into the corridors to enjoy the beautiful weather and the remainder of their only day of the week free of school or work.

"'Work my ass off'?" Dr. Canard chuckled from behind. "Where the hell did you learn your pulpit etiquette, young lady?"

"They leave like they'd been held captive by retractable manacles coming out of the floor," Louisette noted.

Dr. Canard stood up and placed a hand on her shoulder. "They're still young. And it's a lot to learn—and a lot more to live by."

"I just don't think I have the knack for…preaching."

"Of course you do," Canard comforted. "In some ways, you understand the Lord better than I do. Besides, these people need a younger voice. I think they're pretty darn tired of listening to me wheeze and cough for two hours."

"It's not that bad."

"Ahhh, bad enough," he smiled as they began walking toward the stairs. "I'm old. You'd think that alien would've chosen someone else to play Methuselah around here besides me."

"I'm glad he chose you, Leonard." Louisette smiled as she steadied his descent with her shoulder.

As they reached the ground level, Louisette gave him a serious look.

"What?" Dr. Canard lifted his eyebrows trying to lighten the mood.

"You know how much I loved Anna Maria?"

"Yes, I know." Dr. Canard acknowledged the painful subject.

"And you know I'll carry the guilt of what I did to her…or didn't do for her to my grave, don't you?"

"Louise, we've talked about this. You don't need to feel…"

"I do, Leonard. But that's not the point right now. As much as I admired her and cling to her memory, I've come to realize that her approach to her relationship with God was…wrong. Maybe because she wasn't mature enough or didn't have anyone to guide her, but it was as if she tried to swallow her faith in one giant gulp. Force fed. I mean, as much as she understood, she still wound up missing so much! I was reading last night and stumbled upon Luke 6:22, which I've read probably fifty times. But it only hit me last night. It said: '*Blessed are ye, when men shall hate you, and when they shall separate you from their company, and shall reproach you, and cast out your name as evil, for the Son of man's sake. Rejoice ye in that day, and leap for joy: for, behold, your reward is great in heaven: for in the like manner did their fathers unto the prophets.*'

"I remember how alone she felt. How rejected she felt by everyone including me. Yet, if she could have understood this simple passage, it might have kept her from killing herself. I mean, a relationship with God isn't like a course you take in school where you study, take a test, and forget all about it after you pass. It's like any other commitment a person becomes a part of. Just as a husband and a wife learn to live and grow together, that's what you have to do with God. And just like a spouse, you may spend your whole life with him, and never truly, completely understand him. But the more time and effort you invest, the stronger that bond will ultimately become. If she had known that, she might still be with us…helping us today.

"Sometimes I also wonder whether Anna Maria loved humanity just a little too much."

"Well, I don't know about that." Canard rubbed his chin. "As I seem to recall from my reading, God has always loved humanity quite a bit."

"Mom!"

A boy came running up to them with a look of dismay on his face. Louisette paused suspiciously, trying to decipher the expression of her son.

"Mom!" the boy skidded in front of them.

"What is it Matthew?" Louisette took his hand.

"I just saw Lang out in the corridor kissing Victoire Anne!"

"Well," Louisette smiled. "They're going to be married in another month. I don't see anything wrong with that, do you?"

"But this area is a sanctuary!" Matthew frowned. "You said so yourself! You said this is no place for unlawful fornication."

"Fornication?" Louisette's eyes lit up with surprise.

Dr. Canard smiled and fanned his hand. "I got work to do."

"Bye, Leonard." Matthew smiled and waved.

Dr. Canard simply grunted as he ambled toward the exit.

"Matthew!" Louisette raised her voice. "You don't call Dr. Canard, Leonard!"

"Why?" the boy smirked. "You do."

"That's because I'm an adult." Louisette fussed. "Young people should show some respect."

"Says who?" Matthew frowned.

"Says me." Louisette fought to keep her voice low.

"So what about Lang?"

"Matthew, kissing is not fornication. But if it bothered you, I'll speak to him about it."

"Good." The boy smiled and folded his arms.

For an instant, this blue-eyed, towheaded ten-year-old resembled the former Champion so much, that it sent a shiver down her spine. It was clear that the engineers of Victor's genetic dominance had performed their task admirably.

"Now listen to me." Louisette asserted. "Your father has not been feeling well lately. I want you to go up to his room and see to him. Do you understand?"

"He's gross."

"Matthew!" Louisette grabbed the boy's arm. "I don't ever want to hear that again! Your father was a great man. You should be proud. Now see to him!"

Matthew jerked away in disgust and marched out of the hall. Flustered, Louisette combed her fingers through her hair and acknowledged for the umpteenth time that parenthood had become the greatest challenge of her life.

Tightening her fingers around her notes and Bible, she walked deliberately out into the corridor where not entirely to her surprise, she found Lang and Victoire Anne, still pressed against each other in a passionate embrace.

"Lang," she spoke his name authoritatively.

Lang jumped as if he'd been doused by a cold bucket of ice-water.

"Mrs. Hausmeister!" Lang's face flushed with embarrassment.

Victoire Anne also bore an expression of dread and humility. "Sorry, Mrs. Hausmeister," the young lady whispered.

"Lang, I'd like to have a word with you for a moment." Louisette maintained a stoic demeanor.

With loving eyes, Lang bid Victoire Anne to "flee" while she could. Victoire Anne bowed her head to Louisette, then scurried down the corridor and around the corner.

Lang, a tall and muscular young man, towered over the diminutive Louisette. Yet still, he shifted uncomfortably from side to side like a youngster about to be scolded.

"So how does it feel?" Louisette addressed him.

"Look, I'm really sorry..."

"I didn't ask you that." Louisette's face finally broke into a smile. "I asked you how does it feel?"

"Ma'am?" Lang's face appeared nervously perplexed.

"Well, you are going to marry the girl next month, aren't you?" Louisette arched her eyebrows.

"Oh. Yeah." Lang modestly smiled to himself. "It feels good...I guess."

"You guess?" Louisette poked at him. "She's the loveliest, brightest girl in the world."

"Yeah." Lang smiled uncomfortably. "I know."

"Then what?" Louisette sensed something was not quite right.

"Well." Lang's voice quivered. "I really wish my mother could be here to meet Victoire Anne. I mean I know I shouldn't feel this way, but I don't think I'll ever forgive that thing for killing my mother right in front of me."

Louisette was startled by Lang's first admission that he'd watched his mother die.

"She wasn't the greatest mother." Lang continued. "While dad was away on Mars, sometimes she'd send me over to the neighbor's because her...men would come over. In fact, I always felt like she was trying to get rid of me. But now, for some reason, I wish she were here."

Louisette reached up and touched him on the shoulder. "Lang. Don't feel bad about hating the alien. It hurt all of us. But remember what the world was like before it came. And remember why we're not dead too. And as for your mother...well...I'm an optimist. I get the impression she'll see the wedding and like Victoire Anne just fine."

Lang shook his head as he continued to grapple with these difficult personal issues. "Thank you, Mrs. Hausmeister."

Outside, by the sea dock:

"Fuck her!"

"Jean-Paul!" Manda scowled.

"No, really." Jean-Paul sneered. "Fuck…her."

"You have to say good-bye." Manda stomped on the dock.

"No, I don't." Jean-Paul put his hands on his hips. "I said good-bye to Dr. Canard, to Kelp, to you, and all the other people I want to say good-bye to. But Madame Louisette Hausmeister can take her martyred piety and shove it up her ass."

"Jean, you're being ridiculous." Manda raised her voice.

"Am I?" Jean-Paul flung his arms apart. "Am I really? For ten years now, I've rebuilt electrical generators, engineered everything from village greens to food lines, supervised agricultural growth from nothing, built this vessel with my bare hands and tried to convince Louise that she's destroying her life by remaining celibately loyal to that incoherent shell she calls a husband."

"That's right, Jean." Manda shook her finger. "Her husband! She's married! Why can't you face up to that? You're a Christian."

"Yes. I'm supposed to be." Jean-Paul looked away. "But not even my grandfather would have condoned a loveless marriage like the one she locked herself into. Victor was an animal—the living embodiment of everything that made our world kindred to hell itself. And he always treated her like shit! But she still serves him hand and foot, for not even a thank you, I'll wager.

"Stupid me, on the other hand, still loves her! I'll go to my grave loving her. But she refuses to see it, because of him and her screwed up sense of duty. So I've made up my mind: fuck her, fuck them, and I 'pray' they're very fucking happy…'praise the lord'."

Manda took a short stroll to the end of the pier and looked up at the giant sea-faring vessel Jean-Paul and his charges had hammered together for almost seven years. Then she pivoted and returned to him.

"So Africa." Manda changed the subject.

"Just to see how she holds up." Jean-Paul admired his handiwork. "If all goes well, I should be able to radio you from the west coast of Morocco. From there, it'll be a straight shot to North America."

"It's unbelievable." Manda commented. "Ten years ago, a trip to Mars was routine. Now, you're only going to the other side of the world, and it's as if you're leaving the galaxy."

"I guess it's all relative." Jean-Paul shook his head. "I just know I need to get out of here. And those ghost transmissions we got from North America are reason enough to investigate whether there are other survivors besides ourselves."

"You're taking a lot of good kids with you."

"Yes, but you're still keeping some of the best for Cannes, aren't you?" Jean-Paul smirked grudgingly. "Besides, God didn't keep us around this long just to be drowned at sea. And we're packing our Bibles. We should be fine."

"Well I'll be praying for you." Manda took his hand.

"I'll miss you too." Jean-Paul kissed her on the cheek.


The (former) Beneficent Palace:

The room smelled of death (or something dying) as it had for nearly a decade. Makeshift respiratory equipment wheezed and pumped. Occasionally, a desktop clock would toll the hour, taunting the invalid listener with a cyclical chronology, perpetually mocking his lingering paralytic plight.

Sometimes the woman would come and read to him from her wretched book of "curses, fantasies and philosophies". Then she would change his clothing and bed sheets. His mass had dwindled away to so little she could lift him almost effortlessly from the bed to the chair. Though the brown masses of arthritis that had settled into his joints made the movement almost unbearable for his seared nerves. And the chair always ached his bony pelvis and his excrement sores, though his atrophied facial wounds would not allow him to articulate his discomfort beyond a rasped groan.

There were no longer any mirrors. But there wasn't much left to see. The gory sight of his mutilation had induced a heart attack nine years ago. So he wept openly, until all of the mirrors in his room had been removed.

If there was even a glimmer of joy in this joyless, hellish existence, it came from the boy who looked so much like himself...in the old days. But the boy was afraid of him, which was understandable since his body had been butchered into a ghastly contortion of bone and excoriated flesh. Still, the boy's presence, frightened or not, lifted his empty spirit just enough so that he did not will himself to die.

He yearned to tell the boy of great battles and conquests and feats of skill and strength. But tragically, he could no longer speak, thus having no means by which to express his profound, fatherly affections.

Matthew entered the room where his father lay motionless, tongue thrashing about his skinless jaws. Victor struggled to turn his balding head, so as to capture a glimpse of the boy Adonis. The former Beneficent-Champion's face quivered as saliva ran down the sides of his chin with the effort of turning his head even slightly. When he could turn no longer, he forced his watery blue eyes to roll around painfully and search for the boy's face. He never once, wondered why his son always stood at so cruel an angle.

When he finally made out his son's figure near the head board, the vision was blurry and undefined. Though disconcerting, Victor had learned to settle for many things that were not to his liking—and that the boy had come at all was pleasure enough when he considered the alternative.

A look of disgust spread across Matthew's face. If only his mother would stop demanding that he endure this horrid sight. I deserve better than this, he thought. A sneer of evil contempt twisted the boy's features as he decided to make do...for himself.

"Poor father." Matthew spoke disdainfully. "So old and ugly. No one can even look at you without yanking up their dinner. Were you always so?"

Victor felt a sudden sharp pain in the side of his neck that ran downward into his chest.